Dedicated to…

Mickey, who makes it all happen. Thanks, honey.
Terry

Paula and the kids, William, Danielle and Zachary…
Love,
Mark

Acknowledgments

I owe a thank-you to many people, chief among them:

Don Carter, whose vast knowledge of lost treasures sparked the idea; Maureen LaJoy, the first "professional" writer I knew and best teacher anyone could have for encouraging me to go for it; the many folks in my various writers' groups (Nancy, Paul, Peggy, Carol, Cheryl and Kristine, to name a few) who listened patiently and painstakingly to this story numerous times (and rarely complained); Steve & Steve for their insights; Vicki Palmquist, who helped more than she will ever know; Mark Neuman-Scott for coming up with the idea of writing a book together and keeping this thing going, even uphill; and Mickey, who did more than anyone to help me make this dream come true.

Terry W. Lovaas

I also want to thank our original readers for their feedback; Andy and Karen Richards and Francine Kaufenberg for their feedback; my sister, Janet Scott, for editing, critiquing and being honest; TLov, aka Jake, my writing partner in the Jake & Hank series; and my wife, Paula, for reading the manuscript more than once, providing insight on how life really is, providing encouragement and believing in *Lady Luck's Smile*.

MNS

The Beginning
Midnight

After years of working with computers, Anthony Williams no longer heard their incessant, low-grade purr. He gave a shudder against the climate-controlled atmosphere and pulled his cardigan tightly around his thin frame.

Williams sat back, studying the greenish glow from the monitor and smiled to himself. *Serves them right*, he thought. *Serves them right!*

After twenty-seven years of loyal service, he'd found himself on the wrong end of a "staff realignment" because of government budget cuts. There was the semi-veiled mention of an attitude problem but he'd long since dismissed that as an undeserved comment from a know-nothing middle-management piece of shit.

Once a senior programmer in Special Operations with NASA, Williams had been unceremoniously bumped down to the third shift where he worked as a lowly data analyst, overseeing a project using high-orbit satellites to map the southwestern section of the United States. It was a job he could do in his sleep.

And he had. For three months he'd sloughed through the endless, mindless, pointless drudgery of mapping the ever-so-slight changes to the landscape. Out of sheer boredom, he'd secretly tweaked the programming to include search parameters for mineral deposits. Each night, he'd initiate his covert operation, save whatever data he found interesting on his flash drive and then unceremoniously delete his findings. It gave him something interesting to do for a while but not finding anything useful or exciting, he soon grew bored with it.

He was about to give up when a faint little blip appeared on the screen and

7

woke him from his slumbering self-pity. The next night it appeared again, and again the next. When he made a few slight adjustments, it grew even stronger.

He checked. He verified. He researched. It appeared that he'd found a highly concentrated mineral deposit. Further analysis indicated that the deposit was probably gold. Since such a highly concentrated deposit of gold was inconsistent with the geology of the area, he approached this problem from another direction. He studied treasure hunting books and magazines. He studied old stagecoach manifests and railroad bills. He cross-checked those with newspaper accounts and insurance claims. Finally, he came to the only conclusion possible. Anthony Williams had discovered a long-lost treasure. Gold coins? Gold bars? He wouldn't be sure until he actually went out there. But if the newspaper accounts and stagecoach manifests were accurate, he'd located the stolen cache from the Wells Fargo train robbery on July 12th, 1891.

After thinking through all the possibilities, he handed in the paperwork for early retirement. His supervisor, a man twenty years Williams' junior, smiled as he read the form. "We'll miss you, Anthony."

Williams gave a tight smile. S*ure*, he thought. *Sure you will*.

Now there were only two more nights until his retirement. He focused his attention on the screen, searching for the blip. One last time he wanted to see it. The satellite's signal came in. Scanning. Scanning. He pushed his reading glasses up on his nose, studying the monitor. There it was. The blip. Faint, but still there. He cross-checked the GPS coordinates. They were exactly the same as every night before, and the night before that. He typed in a series of commands and the blip, as well as all traces of his freelance adventure, disappeared forever.

Williams' thoughts were broken by the clatter and banging of the approaching cleaning crew. He sat up and punched a few keys. The printer whirred as a page of numbers crept out.

The door opened, making a swooshing noise. Light and warmer air from the hallway flooded the room. A janitor in a dark gray uniform entered. He was pushing a large plastic barrel on wheels.

"Ah, Meester Williams," the man said with a heavy Spanish accent. "Only two more nights. Den you gone?" The man moved to a wastebasket and dumped its contents into the barrel.

8

"Yes," Williams answered. "Only two more nights."

* * *

A vile wind whipped over the ground, creating a choking dust storm. Whitney Cloud coughed as he rolled down the window of his black Bronco and flicked his cigarette into the maelstrom. He guided the Bronco slowly across the ruts and rocks, his own massive bulk keeping him securely in place on the bouncing drive.

Whitney Cloud was equal parts mean and hate with just enough Navajo blood to live on the reservation. He had spent the last three years in prison and now that he was free, he vowed he would never spend another day of his life behind bars or under the heel of the white man's boot.

He couldn't think of a single thing the white man had done for him that was good. With the exception of one person from many years ago, he hated and distrusted every white person. By moving back to the rez, he figured he'd never have to deal with one again.

Until now.

"Owww!" yelled a whiney voice from the back of the Bronco. "My leg. My leg is broken!"

"Shut up," ordered Cloud. "Your fuckin' leg ain't busted."

"I could get an infection," the man protested.

"Shut up or I'll take you back to where I found you and leave you for the coyotes."

The man was quiet for a few seconds and then spoke out of fear and frustration. "Where are you taking me?"

"Someplace you'll be safe." Cloud turned and glared at the spindly white man, silencing him for the rest of their journey.

And silence was just what Cloud needed. He needed time to think, to plan. It was only a few hours ago that he'd found the dehydrated little puke of a man, only a few hours ago that Whitney Cloud's life changed for the better.

Cloud had been deep into the desert hunting rabbits when he found him—Williams—pinned under a rented Jeep. There had been a flat tire and the jack had slipped, trapping Williams. After nearly a full day in the desert sun, he was damned near dead. Cloud had been prepared to rummage through his stuff, take whatever he liked and leave him. After all, the man was trespassing on reservation land. And he was white. It would be months before anyone found his remains.

But then Cloud made an important discovery. He found shovels, a sketchy map of the surrounding area, some electronic gear and an old leather bag with several twenty-dollar gold pieces inside. Cloud didn't know much about gold coins but he knew these must be valuable. Each one was over a hundred years old and looked to be in great shape. He knew a collector down in Gallup. Maybe he could tell Cloud what these were worth.

The next two hours were a struggle of wills and wants. At first, Williams would only admit that he'd found the gold coins "out in the desert." Since Cloud's threats of violence had proved useless, he quietly and expertly began applying some physical intimidation practices he learned from his prison buddies. Williams finally admitted there were more coins, plenty more.

But that is where any cooperation on Williams' part ended. Under no circumstances would he tell Cloud exactly where the stash was located. Williams said he'd sooner take the secret to his grave than give it up now. No matter what Cloud did to him.

"If you don't tell me, I'll get in my Bronco and leave you here to bake in the sun and have your eyes plucked out by buzzards." Cloud's menace-filled whisper hung heavy in the air.

Williams could feel and smell Cloud's hot, bad breath on his face. But Anthony Williams wouldn't give in. "Do that," he gritted, "and you'll never, ever find the rest of the gold."

Then they were both quiet. Only the ever-present wind made any sounds. Cloud realized he wasn't going to be able to beat the information out of the scrawny little white man. Williams, who did not want to die in the desert, realized he was going to have to take on Cloud as a partner. During a temporary break in the windstorm, they looked at each and nodded, forming a tenuous agreement.

After getting Williams out from underneath the Jeep, Cloud gave him some food and water. Once in Cloud's Bronco, Williams told how he'd "pinged" the treasure and, after doing some exhaustive research of old newspapers and insurance records, determined that it was probably from a

Wells Fargo robbery over a hundred years ago. Forty bags of newly minted Double Eagles had been stolen. Using the current price of gold, he figured they were now worth about sixteen million dollars in melt value. Collectors, Williams insisted, would pay much, much more than that for these pristine coins.

But Cloud quickly realized getting these coins into the hands of the buyers wasn't going to be easy. Getting the coins off the reservation would be tricky but not impossible. While Cloud loved his Indian brothers, he had absolutely no intention of sharing this treasure with them—or with anyone. Turning these coins into cash was the biggest obstacle. Selling them one or two at a time would take a lifetime. Selling the whole lot by conventional means would draw unwanted attention—and raise questions. Those questions would bring the authorities. Then the tribal elders. Then the FBI. Then the attorneys and worse, insurance agents.

"So tell me where they are and we'll go get 'em, partner," Cloud proposed. "We'll be rich."

But Williams knew he would be dead the second they got there. "You find a way to guarantee I'll live to spend my share," Williams dictated, "and I'll take you to the gold."

It was in the ensuing silence on the ride to Cloud's hunting shack that he remembered his old friend, Jake Marley. If he could talk Jake into it, he would be the perfect partner. He would be someone Williams would trust, he was ballsy enough to help them get the gold out and he was smart enough to know how to turn it into cash.

Cloud slapped the rim of the steering wheel with the palm of his hand. No matter what he had to do or say, he had to get Jake's help.

1
Jake
Late Saturday Afternoon

Carley Rose Butler shifted in my bed and rolled her naked body toward me. Her fingers tugged lightly at what few chest hairs I have while her toes flirted with mine. "Jake?" Her lips nipped at my ear.

I half-opened my eyes. "Yeah?"

"I was just wondering…" She snuggled in tight, the warmth of her body enticing me.

I opened my eyes and found *the look*. The are-you-really-going-to-leave-me-and-go-play-poker-with-the-boys look. I closed my eyes and tried to ignore the look—and her.

First, I like Carley. I like her a lot. She's the only woman I'm seeing right now, the only one I want to see. But there are problems. She's in the still-married-but-getting-a-divorce-real-soon category and no matter what anyone says that always, always, always leads to trouble. Plus, if she ever did get a divorce, she'd be the type of woman who would eventually want to settle down, get married and decorate a house with lace curtains and pump out a string of kids. I'd purposely and successfully avoided that scenario for most of my adult years and couldn't see why I should change. And, not most of all, but still important, her name is Carley. Mine is Jake Marley. Sooner or later, she'd grow to resent her cutesy, rhyming name—and me.

I quickly slipped out of bed and pulled on my high school gym shorts. They were over twenty-five years old and the color and the logo had long since faded but I figured as long as I could still get them on I was still young and still in shape. Funny what running half a liquor store through your body for over two decades can do to your power to reason effectively.

"Jake?" Her voice sounded like it had been dipped in honey.

I turned and faced her, figuring I was at a safe distance. Her big brown eyes were sad and beckoning and I fought getting lost in them. She sat up and ran her fingers through her too-short hair. The sheet fell forward as she arched one eyebrow. "I just thought that maybe…"

"What?" I asked too loudly. "That maybe I'd skip my game and stay here with you?"

She recoiled, timidly covering her naked self with the sheet.

I looked around my apartment for a t-shirt, any t-shirt I could slip on quickly. "You know how this works. Smiley gets a game together, I have to be there," I said, trying to sound even-keeled. I found my Ten Thousand Waves t-shirt and checked it for stains. "It's like a job."

"A job?" she asked. "You've got to be kidding!"

"I'm not kidding. Besides, Hank said he needed to talk to me about something important tonight. That's going to take a little time."

She stared and swallowed and changed tactics. "How about I drive you down and…" Her puppy-dog sadness was replaced with a half-hearted attempt at cheerfulness.

"Look." I pulled the shirt over my head. "I'd have a hard time concentrating on the cards if you're there. I'd be thinking about you and not about the game."

"You sure there isn't some other reason you don't want me there?"

I posted a full-blown incredulous look. "What? That I'm meeting someone else?"

"It's happened before," she shot back quickly.

"But, not anymore, I've told you. I'm all done running around."

"Well, you've been really distant lately. I just thought…"

I sidestepped this familiar minefield. "There's no one else, Carley."

"Then why have you been so—so quiet?"

"Things. Things that don't concern you."

"Jake, everything you do concerns me."

Now I shot her a look. "Oh, really? You my warden?"

"That's not what I meant and you know it. Quit being a jerk."

13

I shrugged. "This is just something I have to take care of. Myself."

"You're not in some kind of trouble again, are you?"

I was about to give her my "You've got to be kidding" look when I remembered we'd been there and done that more than a couple of times in our relationship. "Just drop it."

She turned away, apparently trying to find another tactic. I turned my attention to why this game was so important.

Poker is how I make my living, how I support myself. My habits. My lifestyle. Smiley's bar has been part of the unofficial southwest poker tour for over thirty years. Cocky cowboys and adventurous tourists know they can find an honest game of cards at Smiley's—as well as similar bars in Amarillo or Tucson or Yuma. My friend Hank and I are regulars at Smiley's—have been for more years than either of us care to admit. When we're not sitting at the bar BS-ing with Smiley or Rufus, we're taking turns hosting these poker games. And while we don't cheat in the traditional sense, we do play as a team. If Hank gets a good hand, he sends me a signal to raise the bet. I do the same to him. We build the pots we know we're going to win and we let the fish win the smaller ones. Cheating? Probably. Do I care? No.

Officially, I freelance for the *Santa Fe Reporter*, writing oh-so-fascinating features about the oh-so-interesting people and the oh-so-popular new places in oh-so-trendy Santa Fe. Tourist crap. Travelogue trivia. And I hate it with an oh-so-purple passion.

But, while freelancing isn't what I want to do, it does provide me with two benefits. It keeps me legal in the eyes of the IRS by providing me with a regular source of income. And, it gives me lots of free time—which is what I need right now.

I have just come into the biggest deal of my life. In another week or so, I will be the newest unofficial member of Santa Fe's millionaire's club and I will never have to write another piss-ant article about emerging artists or new wave spirituality or healing crystals. And all it took was an unexpected phone call from one of the ghosts of my past.

Also, Manny was showing up at Smiley's tonight, too. I didn't know when, exactly. You never did with Manny. He just called and said he would be there with the rest of the up-front money and the numbers for the bank accounts. I knew better than to ask too many questions. Manny didn't like being questioned.

Carley cleared her throat, turned back to face me and locked her eyes with mine. I could feel the tension growing. Like in a poker game. Like when I tell some cowboy that I have a hand that can beat his and he's filled with doubt because he knows it's going to cost him big-time to find out and he's not sure he can afford to lose.

"Okay." Carley bowed her head. "Just so there isn't anybody else."

"Look, tomorrow's Sunday." I gave her a peck on the cheek. "If you can get away, maybe we can take a drive up to Taos."

"Sure." Her voice was soft and weak. She looked up at me. "Jake?"

"Yeah?" I checked the alarm clock. Shit. Not much time. I had to take a shower and get down to Smiley's.

"It's just that I don't want to be alone. Tonight." The sheet came down. Again.

I kneeled in front of her. "Hon, I'd rather stay here with you." My fingers traced a line on the side of her face. "But I have to be there."

She lowered my hand to her full breast. Her eyes asked the unspoken question.

Before I had time to give in, my phone jarred both of us. It rang three times before I regained enough composure to answer it. At first, there was no sound. Nothing. Then I heard the sound of someone exhaling.

"You alone?"

"Sure, Whitney." I snorted at his bluntness, turned and walked to the far corner of my apartment, away from Carley.

"I told you to call me by my Indian name. I no longer answer to the white name."

"I know. I know." I snuck a peek at Carley. She was heading for the bathroom. "What have you got for me, Cloud?"

"I think we'd better do this next Saturday."

"One week from tonight?"

"Yeah."

"Where will we meet?" I heard Carley start the shower and wished I was climbing in with her.

"Meet me in Shiprock at the gas station where 666 comes into town. You know the one?"

"Yeah. Across from that little mall. What time?"

"Midnight."

"Anything else?"

"Make sure you get extra batteries for his GPS. Mr. Computer-fucking-head says his GPS really sucks the juice."

"Ex-tra batt-er-ies…" I enunciated every syllable like I would if I was writing it down. Which I was not. "How are things on the rez?"

"Getting busy." His energy level picked up. "Lots of people this year. Biggest pow-wow ever, some say."

"But the pow-wow is down in Gallup, right?"

More inhaling and exhaling. "Right."

"So we shouldn't be bothered."

"I got it covered."

"You sure?"

"Like I said. Don't worry. I'll handle things up here. You just make sure you handle your end of things."

"Meaning?"

"Meaning, you sure you got the money thing all squared?"

"Don't tell me you're worried about getting your money?" I baited him. "What's the matter, don't you trust me?"

Inhale. Exhale. "I trust you. It's the other guy I don't trust."

"Which other guy?" I played dumb.

"The guy with the money. The guy I don't know. The guy you keep secret from me."

Carley was back in the room, a towel wrapped around her while she sorted through the clothes I'd taken off her an hour ago. I turned so I could watch her every move. God, I loved watching her. I loved that almost as much as I was enjoying baiting Whitney. "You were saying?"

"The money. *My* money!"

"Listen," I turned and lowered my voice so Carley couldn't hear but I didn't lower my intensity. "The money man transferred the money to special accounts at my bank. I've already given you those numbers."

"But we can't get it until Monday."

"Right. The money can't be released until Monday and only with the pass codes I'm getting tonight."

"When you gonna give us codes?"

"Once this deal is over and not one second earlier."

"Two million each?"

"Two million each."

More inhaling. More exhaling. "See you next Saturday." He hung up before I had a chance to get in the last word.

Carley was slipping into her blouse, looking angry about it, and I momentarily forgot what time it was. "You sure you want that on?"

She stopped and stared at me, an incredulous look blanketing her face. "You've got to go *play*, remember?" She picked up her shorts and appeared to be debating whether to put them on or throw them at me. Then, she shook her head and stepped into them. "I just don't get it, Jake." She tucked her blouse in and cinched the belt. "You're *well* over forty. You have no family and you barely even have a job." Her hands fell to her side. "Do you know what that makes you?"

"Lucky?" I shrugged my shoulders, looking for the laugh that wasn't there.

Her mouth gaped open. "You think that's being lucky?" She stood there, first slowly shaking her head in disbelief and then, as if resolving some internal issue, she nodded, like she'd just figured something out. She drew in a deep breath and let it whistle through her lips as she stepped forward. "Life is just a game to you, isn't it? Just roll the dice or deal the cards and see what happens next."

I didn't like where this was heading. "Carley, we've had this discussion."

She didn't back down. "I know! I know! Do you think I like doing this? Do you think I like telling the guy I'm in love with that he's acting like an aging playboy?"

"I haven't got time for this."

She stopped and stared at me. "You don't have time for this? How about me? Do you think I have time for this?"

I held up my hands in protest. "I have got to get going…"

"Okay. You win. I'll stop. For now. But there's going to come a time, Jake Marley, when you're going to have to make some hard decisions about what you want out of life."

"Meaning?"

"For starters," she sucked in a deep breath and let it out confidently. "I'm telling Daryl I want a divorce."

I swallowed. This wasn't what I wanted to hear. "When are you telling him?"

"Soon. Maybe tomorrow."

"You sure 'bout this?"

She nodded. "I know what I want out of life. And Daryl isn't part of it. It's time for me to move on."

"And you want to know if I'm going to be there afterward?"

She shook her head. "No. I just want you to know that this divorce is going to happen, that I will be a free woman again and that we won't have to sneak around anymore. We can be together if you want to—but only if you want to. I'm not asking for an answer now. Just think about what this means. To us."

I stepped forward and put my arms around her. "Worried?"

"Yes. You know what an asshole Daryl can be." She wrapped her arms around me and nestled in close.

"I can go with you."

"No. That would only make matters worse. Besides, this is something I have to do myself."

"What can I do?"

She pulled back and looked deep into my eyes. "Be there for me when it's over."

"Okay."

Her eyes narrowed. "You sure?"

"Positive."

"Good, because I'll be counting on you."

I put my hands on her shoulders and gently pushed her back. "The game should be over by one and I'll need a ride home."

"Okay." She smiled. "One o'clock."

"Wait. Make it two. Hank had something he wanted to talk about, remember? But don't get there any earlier." I smiled. "I don't need any distractions."

She went about the business of leaving, adjusting her clothes and fussing with her hair and makeup. She started to say something a couple of times but stopped. Finally, she kissed me and left.

In the shower, I tried to put her words out of my mind. It wasn't easy. What she'd just told me—what she'd been telling me all along—made some sense. I wasn't getting any younger. There was more to life than poker and drinking and wild women. Everyone needs someone special in their life. And deep down, at some level that rarely saw the light of day, I knew all that. I just wasn't sure I was ready to admit it to Carley—or to myself.

For the past twenty-five years, I'd lived life my own way and done whatever I wanted. I'd salvaged what I could from a failed marriage and a family scandal and went forward. I wasn't one of those people who sat around pissing and moaning about what had happened to them or blaming society or being the middle child. None of that crap. I picked up the pieces, got on with it and never looked back.

But lately, especially with Carley, I was becoming aware that my version of "the good life" wasn't going to last forever. Nor was it preparing me for the future. The job of being Jake Marley hadn't come with a 401K plan. While playing a few hands of poker with the boys on Saturday night was fun, it can't, according to Carley, compare with holding hands during a Tuesday matinee with someone you really care about.

Was she right? Was there anyone out there who was worth changing for? While I wasn't sure Carley was enough of a reason, I also knew I didn't want to live my life devoid of such intimate pleasures.

I shifted my focus to Whitney's call. We were going for it next Saturday. One more week! That made me nervous and excited at the same time. This was such a big deal that I couldn't help but be nervous. Yet, it was so simple and so fucking lucrative that I couldn't help but be over-the-top excited, either.

I shook my head, clearing it of things that needed to be worked on at some other time and started getting my game face on. Me. Hank. Smiley's right-hand man Rufus standing guard over the action, his massive size quietly keeping everyone in line. And three or four cowboys with plenty of money who think they know how to play poker.

To make tonight's game more interesting, a charade of sorts, I'd decided I would be from Kansas City. *Here on business and lookin' for a little* ecessary risk, one that is going to backfire someday. I tell them I pull these little escapades because I don't want the other players to think they are getting set up by a couple of locals. While there is more than a hint of truth to that, in reality, I do it for me. I've been doing this for so long that I'm bored and need to shake things up. I need a challenge. I need an element of danger in my life.

Which is part of the reason I was going to pretend to be from KC. Which is also why I'm sleeping with a married woman. Which is why I'm going treasure hunting next Saturday.

But none of that explains why I think I can trust Whitney Cloud again. That makes no sense at all.

2
Hank
Saturday Night

It was Saturday night and it wasn't unusual for Jake or me to be at Smiley's, either knocking back a few or playing a couple hands of cards. I elbowed myself a place at the rail.

"Evening, Smiley," I called to the owner. Smiley's Old Saloon was dark and smoky, with a poker game in the back room. This was a bar you could call home. The old boy glanced up and flashed me his trademark, a sly smile. His weathered complexion gave him an undeterminable age. He'd been bald since the day I met him, many years before. He kept the fringe around his ears short as a day-old beard; otherwise his dome was bare. Smiley was a big beefy man, with the arms of a day laborer. He was a proud man and took care of himself. His clothes were always clean and pressed.

"So you're the host tonight?" he stated in a hushed tone.

"Yeah, all the fish lined up?" I replied quietly, looking forward to making a few IRS-free dollars and paying off a few bills.

"There are four eager beavers already lined up to play a couple hands of cards. Here comes the fifth player now." Smiley reached across the bar and clapped me on the shoulder as if to give me strength. When I turned around, I was face to face with my good buddy. "Hank," Smiley was talking loud enough for everyone close to the bar to hear. "This is Jake. He's from Kansas City, in town on business. Isn't that right, Jake?" mocked Smiley.

"Oh, so you're from KC. Nice town," I stated sarcastically, playing along with a familiar charade. It wasn't that Jake and I cheated, we just played "partners" poker—like in bridge when you bid. Not something that was out-and-out cheating but not something you made public, either.

Jake had a grin carved so big, I thought he was a jack-o-lantern. His emerald green eyes twinkled mischievously. I've seen more than one pretty lady lose herself, looking deep into those green pools trying to figure out what made him tick. Tonight he even looked like some kind of businessman in a freshly pressed white shirt. He had the sleeves rolled up, shirt open at the neck, and he was wearing a pair of slightly faded khaki chinos. I noticed he had on a pair of expensive deck shoes without socks. A Navajo silver bracelet graced his left wrist. His dark chestnut brown hair had been cut in the last couple days and left just long enough to graze the top of his ears, giving him a slightly tousled look. The new cut was short and hid the gray that had recently snuck in. Jake looked years younger than a man in his forties. He worked out just enough to keep himself trim and muscular. Tonight he looked like a well-heeled yuppie. I felt almost like a slob next to Jake. There was a day's growth on my chin and my dark brown hair hung loose, just short of my shoulders. I gave my head a slight shake to get the hair out of my eyes and pushed some behind my ears.

Jake stepped in close and took my hand, shaking it over-zealously. I could smell Old Spice.

"Nice to meet you, Hank," he said, perfecting his persona.

"You're so full of shit sometimes," I replied softly, looking him in the eye. "I want to talk to you later," I whispered loud enough for only Jake to hear, as I squeezed his hand and made him wince before letting go.

"So let's play cards," he said, trying to maintain a smile.

"Hank," Rufus touched me on the shoulder. "Everyone is itching to get started." I looked around the room at the four prospective players and Jake. I finished my shot of rye and took my place at the table. Anticipation hung heavily in the air. Everyone was acting like a winner.

"Okay, gentlemen, it's time to play cards." Several packs of unopened cards were stacked in the middle of the table. I reached for the blue deck and showed everyone that the seal hadn't been broken. I opened the pack, discarded the jokers and shuffled.

A lone window was open and it helped clear the smoke from the small room. Along the wall was a small bar where Rufus mixed drinks. We sat at an ancient wooden table, worn smooth from many years of use. Rufus brought me a CC and water, which was mostly water. He knew I liked to keep my head clear during play. Rufus asked if anyone else would like a drink.

I shuffled the cards one final time. "Nothing wild, five-card, seven-card games. You can high-low split the pot, but no bullshit games named after states or animals. You wanna play Texas Hold 'Em, go someplace else. This is real poker. You win with pairs, straights, flushes. Ante up fifty, five raises and a two hundred dollar limit. Any questions?" I fanned cards face down across the green felt. "High card deals."

A tourist from Minnesota was on my left. His name was Andy, and he was antsy. He rubbed his hands together and then pulled the nine of hearts from the fan. Next was a short, chunky Texan, Brian, who bought and sold cattle. He worked a large, unlit cigar around in the corner of his mouth. He appeared to be serious about playing cards and having a good time. Seven of clubs was his card. I took the wrapper off a Cuban and bit the end. "Anyone care if I smoke?" Not waiting for an answer, I lit the stubby cigar and savored the first puff. The Texan smiled and followed my lead.

"Ah, Jake, is it?" I asked, playing my part.

Jake drew a ten of hearts. A guy who looked like a real cowboy, named Slim, was next. He needed to beat Jake's ten.

"Slim," I said, when he hesitated, "it's your turn."

He pulled the devil's bedpost, the four of spades. Not a face card on the table. Next, Dave, a music teacher from Iowa who kept humming and singing show tunes, was on the receiving end of the eight of spades. I turned up another spade, the queen, and dealt the first hand.

I flipped the cards around the table. Some of the players picked them up as they were dealt. Others waited eagerly for all five cards before looking at what Lady Luck had in store. I was one of the latter. I believed it was unlucky to pick up your cards before they were all dealt. Tonight it looked like three of the players would be unlucky. Andy, the Minnesotan, was almost taking the cards out of my hand.

"Slow down, partner. They're coming fast and wild," I cautioned and blew a plume of smoke his way. "It's going to be a long night."

The cards were all dealt and everyone was studying their first hand. Five-

23

card draw is a good opening game. You can learn a lot about the players by how they play that first hand. A player who draws three to go with his pair is going to be pretty honest, not a lot of bluffing. I watch carefully to see who knows the game and who goes for the long shot.

Everyone stayed through two rounds of small raises. One by one, they laid their hands down, revealing that nobody had anything to beat Jake's two pair. He grinned in contemplation of raking in the evening's first pot. I had to disappoint my old friend with a trio of threes.

We played a few more hands and it became evident there wasn't a cowboy at the table who knew how to play. They made bad bets and didn't read the other players. "Playing stupid," is how Jake usually referred to it. But everyone was relaxed, having a good time, enjoying the game. Everyone that is, except Slim. He was sipping shots of Southern Comfort and losing. No matter what Jake or I did, we couldn't give him a small hand. I kept an eye on his mood.

I was trying to have fun along with everyone else, to keep my mind off DeDe, the woman I should never have married. Jake had warned me, "You'll be marrying your next ex-wife."

Jake won a couple of bigger pots and I won a few more. The other players took turns winning several small pots. Everyone except Slim. I spread the winning around, not taking too many hands ourselves, but when the pot was big, it usually came to one of us. The way the cards were falling, we would be out of here in half an hour with enough money for the next couple months, and I could finally unload my burden on Jake.

Slim dealt. I picked up the five cards in front of me and slowly fanned the hand; ten, a seven, an eight, a Jack, and a three, all black, all spades, except the three. It was a heart. I tossed the red card. Slim tossed me another card, a black one, the nine of spades. I held the cards close and smiled to myself.

"That'll be a hundred," stated Dave. I pushed a hundred to the center of the table and raised it another hundred. Jake caught my secret signal and smiled slightly. The next two players meet my raise. Jake bumped it another hundred. We were in sync.

Slim was suddenly alive. "I'll see the three hundred," he flipped six fifties from his dwindling stash into the middle of the table, "and that'll be hundred more, if you want to see what I got." He slowly deposited two twenties, a ten and a fifty on top of the growing pile of bills.

Shit. The man had been stewing in his own juices all night. Now, he might have finally dealt himself a hand worth playing. One by one all the players met the raise and then waited for me. I hesitated for a moment. Jake looked like he had just swallowed the canary. He enjoyed this kind of drama. I fanned my five pretty spades all in a line neatly across the table for all to read. A couple "damns" were uttered and hands were quietly folded.

Slim sat staring at his cards. Jake angled slightly to his left and looked at the cowboy. A nasty smirk crept across Slim's lips. His eyes shifted to meet Jake's and then moved back to me.

No one spoke. I could feel the tension radiating from Slim. Sometimes people get funny about losing large quantities of money, especially when they thought it was guaranteed to be theirs.

Jake cleared his throat, breaking the silence. "Well, Slim, you can either beat a straight flush or you can't."

Slim's hands, still cradling his cards, lowered slowly to the table. "I've been sittin' here all night," he began. "I've had nothing more than two pair. I finally get a hand—something I can bet on—and," his fingers opened and let the cards fall, "...and then...fuck me." He slapped the table hard; making a couple drinks spill over their tops.

"Full house, jacks over aces," someone called out as the hand was made official.

"Sumbitch," someone else sighed.

Jake laughed. Out loud. Slim had been a hard case since the opening hand and this was the final nail in his poker-playing coffin. "Guess you couldn't beat it," Jake said.

Slim's eyes narrowed and glared at Jake. Rufus stood up, anticipating trouble, but Slim did nothing but continue his long stare.

"Tough luck," the skinny Iowan nervously uttered to no one in particular. "I guess Hank wins the biggest hand of the night and all I win is the deal." He anxiously reached for the cards while I raked in the twenty-seven-hundred-dollar pot. But before Dave could announce the next hand, Slim pushed his chair back and quickly stood up.

"I'm done." His eyes burned holes in Jake. Finally, after what seemed like several long minutes, Slim slowly turned and walked deliberately toward the door. I kept focused on Slim's retreat. When the door slammed shut behind him, the tension in the room evaporated.

3
Jake
Late Saturday Night

Slim left and Hank's attention returned to the game but not specifically to me. So far as I could tell, no one at the table was even remotely aware that Hank and I were friends—or that we would be playing as a team.

"Suppose that was the rent money?" Hank asked Andy, the Minnesota tourist. A couple of the others chuckled. I said I was ready for a break. Hank took my cue and signaled for Rufus to watch the table. Chairs slid back, people stood and stretched and Hank got busy making small talk. With Rufus standing guard, no one worried about their cash being left on the table. In spite of Hank's and my teamwork, Smiley had a reputation throughout the southwest for running a good, safe game. Rufus' presence complemented that reputation. I headed straight for the john.

As I entered the main part of the bar, I did a quick scan for Slim. I didn't see him but I did see Smiley talking to some fabulous-looking woman half his age—hell, one-third his age. I shook my head. Was Smiley ever going to give up chasing pretty women?

I slowly pushed open the door to the men's room and cautiously headed for a stall. I'd half-expected to see Slim in here—either waiting with a gun or hiding in one of the stalls from his old lady. But for once, the room was empty. Two stalls, a pair of bus-station-sized urinals, a couple of sinks—and me.

Players like Slim were scary. He was clearly out of his league tonight, playing with people he didn't know and with money he obviously couldn't afford to lose. What was it about the prospect of big money that made people do things they wouldn't ordinarily do?

I was washing my hands when the door opened slowly. I shifted my head, using the mirror to see who it was. A shadowy figure with his back to me was shutting then locking door. I panicked. Nobody locked the door unless…

"*Hola.*" The man turned and faced me.

"Manny?" I was momentarily relieved. It wasn't Slim. It was Juan Maniandez, the other person I needed to see tonight. Still, I didn't let my guard down. Not totally. I wasn't sure which would be worse. The devil you know or the one you don't.

Manny was taller than most Mexicans. Large, rough-hewed features dominating his face. An oversized pair of ears, wide-set eyes and a bulbous nose made his face seem caricature-like. He stepped closer and put out his hand. "It is good to see you, my friend."

I wanted to shake hands but mine were still wet. I stammered a weak hello.

"Jake?" He smiled, a gold tooth glimmering in the fluorescent lighting. "Something wrong?"

"I wasn't expecting to see you here—in the john." I gave him my "everything is fine, everything is cool" smile and dried my hands.

"Are you having a good night at the table?"

"Don't I always?" I asked matter-of-factly.

"One way or another, you always seem to come out on top. That's why I like you. You know how to win. You are a lot like me."

I knew he meant it as a compliment. "So tell me," I said, trying to act more nonchalant than I felt. "Am I the only reason you risk coming up from Mexico or did you have some other business to tend to?"

He reached inside his coat. "I came here just to see you, Jake."

I frowned in disbelief.

"Actually, I had a little insurance matter to take care of, something that needed my personal touch." He handed me a thick envelope. I peered into it and found a stack of hundred dollar bills.

He watched me fingering the money. "There should be enough in there for the truck."

I tried to fold the envelope but it was too thick.

Manny pointed to the envelope. "The pass codes are in there, too."

"Any trouble with the arrangements?" I asked without looking up.

"Not for me." Manny suddenly seemed impatient. "When are you going?"

"My man called me late this afternoon and said this coming Saturday would be perfect."

"Saturday…" His voice trailed off and he appeared to be lost in thought. "Then you will be coming to see me on Sunday?"

I nodded. "Sure."

"What time?"

"Shit, Manny, how am I supposed to know that?"

He glared at me.

"Look," I said as I backed off. "I've never loaded a truck full of gold coins before. I have no idea how long it will take. When we're done, I'll call you. That's the best I can tell you."

"And you'll be alone?"

"Just like we agreed. I'll bring you the coins. Alone. You give me three million in cash."

"It's a shame that it's all about money, isn't it, my friend? Up-front money. Special bank accounts. Pass codes. No one trusts anyone anymore. Not like the old days." Manny reached over and felt the fabric of my shirt. "There's some extra—in case things don't go your way the rest of the night."

I smiled. "I'm not worried. Hank's playing."

Manny let go of my shirt. "He in on our deal?"

"No."

Manny frowned. "Does he know about it?"

I shook my head.

"But why? I thought he was your friend."

"It's a long story."

Manny studied me for a while, apparently trying to figure out what I meant. Finally, he shrugged. "Well, be sure to greet him for me. Tell him I'd like to see some of his recent artwork. I may be interested in making another purchase."

I nodded. "After next Saturday, we can probably all…" My words tapered off as I noticed Manny's face had suddenly gone serious.

"Jake, I have just put four million dollars into bank accounts for people I don't even know. I'm giving you three million dollars next week." He pointed toward the money in my hand. "Plus this." A faint smile flashed across his lips but faded before I could measure it for sincerity. "And you still haven't told me who these people are. You know," he growled, "I don't like secrets."

I put my hands up in front of him. "Like it or not, that was the deal." I immediately back peddled. I might snap at Manny but I knew better than to threaten him. I opened my arms and continued. "Three weeks ago I tell you I've got a deal worth at least sixteen million dollars, but it's going to cost you seven million and it has to be handled a certain way. You listen. You like what you hear. You say okay. And you realize you could stand to make a lot more than the sixteen million. Now you come around…"

Manny squared himself in front of me, his eyes burning into mine. "*Si*…"

This was going badly. I couldn't afford having him as an enemy. Not now. Not ever. I lowered my voice and my temper. "Look. Manny. We've already agreed to all of this. You can't come here now and start changing things. Everything's in place. We're this close." I pinched my fingers in front of him. "Besides, what could it matter who the other people are? You know me. You know I won't fuck you over. I trust you. You trust me." I dropped my arms, waiting for his response.

He stared. I stared. Forever. Then, slowly and quietly, he gave me a faint smile. "This had better go well, *amigo*."

Manny turned and headed for the door. As he left, I knew he'd accomplished two things. He'd brought the money to make this deal work and he'd made sure I got his not-so-subtle message. Juan Maniandez could reach out and touch me any time, any place.

I stood there for a few moments, trying to stop myself from getting angry. Didn't Manny trust me anymore? Why the subtle threat? I shook it off. This was no time for doubts. We had a deal. That was that. I'd call him tomorrow and make sure we were still on the same page.

I headed back to the game and was halfway through the door when Smiley stopped me.

"Doing okay?" he asked.

"Doin' fine." I looked the place over, checking to see if any of the other players were in sight. I'd learned a long time ago that when you are running a game, you stick to it. The smallest detail can really fuck you up. Kind of like putting a rock on a railroad track. "Put this in the safe for me." I discretely handed him the envelope. "I'll pick it up tomorrow."

Smiley eyed the thickness and made a face. "Do I need to know…?"

I cut him off and smiled. "Better you don't. Just hold it for me."

He tucked the envelope under his apron while giving me a serious, questioning look. "Sure, Jake, whatever you say."

I looked toward the poker room door. "We just lost one of the fish. Guy named Slim. What was the story on him, anyway?"

"He checked out okay. Why?"

"Don't know, exactly. Seemed kinda weird." I thought about it and then shrugged it off. "Must have been wrapped too tight for these stakes."

"Your new pigeon is already at the table."

"He check out okay?" I asked nervously.

"Knows Clarence in Amarillo. What more do you need to know?" he said as he turned and headed back to the bar.

I left a moment later and slipped into the back room. The rest of the cowboys and Hank were standing in a small circle, busy talking to the new player. I made my way over to the group, giving Rufus a private wink. Edging my way around the chunky Texan, I extended my hand toward the new guy without really looking. "Jake Marley."

The new *guy* turned and faced me. *Her* hand reached for mine, which she held gently in hers.

"Karen." She smiled, slow and sly-like.

I froze. This was the same woman Smiley had been talking with at the bar. And now she was going to play poker? With us? I hoped Smiley knew what he was doing.

She angled away from the other players and positioned herself in front of me. She was half a head shorter than me. "Smiley said there was an opening." Her hand still lightly held mine. "Do you mind?"

Suddenly, Smiley's grin made sense. Smiley hadn't said anything about the new fish being a woman.

"I'm looking forward to it," I said.

She was beautiful, gorgeous, in fact; the kind of classic beauty that immediately held your attention. Her green eyes sparkled with a hint of elfin mischief. A quick glance south revealed two nipples teasing the fabric of her silk blouse—and every cowboy in the room. Was that part of her game? Get the cowboys staring at her breasts so they'd lose their concentration? I made a mental note to pay more attention to my cards than to her.

I wanted to make the usual small talk. Where you from? What kind of work do you do? How long are you in town? Married? Got a boyfriend? Wanna see my collection of Impressionist paintings? But I was speechless. All I could think about was how absolutely beautiful she was. And how I was immediately and entirely filled with lust.

"Did you say your name was Jake Marley?" Even with such a straightforward question, her smile radiated a sexy warmth.

I managed a semi-intelligent-looking nod.

"Jake Marley? As in Dickens' Jacob Marley?" Her green eyes lit up, sparkling with curiosity.

"Yeah." I slowly moved her away from the others.

"Did your parents do that on purpose?" Her eyebrows arched with the question.

"It's kind of complicated."

"So what's your brother's name, Tiny Tim?" She laughed like she was certainly pleased with herself. If I hadn't heard the same question a half-million times I might have thought it was amusing, too. But I had and it wasn't. My displeasure must have showed.

"I'm sorry," she offered. "It's just that it's so unusual. Your name, I mean…" Her hand lightly touched mine. Her eyes sought mine. All was immediately forgiven.

Hank called us all back to the table. "We have a new player," he announced. "She told me her name is Karen and that she comes from west Texas. I told her my name is Hank and that she and her west Texas money were more than welcome in Santa Fe. I also told her we play for keeps."

I was surprised by Hank's sense of humor. I knew he had one. It's just that he seldom ever uses it with people he doesn't know well. He prefers the solitary life. Claims it suits him and helps his art. He could go days without seeing anyone. Now, he was acting like the emcee at a Friar's Roast. I wondered if his good mood had anything to do with that lawyer-bitch of a wife getting any closer to leaving him. I'd warned him…

Whatever it was, I was sure he'd be telling me about it—after the game.

* * *

Less than an hour later, Karen, who hadn't been winning, announced, "I'm sorry but I've only got time for one more hand." A slow smile crept across her face. "What do you gentlemen say we raise the stakes?"

Hank immediately gave his approval. "It's all right with me, hundred ante and five hundred raise?" His eyes traveled around the table. Finding no objections, he turned to Karen. "Okay?"

"Just what I was thinking."

She didn't hesitate with her answer and I liked that. Most of the women I know offer little except sweet compliance. Karen seemed like she knew what she wanted and went right after it. That intrigued me.

Hank dealt straight seven, a good betting game—one that insured the last hand would be worth staying to the end. I held a pair of tens in the hole with a third ten arriving on the next round. Not bad. Three cards, three tens. I sent a private signal to Hank.

The next three rounds brought more good news. I hit my full house on the sixth card and continued raising. Karen had a pair of aces showing and raised me back at every opportunity.

The room was getting tight. It was like we all suddenly realized that someone was going to walk out of here with over ten grand from this one hand. Even Rufus edged forward in his chair, craning for a better view.

"Last card, down and dirty," Hank announced the perfunctory statement as each card nestled in with its predecessors. "Aces bet." He nodded toward Karen and then added, "May the best man—player—win."

Without looking at her last card and without hesitating, she bet five hundred. Was she bluffing?

Dave passed. Hank and Andy immediately bumped another five hundred each. Brian called and I quietly added my money, not looking at my last card. I'd be seeing it soon enough.

Karen lifted the edge of her last card. Her eyes widened momentarily and I thought I heard her gasp. She looked at Hank, her eyes narrowed and then back to her cards. After a long and quiet half minute, she turned her cards face down and sat back in her chair. "I'm out."

I was stunned. Had she been riding a pair of aces and bluffing the whole time? If that was true, I had to give her credit for guts. I'd figured she had the best shot at beating me and now she was out.

Everyone anted what they owed and put their hands on the table. My full house triumphed and I silently raked in the biggest pot of the night.

Hank stood up and grinned. I wasn't sure if it was because it was such a spectacular round or because he knew we'd both be pocketing a several grand from this hand alone. The others shook hands and recapped the last hand—and the night. Most players seem to find pleasure in retelling or reliving certain aspects of the evening. I wasn't like that. For me, win or lose, the game was over. It was time to move on.

While people started getting up and stretching, I did what most winners do and stuffed a couple of bills in the house jar and called Rufus over. As I handed him his tip, I asked, "Where can I stash this?"

"Mr. Smiley has a safe for just that reason," Rufus answered loud enough for the entire room to hear. "I'm sure he'd insist that you keep your money in there until tomorrow. I'll get you a receipt."

We shook hands and he went about the business of helping me protect my money. I'd learned a long time ago that a little bit of timely prevention saved a lot of potential trouble later.

I'd won the hand, now I had to choose between having that talk with Hank or getting to know Karen. Then I remembered Carley. Shit! I checked my watch. It showed a few minutes before one. I realized I did not want to see Carley. Not now. Not tonight. I still had time to give her a call and tell her not to come down, tell her that Hank was going to give me a ride home, tell her something. But before I had the chance, Karen stepped in front of me.

"Buy me a drink?" Her question was soft enough to sound enticing, loud enough for everyone else in the room to hear. The lady had made her choice. I'd made mine. My talk with Hank would have to wait until tomorrow. As for Carley, I'd see what this gorgeous woman from west Texas had on her mind first. Maybe I could have a quick drink with Karen and send her on her way before Carley got there. It was looking like a win-win situation for me.

I scooted by Hank and led Karen away from the poker table and into the main room, checking for an isolated table. I found an empty booth and signaled for Irene.

"Two brandies," I ordered as she drifted within earshot. She took my order, smiled like she would for any out-of-town-businessman and then headed to the bar. Like most of Smiley's regulars, she knew I was playing a role tonight. She also knew enough not to be the one to blow it for me. I liked playing my little games. She liked getting big tips.

After a few moments, Karen reached for my hand. "Let me see your palm."

I resisted, just a little.

She did that thing women do whenever they run up against male stubbornness. She rolled her eyes, took in a deep breath and slowly, patiently continued. "You might not believe me, Jake Marley, but I'm pretty good at telling people things about their future. And their past." Her eyes were locked with mine.

Something about her looking me squarely in the eyes demanded I at least give her a chance. She seemed like the type of person who swung for the fences. I liked that.

"Relax." Her tone became friendlier, almost seductive.

Irene arrived with our drinks and a private smile for me. The she headed for her next table.

"So what am I going to be when I grow up?" I asked.

Karen cradled my right hand in hers and studied the lines, first with her eyes and then with the tip of a fingernail. Closing her eyes and squeezing my hand, she took in a deep breath and slowly let it out. Without looking up, she began. "I see travel." Her fingernail stopped at the confluence of two lines I never knew I had. "Someplace hot and dry. This journey will be very soon."

I pulled my hand away and looked at it. "Where do you see all this?"

She took my hand back and pointed. "Here." She guided my attention to a big line in the middle of my palm. "This is your fate line. Over here," she said, raising the outer edge and pointing to the base of my little finger, "is love. Marriage." Another not so gentle twist. "Right here, along the thumb. Your lifeline. Up here, where they meet, is the start of your head line. See how they cross, how they get deeper, how they have little breaks in them?"

I couldn't really see what she was pointing out but nodded anyway. I'd never met a palm reader before—at least not one that I'd ever thought was doing more than telling me what I wanted to hear.

"Okay, okay." I lied. "I believe you."

"You want me to continue?"

"Sure. Why not?" Sure, why not, we were in New Mexico and hot and dry was not seeing the future, and travel, well, a trip to the grocery store was traveling.

She went right back to work. "I see money—lots of money." Her eyes rose slowly and met mine. "I also see danger…"

I swallowed. So far, she'd more or less outlined my impending excursion into the desert. Travel. Hot and dry. Lots of money. But danger? This thing, this deal, this was supposed to be easy. I had it all worked out and I'd taken every precaution. "What?" I smiled, masking my apprehension. "Like I'm going to lose my wallet?"

"Look," she stated. "You can either believe me or not. It really doesn't matter. But I *do* have this ability. I read palms. I do star charts. I can see things…"

"Like?"

"Like there's a lot of pain in you." Her hands reached for and found mine. She closed her eyes, concentrated and a moment later whispered, "A bank. I see a bank. An old man. A young woman…"

A chill crawled up my spine and crinkled my neck. I tried to pull my hand away but she held it tight. Her eyes opened and she looked at me, wondering if she'd come close. The look on my face told her she had.

"Want to talk about it?" Her hands were now soothing mine.

"No." Things, personal things, got buried for good reasons. While I could handle just about any situation, I'd never been good at dealing with certain portions of my life.

We sat quietly—I'm not sure how long—when a large shadow blanketed our table. It was Rufus.

"Mr. Marley? Mr. Smiley over there," he pointed toward the bar, "would like to see you for a minute."

I looked up at him, knowing he was still helping me perfect my charade for the evening and was about to politely decline, to tell Rufus that Mr. Smiley would just have to wait. Then I saw the serious look on Rufus' face. Something was up.

I nodded an apology to Karen and followed Rufus to the far corner of the bar where Smiley waited. I immediately started to express my concern that we shouldn't be talking when he waved me off.

"Relax, Jake, the other fish have all left. Just your lady friend is left."

I looked around, more out of nervousness than disbelief. If Smiley said they were gone, they were gone. Besides, it was so dark that I couldn't have picked anyone out anyway. Only the pool table area was lit well enough to see faces clearly and it was nearly empty, just two big Mexicans and none of the regulars. That was unusual. This was Saturday and Smiley's pool tables were always busy on Saturday night. It was like something—or someone—had scared everyone away.

Smiley handed me some cards. Keeping them close to my body, I peeled them back, revealing an eight, a five, a ten and four aces!

I looked back up at Smiley. "This what I think it is?"

He nodded. "Rufus picked up her hand after you left. He told me. I thought you ought to know."

"Shit." I muttered. "Hank know?"

Smiley shook his head. "Not yet."

"And you're sure she's okay? You checked her out, right?"

He gave a slight shrug. "As sure as I am with anybody." He looked over in her direction and then back at me. "She knows Clarence. What more do you want?"

He was right. If Clarence had said she was okay, that should be good enough. Besides, if she was the law, we'd all have been busted by now. But if she wasn't the cops, then who was she?

I patted him on the shoulder, told him thanks for the good news and turned back toward Karen. Shit! The two Mexicans who had been playing pool were now hovering around our booth. I sped across the bar and came to within a few steps of them before I slowed my pace. I'd walked into a hornet's nest before but I'd never *run* into one. As I drew closer, I noticed Hank was sitting in the booth with Karen. I felt better already.

"We jus wanna dance with de lady." One of them was in Hank's face, attempting to stake his claim on Karen.

I tapped the shoulder of the other man. "There a problem here?" I gritted my teeth. I'm not a big guy but I can *attitude* like one.

Both men turned and faced me. Neither spoke. They just stared. So be it. Right or wrong, win or lose, I didn't back away from trouble. I stepped closer without questioning whether Hank would back me up. He was here. That was all I needed to know.

"If she wanted to dance, it'd be with me, not you." I stopped right in front of the bigger of the two men. I never blinked. Neither did he. The bar was filled with a deadly silence.

The bigger man grabbed my arms. "Go away, leetle man." His face was directly in front of mine and I hoped he wasn't half as mean as he looked. "Dis ain none a your beeness." His eyes were filled with menace.

Hank stood up next to me and suddenly I felt the presence of a third person. It was Rufus. He'd edged his way to my right and the three of us formed a threatening triangle.

"This ain't gonna happen." Rufus' voice was calm yet powerfully effective.

The entire bar was stone still and unearthly quiet. The big man let go of my arms. "C'mon, Miguel," he muttered to the second man. "We don need dis shit."

Miguel blinked, turned an inch to his left to look at Rufus and then returned to me. He smiled, revealing a whole crop of bad teeth. "We will meet again."

"Yeah?" I leaned closer. "Next time, make sure you bring your balls."

The one named Miguel smirked, turned to his right and looked at Hank. "You shoulda let us dance with de pretty lady." They headed for the door, knocking over a couple of chairs in the process.

Hank looked at me. "Bring your balls?"

I smiled. "Yeah. I thought maybe we'd go bowling."

Rufus shook his head in disbelief and headed back toward the bar.

I scooted into the booth next to Karen. She was still shaken. "Are you nuts? Talking like that? There were two of them!"

"I'm sorry." I feigned sincerity. "Did you want to dance with them?"

She stared for a moment and then turned away. I downed my brandy and signaled for another.

Hank leaned toward me. "Rufus isn't always going to be around." Hank backed off, remembering we really weren't supposed to know each other.

I knew he was right but it wasn't what I wanted to hear right now. Once again, I'd taken a big chance and beat the odds. I was still high from the rush, from the excitement. "But Rufus *was* here and that's all that matters."

Hank frowned. "You didn't make any friends here tonight. What about the next time?"

"Never happen." I looked to see where Irene was with my drink. "Two drifters coming through town. That's all. By tomorrow, they'll be a couple hundred miles from here."

Hank half-smiled and gave me his "you're full of bullshit" look and then turned his attention to Karen. "I didn't mean to bother the two of you but I just wanted to tell Karen how much I enjoyed playing cards with her tonight and I wanted to invite her to come back and play anytime she's in Santa Fe." Obviously, Hank was trying to cover for his gaff.

I smiled back at Hank and then at Karen. I could continue this charade, too. "If either of you are ever in KC, you might want to stop in at Builder's on the east side. They've been known to have a game or two. Just mention my name."

We fell into one of those awkward moments where no one knows what to say next. From Hank's concern over my well being, it must have been obvious to Karen that we hadn't just met tonight. But, so far, she hadn't reacted. If she wasn't going to bring it up, neither was I.

I looked at Hank and was torn between telling him to leave and asking him to stay. I was totally wrapped up with figuring out Karen and I didn't want to deal with whatever potential problems Hank carried to the table. On the other hand, things had gotten more than a little weird tonight. Spooky-actin' Slim. Manny's attitude. Karen dropping with four aces. And those two *hombres*. Hank was the only person I trusted and I might need him. I wasn't so sure what I was up against.

I slid in closer and whispered to Hank. "Karen says she can read people's palms. Says she's a psychic."

Hank snickered and put his hand in Karen's. I detected some hesitancy on her part but she soon started examining Hank's lines.

"I see that you are an artist." Karen's voice was professional and held the air of confidence. "I also see that you have a friend..." Her fingers traced a line across his palm and then she raised her eyes to meet his. "This friend isn't being honest with you."

Silence. This was getting more and more strange. She was right. Dead right. I'd kept my excursion a secret from Hank. Not that I wanted to. I didn't. But he'd told me a long time ago to never involve him in any of my illegal or semi-illegal activities ever again.

I reached for Hank's hand and angled it towards me. "I see something here." I studied some lines. "I see that Hank has someplace to be right now. Yes. Look here." I pointed out a line in Hank's hand to Karen. "See. Right here. It says he's already ten minutes late."

Karen leaned in, picking up on my strategy. "I think you are right, oh Great One." I noticed her previous tension had all but evaporated. Or was it just hidden?

I smiled and winked at Hank. "It was nice meeting you."

He stuffed any additional comments, offered a weak grin and scooted out of the booth. He knew what was going to happen next and he knew that he was in the way.

We finished our brandies. We didn't talk much, not about anything important. Mostly, we just sat there and looked at each other. I marveled at how the light from the candle emphasized and shadowed her beauty, how her diamond earrings sparkled, how her perfume was slowly, surely enveloping me.

I had no idea what she was thinking but I was having a world-class debate going on in my brain. I wanted her. In the back room. Or out in the parking lot. Anywhere. There was something incredibly intriguing about her and I *wanted* her.

Still, another part of me said *stay away*. She was trouble. She was too smart, too beautiful, too good to be true. I doubted she just walked in here looking for a card game. I even doubted she was from west Texas. And, most of all, I doubted that this was some kind of chance encounter. This was a woman with a purpose.

What was it? Then, it hit me. She'd tossed away the winning and the pot worth eleven grand like it was nothing. That might mean she had more money, lots more. I cocked my head and looked at her in a whole new light. If she had lots of money, I wanted to know about it. And as long as I kept one step ahead of whatever game she was playing, what could go wrong?

"Jake?" Her voice was soft and fluid and held the promise of untold pleasures. Her nipples were hard against her silk blouse.

"Yeah..."

"We could sit here and get drunk or..." Her hand reached under the table and stroked my thigh. "...or we could go someplace else."

Okay. We could do that. I could get to know her a little better, see if I could find out why she tossed in the aces, find out just how much more cash she had around. Okay. We could do that. Nothing I did tonight was going to interfere with what was going to happen later this week.

She stopped stroking my thigh, glanced toward the bar and then back to me. "I think someone wants you."

I turned. It was Carley. Shit! I'd forgotten all about her. She was glaring at me, her anger coming off in measurable thermals. I swiveled around, asked Karen to excuse me for a moment and headed for the bar desperately trying to think how I was going to handle this.

I stopped a few feet in front of her and we both stared. Finally, she glanced back toward Karen. "She's very pretty."

"Carley, listen…"

She faced me. "Now I understand why you didn't want me here early."

"You've got it all wrong."

"No, Jake, I've got it all *right*." Her face was a study of controlled rage and crushed feelings. "Who is she?"

"No one you know. We're just having a drink."

She took in a deep breath and exhaled slowly. "Just a drink?"

"Just a drink."

"I know you, Jake Marley. You don't have *just a drink* with a woman who looks like that."

"She played in the game tonight…"

"Don't lie to me!" she snapped. "You think I'm stupid? You think I can't see what's going on?" Her eyes burned into mine. "I didn't just walk in the door, you know. I came early, sat in the shadows in the back, watching the two of you!" She waited for my reaction but I didn't have one. At least, not one she would want to hear. "Have you forgotten this is how *we* met?"

I shook my head. "No. I haven't forgotten."

"Then stop lying to me."

She had me in her cross hairs and her finger was squeezing the trigger. If I told the truth, maybe she'd go for a clean, painless kill. "Okay."

"You're going home with her, aren't you?"

"Yes."

She flinched and closed her eyes. "You're a real bastard." She nodded her head. "Right now I hate you more than I ever hated anyone in my life."

"Carley, I never intended…"

"Shut up! Just shut up." She put her palms in front of my face. "I don't want to hear about it. I don't what to hear any more lies. Not now. Not ever." She dropped her hands and started backing away. "The thing of it is, I knew all along that something like this was going to happen." She sucked in a deep breath and let it out slowly. "This is what you do. This is who you are. You can't be trusted."

I couldn't argue with her.

"Jake, I am the best thing that could ever happen to you and you don't even realize it. You're going to regret this night for a long, long time."

Carley Rose Butler turned and walked toward the door, never stopping to look back. Some small, mostly ignored segment of my psyche told me she was right. I *was* going to regret this.

I slowly headed back to the booth but instead of sliding in next to Karen I sat across from her on the outside edge of the seat.

"Is there a problem?" she asked softly.

"No," I lied.

"If I'm in the middle of something, I can just go."

"No. Stay."

Then we were quiet, both of us staring at far off points. I had no idea what Karen was thinking but I'd mentally drawn my sword and was busy slaying the Carley Dragon one final time. I liked her but not as much as she liked me. She was, after all, still married. She would want me to get a real job and settle down. She'd want to have a house and kids. She'd want me to be her version of a suburban husband. I felt bad for the way it'd ended. She deserved better.

Karen leaned across the table. "Do you still want to do something?"

I kicked the Carley dragon over the cliff. "Sure. Your place or mine?"

She arched an eyebrow and smiled. "I'd like to go to your place but not if we have to drive all the way to Kansas City."

I chuckled and wondered when, exactly, she'd figured out I wasn't from KC. "You see, I'm here so much that I actually have an apartment on the north side." The lie flowed effortlessly, almost automatically out of my mouth as I nodded my head in the direction of my apartment. "It's not far."

She continued her stare. I wondered if she believed me or if it really mattered or if what we were about to do had anything to do with geography.

"One problem," I confessed, changing the subject. "I don't have a car."

"That's not a problem." She fished out a set of keys and handed them to me. "There's a brand new, red Grand Prix just waiting for us."

I handed them right back. "Actually, I do have a car. It's the license I don't have."

I smiled. She smiled. In a few seconds, we were on our way.

4
Hank
Saturday Night

"Smiley, bring me another shot of rye and a Guinness." I had just drained the bottle of stout in anticipation of another.

"How much you going to drink? I'm not going to stay open all night just for you."

Winny gave a yelp in reply to her master's statement, as if she agreed. The English bulldog was a fixture at the bar. Sometimes patrons felt something breeze by their feet and reached down to brush it away. When they did, they were rewarded with a wet tongue. I've heard more than one person give out a shriek when Winny pulled this routine.

I gave Smiley an incredulous look and leaned over the bar to find the dog. "I ain't even drunk yet, Winny." But I wanted to be.

"Yeah, well…" Smiley moved down the bar to pick up a few empty glasses and wipe up a spill.

The bar was almost cleared out. Jake and Karen had left twenty minutes ago. The stale smell of cigarettes and beer hung in the air. Smiley kept the overhead fans spinning, which helped, but I would still smell like a bar the next day. A couple making goo-goo eyes at each other giggled in one of the booths behind me. Otherwise only half-finished drinks and plates with puddles of ketchup remained. The clatter of pool balls being smacked around was now silent, but the jukebox played a country western song whining about lost love and lost chances. Rufus was helping the waitresses clear the tables. I was the only one sitting at the bar.

"Smiley, you know I quit smoking over fifteen years ago. Me and Jake quit at the same time." Smiley looked my way to indicate he had heard me. "Hey, Smiley, you got a cigarette?"

Smiley made his way back to my spot, grabbing a couple more glasses along the way and placing them in the sink under the bar. "You and Jake made a few bucks tonight." He wiped at a wet spot. "I just wish Jake didn't like to play visiting businessman. Some night one of the locals is going to blow that little charade of his."

"Or one of his girlfriends," I interjected. "Carley probably did it tonight."

"And then who knows what trouble there will be?" replied Smiley. "Jake shouldn't treat Carley that way. The girl loves him. Beats me why."

"She's still married to that Daryl with one L." I blew an imaginary smoke ring into the air. We were both silent for a moment.

"You'd think Jake would get enough of a thrill out of taking money off these yokels. But no, he has to be fucking Jack Nicholson. He should have been an actor," I said laughing. "That cowboy tonight…" I shook my head to clear it, trying to remember his name.

"You mean Slim?" Smiley filled in my memory.

"Yeah, that's him, Slim. He was squir-rel-ly. He ever been in here before? He isn't going to be a regular is he?" I took another drag off the ghost cigarette. "'Cause if he is, he'll find out Jake ain't from Kansas City. Smiley, you tell Jake he can't play no more if he's goin' to be from out-of-town."

Smiley gave me a big grin. "You're starting to sound drunk." He grabbed the empty Guinness and put down a glass of clear liquid. "Here, have some water. It'll help the hangover you're going to have in the morning."

"I never have a hangover," I stated seriously.

Smiley shot me a doubtful look. "Anyway, Slim was all friendly and full of jokes at the bar. Said he was passing through. He's on the rodeo circuit. So it *is* possible he could be in here again sometime. Just like any of those other jokers could be back. I'll talk to Jake." Smiley wiped circles on the oak countertop until it shined.

"Yessiree," I sang. "Slim was carrying a knife." I smiled and waited for Smiley's reaction.

He quit wiping the bar for a second and listened.

"I saw it, stuck in the top of his boot. But, I'm not going to get in a knife fight over cards. No, *Señor*."

Smiley laughed. I could hear Rufus' chuckling from across the room.

"No, not you," Smiley mocked. "I remember replacing some broken furniture from more than one fight you've had in here. I told Rufus to keep an eye on that ole cowboy just in case."

"Thanks, Smiley. I really did see the knife and I quit drinking as soon as the game started."

"Yeah, sure. We're not going to let anything happen to you or Jake." Smiley raised his eyebrows. "Those other two guys, what was going on? For a minute it looked like there was going to be a fight."

"You mean those two pool players? They were drunk. They wanted to dance with that blonde. Rufus scared them off." I waved off Smiley's concern. For a second it looked like Smiley was going to comment, but he changed the topic.

"Don't you ever have to be home? That cute little wife of yours is going to wonder why you're here and not there."

I gave Smiley a long look.

"Sorry. Touchy subject?"

"Shit, I called Jake and said I wanted to talk and I end up playing poker."

"Yeah, well." Smiley sounded almost apologetic. "You know there's a game almost every Saturday. Jake gave me a fat envelope tonight," Smiley said in a hushed tone. "Has to be full of money. Where do you think he got it?"

"I have no idea. Probably full of ones," I chuckled. "What were you thinking, putting that blonde in the game tonight?"

"She asked. She had money. And this ain't the 1890s. Women play poker. Anyway, I wished I'd seen the look on Jake's face. I don't like his play-acting much either. And she was mighty friendly and pretty. But now I'm sorry I let her play."

"Yeah," I stated with some disgust, "but that's not a very good reason to let her play. That sounds like Jake's thinking."

Smiley shrugged. "She asked if she could sit in. I told her I didn't know what she was talking about." Smiley leaned his elbows on the bar and gave me one of his smiles. "Then she mentioned Clarence."

"She could have been a cop."

Smiley gave me a doubting look. "I've been sizing up players long before you and Jake started believing you were the Maverick brothers. You're not the first people to win a hand of five-card in that room. There was a game long before…oh shit." Smiley gave a belly laugh. "There were some times." He shook his head, sending memories I knew only as legends on their way.

"It just seemed strange the way she homed in on Jake."

"Maybe she could tell you were married."

My look was my reply.

"Maybe she thought Jake was cute. I don't know. This isn't the first time a woman took Jake home." Smiley leaned forward on the bar and checked to see if anyone might be eavesdropping on our conversation. "If you think it seemed strange that she picked up Jake, the four aces she dropped in the last hand were even stranger."

"What?"

"She dropped with four aces."

"I don't believe it!"

"Rufus brought me the hand."

"She was a cop!"

"No way. That I'm sure of. I know a cop when I see one, even one undercover. And this dolly wasn't a cop."

Smiley sounded like he was sure and I didn't say anymore on the subject. But dropping with four aces is more than strange. I would have to ask Jake what he made of this stupid move.

Smiley had the bar cleared and cleaned, except for my lone glass.

I scratched my head and finished the water. Holding up the empty, I said, "Another, my good bar-keep."

"Okay, but that's your last. Then I'm cutting you off. I'm tired and I'm not staying all night so you can work your way into a funk."

"She was a pretty one." I whistled through my teeth. "Yes, sir." I licked my lips.

I received a gentle slap on the back of my head. When I turned, Irene was standing there smiling. "You mind your manners, hot rod." She had a towel over her shoulder and a fourteen-hour day behind her. Irene was fifty-two and looked thirty-five. She'd been married more times than me. Her last husband had died two winters before of a heart attack.

"Hank Djumpstrom, you're a married man. If you're going to go ordering off the menu…" She gave me a wink. Smiley watched us as he went about putting bottles back in their correct places along the mirrored shelves behind the bar.

I returned Irene's smile, reached out and took her hand. "I'm a single man again, Irene. There's nobody out on the farm these days but me." Irene stepped towards me.

"Where's DeDe?" There was an ardent tone in the question.

"She's long gone and won't be coming back," I said playfully and returned her wink. We exchanged questioning looks. "I'm a free man." I tried to sound serious.

Irene smiled, trying to read me.

I gave her a long look. My face showed my statement was true. When I kissed her full on the mouth, she returned the affection. I could feel her breasts push against my chest. I had wanted to kiss Irene for a long, long time.

5
Jake
Sunday Morning

My first conscious thought of the day was that my head was wracked with pain. My second conscious thought was that I wasn't alone. A woman was in bed with me. Carley? No, that couldn't be. Not after last night. Then who?

Okay, Jake, I told myself, *it's time for a look, time to put the puzzle together.* I half-opened my eyes. They hurt, too. How much had I drank? Slowly, ever-so-slowly, I started turning my aching head.

I've been told that there are lower life forms that depend on their ability to move slowly, carefully and quietly. It's how they hide from larger animals or stalk smaller ones. I couldn't help but think that they would have been impressed with the way I inched my head to the left, trying to get a look at my companion.

For a while, it seemed like I wasn't getting anywhere. I wondered if the earth and I were rotating—or was it revolving—at the same speed, making it a physical impossibility for me to ever catch up.

Then, finally, she came into view. Her hair first. Blonde. Sort of. Fallen-down blonde hair, half covering her face. Not Carley. But who?

I thought that might be a blessing in disguise. In these Sunday morning encounters, one person always wound up disappointed. Mostly, it'd been me. I was the one who vowed to be more selective *next* time. I was the one who muttered, "Got-to-leave-can't-stay-for-breakfast-call-you-later," pulling my pants on as I headed for the door.

Usually. But not always. There had been a time or two when I'd have made breakfast, lunch and dinner, quit my job—or got one, whatever she wanted—and written bad checks all across New Mexico just to get her to stay awhile.

She stirred. She rolled toward me. Her arm slid up and rested on my chest. For a brief moment, the sort-of-blonde hair parted and revealed her beautiful face.

My eyes trailed the contours of her body. Her breasts were full, her waist was slim and her stomach flat. The sheets guarded the rest.

Just as I noticed I was getting hard, her hand slowly traced a path from my chest to my stomach to just beneath the sheets.

"Look who's awake..." she murmured. Her hand was already at work.

She rose up on one elbow and looked me square in the eyes. Maybe it was her turn to re-evaluate her drinking career, make a hasty exit and start going to church.

Maybe not. She smiled. I smiled.

That smile. Now I remembered. Last night. The poker game. Folded with four aces. Said she could tell me my fortune. Said she saw travel and money and danger. Without knowing it, she'd nailed next Saturday's deal. Not the finer details, but enough to make me wonder about this palm reading, psychic shit. And about her.

And I remembered thinking—no, *knowing*—this woman was trouble—that I should just get up and walk away.

But she had *that smile*. The smile you don't see very often. The one that comes from a woman who already knows what's on your mind—and knows how to make it happen. That slow, sly smile that holds a whole universe of enticing promises.

I ran last night's choices through my muddled brain one last time. Trouble? Sex? I smiled at the thought of debating it as long as I had. Hell, I would make sure she was long gone *before* she got to be any trouble. There was no way I was going to let some wench—no matter how *interesting* her smile was—get in my way.

I remembered that I had noticed something else in that smile, too. Something I couldn't quite put my finger on. Something that made me uneasy.

I was usually good at reading people. Had to be when you made your living playing poker. Hundreds, even thousands, of dollars rested on being able to tell if a cowboy was bluffing or not. But I remembered that I just couldn't get a good read on her.

And Carley. Best I could remember I'd blown her off. Wait. Had she blown me off? I decided to let the Carley situation go for now. I would see Hank later and find out what he thought. He'd been there last night. He'd seen what had happened. He could help me put "the night before" back in some semblance of order. He was good at it, too. Said I'd given him plenty of practice.

Her hand stopped teasing and gave S*eñor* a squeeze, bringing me back to the here and now, to her lips, her breasts, to her beautiful naked body.

Fuck Hank. Fuck thoughts of Hank.

Suddenly, hangover and all, I was *very* busy.

6
Hank
Early Sunday Morning

The phone rang three times and then I heard a click and the answering machine started its message. I waited for Jake's latest version of "Aren't I funny, aren't I clever" to end.

"Yes, Jake, you are a very funny guy. Maybe you should try being a stand-up. It'd be a regular job." I paused, leaving a long blank space in the tape. "Since you're not answering your phone, you either got lucky and are enjoying the bliss I imagine the blonde from last night could bestow or, she read your palm again and found out what a pig you really are and dumped you, and you are now sleeping off a screaming hangover all by yourself, which you deserve for saying I had other places to be, which I didn't." The beep signaled my time was up.

I slammed down the phone and stared at it for a few seconds. "I wonder if Alexander Graham Bell knows what he did to the human race?" There was no one to answer my question. I thought about trying Jake's cell phone again but I'd already left two messages on it. What was the point?

I opened the refrigerator and stood with the door wide open. The sudden rush of cool air felt good against my bare chest. It was only 7:30 a.m., but the day was heating up to be another blast furnace. I pulled my hair back into a ponytail, fastening it with a rubber band and surveyed the few staples the fridge held. I was famished and a couple of eggs seemed like a tasty idea. There was a wire basket with a dozen or so brown eggs, which I grabbed, along with a large chunk of Colby, a tomato, an onion and a can of beer. I scrambled three eggs in a bowl and diced the onion. In a frying pan I melted some butter and tossed in the onion. Next I sliced the tomato, cut a couple chunks of cheese and popped open the beer. I took a sip and poured an ounce or so into the eggs. The onions were beginning to sizzle so I turned down the heat and tossed the rest of the mixture in.

While the eggs cooked, I rummaged through the CDs in the living room until I found *Court and Spark*. Joni Mitchell started singing the title tune. Her words were like sweet poetry. This met my mood. I was feeling a tad depressed and Joni would help me enjoy it.

I dialed Jake's number. "It's me again and your damn machine is still on. I talk to it more than I do you. I suppose you could be in a ditch—dead. But you're not. You are in bed with that lovely lady, telling yourself you'll get a job. You'll join a church. Or, you're telling yourself that you are really in love. It'll last a day, two at the most. Who are you kidding? Yes, my opinion is that she is—she was—stunning and that she spoke in complete sentences. That's a good start. What she saw in you, I'll have to ask her sometime." The beep. Damn. I hung up the phone and I finished the beer before I ate the eggs, along with wheat toast and a large glass of orange juice.

Joni Mitchell sang another song as I sat in silence stroking Fred, who had hopped up on my lap hoping for a morsel. The big yellow tom had come to the door one day and stayed. He had his life and I had mine, but he spent a bit of time with me every day, mostly because he enjoyed being fed on a regular basis.

I noticed the Robert Cray CD Irene had played the night before. I put it on. He kicked out "Smoking Gun." Robert's guitar playing made me smile. "Now that's playing, Fred." I did some air guitar for my audience of one. The big tom just blinked his eyes and gave a silent meow, mouth moving but no sound. I cranked the volume and did a few more licks on the air guitar, much to Fred's satisfaction and mine. I was working up a sweat when I thought I heard a knock at the door. I turned down Robert and went to see who was out and about so early.

I looked through the window and saw DeDe standing there. She had an impatient look on her face. When I opened the door I noticed a suitcase in her hand. Her hair was in a French braid and her sunglasses were pushed up on top of her head. Her gray tee shirt and blue jeans with the knees torn out made her look even younger than she was, and made me feel even older. We stood for a few seconds exchanging looks.

"It's about time you finally answered the door," she eventually said. "Nice outfit." DeDe sized up my old striped pajama bottoms, which was the only clothing I had on. Then she looked down at her suitcase. "Don't worry. I'm not moving back in. I just came to pick up the last of my clothes."

There was a long silence. I waited, blocking the doorway.

"Hank?" She looked quizzically at me as if I didn't remember who she was.

"Yes," I answered the woman that I'd lived with, on and off, for almost the last two years.

"Hank?" she asked a second time. "May I come in?"

"And who might you be?" I growled.

"You don't need to be an asshole, especially so early in the morning," she growled back.

"I don't need to be an asshole? You show up here at the crack of dawn and wake me up," I attacked.

DeDe shook her head, "Woke you up? I heard the music." With that she pushed by me. I wanted to tug her braid as it bounced with her step. But I avoided the childish prank.

"Man, what a mess. But, then, why am I surprised?" She stepped over a pile of clothes and some CDs in the living room that I hadn't put away.

I followed DeDe to the bedroom and found her already in the closet rummaging around. All I could see was her, bent over and tossing shoes in the direction of the open suitcase. There was a time when I would have found the pose provocative. Now I just wanted to kick her ass.

"I didn't know you owned so many shoes," I stated sarcastically.

"There are a lot of things you don't know about me," came the snide reply. I rolled my eyes.

DeDe stood up and started pulling blouses off the rod. "I'm leaving for good, Hank." She ended the sentence with a huff.

"See ya," I replied, with no surprise in my voice at what she had said. This stopped her. She held an armful of clothes and looked at me for a second.

"Well, I can see you're all broken up."

"I thought you had already left."

DeDe continued to look at me. When I didn't say anymore, her face flushed and I wasn't sure at first if it was anger or hurt. She just examined me for a few seconds before she spoke. "I did." She dropped the clothes in her arms in the suitcase.

"Then I *guess* its official."

"We've had this conversation already." Now there was definitely anger in her voice.

"So fucking what?" I returned. "Then why are you here? And, so early in the morning? Guilt starting to set in? Or did you just run out of clean clothes?"

There was a long pause. I waited it out.

"Guilt, Hank?" She let out a sigh. "I just didn't want it to end like this. I wanted to see if we could agree. We're just not right together. Once I moved out to *your* place, I thought it might be different. But you're wrapped up in your art. You don't want a wife. You want a groupie or something. You just don't…"

I interrupted. "No, no, no. Don't give me that bohemian lifestyle shit. That's what attracted you to me. You didn't want a suit, the 9 to 5 guys you'd been going out with. You," I emphasized, "didn't care if…"

"Don't start again. It was great when I was just staying over a couple times a week. But it's not enough for a marriage. That's why I kept the condo. I thought if I wasn't here all the time…" Now she was shouting. "You don't want me here any more than I want to be here. You just don't want to have to admit you were wrong." Suddenly DeDe stopped and just looked at me for a long moment. Her dark brown eyes glistened and a tear ran down her cheek.

"I was wrong." Her voice was soft. "You were wrong. We were both wrong. We were great lovers. But we should have left it at that. We just weren't friends anymore. Great fucking doesn't make a marriage."

I thought I heard a sniffle.

"I've got to get going." She bent over to start packing her bag. "Jake told you before we got married. He may be a prick, but he was right. And, that's why you're being such a shit. Hank, you're a great guy. You're just not the great guy for me. Now let me pack in peace, before I start to really cry."

It was too late. I left the bedroom and shut the door, leaving DeDe to pack.

She was right. She was right about everything. I was fighting her out of pride. Stupid male machismo pride.

I went into the kitchen, sat down and patted my leg. Fred jumped up and arched his back. I stroked him until he started to purr and nip gently at my fingers.

A few minutes later, DeDe emerged from the bedroom with her suitcase and the fish lamp. The base was clear and filled with water or something. Little plastic fish of different colors floated in it.

"I thought I'd take the lamp." She questioned if it was okay with her eyes.

"Take the lamp." I stood up and walked toward her. "Just let me tell people I broke up with you, say we had a big fight."

DeDe blubbered a laugh and started to cry. I took her in my arms and held her. The lamp dug into my back.

"Hey, it'll be okay," I heard myself say.

"Yeah, I know," she said through sobs. "I just hoped we could be friends again."

Friends?! thought. Friends and sex. Didn't seem they went together too well. Sex screwed up the friendship eventually.

DeDe kissed me goodbye and left with my fish lamp.

I looked out the window and watched her get into her brown BMW and drive away.

"A Beemer never belonged out here anyway, Fred." He did the blink thing and started to lick a paw. I turned Robert back up just as he broke into "I Guessed I Showed Her." I sat down to listen and when the song ended I picked up the phone and dialed.

Jake was going to react with a smile and say, "I told you so," just as DeDe had predicted. I just hoped I didn't have to hear him say it too many times.

It wasn't really Jake that I was angry at. It wasn't even DeDe. I was mad at myself. Mad and embarrassed. Mad, because I should never have married the woman in the first place and embarrassed because I knew it at the time. Now Jake was going to serve me some humble pie.

Jake thought himself to be a modern day Koko Pelli, the mythical flute-playing trickster and seducer of women from Navajo legend. When it came to love, Jake followed his pecker.

Me? I wanted to believe I followed my heart. But, I knew that it had been

DeDe's youthfulness and her curves that made me fall in "love," not what I felt in my heart.

Jake was a fool, I was a fool, we were just different kinds of fools.

"Listen you shit of a friend, DeDe is gone. She left. I'm sure you're not surprised. I'm certainly not."

There. It was said. I gently hung up the phone, stopped Robert and restarted Joni.

7
Jake
Sunday Morning

I poured milk on my cereal and stared at my unmade bed.

Karen had split an hour ago or so and left a short note saying that she'd had a *wonderful time* and that she'd call me *real soon*.

Her *i*'s were dotted with little hearts and that threw me for a second. The cute little artwork seemed childish and there was nothing child-like about this woman.

I fought the strong urge to check my stuff. She didn't seem like the poke-and-pilfer type. Yet, since I had been in similar situations once or twice, I knew I shouldn't take the chance. My eyes casually panned my apartment. About halfway through, I started to laugh. Out loud. I had a couch, a CD player, a brand new computer and a TV, all of which were still in place. There wasn't anything else worth stealing. Well, actually, there was. I just wasn't foolish enough to keep it in my apartment.

I walked over to the stack of clothes near the bed and pulled out my jeans. The two fifties I'd kept from last night were still in my front pocket. She hadn't seduced me just to take my money. Hell, if I remembered correctly, it should have been *her* money.

I tried putting it all together. The bar. Hank. Poker. Carley showing up and then leaving. For good? I winced at the thought of how I'd treated her. She'd been one hell of a lot better to me than I'd ever been to her. I felt bad, like I needed to call her and tell I was sorry, that I'd make it up to her. But I couldn't. Deep down, I knew I do the same thing some other time. Maybe this was best. At least this way, I'd stop hurting her.

My mind shot back to Karen. The poker game. Folding like that. Just throwing away eleven grand. And then asking me to buy her a drink, asking me to take her home. It didn't add up.

I've been with plenty of women. It was just that most of these women weren't the kind you brought over to Mom's for Sunday dinner. Dad, if he were still alive, would have enjoyed their earthy company, but Mom's gravy would have curdled or separated or whatever it is that happens to gravy when it doesn't turn out.

But this woman, this Karen, was something else entirely. What, exactly, I wasn't sure. Was she the mythical woman I was waiting for? Judging by the note, it looked like I'd be getting the chance to find out. *Real soon.* If I wanted to.

I had to remember I had other, more important things to think about. I also had to keep reminding myself that she was trouble. If I saw her again, fine. If I saw her again next week, better. I resigned from making any further speculation. After all, how objective could I be when the thought of anything that happened within the past six hours caused Señor to think he was seventeen again?

The cereal tasted odd. I spit it into the sink and reminded myself to check expiration dates *before* I poured the milk on my Wheaties.

Hank. I should call Hank. He'd wanted to talk to me about something important and I'd dropped him like a bad habit as soon as Karen sat down. And even though I knew that he *understood*, I still owed him the courtesy of a phone call.

I saw the light flashing on the machine and a pale green "6" telling me I had a half-dozen calls circling and waiting for clearance to land. I wondered why I hadn't heard the phone ring. They weren't there when I got home last night. I checked the volume dial and found it set on the lowest level. I didn't remember doing that. Had Karen? If so, why?

While I fumbled with the various buttons, I accidentally hit erase. In my uncoordinated stupor, I hit a few more buttons trying to make it stop but that only made it worse. Finally, in frustration, I just set it down and let it run its course. Whoever had called would eventually call back. We could chat then.

I dialed Hank's number. The phone was on its fifth ring when it occurred to me what Hank had wanted to talk about. DeDe had left him. Or was about to. The last time I saw them together it looked as if they were both wearing the marital death mask. It wasn't working out. Whether she'd already taken the good towels or not was a moot point. DeDe, wife number three, was history.

DeDe was a beautiful woman. Successful, if being an assistant District Attorney at twenty-nine was still considered successful. She'd built an impressive conviction record, topped off by winning the biggest trial this town had seen in years. At any rate, DeDe was going places and, like lots of other "successful" people in Santa Fe, she had a thing for the arts. Real or manufactured? Who could tell? But that's how she met Hank.

While DeDe was soaring to the top of her chosen profession, Hank was enjoying his own successes. Despite a decades-old art scandal—which I helped create—he'd become a respected artist, regularly contributing to some of Santa Fe's more popular shows.

Storybook romance? The hippie-artist and the on-the-move DA? Hardly. There were problems right from the beginning. There was the age thing. It had been quite a few years since Hank had seen twenty-nine. And while Hank wasn't a hardened criminal, he wasn't a Boy Scout, either. His police record could be a serious impediment to her career. There were strenuous objections from her wealthy family. Some gaps are just too wide.

Neither of them seemed to care or notice. They continued seeing each other. One day, Hank had told me later, they just decided to get married.

Thinking about being married brought a sudden flash from my own marital past. And pain. After all these years, the pain was still there. I quickly banished the thoughts, sent them back to the festering crevice they'd escaped from and re-buried them, sealing them once again.

By what must have been the ninth or tenth ring, neither Hank nor his machine had heeded my call, so I re-cradled the phone and planned my next move. Hank, no doubt, was out in the barn or in his studio, doing art in his own desert version of Superman's Fortress of Solitude.

I'd tried to talk him into getting a cell phone for years but he adamantly refused. "Why would I want to talk to you more than I already do?"

"But what about emergencies?" I'd argued. "What if someone breaks into your place?"

"That's why I have guns," he'd stated, ending any further discussions.

To atone for dumping him last night, I decided I'd grab a cab, head over there and check on him. He'd been there for me plenty of times. Now, it was my turn to play the good guy.

Only Hank hadn't tried driving after one too many at Smiley's and lost his license for the next six months. So, since he could drive his own self and I had to take a cab, did that make me a better friend?

Such unsolved mysteries would have to be dealt with another time. I needed a shower. Hank needed a friend. Everything else would have to wait.

8
Hank
Sunday Morning

The sun had hit a quarter of its daily ascension across the sky and had already heated the day to a frying sizzle. This was rare for Santa Fe. At 7,000 feet, we usually avoided the oppressively hot days that much of the state took in stride.

I went out on the porch and listened to the occasional car on 590 taking the curves, coming over the hill, heading north to the main highway. Two decades earlier, I'd left art school in Minneapolis and moved to New Mexico after having a dream about a beautiful Navajo woman. I had also come looking for the same inspiration that Georgia O'Keefe had found in this desolate land of sand and cactus. My first stop had been Taos, where I hoped to find the great painter or the beautiful Navajo woman of my dream.

I learned Taos was merely the subject matter for many of O'Keefe's paintings. She actually lived over in Abiquiu, a dusty little wide spot off the main road. I found the church that she had painted so many times, but not her. She'd died years before. I settled in Taos for a year and tried to sell my pottery to the tourist trade. Eventually I tired of the art community crap and moved south, where I found the house I now live in.

The house sat on the same property as an infamous junkyard belonging to W.E. Buggs. At the time, his junkyard was considered to be out in the sticks. There were two white adobe houses on his twenty acres of land. His mother and father had once lived in the larger house, while an uncle had lived in mine. The place was just what I was looking for, simple, and there was an outbuilding I could use for a studio. The rent had been right and W.E. said he'd be happy to sell me the house if I ever wanted it. I bought the place shortly after moving in; paid in full with some ill-gotten cash. W.E. never asked a question. He just took the money and handed over the deed.

W.E. Buggs seemed as old as New Mexico. He'd never lived anywhere but the house in the middle of his junkyard, except for his many years in the army when he toured the world. W.E. said people had told him in recent years to drop "junkyard" and use "recycling center." "But it *is* a junkyard," he had responded. And that's what the sign said: "W.E. Buggs—Junkyard." It was carefully spelled out in weathered pieces of mesquite. When you first saw the sign it was hard to see what it actually said. It just looked like pieces of twisted wood. I had carefully constructed the artwork years ago for W.E.'s birthday.

A six-foot-high fence decorated with hubcaps fortified the junkyard. The hubcap fence had been there for as long as I had known him. I once asked him how many years it took to build the fence. "I'm still building it," he'd answered. And so he was. Whenever a junker would come in with hubcaps W.E. fancied, up on the fence they'd go. If a patron came looking for a particular hubcap, he could point to the exact location where the matching hubcap could be found.

W.E. was sitting up on his porch as I made my way through the skeletons of dilapidated cars. He was busy picking on an old guitar. As I approached, I could hear the chords to an old Robert Johnson blues song being soulfully played.

As was his nature, W.E. ignored me until I had reached the shade of the porch. I wiped my brow with the back of my hand and waited a moment to see if he would greet me first. I placed a carton of eggs on a small table next to the old guitar picker. He responded with a stream of tobacco juice that cleanly cleared the porch rail. Then he looked up at me.

I greeted him first. "W.E."

"Hank."

"That Robert Johnson?"

"You know it is." The old man squinted at me with one eye. "You should be wearing a hat in this sun."

"Brought you some eggs."

"Eggs. I can see." W.E. sounded irritated that I'd pointed out the obvious. "You know I got chickens around here," he growled.

Yeah, he had a couple of old Barred Rocks that scratched around the junkyard. If they laid any eggs, it was anyone's guess where. And if you found an egg, there was no telling how old it was.

"Ya didn't need to bring a full dozen. I can only eat so many eggs. Cholesterol."

This made me laugh. "How do you know there is a full dozen in that carton?"

"'Cuz you always bring a dozen." W.E. plucked a few more notes.

"And they'll be gone in a couple days." I responded in a monotone, not rising to the old man's bait. He would eat eggs twice a day and feed a couple to his dog.

"How those lambs comin'?"

"They're fattening up. Why do you ask?" I knew why.

"You should raise a pig or two."

"No porkers, W.E. I don't like keeping pigs." We'd had this discussion before. "There'll be some lamb for you." I raised my eyebrows to emphasize the point.

"Well, I had some vegetables growing, and I'd a had some for you, but that goat of yours got out and was over here eating the broccoli." He paused, waiting for my apology.

I kept silent and continued to listen to his story.

"Damn, I hate that goat. Why don't you get rid of that animal?" He was testy as usual.

"Because I like Mildred," I said in protest.

"You don't even milk that old nanny. If you want a friend, you should get a dog like a normal person." His fingers broke into a Willie Dixon tune and W.E. hummed along to the chords, every so often singing "I'm your hoochie coochie man."

I enjoyed the playing and I enjoyed W.E. When I first met him, he was a young man in his fifties. He had become my materials supplier, my adversary, my mentor, and my friend. Now he was a withered, little old man and I loved him dearly.

"Where you been?" he questioned.

"I have been around. You miss me?" I knew that an affirmative answer wouldn't be coming.

"No. Just have a couple cars that need parting out," W.E. responded somewhat shyly.

When my pottery was slow to sell, I turned to creating large pieces of metal sculpture, hoping to sell them to the rich art patrons for their yards. The junkyard had become my source for finding pieces of scrap metal. W.E. and I had started off as buyer and proprietor. When he saw my torch skills, he had occasionally hired me to help in his welding business. Over the years I had worked more and more in the junkyard, helping the old man out.

W.E. stopped strumming and looked up. "Listen to those cars goin' by. Probably more of those rich bastards goin' up to their big houses in the hills."

I knew he hated the new homes that were going up in "our neighborhood." When I first moved in there were very few places out on 590. The Bishop Lodge was several miles south, and Smiley's had been just a small bar at the time. Now there were several large developments, planned communities, million dollar houses and strip malls encroaching on our territory—and the requisite numbers of people to live and work in this new area.

While a few of our new neighbors had found their way into Smiley's, most didn't find it to their liking. Smiley's was an old-fashioned bar for drinking, burgers and Saturday-night poker games and not some trendy glass-of-chardonnay-with-a-romaine-lettuce-salad-for-lunch café. Not very many people came back a second time.

W.E.'s junkyard was even less popular. The "squatters," as W.E. called them, had been a bane to his business. He felt there was a conspiracy brewing to get his place torn down. Some of the new neighbors had said the junkyard was a blight on the area and probably a health hazard. "This junkyard ain't no health hazard. Those houses perched on the hills, destroying the natural balance of things, those are the real environmental hazards," he'd stated more than once.

I kept silent. I knew what he was talking about and we'd had this discussion before, so I changed the subject. "Hey, I've got a couple chickens ready for the grill."

"So?" he responded.

"I thought you might want to come over this evening and eat."

W.E. plucked a couple notes and looked up at me.

"You read the paper yet?" W.E. asked.

"Me? I don't get the paper."

"Hank, you need to stay up on current events." The old man started his song over. "Remember that plane crash up on the reservation?"

I nodded that I did, because he had told me about it.

"Couple NASA guys in that plane," he raised his eyebrows and spit a line of brown juice over the porch rail. "They didn't identify them by name. Just said they were with NASA. I told you there were some strange goin's on." W.E. nodded to himself. "Of course they're not providin' any details. It's under investigation is what the paper said. Now, what do you think NASA is doing flyin' around out in the desert?" He didn't wait for an answer. "They're probably investigating some alien sightin', and I don't mean the kind that comes over the border to the south. We ain't gettin' no details 'cause a how they died."

"And how would that be?"

"Got too close to the spaceship and *zap*," he stated very matter-of-factly. "Prob'ly the same as happened to that coin dealer last week. Out diggin' around in the desert and stumbled on someone or something he shouldn't have. There's lots of strange shit going on at the rez these days. Now he's dead, too."

I smiled at the theory. "Now how do you know this if the papers aren't giving any details?"

"There's people I know who know things. Remember those cows that were mutilated up in Utah back in the seventies? People thought it was aliens. The government tried to cover it up sayin' it was something else. Yeah, something else, something like alien activity! Those mutilations were scientific autopsies." He shook his head, not caring if I agreed. "And then, when that spaceship got near Mars, all of a sudden there were no pictures comin' back. NASA didn't want us to know they found aliens. The government was behind that decision. You know the government's got spy satellites that can see you right here on earth. They can zoom in and see you smokin' a joint on your back porch."

I laughed. When W.E. started rolling there was no stopping him. W.E.

loved a conspiracy and the government hiding the existence of aliens from the American public was his favorite.

"Wasn't it in South Dakota where they found those cows, out by Devil's Tower?" I asked.

"Devil's Tower's in Wyomin', Hank." W.E. gave me a look like I used to receive in school when I didn't know a simple answer. "There are reports from thirty-six states of animal mutilation without an explanation; including some in South Dakota and Wyomin'. You could a said just about any state and been right." W.E. plucked a couple notes. "They're probably coverin' up any mutilations in the other fourteen states."

"Whatever," I said. "I think you are getting movies mixed up with reality."

"I am not," the old man protested. "Thirty-six states. That's a lot of unexplained phenomena. And don't forget Roswell in '47 when that spaceship crashed. The government even had a live alien at one point," he shook his head in disgust. "And they said it was a weather balloon. Hell, I was in the Army for over twenty-five years. I can imagine what the brass was tellin' them boys to keep 'em quiet. You know that was the 509 Heavy Bombardment Unit down there. They had *the* bomb. Those men didn't mistake a weather balloon for a UFO. There's plenty of evidence of us being visited in that one incident. The damn government just ain't telling. Except some cockamamie story that comes out about it being a special government project called MOGUL. You should read some of the articles in the stuff I got from MUFON. MUFON has the straight dope about the government."

I smiled and shook my head. MUFON. The Mutual UFO Network. I knew the drill, but there was no stopping him.

"The government has known about life on other planets for decades. In fact, that 'War of the Worlds' thing was government sponsored. They wanted to find out how the public would react, so they commissioned old Orson to put together that radio broadcast." W.E. stopped just long enough to see if he had my attention. "And the public's reaction just proved they couldn't handle the possibility of outer spacemen. People panicked. They jumped out of windows, shot 'emselves they was so scared. If people today thought there were life forms from other planets, they would demand space weapons, like Reagan's Star Wars bullshit project. What'd the religious leaders say if it was proven there was a higher life form out there?"

I smiled to myself. Organized religion was another favorite target.

"No, the government will never admit there are aliens. People couldn't handle it. Believe me, you can't trust the government. They're hidin' something concernin' this plane crash." The old man just gave me one of his long glares, indicating I was just one of the uninformed. He started working his way through the old blues tune, and I listened for a few minutes before I changed the topic back to chicken on the grill.

"DeDe's gone. She left." I paused. "So the coast is clear." I knew W.E. felt more comfortable coming over when she wasn't around.

"Huh. I never liked that woman. Never could see keeping any woman around full-time."

"I know your feelings. They've never been a secret," I responded.

"Shit, it'd be better to keep that goat than her," W.E. replied with disgust. "Why she's young enough to be your daughter."

"Maybe if I'd had a daughter when I was in junior high." One of the main reasons W.E. resented DeDe was because she was an attorney, and worse she was an assistant DA—worked for the government, even if it was only city government.

"The only thin' you saw in her was that cute little behind." W.E. thought for a moment and smiled. "She is a looker, though." Breaking into a laugh, he raised his hands to his chest to indicate large breasts. He looked for my reaction.

"Yeah, yeah."

The old man was now grinning from ear to ear.

"I know you really liked her," I responded.

"Yeah, sure, but what a mouth on that woman." He was still laughing.

"Jake's going to miss having her around, too," I stated sarcastically.

The laughing stopped. "Jake Marley. Now there's a piece of work." He shook his head and started another story I had heard a million times. "When he was a kid, he used to come out here and haggle over the price of a car. Finally, he'd buy the thing. Then he'd be back lookin' for a radio or gearshift knob or something a few days later. Shit, then that kid'd be back three months later sellin' me the radio, then the hubcaps and finally the whole fuckin' car for less than he had paid for it. He never understood business. Thought I was runnin' a pawn shop or bank like his old man." W.E. looked off in the distance. "Jake," he snorted. "He always lookin' for a quick buck. I made more money sellin' Jake cars and buyin' them back. That kid wasn't born with any sense. Shit, his old man..." He didn't finish the sentence and actually sounded melancholy at the memory.

W.E. started another song, and I just listened for a while, without trying to start up the conversation again. I knew he felt bad for my hurt, even though he hadn't said as much. Later he'd tell me I should have kept Francine, my second wife. Whenever DeDe and I were on the outs, he would remind me how much he liked Francine.

"Yeah, I'll come and have chicken. You still got that big ole yella tom cat?" He knew I did.

9
Jake
Sunday Morning

"Hank?" I called as I walked through the studio in Hank Djumpstrom's back yard, trying to remain civil. But how could I be expected to remain civil when I'd cabbed it all the way over and he wasn't even home? All that effort and all I was getting was hot and sweaty. I wondered if he was in the house but just ignoring me. Or, was he passed out in one form of coma or another?

Maybe he went looking for DeDe. A last chance, desperate, nothing-to-lose "Hail Mary" reconciliation attempt that would either put him in the Lover's Hall of Fame or humiliate him even more. I gamble for a living and I already knew where my money would be.

I decided to see if his truck was there. One thing I'd always been good at was sorting things out and getting to the heart of a matter. Start at the top, eliminate the unnecessary shit and work with what's left.

The red Ford, smart enough to be nestled in the shade of the house, sat there quietly. There weren't any tracks behind or in front of the tires so I reasoned that it hadn't been moved recently.

Now I was getting a bit pissed. I went up to the house and called out as loudly as I could, "Hank? Are you in there?"

The door opened without so much as a quarter turn of the knob. If Hank wasn't home, he'd gone without locking his door.

"Hank?" I edged my way into the kitchen. I'd lowered my voice though I really didn't know why. I'd already made enough racket to alarm anyone within a hundred feet. Still, this was getting weird.

Everything looked like it was in order. There weren't any chairs turned over or pools of blood congealing on the floor. "Hank? Get yo' skinny ass outta bed." I did a quick walk-through, calling out once or twice and was finally convinced he wasn't home. I went back to the kitchen and opened the refrigerator. A wave of cold air swept over me while I looked for a beer. Two egg baskets sat on the top shelf one filled with already washed eggs and the other nearly empty.

Then I knew. He'd brought eggs to that asshole Buggs.

I let the refrigerator door swing shut and walked over to the window that faced Buggs' place. I couldn't see anything definitive through the overgrown vegetation. I didn't have to. Hank was there, cozying up to that bony old bastard like he was some sort of father figure. I thought about going over there but decided against it. I'd come out here to talk to Hank, not listen to that old coot's loony theories.

It didn't make sense, Hank liking that old man. Hank was smart. He had talent, art-wise. He could *see* things in his head and then make them into something real. What he saw in that money-stealing, low-life waste of skin I could never figure out.

It was probably the only other thing that was off limits for Hank and me. He knew how I felt. He'd heard my stories about how that old coot had ripped me off every time I'd bought a car from him. Nickel and dimed me to death damned every time I saw him. Finally, Hank said he didn't want to hear another word about it. Ever.

So far, I'd complied. I'd kept Hank out of my semi-illegal endeavors and I stayed away from Buggs, verbally and physically.

I went to the refrigerator and grabbed a cold beer. I popped the top and downed it in one long pull. I tossed the can in Hank's recycling box and grabbed another for the road. My cab was probably halfway back to civilization by now and that meant I had a long wait or a longer walk. I thought about waiting but Hank had been known to stay quite awhile at Buggs' place. Sundays, Hank had told me once, were good days for parting cars. I reckoned that this might be one of those days.

I decided to walk to Smiley's. It wasn't that far and I could use the exercise. Besides, our winnings from last night and Manny's envelope were sitting in the safe and now was as good a time as any to pick them up.

I scribbled a quick note to Hank, grabbed one more beer and headed for the road.

* * *

Somewhere between here and there, as I walked with my thumb only half-heartedly extended, I heard a car approaching. I turned and searched the road. It was hard to see anything definitive because the road bends and curves so much, barely a stretch that's straight for more than a quarter of a mile.

But I heard it again. That low rumble of a big car with a powerful engine. It was back there, somewhere. I just couldn't see it yet.

I strained to locate the source of the motor noise. Finally, a black car came over the crest of the last hill. But something was odd. It wasn't acting like it knew where it was going. It slowed momentarily and came to a stop, the sound of its engine fading with the wind. It just sat there, at the top of the rise. I strained to see something. Anything. One driver? A passenger? Someone getting out to take a leak? Or pick up a rock? Take a picture? A lost tourist? What?

Then, slowly, steadily, it accelerated, picking up speed. The engine noise became more powerful and I heard it fill the countryside with a mighty roar.

As the car rocketed closer, picking up more and more speed, I could almost see the silhouette of the driver, both hands gripping the wheel. I took an instinctive step backward. And another. The front wheels made a slight yet certain move toward me. For a nanosecond, I froze and a very small and foolish part of me wondered if this is what a deer feels like just before it becomes road kill.

The larger, saner part of me made a quick move for the center of the road, then quickly back to the near side and dove headlong into the brush. The screeching tires told me that the driver had tried to follow my moves but couldn't adjust fast enough to hit me. He shot past my thorny sanctuary, brakes locking up, finally screeching the black beast to a stop.

I hunkered down, listening for any sound that would tell me what was happening. I heard a motor race but I couldn't tell if it was going away or coming closer. It sounded like both. I rolled over for a better view. Peering through the thick brush I saw the same car, a black LTD or Thunderbird that had tried to hit me. It was backing up. I dropped down. Think! What could I do?

The car stopped. Shit! I heard a door open. Fuck! Then, from out of nowhere, I heard another car. It could have been the devil himself but, at this point, I didn't care. It meant a distraction and that bought me more time.

The second car slowed and stopped. I heard a door open. A man called out in a loud, clear voice. "Is there a problem here?"

A door slammed. An engine roared. Tires peeled. From the first car? Or the second car? Then, I heard someone talking. The same voice as moments ago.

"Hello?" A pause. "Are you okay?"

I heard a woman's voice calling the man back to the car. "Honey? Come back here. I don't think we should get involved."

"What if he's hurt?"

"Come on, let's just go, please."

I hunkered down even further. I didn't know who was out there. I wasn't going to stand up and find out, either.

I heard more talking but it was too low for me to make out. Then, a door closed, followed by the gentle, steady acceleration of a car not in a hurry. Then, quiet.

I waited until I was sure I was alone. I stood up slowly. I re-assessed. The car had been coming at me, hadn't it? I mean right at me! It really had turned when I turned. It had been *aiming* for me. I'd swear it.

I inventoried my recent history. No outstanding gambling debts. At least not sizable enough for this kind of treatment. Enemies? Of course, but none who would do something like this. Cowboy Slim from the poker game? Or the two Mexicans from last night? Impossible. There was no way they could have followed me out to Hank's. To the best of my knowledge, Carley was the only married women I'd slept with recently and I didn't figure her or her husband for the type who would try to run me over.

There were only two things I could think of that could possibly have led to someone trying to take me out. One involved Whitney Cloud. The other involved Karen.

While I couldn't remember much about last night, I did remember that

Karen drove a red Grand Prix and not some black battleship. Did she have a boyfriend? A husband?

And I had no idea what to think concerning Whitney Cloud. There's no way he'd be trying to take me out. He needed me. I was his key to getting a two million-dollar payday.

I felt sick to my stomach. I was a few days away from being a millionaire and I wasn't about to let anything or anyone get in the way.

I edged my way out to the road, looking carefully in both directions. A moment later, I heard the sound of another vehicle approaching.

10
Hank
Sunday Afternoon

I drove twenty yards past Jake before I rolled to a stop. In the rearview mirror I watched his face as he turned to see if I was going to pick him up. He had a look of disbelief. I kept an eye on him as he slowly ambled toward the truck. He seemed cautious as he approached, twice looking over his shoulder, back up 590.

"I didn't know if you were going to stop." Jake seemed out of breath from his short hike.

"What I should have done is hit you," I snorted and put the old truck into gear. It hesitated at first and then jerked a couple times as I eased down on the gas. We rode in silence for a quarter mile.

"I'm not going all the way into town, just to the liquor store."

Jake sat back in the corner of the cab and gave me a look of horror.

I laughed. "Don't worry. I'll give you a ride into town, unless you're interested in eating some barbecued chicken."

No answer came from Jake.

"Or not." I glanced at his face waiting for an answer. "You got a couple scratches on your face and some blood," I said.

Jake sat up and moved the mirror so he could see his face. "I suppose that old buzzard's coming over," he replied while dabbing at a cut.

"Yes. And yes, you could have stopped over, saved yourself the walk back to town. You two could learn to get along. You've known W.E. longer than I have. And you both enjoy beer."

This time Jake snorted. "No, I don't think so, not tonight. Thanks, anyway."

A 'thanks' from Jake? He's been out in the sun too long. "What got into you last night?"

"What do you mean?" Jake answered innocently.

"You know exactly what I mean. Jake from Kansas City. Running off with that blonde, and that scene with Carley. I wanted to talk to you last night."

"Well, we did okay," Jake said in his defense. "I thought we'd play some cards, win some money and then talk."

"What I wanted to talk to you about last night is that DeDe's left. This time for good." I shot a glance to see if Jake was listening. "To no one's surprise," I added.

Jake smiled. "When did she leave?"

"Last Monday."

"Huh. You took your sweet time in telling me."

"I was going to tell you last night." I shrugged. It didn't matter now.

"Yeah, well, that's why I came out, to see what you wanted to talk about," Jake said even more defensively.

I continued my tale of woe. "I knew it was coming. She'd been spending more and more time at that condo of hers in town. When she kept it after we got married she said it was only for convenience, when she had to work late. But once or twice a week turned into four and five times a week." I paused for a response, but there was none. "Now that she's gone, I'm glad. I really am. I just don't relish going through all the breaking up stuff." I was waiting for Jake to tell me that he had warned me more than once, but he seemed to be lost in his own world.

"You listening?"

"Yes, I'm listening. I told you not to marry her."

"Well, fuck you, Jake. I know you told me. You know, sometimes, you can be a real asshole, as opposed to the fake asshole you normally are." I was somewhat hurt that he seemed so disinterested.

"Hey, I'm sorry." Jake's voice showed it. "Shit. DeDe was no good. She was a self-centered bitch. That girl was a b-i-t-c-h." He laughed, trying to lighten the moment.

First a thanks, and now an apology from Jake. Something wasn't right.

"Well, you and W.E. have your love for her in common. It doesn't look like anyone is going to miss her. Fred didn't even like her. He used to hiss at her." We both laughed. It didn't look like Jake was going to give me his "I told you so" monologue after all.

"So, old Buggs didn't like DeDe, either?"

"Not really."

"Maybe the old buzzard ain't so bad."

"So how'd you get out here?"

"A cab."

"A cab?" I raised my voice and whistled through my teeth.

"Yes, a cab!" Jake responded somewhat indignantly.

"So Jake does have a heart. He was worried about Hank. Ah, isn't that sweet," I said in baby talk.

Jake responded with a hearty laugh.

"Or was it guilt? A human emotion from Jake?" I stated smugly.

"Guilt? I've never felt guilt in my life." Jake looked like he was going to pout. "And I wasn't worried."

"No, you just took a cab out here. Probably cost you fifteen bucks."

"Eighteen."

"Eighteen? Did you tip the driver?" I questioned, self-satisfied.

"Well, I'm glad to see you're in such good spirits. I needn't have worried."

"So you were worried."

"I wasn't really wor-ri-ed," Jake responded with a half smile.

"So what were you doing out here then? Hiding from Karen?" This got Jake's interest.

His tone changed, "Why do you say that?"

"I don't know. Last time I saw you, all you cared about was getting in her pants. 'Oh, yes, Hank's got somewhere to go. In fact, he's ten minutes late,'" I mocked in my best impersonation of Jake's voice. "Have you ever heard of AIDS?"

"Fuck you."

"Not me, too. Didn't you get laid? Now you want to fuck me?" I laughed.

"Hey, Hank." Jake sat up and pointed. "You just passed the liquor store."

"I thought I was taking you home."

"Yeah, but weren't you going to the store?"

"What? I should stop now so you can drink my booze all the way to your apartment? Don't you ever sober up?"

"I'm sober now." Jake slumped back dejectedly.

"Okay, I'll turn around."

"Forget it. I spend eighteen bucks coming out here and you're worried about me drinking your lousy six-pack of beer."

"Fine. You want me to give you eighteen bucks?"

"Yeah." Jake's face had a glow of hope.

"I'm not giving you eighteen bucks," I responded sarcastically.

Jake shook his head in disbelief.

"I'm not."

"Okay, okay, drop it already. It's stupid that we are arguing about eighteen bucks, after the money we won last night."

I had to agree. "Yeah. It was nice to pick that up. You've been scarce lately. What's up?"

Jake didn't respond at first, and when he did, he avoided the question. "What'd you think of Karen?" A big grin grew across his face.

"The woman last night? She…she was bow-wow. Walk on by, get a bag. You musta been stone blind. Ruff, ruff," I barked.

"Yeah, sure." We both laughed.

"Okay, she must have been the one who was stone blind." We both laughed harder. Laughter always came easily when I was with Jake.

"So, ah, do you remember Karen saying anything about a husband or a boyfriend?"

This brought a hoot and a howl. "A husband?" I laughed. "So that's why you came out here. You were hiding."

I wiped away the tears of hilarity and looked at my friend. He wasn't laughing with me and there was a pensive look on his face. "What's wrong?"

Jake took his time.

"Before you stopped and picked me up, did a car pass you?" Jake's tone didn't have its usual devil-may-care attitude.

"There was a dark-colored car that came shooting past just as I turned onto the highway." I watched for Jake's response.

"A black car? Do you know what it was?"

I thought for a second. "It could have been anything. It was a few years old and dirty. It was big and black. Why?"

Jake blew out a stream of breath. "I think it tried to hit me." He was entirely serious.

"Tried?"

"Yeah, tried. I'm sure the fucker aimed right at me." Jake gave me a dead-on look. "He was trying to hit me, I'm sure."

"Sorry, Jake, I just noticed that he was going awfully fast. But the car had to be a few years old because of the grill work."

"Hank, I would think with all the cars you've cut apart in that junkyard, you'd recognize what kind of car it was." Jake sounded perturbed.

"Well, excuse me." I racked my brain to bring back the car's image. All I remembered was the big silver grill catching my eye and how fast the car blew by me. "If I had to guess, I'd say it was a big Ford. Probably an LTD, or maybe one of those boat Thunderbirds, but I don't think it was that old. I do know one thing for sure; it didn't have New Mexico plates. Texas," I stated with some satisfaction.

Jake thought for a moment without saying anything.

"Texas plates." Then I remembered Karen. "Karen said she was from west Texas."

"Texas is a big state. There are a lot of people from Texas who come here," Jake stated, trying to sound convincing.

I took the left turn onto Artist Road. "That's why you asked about the husband," I said almost to myself. "You must have really been out of it."

"Well," Jake said, sitting up straight in the seat. "Shit, Hank. She didn't say anything about a husband or boyfriend. At least I don't remember anything." Jake shook his head slowly. "No."

"Well, whatever. A husband or boyfriend is a good possibility, but it doesn't have to be Karen's. You've got enough enemies. Maybe Carley's husband."

"That little worm doesn't have the guts for it. Besides he's supposed to be out of town."

"Supposed to be?" I asked.

Jake just looked at me.

"So I guess you and Carley are done after last night. She didn't seem any too happy," I said.

For a second Jake continued to stare out the window. "Yeah, that was not a good thing. I'm sorry it had to happen."

"Well, maybe it is my turn to tell you something. Carley cares about you and you screwed it up by following your dick again," I said.

Jake turned back to the window and was silent. I made the right onto Otero Street. "What about that cowboy last night? Slim? He wasn't too happy when he left the better part of a month's wages behind. And I think he was from Texas."

"Slim?" laughed Jake. "That loser's the kind of guy who'd be waiting in the can or parking lot for a sneak attack. He wouldn't dare do anything in the daylight."

"Yeah, I know what you mean." I thought for a moment. "How about the two pool players?"

"Nah. Couple bar flies blowing through, puffing up their chests, trying to look macho. All show, no go," stated Jake with confidence.

I remembered how Jake had reacted the night before with the two of them. Now he sounded pretty cocky. "I hope you're right," I replied, trying to think of someone who might have it in for my friend. "There isn't anyone else looking to put your ass in a sling?"

"No. I've been a good boy lately." Jake smiled at me.

"Yeah, sure. Except that Carley's a married woman. 'Thou shall not covet thy neighbor's wife.'"

Jake just stared out the windshield, thinking about something he wasn't sharing.

"Is there something else you want to tell me?"

"Well, after the game," he hesitated for a second. "After the last hand, Smiley showed me Karen's cards. She folded with four aces."

"Yeah, I know. Smiley told me last night after you two had left. I was going to ask you about that. That seems really strange."

"Yeah, can you believe it? She dropped with four aces, giving up eleven thousand dollars."

No, I couldn't believe it.

"I don't understand," Jake said, "Am I missing something?"

"Did she say anything later?"

"No."

I shook my head. "Then I'd ask her about that. If you ever see her again."

Jake was gone, staring straight ahead, probably playing that last hand over and over. Searching for the missing something.

I pulled the truck to the curb and parked in front of Jake's apartment building. The building was an old four-plex that he'd lived in for as long as I had known him. I sat for a second and studied the street. When I looked at my friend he was doing the same. I followed his line of sight. Checking the cars, looking for a big black car. Maybe an LTD. Maybe a Thunderbird. The street was empty in the noonday sun. No one wanted to be out in this broiler. The truck's cab was heating up now that our movement had ended and there was no breeze.

"You want to stay out at my place for a few days?"

Jake looked at me. I could see that he did, but he wouldn't. He shook his head no.

"Want me to come in?"

"No, I'll be okay. Thanks for the offer."

"Jake, it was probably nothing. Some drunk having a little fun or some crazy kid showing off. At worse, someone's husband, maybe Daryl." There was no way I could know this, and Jake knew that. But I didn't know how else to make him feel safe. "Probably nothing. And if it was Slim, well, he was all show, no follow through. That is the last you'll see of him."

"Yeah, probably." Jake was thinking, his eyes indicating he was off somewhere trying to figure this out.

"If you change your mind, give me a call."

* * *

It was past noon when I got to the liquor store. I pulled into the parking lot and shut off the engine. Jake's episode on the highway had occupied my thoughts the whole way back. Who would want to run Jake over? There were plenty of people who would bust his head if they got the chance. But to try to kill him? That was serious.

Not that Jake was a stranger to trouble. In fact, trouble seemed to follow him. Occasionally it was an adventure at Smiley's Old Saloon. More than once I'd ended up in a fight, just because I was sitting with Jake. Instinctively, I felt the back of my head with my fingers, searching for the scar that crossed my crown. A drunk had laid open my skull with a bottle of Jack Daniels one night when I got between him and Jake. My forefinger felt the crease that cut into my scalp. Jake had knocked out the drunk's front teeth, and the scars on his knuckles proved our friendship.

Since the bar had been our regular watering hole, anyone looking for Jake would know right where to find him. We had both spent a lot of time in that bar, eating and drinking off an ongoing tab that might never be paid in full. Smiley never complained, treating us more like family than customers. He enjoyed having us host the back room games and keeping his bar on the circuit.

But Jake nearly getting killed wasn't some Saturday night bar fight. No one had come looking for Jake at Smiley's. They'd waited until he was alone, out on 590. Jake believed someone had tried to kill him, and he wasn't one to panic without good reason. There was something going on. I could feel it. And Jake wasn't including me. Why?

"Jake, Jake, Jake," I said to no one.

A movement caught my eye and I looked up to see a woman stooped over in the bed of a blue pickup, decades newer than mine. She was wearing khaki shorts and a black sleeveless blouse. The blouse showed off the well-toned muscles in her arms. I looked at her taut thighs as she bent over from the waist, searching in the truck's bed for something. "Stand up," I said out loud. I wanted to see her face.

Finally, she stood and straightened her back. Her hair was pulled back in a tight ponytail that hung well past her shoulders. It was raven black in the midday sun. A pair of large sunglasses hid her eyes. I was staring, and then I realized she was staring right back; probably wondering who this nut was sitting in a truck. Quickly, I acted as if I were searching for something. I opened the glove compartment and turned over a New Mexico map several times. When I looked up at the woman, she was bent over again, rearranging the back of the truck. It looked like she was moving a cooler. There was something familiar about her, but I couldn't place it. I had to get out and introduce myself. If I didn't, she would haunt me forever.

As I got out of the truck, a dark-haired man came out of the liquor store with a case of beer and headed for the woman in the truck. She stood up. "It's about time. What took you?"

"I was getting cooled off in the air conditioning." He laughed and handed the case of beer to her.

"Oh, thanks. Leave me out here in this heat," she said, laughing, too. "Where's the ice?"

"Shit, I forgot it. I'll go back and get some."

I shut the truck door as the man re-entered the liquor store. The sound made the woman look in my direction. I pushed my sunglasses up on my nose and studied her. Where did I know her from?

"Hi. Pretty hot. You from around here?" I said.

She looked at me before she answered. She smiled. "Yes, it's pretty hot."

I smiled back. "This is going to sound stupid, but I think I've seen you somewhere before." Then I noticed the truck had Arizona license plates.

"Maybe," she was looking right at me.

"Oh," I responded. "I thought, ah, the Arizona license plates…" There was a glow about her, an enchantment that drew me to her. I shaded my eyes with my hand and looked up at her.

"The truck belongs to my brother. He lives in Arizona." She jumped down from the truck's open tailgate. She was five or six inches shorter than me. I liked this view better. "My name's Molly Kiyanee." She held her hand out.

"Hank Djumpstrom."

"Yes, I know. I saw you about a year ago."

My face must have shown the complete blank my brain was having.

"You had a show at Frank Galleries. I was there."

"Did we meet?"

"Not really. You were busy talking to potential buyers. As I recall, you had your arms around one of them, an attractive brunette."

"Well, there have been some changes with who I hang out with these days." A big smile broke across my face. "How would you like to come out, see my studio and some of what I am working on?"

Molly returned my smile.

83

11
Jake
Sunday Noon

I'd been sitting in the shade of my apartment's courtyard for ten, fifteen minutes watching for cars, big black cars in particular. For once, the courtyard was empty, which was good. I needed some time to rest—and to think.

Two trees provided enough shade to keep the sun at bay and a gentle breeze did its best to cool my overheated paranoia. I was pretty sure someone had just tried to kill me and I knew I'd better figure out who and why before they had another chance.

I'd been lucky Hank had come along when he did. I might still be out there and maybe that LTD—or was it a boat Thunderbird?—would have come back.

Hank thought that it might be Slim or those two Mexicans from last night. But how would they know where I was? How would anyone know I was going to be on that stretch of 590 at that particular time? Had someone followed me? Hank said Smiley had told him that Slim was with the rodeo. That would be easy enough to check out. The Mexicans? Just drifters, I hoped.

Hank had proposed a few other theories. Some drunk out of control. Carley's soon-to-be-ex-husband Daryl. Or some asshole kid trying to have fun at my expense.

I thought about it. It could have been a prank, but I sure didn't think so. It *aimed* right for me! Didn't swerve or dip or lean. It *aimed*! And, it'd backed up for another shot. If that second car hadn't come along…

Someone had tried to kill me. But who? And why? I honestly couldn't think of anyone who wanted to do me in.

It just couldn't have anything to do with my Shiprock deal. There were only four of us involved, Manny, Cloud, Williams and me. Without me, there was no deal, there was no multi-million-dollar pay-off. If I'm dead, then so is the deal.

Karen? I shook my head. It didn't figure. Besides, what was her motive? Was I a lousy lay? Was she married and worried that I'd tell? Was she was one of those psycho bitches they make bad movies about? It couldn't have been her driving. The shadowy figure I'd glimpsed behind the wheel was much bigger than Karen. Had she hired someone to do her dirty work?

I wished I could mull all this over with Hank. But that would mean telling him about partnering with Whitney Cloud and Manny, my impending trip to Shiprock, and sixteen million dollars in gold coins, and that was more than I could do right now. Once it was over, I'd see to it that Hank knew every single detail.

I suddenly realized that I'd been having to ask Hank a lot of things lately. That was usually a sign for me to stay home a few more nights a week. I resolved to get some rest, call Hank a little later and see if he had any other ideas.

I'd have to ask him more about DeDe, too. He'd wanted to talk about her, but I'd been too preoccupied with that black boat trying to make road kill out of me. Lately, Hank was being a better friend to me than I was to him.

My stomach churned and gurgled and told me it was time to get off my ass and get some grub. I headed toward the apartment, wondering what I'd be able to scrounge up. "Remember to check for those expiration dates," I reminded myself.

I headed around the back and started climbing the stairs when I heard music. I was just about to curse the neighbors for playing their shit too loud when I realized that it was my shit I was hearing. Pink Floyd was spilling out of my apartment. My door was open. The lights were on. Was that bacon I smelled?

I eased the door open ever-so-slowly. Most people who were about to kill you, rob you or do you some sort of bodily harm didn't turn on your favorite music and fry bacon first. Was that the smell of french toast?

"Wish You Were Here" came to an end. I opened the door the rest of the way, revealing the whole apartment. Karen stood at the stove, flipping the battered bread.

Click. "Wish You Were Here" came back on. She had the song on infinite repeat. Let us meet during some other set of circumstances and I *could* like this woman.

"Looks like I got *my* wish," she said without looking up from her chores. I walked in and closed the door. What the hell was she doing here?

"Your neighbor let me in," she answered before I could ask. "I told him we had *relations* together."

She looked up for the first time. Her hair was pulled back and for the first time I noticed her tiny ears. She was wearing one of my white shirts and, from what I could see through the thin fabric, nothing else. I was apprehensive as hell but couldn't help but smile.

"Breakfast is served." She motioned for me to sit down and it was then that I noticed the table had been set with my finest mismatched plates, gas-station glasses, silverware and the usual paper towels for napkins. Except these had been folded into some sort of shape that made them look much better than they actually were.

"Breakfast?" I asked. I would have sworn that shirt had buttons the last time I wore it.

"Okay, lunch, then." She'd joined me at the table and started dishing up her own plate. She noticed I hadn't started. "Aren't you hungry?"

"Starved would be more like it. But I'm also confused."

"'Bout what?"

"How'd you know I'd be here? Now?"

"I heard you get dropped off and I saw you sitting in the courtyard. I figured it wouldn't be too long before you came in."

I buttered two slices of french toast and then drowned them in syrup. As I reached for the bacon I wondered if she had brought it with her. After a quick mental inventory of my food shelves, I realized she'd brought the whole meal. Who does that? And why?

Okay. What was this all about? Was this an intricate little chess game? Was she calling the shots, controlling everything that happened? Questions raced through my mind. *"Who are you?" "What are you doing here?" "What do you want with me?" "Do you know anyone who drives a big, black Ford?"* But I just couldn't bring myself to ask them. If I scared her off, I might never know and there was way too much riding on this to be left in the dark. I'd have to find another way to learn her secrets.

She leaned forward to reach the syrup and her shirt—my shirt—gaped open, revealing the tops of her breasts. I immediately remembered how her nipples stiffened under my fingertips, how she moaned when I kissed them. Man! I'm in my forties and I'm still getting turned on like I was looking at my first *Playboy*. I wondered who was really in control, Karen, me or *Señor*?

I pointed. "Didn't anyone ever teach you how to button a shirt?"

Her other hand clutched the material together. A faint smile appeared, then disappeared. "Are you complaining?" She lightly fingered the buttons.

"No."

We stared at each other. A thousand thoughts drifted in and out and back again. I needed to know more about her—a lot more—but I found my hard-edged curiosity slipping away. She was beautiful. Sexy green eyes. Creamy skin, the kind you don't see much of around here because of the dry air. And a smile that made you want to do the same in return.

We ate without talking. It's better that way. Sometimes.

* * *

We both cleared the table and did the dishes. She made some attempts at small talk but I wasn't playing. When the last plate was put on the drying rack and the towels were hung up, I turned to her and asked the most simple yet powerful question I could think of.

"Who are you?"

She stared for long moments, her eyes probing mine. "What are you asking? Exactly?"

"I want to know who you are. It's just that simple."

"Nothing's 'just that simple.'"

"Oh, but it can be."

She dried her already-dry hands on one of the towels and headed for the couch. "I'm Karen Meyers and I come from west Texas."

I followed her. "And?"

"And what?" She sat down, pulling her legs up under her.

"And the rest. I'm sure there's more to you than that."

"Of course there is, Jake. But what makes you think I want to share it with you? Or with anyone?"

"If you don't, then I'm afraid you'll have to go."

"Go?"

I nodded. "Things are happening. I need to know."

She stared for long moments. A subtle fear etched her face and then quickly disappeared. "Okay. What do you want to know?"

"What kind of poker do they play in west Texas, anyway?"

She swallowed. "Why?"

"Why?" I sat down next to her. "Around here, four aces are considered a pretty good hand, almost a winning hand…"

She studied me before answering. "I thought Hank…" her voice dropped to a whisper, "…*dealt* them to me."

I shook my head. "You mean cheat? We don't cheat."

"And how was I supposed to know that?" She threw her arms in the air. "I mean, shit, how often does a person get four aces? How often do you get a chance to make that kind of money?"

"So why'd you throw them in?"

"I thought he was *giving* me that hand." She hesitated, like she was unwilling to tell me any more.

"Why? Because he wanted to get in your pants?"

"Maybe." She sounded defiant. "Men have done a lot of things to get my attention."

"I don't doubt it," I replied. "But not this time. Not Hank. And certainly not for eleven thousand dollars. Hank and I do this for money, not for…" I stopped short. She knew what I meant. I leaned forward. "So why?"

She held my gaze, took in a breath and answered, still whispering. "Because I've seen what happens to cheaters."

No way. I'd seen what happens to cheaters, too, and it wasn't pretty. But I still wasn't buying it. My continuing glare sent my message.

"I got scared. I had this good hand going and then all of a sudden it looked *too* good. It just seemed like the best thing to do."

Maybe. Just maybe. She didn't seem like a woman who scared easily and she hadn't played the last hand like she was scared. She'd raised on every card like the pot already belonged to her and then suddenly dropped so that part made sense.

"It was a gut reaction. Something you can't explain but you do it anyway because you *know* it's the right thing to do."

Okay. I'd gone with my gut hundreds of times. But for eleven grand, it had better be a fucking earthquake telling me to quit.

I looked at her, more to evaluate than to interrogate. If she was lying, and I still wasn't sure how much of her story I bought, she was doing a damn fine job. Under other circumstances, I believed I could actually work up some full-fledged admiration for talent like hers.

"Satisfied?" Her eyes locked with mine.

"For now."

"Anything else you want to know?"

I thought for a second. "You married?"

She turned away. Her arms folded into each other. "And if I am?"

"I don't know. Maybe you'd better tell me about it."

"I am married."

"*Married* married?"

"What do you mean?"

"I mean like married as in 'until death do us part' and this is just some little distraction while hubbie is out of town?"

"No, Jake, nothing like that."

"Then what?"

She paused. "I'll be getting a divorce."

"So this is just happening? This is right now?"

"Yeah." She reached for my arm.

Okay. Now some things made a bit more sense. Like my wondering why she wasn't married. She was. Like why I hadn't seen her around. She just got here. Like who she was. Well, the jury was still out on that one.

"Who's the guy?"

She leaned back and took in a deep breath. "It seems so long ago, but…" She closed her eyes and did the marriage math. "But it was only seven years. Seven years that started out with love and hope and promise." She turned and looked at me, wondering if I was following.

89

I nodded. I knew of such things, too.

"We met in college and got married right after graduation. His name is David. He is, without a doubt, the smartest man I have ever known. A math genius. He sees the world as formulas and patterns with obtuse relationships to each other."

The Beauty and the Geek? I thought. I could not imagine her falling for a numbers nerd.

"About this time last year, he came up with this idea that he could build a program to predict the outcome of football games. He'd spend hours and hours at his computer, running different scenarios, altering the formulas, tweaking his program. Then, every Sunday afternoon, he'd watch the results come in and spend even more hours making additional adjustments."

"And it worked?"

Her eyes grew large and she slowly nodded. "By the time the season ended last year, he figured he'd perfected his system. He made a few parlay bets and won some nice money."

This was getting interesting. I'd tried football parlay bets but always came up short. While the payoffs were fantastic, like eighty to one or even one hundred to one, it was nearly impossible to pick ten out of ten winners. Anyone who could do that could make a ton of money. They'd also be likely to draw the attention of the underworld folks who paid out that money. Most bookies are basically honest guys. They know the average Joe who bets on a couple of games every week is going to lose more than win. They take your money and they pay you money if you win. They get their percentage of the action. But if the payoffs get too big, they have to go to their backers and that's where it could get dangerous. Those boys are not in business to lose money and they'll come looking for whoever is hitting it big.

"How much did he win last year?"

"Ten thousand. But the guy he placed his bet with told him he wasn't going to take any more parlays from him and that he was going to spread the word to the other bookies he knew. Said it was for his own good."

"So he's got the perfect system but he can't find a bookie in the whole state of Texas who'll take his money."

"Ever hear of Las Vegas?"

Vegas! The wheels in my brain stopped spinning and locked into place, with dollar signs three across. The first pre-season games were last weekend. "How much?"

"He placed some sizable parley bets at five different sports books."

"How much?"

"Two hundred thousand dollars total."

"Holy shit!" I exclaimed. "You hit the jackpot."

She wasn't sharing my enthusiasm. "There's a problem…"

"Problem?" Placing bets with a bookie is illegal but gambling in Vegas is okay. They take your bet, they *have* to pay you.

"Ah, yeah," she whispered as she looked down at her hands. "David had few celebratory cocktails and mentioned to a couple of people that he had a system for picking football games and that he'd be back next week to win even more money."

"And those people worked for the hotel?"

She nodded. "I suppose. Later that night, we got a visit from the hotel manager congratulating us on our winnings and offered to take us out to dinner, front row seats to their hot show and put us up in one of their high roller suites."

"They wanted to go through your stuff."

"Smooth, huh? They smile and shake your hand and give you a penthouse suite—just so they can search your bags."

"When did you notice?"

"The next morning. David's laptop was missing."

"He had his system on it?"

"Yes."

"Did he make a back-up copy?"

"Not of the most recent version."

"You've got to be kidding me! A computer geek who doesn't back up his work."

"I know. I know. Maybe it was the heat of the moment. Maybe he ran out of time. I don't really know. He just never made a copy of the latest version, the one that worked."

"Shit."

"But I did."

* * *

I spent the rest of the afternoon listening to the rest of Karen's unbelievable story. She said David got all paranoid and flipped out when he found his laptop had been stolen. He got so bad that the hotel security had to intervene. When they couldn't calm him down, the police got involved. They eventually had him brought to the local hospital. She'd gotten so scared that she grabbed the money, rented a car and took off. She drove non-stop, hoping to get back to Amarillo but along the way she decided going home wouldn't be the smartest thing to do. If people from Vegas were looking for her, that's the first place they'd look.

"So you pulled into Santa Fe to think things over?" I'd asked, looking for anything that would prove her story—one way or another.

"More or less," she'd answered.

"And then you thought, 'Hey! As long as I'm here, I might as well get into a poker game?'" I'd said in a mocking voice. "That makes absolutely no sense."

"Wrong."

"Wrong? Your story is what's wrong."

She squared herself in front of me. "Think about it, Jake. I have a program that predicts football games. It's a license to print money. But I can't use it."

Okay. Maybe. Just maybe this *was* making sense.

"No one in Vegas is going to take my bets."

"That doesn't explain how you got to Smiley's, how you got in the game."

"I got in the game because I know about the poker circuit, because I know how to play cards and, mostly, because Clarence just happens to be a very close friend of my father's. I've known him all my life."

"So you get yourself into the game Saturday night but you're not really there to play cards as much as you are to find a new partner? That about it?"

"That's close enough," she'd admitted. "Know where I might find one?"

12
Hank
Sunday Afternoon

As my truck came around the bend I could see the flashing red and amber lights. A county sheriff's car was blocking the left side of the road going north. Closer to the ditch was an ambulance. Up in the junkyard was another sheriff's car. Its flashers were off. A county uniform was standing on the center lane waving cars around from the left lane. After a couple of cars swung by the cruiser, I was waved on. I quickly took the left turn into the junkyard.

I was immediately relieved when I saw W.E. sitting up in his chair on the porch. Standing next to him was another of the county's finest. I hopped from the truck and slammed the door. The sound focused their attention on me and then, suddenly, a siren broke everyone's concentration and the ambulance pulled from the ditch and headed south on 590. An old mangled blue bicycle was left by itself.

W.E. looked up at me as I stepped onto the porch. His face was red and covered with sweat. His breathing was labored. He was distressed.

Deputy Sheriff Wayne Wayne looked me up and down. He was several inches taller than me. Over the years he'd added a several extra pounds around the middle to his sturdy build, making the buttons of his uniform shirt pull a bit. Wayne was still an imposing figure.

"Hello, Hank." His tone was full of disgust. Wayne didn't like the junkyard, he didn't like W.E. and he certainly didn't like me. The only things I knew he liked less were Jake and horses. Wayne hated horses because the sheriff's department would be called out whenever one got hit on a road. The horse was usually not dead, just left lying there, struggling to get up, until the patrol car arrived. The deputy sheriff had to pull out his revolver and place the muzzle between the poor beast's eyes and blow its brains out. "Stupid animals," I heard Wayne say on one occasion. He'd said it with as much repulsion as he had when he greeted me.

Smiley's Old Saloon was in Wayne's district and he regularly came swaggering through the bar, eyeing the patrons and generally making everyone uncomfortable. Whenever he saw Jake and me, he'd give a long look that summed up his feelings. Generally, he was more bark than bite.

Wayne's offense with the junkyard came from his belief that it was a blight on the countryside. He liked the idea of the expensive housing developments moving out this direction. Wayne Wayne really wanted to patrol nice, quiet, tree-lined streets, not dusty bars and miles and miles of lonely highway. He thought the rich who were building their homes into the side of the foothills were going to treat him with the respect he felt he deserved. I knew he was mistaken, but he was just too fucking dumb to know it. It wouldn't be too long before they'd see him for what he really was.

"Yeah, Wayne," I replied with equal friendliness. "What's going on?"

"Elmore got hit by a car," W.E. responded before Wayne could. "He was coming here to teach me some more blues, just riding his bike…"

"Against the traffic," Wayne interrupted. "Crazy old Neg-ro riding out here on the wrong side of the road in the noonday sun. Probably had a heat stroke and swerved into the traffic." Wayne shook his head, snickering to himself. His reddish flattop glistened with sweat.

Both W.E. and I glowered at the big man.

"I'm just trying to find out from your old friend what happened. I had to bring him up here before he'd had a stroke out there in the sun." He leaned back and shot a mouthful of chew on the ground, the last bit staining the front of his shirt.

We both ignored Wayne. W.E. continued his explanation of what happened. "Hank, Elmore was ridin' over here like he always does," he took a deep breath and looked at Wayne, "against the traffic, because he don't like the cars sneakin' up behind him." W.E. returned his attention to me. "I'd been sittin' out here on the porch waitin' for him. While I was out here I seen this big black car go by real fast headin' towards town."

Suddenly, I felt a cold chill crawl up my back in the midday heat.

"Then sometime later you come by, Hank. There hasn't been much traffic today." He paused, still looking at me. "Then that same car comes back, maybe fifteen minutes later goin' north again. But this time he's goin' kind of slow. I figured he's lost. 'Bout a half hour ago, I'm watching for Elmore, and that big black car is comin' down 590 lickety split. Well, Elmore come around the bend and he's almost here. That car goes flyin' by and next thing I know Elmore's in the ditch and that car just kept goin'."

"The ole fart got a bump on his head from de fall. It looks like his right hip and maybe leg is broke. Might be some internal injuries," Wayne added flatly. "Now, W.E., did you know what kind a car that was, or maybe something about the driver you seen?"

W.E. sat silent for a long time thinking. "Not for sure. It was a big Ford, black. But it was going so fast…some kinda big Ford, probably a Thunderbird." The old man sat back in his chair and wiped his brow.

"W.E., let me get you a glass of water." I stepped past Wayne and into the living room. W.E. kept his house very tidy. Out of the sun, the house felt cool. He never had added air conditioning, because he felt a person would never go outside again after getting used to it. The kitchen was directly behind the living room. Breakfast dishes were neatly stacked in a dish drainer. I opened the cabinet on the left-hand side of the sink and took down a large plastic Jurassic Park glass W.E. had gotten, by the advertising on it, from McDonald's. I let the water run until it was cool.

"Here, W.E., drink this."

The old man took the glass. I could see his hand shaking slightly. Elmore George had been W.E.'s closest friend for over seventy years. The two of them had joined the army together and both retired as sergeants. Because of their color difference, they'd each gone in different directions during those military years, but they'd stayed best friends.

After their service years, they both moved back to Santa Fe. W.E. moved back into the only home he'd ever known outside an army barracks. His mother died shortly after that and since then he'd lived alone.

"I think I also saw that car," I interjected.

Wayne looked up from the porch railing where he had placed his three hundred pounds of bulk. I was surprised the railing held him.

95

"What car?"

This man was as dumb as I thought. "The car that W.E. saw. If you remember, he said the black car went by, and then he saw me go by a bit later. Well, I was waiting to turn on to 590 and I saw a big black car go shooting by real fast. When you are sitting waiting to make a turn, you watch for cars approaching." I said this real slow, hoping this blob of goo would understand me. "I think it was an early eighties LTD or maybe one of those big-assed Thunderbirds. Either way it had Texas license plates. The driver was probably a man. I'm not sure if there was a passenger."

Wayne was scribbling in a notebook as fast as his fat fingers would allow him.

"Anything else?"

"Nope." Except Jake and his close call with the black mystery car, a piece of information I would be keeping to myself.

Wayne and the other deputy finally left and everything was quiet at the junkyard. W.E. and I sat in silence for fifteen minutes on the porch, watching an occasional car pass by. Then I listened to W.E. tell a story about him and Elmore in Paris. It was a risqué story about their exploits, when they met on leave with a couple young Parisian women. He laughed as he told the story, truly enjoying himself. I'd heard the story several times before but listened attentively.

About five o'clock the other deputy returned to ask if we'd seen the black mystery car again.

"No."

He told us that the hit-and-run report on Elmore had been filed and an APB put out on the car.

We sat for a couple hours talking, W.E. telling me more stories I'd heard before. The time together seemed to calm him. The sun was just beginning to set behind the house when I finally left the junkyard. I had called the hospital a couple of times. Elmore had gone through several hours of surgery to repair his broken pelvis. He didn't have a broken leg but had broken his right wrist and he was suffering from a slight concussion. They wouldn't allow visitors until the next day.

The day had taken its toll on W.E. He didn't want to come over and barbecue. I left him sitting in his chair on the porch.

When I pulled into the driveway, I stopped at the mailbox. As I emptied the box of Saturday's junk mail, I listened for the goat. I figured she'd be calling for me, wanting to be fed her grain. No cries reached my ears. I pulled the truck in between the house and a stand of mesquite.

The back door swung open at my slightest touch. *Damn Jake, he hadn't even bothered to shut the door tight,* I thought to myself. I tossed the junk mail towards the kitchen table, but it landed on the floor. The thud made me turn to see what had happened. In the shadows of evening, I could see the table had been moved. I switched on the light, revealing a rearranged kitchen. The table had been pushed aside, chairs turned over. The food from the refrigerator was scattered around the kitchen.

"What the fuck?" This made no sense.

Several cabinet doors were open and their contents dumped on the counters and floor. The floor was littered with broken glass.

The ringing phone made me jump two feet in the air.

"Hello."

"Hank?"

"What?" I recognized the inquiring voice.

"Hank, its DeDe." Her voice was soft and filled with question at my gruff greeting. It must have set her back.

"Didn't I just see you earlier today?"

Her normal commanding tone returned. "I just called to say I was sorry I left like I did. I just don't want to go through the bullshit again."

"Fine."

"Fine? That's all you've got to say?" she asked, sounding stunned.

"Yeah, fine." I was angry and preoccupied with my house being ransacked.

"Listen, I know it wasn't nice just showing up this morning without calling you first, but…" She let it drop.

"Are you the one who trashed this place?" I knew it was a stupid question before the words even left my mouth.

"What are you talking about? Have you been off drinking with Jake? Or have you been sitting smoking pot with W.E. all day?" She met my anger and raised it.

"Neither. When you left this morning did you see a big black car, maybe a Thunderbird hanging around?"

"Yes. Why? What's going on?"

"Elmore got hit by a black car out on the road today. Some crazy driver. Do you remember anything else about the car?"

There was a short pause before she simply answered, "No."

"Listen DeDe, I have to go. It's been nice knowing you." I hung up before she could respond. Had it been just a crazy driver? For a moment I wondered.

I stepped through the living room. Chairs had been overturned, the couch slashed open and some of the stuffing pulled out. A few books had been hurled from the shelves, the TV knocked to the floor and records and CDs tossed every which way. When I switched on the light in the bedroom, I saw this room had gone through the same hurricane. The phone rang and I jumped again.

"Hello."

There was a long silence and then a click. I hung up the phone and wondered for a moment. I went into the bathroom. It had been thoroughly searched, too.

I stepped out on the back porch and looked around for more destruction. My troubles weren't going to get me out of feeding the goat. Mildred would be complaining until I showed up, chewing her cud and stamping her hooves.

The outside barn light flickered on just as I stepped out the back door. It would take the mercury vapor light a good five minutes to warm up and illuminate the yard. There were still rays of setting sun crossing the yard. The day's heat had not dissipated yet. I opened the gate and walked around the barnyard, expecting to be greeted by one angry nanny, giving me her "you're late" look. She was nowhere in sight. Probably gone off to eat the rest of W.E.'s garden, I thought. It would be a fitting crown to the day.

I looked in the barn for the missing goat. What looked like her outline, lying on one side, was in one of the stalls. I flipped on the light. Her brown back was pointed in my direction.

"Mildred," I called.

She didn't rise as I approached her. As I got closer I could see she was lying in a pool of dried blood. Small flies covered it. One dead eye stared up at me. A large ugly hole in the middle of her head was the source of the blood. Tears welled up in my eyes as I stooped to gently raise her head. "Mildred?"

Teardrops fell on my jeans. When I looked up to wipe my eyes, I noticed that a few bales of hay had been thrown around the barn. Even the barn had been searched. I waved my hand to scatter the insects that had come for the feast. Gently, I lowered her head back down. She had already started to stiffen.

Someone had come into my day and destroyed it. Nothing made any sense. Killing my goat—that was cold-blooded. They must not have found what they were looking for and had taken out their frustrations on Mildred. She had probably come up to whomever and affectionately rubbed against him, looking up expectantly and then had received her death call.

For the second time that day a cold chill crawled over my body. I ran to the house. I punched the numbers as fast as I could. The phone rang and rang. I didn't even get Jake's damn machine.

After fifteen rings I hung up and dialed W.E. His phone rang ten times before I gave up and ran for his house.

13
Jake
Monday Morning

Karen finished making breakfast while I anxiously sipped my coffee. I'd asked her to stay last night with me rather than have her return to her hotel room. It seemed like the right thing to do. If someone from Vegas was after her, they could find her by tracing her rental car. While I wasn't sure how quickly they could do that, I didn't want to take any chances that they could do it fast enough to find her this week.

I also wasn't sure about her story. A math genius husband? Software that predicts footballs games? A timely escape from Las Vegas? An old friend of Clarence's? I made a call to Smiley and had him call Clarence to double-check this story. Maybe he could make a few calls to his friends in Vegas, too. True or false, I needed to know—now!

We were both exhausted from our long trip and went to bed early. After a good night's sleep, we were both in a lighter mood—probably out of necessity. I wasn't built for stress and I suspected she wasn't, either.

Without looking up, she asked me, "Is your place in Kansas City this nice?"

"Come on." I opened my arms wide. "How could anything in Kansas City be as nice as this?"

She looked around my stark apartment. "It'd be hard to imagine." She frowned and then faced me. "Have you ever even been to Kansas City?"

I smiled. "Yes."

She waited for more information until she realized I wasn't going to offer any. "But you're not from there?"

"No."

"What was that all about then?"

I shrugged. "Part of the game. That's all."

"You play poker and *pretend* to be from KC?"

"Sometimes."

"Why?"

"I don't want the other players to know Hank and I are friends."

"Is that all?"

"No. I like the challenge. It adds an extra element."

"A game within a game."

"Never thought of it like that before."

"Ever get caught at it?"

"Not until now."

She munched more bacon while digesting my answers. Finally, she swallowed and changed the subject. "Sooooo," she smiled, "I'm still curious about how you ever got a name like Jacob Marley."

"I didn't have anything to do with it," I answered calmly. There wasn't any big secret to it. It's just that I'd heard that same question and all the baggage that went with it since before puberty. It'd been a long, long time since I regarded it with anything but contempt.

"What were they thinking? Your mom and dad, I mean."

I breathed in and slowly exhaled. Okay. One more time. I even smiled and acted like I enjoyed telling how I was really born Jacob Druess and that my father, Wilbur Druess, died when I was a baby. A short time later, my mother married Ken Marley. He insisted on adopting me, his attempt at family unity. "And that, my sweet, is how I became named after one of the more notable figures in classic literature."

"Did they know? At the time?"

I shrugged. "Mom wasn't what you'd call well read. Even so, it wouldn't have made any difference. Ken was going to 'have one family under one roof' and that was that."

"Are they still alive?"

"Mom is. Ken died years ago."

"Is your mother still around here?"

"No. She went over to Sun City a couple of years ago. Married some asshole named Bob," I said curtly. I felt Karen back away slightly. I hadn't meant to take my old anger out on her.

She faced me, studying my features for a while and finally asked, "Who gave you those green eyes?"

"Ken."

She giggled. "No. Really."

I nodded. "Really. They were rumored to have had an affair. It was quite the scandal, so much so that Mom and Ken eventually moved from Albuquerque to Santa Fe."

Karen sat back. "So you hate it, don't you? Your name."

"Yeah. Mostly."

"You could have changed your name, you're an adult."

"I've lived in Santa Fe most of my life and I've always been Jake Marley. No one calls me Jacob. Let's leave it at that." I smiled tightly. "Just call me Jake and we'll be okay."

We finished eating in a comfortable silence. Karen picked up the dishes, neatened the kitchen and got ready to leave. She was going to get a few things at her hotel room. I had some errands to run. We made plans for meeting at Porter's House for lunch in a couple of hours. I gave her directions.

"You sure you'll be all right?" I asked. "No bad guys?"

"Should be."

"And if you see anyone hanging around?"

"I'll turn around and come right back."

"No. You'll turn around and make sure no one is following you and then you'll come right back."

"Okay, boss." She kissed me. "Whatever you say."

* * *

As I watched from my second floor window as she drove away, I started questioning my decision. Instead of looking at it from my point of view, I turned the tables.

What did she see in me? Hell, I lived in a dump, didn't have a real job, had no license and spent more time drinking at Smiley's than even I cared to admit. Not the kind of stuff you put on a marital resumé. Yet, she was here and acting every bit like that's exactly where she wanted to be.

Did her showing up now have something, anything to do with Shiprock? Not likely. The lid on that was tighter than a year-old bottle of maple syrup. I was the only one who knew the identities of all the players were. None of them had anything to gain by bringing in another person. It made no sense.

I shrugged and put it off to coincidence. Mostly. If she was somehow involved in this deal, and that's almost totally unlikely, then maybe it was better to have her right here next to me where I could keep an eye on her.

Enough. For now. It was time to do the list. I have only a few rituals but making a weekly list every Monday morning was one of my strongest.

I checked the time. I had a few minutes before I had to call Cloud so I grabbed my legal pad, fished through the junk drawer for my Onyx Fine and headed for the table. I scanned last week's column of mostly undone items.

THINGS TO DO: WEEK OF: AUG 2
call Fenter Press about article
write article (if they want it)
call Mom
Cloud
truck stuff
AA / Thursday / 7:00
laundry
W.O.N.

As my eyes read from top to bottom, I realized I'd only done one of the items. I had made it to my court-ordered AA meeting. Getting a few million next week was one thing. Being able to drive somewhere and spend it was another. I wanted to get my license back so I listened to drunk stories for an hour a week, held hands, said the prayer, cabbed it over to Smiley's and had a few drinks.

I checked the clock and saw that it was time. Whitney Cloud would be at the Shiprock Trading Post, waiting for my call. I hit a string of numbers and, a few seconds later, I heard Cloud's husky voice. "That you?"

"Who else would it be? You don't have that many friends," I quipped. Silence. Cloud evidently wasn't in the mood for humor. I returned to the straight and narrow. "Are we still on for Saturday?"

He paused before answering, sounding like he was taking a drag off a cigarette. "I've been thinking about that. If we wait until Saturday, we're gonna be asking for trouble."

"Why? What's wrong?"

"Nothing's wrong. It's just that there are a lot of people coming in for the pow-wow this year. Some are here already but most will be coming on the weekend."

"But you said they'd all be going to Gallup..."

"I know what I said." He cut me off, the tension growing between us. "But I can't guarantee that they'll all go to Gallup. There's always a few who don't go."

"When, then?"

More silence. More cigarette sounds. Finally, "The sooner we go, the better. There'll be fewer people and there's a full moon this week. We could use its light."

"Aren't you worried about being seen?"

"No."

"Why not? I'd think..."

Cloud laughed. "You haven't spent much time in the desert at night, have you?"

I scoffed. "Not for a long time."

"Then you've forgotten how dark it gets when there's no moon."

That was true. I had forgotten that there had been times I couldn't see my hand in front of my face. The moonlight would help. "But wouldn't someone..."

"No," he interrupted, "we're going to be in the middle of fucking nowhere. It's the getting in and the getting out that I'm worried about. The fewer people in town, the better. Understand?"

"I understand."

"How's my money?"

I sighed. We'd been through this a couple dozen times since Cloud first called me. "The money's there. Two million for you. Two million for Williams."

"And we get the numbers after delivery?"

"That's the deal. Everything's in place."

Cloud paused. "How do I know you won't take the pass codes and keep my money for yourself?"

"I don't have the bank account numbers, Whitney, and as easy as it is to get information these days, those bank numbers are pretty hard to come by."

"Even for a sweet talker like you?"

"Yeah. Even for me. What else is bothering you?"

"It's just that I don't know who the money man is and that makes me nervous."

I dealt with this latest attempt at uncovering the fourth partner's identity the same way I'd done it before. "The money's there and you trust me, right?"

"Okay. Okay." Cloud quit his pursuit before it began. "But there better not be any slip-ups…"

While Cloud ran through a short list of what he'd do if he was double-crossed, I toyed with the idea of telling him that the money man was his old enemy, Juan Maniandez. Manny was the one—and possibly only—person Cloud feared. Cloud had crossed Manny years ago. I never knew all the details but I'd suspected that Cloud had returned to the rez for more than a celebration of his tribal heritage. I'd always thought he was hiding there from Manny.

"Don't worry about it, Whitney. The money is there. By Monday, we'll all be living large." I enjoyed this one little advantage I had over Cloud—and over Manny. While both of them may have had their suspicions, neither knew for sure that the other one was involved in this deal. It gave me an edge, my own little private piece of the puzzle, one I could use if I had to.

"And you're telling me that he doesn't know who I am, either?"

"That's right. That's the way I set this up. It protects you. It protects me. And most of all, it gets Williams to cough up the GPS numbers."

"I know. I know."

"Now when are we doing this?"

Cloud didn't speak for a while. Finally, "I'll have to call you back." He hung up.

I cradled the phone, took in a deep breath and told myself not to worry. This was going to work. I wasn't going to let anything get in the way. Not now. Too much was riding on this.

Enough. It's under control. Nothing can go wrong. Move on. You've done everything you can. It's a good plan.

Resigned that I'd put all the demons to bed, I crumpled the old list and launched it toward the wastebasket. I didn't hear any noises on that end of the room so I concluded a swish had taken place. I cleared my head and returned to my legal pad, my list.

THINGS TO DO: WEEK OF: AUG 9
laundry

If nothing else, I needed to wash my socks and underwear—or just buy some new ones.

articles

I decided to combine all writing ventures, except my novel, into one category. This saved time and ink. I wasn't going to call or write or research anything anyway this week. Having one word—articles—on the list made it easier to ignore.

W.O.N.

Work On Novel. What I really should be doing. What I really wanted to do. I was a writer. A good writer. The fluff-stuff I did for the *Reporter* was okay. It paid the rent. But what really burned within me was the desire to write something bigger, something more. I'd started and stopped more novels than I cared to remember. I figured I lacked the discipline, the stick-to-it-iveness, to see it all the way to the end. Hank disagreed. He said that what I needed is what all artists need. He said I needed to have something to say. Without that, it's only clay or metal or words or paint. It's just material. It's what powers your hands that's truly important. Then, he'd smile and tell me that he believed with all his heart that I'd find it someday.

T.A.N.

I resolved, in my spare time, to *think about novel*. That would be all I could do. Once Shiprock was over and done, I'd be able to spend the rest of my life writing.

truck stuff

I'd call Ed and make sure the truck would be ready. When I'd talked to him last Friday he'd said the truck was coming in on Monday and they had the usual dealer prep work to do. He also said they were going to need an extra day to make sure it'd handle the extra weight I wanted to carry. When I'd told him "no problem," I was assuming I'd be going up to Shiprock on Saturday. Now that it looked like we were going midweek, I had to make sure it'd be ready. No super-truck, no way to get the gold out in one trip.

I smiled at the thought of Ed as we calculated how much weight I'd be carrying. He never said but I knew he was trying to guess what, exactly, I was going to haul. All I'd told him was I needed to be able to put just over a ton of "material" in the back and transport it over some very rough terrain. I'd also told him I didn't want to run out of gas, break an axle or ruin my kidneys in the process.

I was sure he suspected I was doing something illegal but, being the commission-type salesman that he was, he knew when to stop asking questions and start writing purchase orders.

call Mom

I could just pick up the phone right now. I could just hit the buttons. I could make small talk for a few minutes, find out how she was doing. I could tell her I'd just met someone, someone I could bring home for dinner. I could do it. Right now.

My arms didn't move, didn't obey my brain's guilt-driven commands. For what, the fourth week in a row? Or was it the fifth? It wouldn't be so bad if I didn't think shithead would answer the phone. Bob. Bob the batterer.

I remembered our last get-together. They'd driven in to visit some of

Bob's relatives and Mom had called. She'd wanted to see me so we'd met at Porter's for lunch. The first hour or so had been terrific. We talked and laughed and were enjoying ourselves. Then, I asked if he had kept his promise. The look on her face told me he hadn't.

"Mom," I'd pleaded, "you have to get away from him. You can't let him treat you that way!"

She'd smiled and said it had only been once and that he'd been truly sorry and that the counseling seemed like it was helping and that, after all, he was her husband.

Then it had occurred to me. This was one of the differences between our generations. She believed in staying married, in keeping her promise to her husband. No matter what. My generation believed in keeping promises, too. But not to an abusive asshole like Bob and certainly not at the expense of one's dignity, or one's life.

We'd ended our conversation with me telling her that I'd knock him into the next decade if he ever hurt her again. She'd ended it by asking me if I'd given any more thought to finding a nice girl and settling down.

We each had our own agendas.

I promised myself I'd call her before I left for Shiprock. Otherwise, I might not get the chance...

AA / Thursday / 7:00

If I wasn't up in the desert, I had to go. If I didn't, I'd have my probation officer crawling up my ass.

Hank

I had to be careful on this. I needed to tell Hank that I was taking off for a while without telling him where I was going or why. The last time I'd taken off on a secretive venture, he'd gotten pretty worried about me. Thought I was dead. Spent the better part of the weekend looking for me.

I wished I could tell him more, but I couldn't take the chance on getting him involved. If this thing blew up, I didn't want any of the shrapnel hitting him.

Yet, I ought to tell someone. I had to leave a clearly marked trail in case this doesn't turn out as planned. But who?

Carley was now out of the picture. I hadn't known Karen long enough to even consider involving her. Hank was the person I trusted more than anyone else. Hank was it. My benefactor. My confessor. My silent partner.

I didn't care about the warnings from Manny not to let anyone else know about this. This was *my* plan and I'd do whatever I felt like doing. I'd write out everything. How it got started. Who was involved. Who to call if…

Then, I'd put that letter where no one could get to it. Except Hank. Just last week, I'd drafted a will and named Hank as my executor, so he'd find it eventually. That way, worst case, Hank would know what happened.

KAREN

Not exactly sure what she was doing on the list. I guess it gave me a sense of control over her. Like if I put her on the list, I'd be able to decide how and when I dealt with her.

I capped the pen and put it down. There were things to plan that couldn't go on this list. When Cloud had contacted me, told me about the gold coins, I'd made it clear that there was only one way to pull something like this off. I told him I'd develop a plan where no one knew more than his share.

When he'd questioned me about that, I told him when people learn what someone else knows, they start thinking the other person has suddenly become expendable. And if the other person wasn't necessary, that meant a bigger split. And while I was into making easy money, I was also into staying alive. We'd keep it simple and secret or we wouldn't do it at all.

"Gold," I'd warned, "does that to people. If you don't believe me, just ask yourself if you haven't already had some of those same thoughts." I'd made my point.

When Cloud brought me in, he had two main problems. One, Williams needed a guarantee that he wouldn't wind up dead the second he pinpointed the treasure. And, two, what to do with the gold coins once we had them.

The first problem was easy to fix. Williams feared Cloud and with good reason. The man's greed made him unpredictable and vicious. But when I told them they'd both get two million dollars cash for one night's work, Cloud mellowed and Williams agreed to give up the numbers. I'd taken away any reason Cloud would have for killing Williams.

Fencing the coins was another matter. Manny was the only person I knew who could put this together. He had the up front money and he had a genuine interest in the coins. But he was also the sworn enemy of Whitney Cloud. I had to be very careful about not mentioning his name in front of Manny.

There was a third, unspoken reason. While Cloud had a lot of cohorts, he didn't have anyone he could trust with something of this magnitude or anyone who could handle turning twenty-dollar gold pieces into walking around money.

Manny hadn't been an easy sell. He was shrewd and didn't invest seven million plus without good reason. But when I laid out the entire deal, he realized it was the kind of investment he could get behind. Manny and I went back a long way together. Maybe it was my attitude or my smart-assed approach to life, but he had taken a liking to me a long time ago. And that was something he couldn't afford to do very often. Manny claimed everyone he knew had an angle. They wanted something from him. They wanted a favor. They needed money. All without giving something back.

That was a line I'd never crossed. I actually liked the man. Despite what he did for a living, Manny was cultured, well educated and very, very generous to his friends. Over the years, we built a friendship and shared many things. We had history.

This was why I could tell him I needed seven million dollars and get it.

It all hinged on trust. Me. Manny. Williams. And Whitney Cloud. If there was a weak link, I figured it was Cloud. Radical. Dangerous. But mostly, unpredictable.

Whitney Cloud always claimed to be a full-blooded Navajo but I had my doubts. I met him when we were kids. We started the eighth grade together by getting into a fight. He kicked the shit out of me in about two seconds. I figured it'd be better to have this kid on my side so I worked at becoming his friend.

His family had just moved in from the rez. Seems his old man was in some kind of trouble with the elders so they moved to a trailer park on the outskirts of Santa Fe.

It was rare for a white kid and an Indian kid to hang out together back then. Partly because of the miles we each had to travel, but mostly because of the distances between our cultures. My folks disapproved. So did most of the people I knew. His folks either didn't know or didn't care. He wouldn't talk about it. Somehow, we'd found a way. Hell, we were just two kids looking for quick money and easy pussy. What did we know about how the world was supposed to turn?

After high school, I went to college, played baseball and got married. Whitney stayed in Santa Fe, got in trouble and got arrested. The local cops nailed him for selling drugs. He claimed the charges were bogus, but he did the time anyway. Immediately after he got out of prison, he headed directly there.

Then it was my turn. The scandal. The newspaper headlines. The suicide. Everything wiped out. Everything ruined. All that work. All that time. Marriage. Baseball. The possibility of a pro career. All gone. I immediately looked for and found the proverbial bottom. If it wasn't for Whitney Cloud, I might still be there. Or dead.

Cloud was in Santa Fe one night and he found me at our old hangout. He sized up what I was doing and did the same thing he did when we first met. He kicked the shit out of me. Said he'd do it again if he ever found me wasting my life away like that. Then, he took me to the rez and kept me there until my head was facing forward again. He took some shit for bringing a white man to live on the reservation. Some, but not a lot. Most people didn't argue with Whitney.

He introduced me to Manny and taught me how to run dope across the border. In just one year, the two of us made enough money to take care of us for years. Never even saw a Fed. Whitney Cloud had learned a thing or two in prison.

Then, suddenly, Cloud got pride. Or said he did. Words like *heritage* and *tribal* and *respect* became a regular part of his everyday vocabulary. He told me drugs and alcohol were killing his people. He broke with Manny and quickly headed back to the rez. He never admitted to me that the money he had with him had been stolen from Manny.

I'd continued working for Manny. I'd tried a couple of times to contact Cloud but the timing or something wasn't right. Eventually, I just gave up. It'd been years since I'd even thought of him.

Then, three weeks ago, I got this call. "I want you to come up to Shiprock. I'm into the biggest deal I've ever seen and I need your help."

I went. I met Anthony Williams and heard his story. Cloud was right. This was big.

I grabbed another cup of coffee and headed for the computer. It was time to tell Hank the first part of a story he wasn't going to believe.

Hank,

If you're reading this, I'm dead.

I know. I should have told you that you were my executor but that would have raised some questions that I didn't want to answer. If this is too much for you, I'm sorry. There isn't anyone else I trust as much as you.

My old friend Whitney Cloud and our old "business" pal Manny are in on this deal. Only neither of them knows about the other. There's also a computer guy named Anthony Williams. Stay away from them. Do not agree to meet with any of them. No matter what. One of them—or all of them—would be primary suspects in my murder.

Go about your normal business. Act as if nothing out of the ordinary has happened.

Have me cremated (if there's a body) and scatter my ashes in Buggs' junkyard. And don't tell him until after it's been done.

Do not take anything from this safe deposit box with you when you leave the bank today. All of the real information has been hidden over at Buggs'. There's a big section of Chrysler caps on the north fence. In the fourth row, look for the second hubcap from the east end. It's a big gaudy one from an old Imperial, I think. There's a plastic bag taped to the inside. In it, as Paul Harvey likes to say, is the rest of the story.

Hank, I'm sorry it has come to this. I want you to know what happened and how it happened. And I don't want you to get hurt in the process. If you follow my instructions, nobody should ever find out that you know what's going on. I also want you to get my share of the gold if that's possible. If you do, give a bunch to my mother if she agrees to leave asswipe. The amount is up to you.

Or, you might decide to turn this all over to the police. Just don't let that dipshit Wayne get involved. Otherwise, I'll come back and haunt you.

Hank, I miss you already. See you on the other side.
Jake

Remember, don't take any of this with you when you leave. Just tell the clerk that ol' Jacob Marley must have found a way to take it with him because the box was empty.

I hit "print" and watched as my words were lasered noiselessly onto paper. When that was completed, I exited the screen. The prompt asked me if I wanted to save this document. "No, you ignorant piece of shit. The only thing I want to save is Hank's life." I hit "no" and wiped Hank's letter off the screen. Since it had never been made into a document, I didn't have to worry about it residing in some deep crevice of my hard drive. In another hour, this letter would be in my safe deposit box. It wasn't the most expedient way to communicate with Hank but it was the only way I trusted.

I had one more letter to write to Hank. The one with the rest of the details. That would have to wait. I had to get to the bank.

* * *

After I was done at the bank, I had my cab drop me at Porter's House. It was my favorite place to eat. Most of the rest of Santa Fe's eateries had gone trendy, substituting over-done greenery and weird stuff hanging on the walls for good food. They had perky *waitressii* whose names were spelled more phonetically than traditionally. Aimee. Aleesha. Karee. Sharee.

But not Porter's. I counted the two Marys and one Linda on the staff, plus Betty who owned the place. Kind of like looking at the names in my yearbook. Made me feel right at home.

I usually ate here because even though I liked good food, I still lacked the primary ingredient. Labor.

I figured it this way: As long as I could peel a few bills off my money clip,

I couldn't see any reason to slice or dice or mix or simmer or whatever it was that people do when they cook. It just wasn't for me.

Hank, on the other hand, was good at cooking. And he liked it. Kind of like his art. He took raw materials and made something out of it. Something good.

Me? I'm a capitalist. You have money, you spend money. You want something, you buy it. It's what makes the economy go. The last time I checked my stash, I had plenty. Add what I'd won Saturday night and I was doing okay. The Shiprock deal, however, would set me up for life.

The waitress I called First Mary came and took my order. She was a plus-sized woman old enough to be my mother. Tall and dark-skinned, she'd watched over me for more years than I could remember. I'd asked her once or twice what part of the country she came from but she'd never even come close to answering me. From the way she spoke, I suspected the Deep South. From her facial bone structure, I thought maybe there might be a bit of Indian heritage. Something in her dark eyes hinted at a Mexican gene pool. Maybe one day she'd tell me. Maybe not. Wherever she came from, she carried the gentleness of an angel in her every action.

"Took my order" was really just a phrase for the process of getting me something to eat—a process that had been refined by the two of us over the years. She'd walk over to the table, greet me by name, make a modicum of small talk and then leave. A few minutes later a plate of food would arrive and I'd eat it. She claimed she could tell what I needed just by talking to me. She knew I didn't cook for myself and said that she wanted me to have good meals. She must have been right. In more years than I care to remember, I had never sent anything back. I damn near called her Mom.

Second Mary and Linda had tried doing this with me but it didn't work, mostly because I wouldn't let it. I didn't trust them, didn't think they knew me well enough.

"Miss Carley was in yest'day," she stated quietly but firmly.

I shot First Mary a stern look. If she was going to start lecturing me, I wanted to cut it off immediately. The last thing I needed was a what-in-the-hell-is-wrong-you-Jake-Marley-reprimand from my surrogate mother.

"I know you don wan' to hear it," she huffed, "but she is one fine woman. She the best yo'll ever be getting. Yo betta think two times 'bout it."

First Mary left with my "order" and I sat back in the booth. First Mary was right. And wrong. Carley was a good woman. Maybe that was the problem. She was good. I wasn't. Or I wasn't good for her. I shook my head. From what had happened Saturday night, it didn't really matter anymore. Carley Rose Butler was out of my life.

I looked out the window and examined the new day. The sun was well on its way to warming up Santa Fe. Another hot one. Unusual but not unheard of. Even though we were up in the mountains, we were still surrounded by desert.

I thought about my early morning visit to the bank. It wasn't very often I went there. Since I'd lost my driver's license, I did most of my banking online or at ATMs. And it was even less often that I was the first person there. I had to wait for the doors to open, in fact.

I'd headed right for the safe deposit room and, after going through all the shit you have to go through, put my letter to Hank in my box and made my exit.

By putting Hank's letter in my box, he was now a part of the team. Kind of. I'd have to die first. Then, he'd have to make a choice. Run like hell? Call the cops? Both?

I turned upbeat and thought ahead to when this deal was successfully completed. First thing, once I knew the dust had all settled, I was going to take Hank to Smiley's and tell him the whole story. Then, I was going to ask him where in the world he wanted to go for a couple weeks—or a couple of months—and then we'd go.

First Mary brought me silverware and a glass of cold water. She looked like she was going to say something but didn't. I was wondering what it might have been when I caught a glimpse of a familiar black car coming around the corner and heading slowly toward Porter's. I tensed. Was it the same car as yesterday? I craned my neck and scanned the front end, looking for the plates. Texas? Just when I was about to get a good look, Linda walked past me, blocking my view. I jumped up and edged my way toward the big front window, dodging Linda and a group of newly arrived customers. By the time I got to the window, the car was parallel to Porter's with the driver on the opposite side. The car slowed, not like it was going to turn into the parking lot, but more like the driver was looking for someone. Bit by bit, second by second, I grew certain that this was the same car that had tried to kill me. Same huge grill, same dirty black surface, same dark-tinted windows. It *was* the same car! A mid-80s T-Bird.

The car slowed even more, nearly to a full stop, the driver looking toward Porter's and not at the traffic. I moved away from the window and hugged the wall, letting the morning logjam of customers become my shield. If "they" were trying to find me, I wasn't going to make it any easier for them.

I lost my cool. I panicked. I wanted to run. I wanted to get out of there. My heart was racing and I could feel the sweat beading up on my forehead. I realized I was in a hell of a lot of danger. Someone *was* trying to find me. Someone was trying to…

"Hey!" a shrill voice pierced the air.

I turned. It was Betty Porter, leaning against the cashier's counter.

"You tryin' to sneak out without payin' your bill?!" Now she was walking toward me, shaking a chastising finger.

It took a moment for me to understand what she was saying. Her words had startled me even more than the car.

The car! When I turned and searched the street, it was gone. I looked again. Gone. I was about to go outside, but stopped myself. I was reasonably sure they hadn't seen me so there was no sense in making myself an easy target now.

"Sorry, Betty," I said, turning back toward her, still distracted from the incident. "I was just looking at something…" My words trailed off as I automatically looked up and down the street.

She waved me off, evidently satisfied with having given me a piece of her mind. "Just take care of your waitress like you always do. My girls work hard for their money and the tips you give them are…"

Her words faded away as she went through the double doors and into the kitchen. She might continue talking for another couple of minutes and then move on to another topic. And she might not. As long as I'd known her, she talked and talked and talked. It didn't really matter if anyone was listening.

I reached for the phone behind the counter and punched the numbers for Smiley's. I knew it was too early for Smiley to be in but I had some things I wanted him to check on for me and now might be the only chance I had to get a hold of him without Karen around. I left my requests on his machine and then checked the street one more time for oversized black cars.

"You all right?" First Mary asked as I neared my table. "You lookin' like you jus' seen a ghost or somethin'."

Had I? If not a ghost, then what? "I'm fine," I lied. "What did you bring me today?" I slid into the booth.

"Steak 'n' eggs. You look like you be needin' something sub-stan-tial." She pronounced every syllable like it was its own word. Sub. Stan. Shall.

My mood lightened a bit. "Shame on you, First Mary. You've been peeking in my bedroom windows again, haven't you?"

She was long past blushing at my words. "An' if I was?"

"If you was, you might learn a thing or two." I checked the street one more time. No sign of the T-Bird.

Her eyes followed mine to the front window but didn't ask what I was looking for. "An' at my age, what ever would I do wit such car-nal knowledge?"

I smiled at her. "I suppose you'd take Milton to a motel and show him a good time."

She scoffed. "Milton? In a motel? Only if it had free HBO. An' then he'd jus' stay up late so's he could watch those movies with those pretty, young, nekkid ladies in 'em."

I leaned forward and whispered, "And what's wrong with pretty, young *nekkid* ladies?"

She topped off my coffee and shrugged. "I ain't one no more!" She turned and headed for the kitchen, her ample frame cutting a wide path as she went.

I slowly worked over my eggs and took a few bites of steak. The toast and juice rounded out what would have been a damn good meal if I'd have had any appetite left. But seeing the T-Bird again had taken care of that. Someone *was* trying to get me. I was sure of it.

Was I being paranoid? Probably. A little. But, so be it. I'd rather be a live paranoid than an overly-confident dead man.

Review.

I was sure a man had been driving both times. I was reasonably sure it wasn't Slim. While I hadn't been able to see his face, I could tell he was a big man. Slim was just too skinny to have been the driver. Was it one of his rodeo buddies? Or the Mexicans?

At least Hank's letter had been safely tucked away. That made me feel a little better, like I actually had some control over this mess. Why did it seem like everything was falling apart?

Manny would be calling around eleven and I could tell him about our change in plans. Or not. I'd have to think about that.

More review.

As much as I like to think I lead an exotic life, it basically isn't true. I wasn't as predictable as the sunrise but close. Now, however, there were two new elements in my life: Shiprock and Karen. I'd tried to keep the Shiprock deal simple and safe but now it looked like my careful plan was starting to unravel. At least it would be easy to find the culprit. Shit, there were only four of us who knew about it.

But what if what if there was a fifth person? Maybe a sixth? Or seventh? Or more?

I wondered who talked. It wasn't me and I doubted Cloud would say anything. But then I remembered that he'd double-crossed Manny. And, there were sixteen million other reasons lying out in the desert.

I knew Williams wouldn't talk. Hell, *couldn't* talk was more like it. I was sure Cloud had him cut off from the real world ever since he found him in the desert.

I seriously doubted that Manny would risk trying for the whole enchilada. As it was, his take was already larger than everyone else's. If you figured the price of gold at about four hundred dollars an ounce, he was looking at sixteen million dollars in melt value. If the price was lower, then less. But only a fool would think about melting it down. You had to look at the real value, the numismatic value. Manny was sitting on at least fifty or sixty million. And all he had to do was put up seven million and then sit back and wait while we did all the work.

And if it was Karen? Did she have Vegas heavies after her? Had her husband trailed her here? Had they seen us together and now they were after me, too? I'd already had Smiley making some phone calls to check on Karen's story. That would tell me what I needed to know about her. If her story didn't check out, then I'd dump her faster than last week's garbage. If her story did check out, then...

"Mind if I join you?" A bright voice broke my concentration. I jumped. It was Karen.

"Ah, sure…"

"You okay?" She slid into the booth and reached for my hands.

"Yeah. Just thinking about something."

"Me?"

"You *are* psychic." I leaned toward her. "Any problems? Anyone following you?"

"I don't think so," she answered after thinking about it. "Maybe I'm just being paranoid by all of this."

"It's going around."

"Huh?"

"Nothing."

The shadow of First Mary arrived an instant before she did.

"Jake?" First Mary asked, towering over the two of us, her eyes frowning at my partially-eaten breakfast. "How are your eggs?"

"The eggs are just fine."

First Mary nodded her head toward Karen, smiled and asked me, "She the one?"

"The one?" I asked cautiously, hoping First Mary wasn't going to make a Carley-inspired scene.

"She be the reason you be needin' steak n' eggs this mornin'?"

Her question made me relax—and smile. "Yeah," I mumbled, using First Mary's speech pattern. "She be the reason."

Her eyes went back to Karen, gently evaluating her. I could feel Karen squirm. Then, in her most business-like voice, First Mary asked if "the lady would like to see a menu." Karen declined and First Mary huffed as she left, her vacancy creating a huge void.

Karen's smiling eyes lit up the room. "Steak and eggs, huh?"

"Yeah," I mumbled, still distracted by the events of the week.

"Maybe I should look at a menu after all." She was trying to be upbeat.

I noticed First Mary standing by the cash register, still evaluating Karen. If I'd learned anything in all these years it was to listen when First Mary spoke. And while she wasn't speaking any words, her silence was screaming her concern. What could she see that I couldn't?

I turned back to Karen. "Why'd you shut my phone off yesterday?"

"Oh. That." She lowered her head. "It's an old habit. I don't like interruptions while I…" She shrugged, letting her blushing face finish her sentence. "I'm sorry I forgot to tell you."

Okay. I could buy that.

She looked up. "Anything else? Any other questions you need answers to?"

Back to square one. "What do you want with me?"

She leaned back. Her eyes dropped and focused on the table. "I'm not sure what I want, Jake." Her voice was louder than before, showing signs of exasperation. "It started off with needing a partner, someone who can help me make parlay bets and while that's still true, it's sort of changed."

"Changed?"

"I, um, like being with you." She looked up. "I want to get to know you. Better."

I listened to her words. I studied her face. I checked my own gut. Damn! Despite everything, despite Shiprock, despite Vegas bad-asses, despite the improbability of it all, I still wanted her. More than that, I wanted it to be all right that I wanted her. Half of me wanted to smile, to say, "Okay," to ride off into the sunset together. The other half? The other half just wanted to get up right now, walk out the door and chalk it up as a nice time but nothing more. Why now? Why this week?

She reached for my hand and turned my palm face up; just like the night we met. I played along. Just like I did the night we met.

"I see some trouble in your life." Her finger traced a line that ran from my index finger to my wrist. "You have a hard time trusting people, even when you want to, even when you should, even when it would be really good for you. You fight it."

I shrugged. She was softening me. "Half the people in Santa Fe could tell you that. Tell me something I don't know."

Her eyes remained on my palm, her hands cradling it like it was something special. "I see that you are about to go on a journey…"

"You told me that Saturday night and yet I'm still here."

She squeezed my hand, cutting short my smart-assed protest.

"I see that you are about to go on a journey…" her head turned toward the window, "…a very fast journey in that red Grand Prix…" Her head nodded at the bright red convertible parked two spaces from the front door.

She looked back and smiled. It was that same inviting smile that had captivated me Saturday night. "And Madame Kar-ren," she intoned in her worst gypsy-like accent, "ees never wrong."

I checked my watch. Manny wouldn't be calling until one so I had some free time. "A journey, huh?"

Her eyes brightened. Her smile got even better. "That's what it says in your palm."

"Where to?"

She leaned forward, whispering, "It doesn't say exactly. You'll just have to *trust* me." I noted the emphasis. "Besides, you sure ask a lot of questions for a man who came this close…" she showed me with her fingers nearly pinched together "…to not getting anywhere, or *anything*, at all."

I went back to my previous question. "A journey, huh?"

She nodded, smiled, picked up her purse and headed for the door, stopping to check for quarters in the pay phone. I got up to follow. I peeled off a twenty and left it on the table. I glanced one last time at First Mary. She was standing near the cash register, hands on hips, watching me in stone silence.

14
Hank
Early Monday Morning

I woke with a start. For a split second I wasn't sure where I was. My neck was sore. I had been sleeping sitting up with my chin on my chest. My legs had fallen asleep from the weight of the twelve-gauge that was lying across them. I felt sticky with sweat. I put the shotgun aside and pushed up from the old couch. Immediately, a thousand needles attacked my legs as my blood returned to its normal flow.

It was early; a sliver of sun was just starting to creep across the horizon. In another room I could hear W.E.'s heavy breathing. It came in an even pattern; a wheezing sound, pause, and then a long exhale. He was obviously having no problem sleeping.

When I had come running across the junkyard the evening before, W.E. was sitting on the porch right where I had left him. The story of how I'd found my place and the *murder* of Mildred concerned him as much as it did me. When I told him his life might be in jeopardy, he just pooh-poohed me. "Isn't got nothin' to do with me. Anyway, I can take care of myself." I told him about Jake's narrow escape from the killer car. He agreed that the black car and the scene at my place might be related. "Some crazy who's pissed at Jake, lookin' to get back at him for somethin'. Or that guy from the poker game you were tellin' me about. Slim. Damn near killed Elmore," he responded. "You shoulda told lard-ass about him."

These events were somehow connected. But how? W.E. and I had argued for the better part of an hour on what we should do.

"Let's say you're right, Hank, that this crazy driver did kill your goat. Why? How's that get back at Jake?"

"I don't know. If it was Slim, then it's 'cause we took his money."

"So why'd this guy try to run down Jake?"

"I don't know. If it was Slim, same reason. Or it could have been those Mexicans." *Or even Daryl*, I thought.

"What's Jake into now?"

My mind kept flipping back to the poker game, and Slim, and to Karen.

"Jake met this woman at Smiley's."

The old man raised his eyebrows in interest.

"She was playing poker with us." I hesitated for a second. "And she dropped out of the last hand when she had four aces. Dropped out of a pot worth well over ten thousand dollars."

W.E. let out a howl. "Women don't know how to play poker. What kind a pussy games you playin' there?"

I waited for W.E.'s laughter to subside before I continued. "This woman knew how to play poker. And later she read my palm, told me a few things that hit a little too close to home."

This statement gave W.E. a thought to ponder. "There are people who can see the past and future. But most human beings are too narrow-minded or scared to believe in those types of powers."

I just nodded, considering the possibilities. I was surprised W.E. hadn't concocted some kind of conspiracy. He seemed to want to dismiss the whole thing.

"This woman go home with Jake?"

"Yes."

"Probably a jealous husband or boyfriend tried to flatten his ass. And instead they damn near killed Elmore," W.E. said angrily.

"I don't think so."

"Why?"

"I don't know." But the possibility did seem to be there.

This conversation kept repeating itself. W.E. would ask a question and I would answer, "I don't know."

W.E. finally announced he was going to bed. I told him I was going to spend the night. He snorted and said he didn't need a guard, but I could sit on his couch all night if I wanted. And that's what I did.

I had spent the night trying to figure out what I was going to do next. Several calls to Jake's house and cell phone went unanswered. I did catch Smiley and asked him if he had seen Slim again. He said no and asked why. I brushed off his question and went back to my vigil, trying to figure out this mess. The one thing I knew for sure was, whoever had blown out Mildred's brains was not someone I wanted to meet without a gun in my hand. W.E.'s Winchester Model 12 had sufficed for the night. But I wished I had thought to look for my 9mm Browning before running out of my place. I had purchased the automatic many years earlier to replace an old Colt .45 revolver my father had given me.

When I had first met Jake, he was always trying to think of a way to make easy money. In the time I'd known him, Jake would alternate between legitimate jobs and those just shy of prison time. One his ideas involved a bogus art critic and my first art show in Santa Fe. We made some money on the con, but we didn't get rich. Then we started running pot over the border. Jake said it was good money for little work. There was nothing wrong with pot, as far as I was concerned, or with making a quick dollar. Fortunately, Jake and I were smart enough to get out of the dope business before we got caught and went to prison for a long, long time. I had put aside a tidy nest egg from our success and turned my full attention to my artwork.

Then Jake came up with his *best* idea. He made everything he was involved in *sound* legitimate.

One of the interviews Jake did for the *Reporter* was with an archaeologist. A dig was taking place up on some public land near the Four Corners in southern Utah. It was believed to have been an Anasazi community. The Anasazi had disappeared around the thirteenth century and no one knew why. But what the archaeologist found was much, much older than the Anasazi.

The pubiic's keen interest in the dinosaur fossils intrigued Jake. The money that private collectors were willing to pay for these fossils was even more intriguing. It wasn't long before we were traipsing off into the desert every weekend. I was surprised that it wasn't all that hard to find fossils along the dunes where the wind had blown the sand from the rocks.

The fossil business was fine and would have been fine if we had remained on private land. But staying on private land meant negotiating for the land rights. Land rights meant spending money. Jake wasn't good at spending money on *maybe* finding an old dinosaur bone or two, especially when he could just take it. So I bought the Browning automatic to protect myself from irate landowners who frowned on trespassers. I never intended or needed to use the gun on anyone, but I sure could have used it on Jake.

When we weren't poaching on private land, Jake led us onto public land, or worse, reservation land. Taking fossils from public land or a reservation is a federal offense, but usually results in a wrist-slap and a warning. That is, if you are a tourist. We weren't tourists, as Deputy Sheriff Wayne Wayne was quick to testify at our hearing. A plea bargain brought us each six months in the county jail and a year's probation, which tested my friendship with Jake. My interest in easy money ended there, along with my marriage to Francine. Francine had said "enough was enough," that our home life was not the proper atmosphere in which to raise a child. She left with Alice and we were divorced as fast as the New Mexico courts could process the papers.

I rubbed the sleep from my eyes and ran my tongue over my teeth. They needed brushing. The one thing I had been able to decide for myself, the night before, was that calling the sheriff's department would not help. It would only make matters worse. Trying to get help from Deputy Wayne would have been like getting directions from a blind man. Wayne believed that Jake and I were criminals and it was only a matter of time before he put us back behind bars. It had really riled Wayne when he had heard about the two of us being picked up with shovels in hand and a truck full of *hot* dinosaur fossils. We'd been out of his jurisdiction, picked up by a couple of reservation police officers. When we went to jail, Wayne Wayne had been there to hear the bars slam shut; with a shit-eating grin stretched across his fat jowls, enjoying the moment.

I went to wake W.E. and get the day started. The old man was fast asleep. I felt bad about waking him, but I wanted to get going. A couple of gentle shoves did nothing to rouse him. So I pushed harder. One eye came open and looked up at me.

"What?"

"It's time to get up," I said softly.

"No, it ain't." He closed the lone eye.

"W.E., I've got to go."

"So, go," he barked.

"I don't want to leave you asleep."

"Ya keep talkin' to me and I won't be."

I laughed. "Come on, W.E."

He sat up suddenly and rubbed his eyes. The old coot had on a white t-shirt gone gray with age. It was several sizes too large and was stretched badly at the neck. "Hank, I been through World War II before you was even born. So, the one thing I don't need now is you standing around guardin' me. You wanta go? Go." He threw back the sheet, revealing his bony white legs. "Get out of my way." I stepped back and he pulled on a pair of faded jeans from the foot of the bed.

I followed him into the living room where he fetched his shotgun. He then walked on out to the porch and sat down in his chair. The shotgun rested across his legs. "Now get." He waved me off with his left hand, as if shooing flies.

I stood looking at the old man. "W.E.?"

"Hank," he said as if I wasn't listening, "I'll be all right. I got my gun." He patted the shotgun. "Nobody gets up here I don't see first. Now get. I'll see you later." With that proclamation, W.E. sat back in his chair and stared out at the road.

I took one last look and he gave me a wink and a wave. I headed home.

* * *

The sun was just over the horizon as I stood and surveyed my place. Several chickens scratched around, raising dust, searching for a bug or two. I hesitated before entering the house, preparing myself for the destruction that had taken place.

Everything was as it had been the night before—chaos. The first thing I wanted was my gun.

When I first bought the Browning, I had searched for a good hiding place because of my daughter. And even though she hadn't lived with me since she was three, I still kept the gun tucked away. I had grown up in a family where guns were kept. My father had taught me to properly use them and to respect their power. Part of that respect was keeping them out of the hands of those who knew nothing about their dangerous nature. I ran my hands over the boards at the back of the closet and pressed. One popped free and there was the Browning, snug in its holster. I checked a clip, snapped it into place and put the gun in the holster. The shoulder holster made me feel silly, so I put it back in the hidey-hole and tucked the gun in the waistband of my jeans.

I searched through the house trying to see if anything had been taken. There was one big mess and some damage, but nothing seemed to be missing, other than the fish lamp that DeDe had taken. Then I had a sinking thought. I ran through the house and across the backyard, scattering chickens on my path to the shed. I had turned an old tool shed into my studio when I first bought the farm. The padlock had been busted off the door. I pulled open the door. An easel with a painting had been knocked over and the canvas torn. The cabinet doors stood open and some of the supplies were spilling out onto the floor, all in all, not as much destruction as in the house.

I went and threw open the large double doors that looked out to the east. They revealed a large metal sculpture in progress. It stood higher than the shed, partially blocking the sun. The sun shone through the sculpture's right angles, blinding me. It was fine and I relaxed a bit as I headed back to the house.

Who could have done this? I couldn't think of any reason why I had been singled out. Jake had something to do with this destruction—I could feel it. I knew he hadn't attacked my place, but his involvement in something I knew nothing about had led to this destructive force visiting me. Jake had been out to find me, but I hadn't been home. Had he hidden something here? If he had, I hoped it had been found and there wouldn't be a repeat search.

The wall clock in the kitchen showed it was almost eight o'clock. I reached for the phone and called Jake. The phone rang three times before the machine answered.

"Goddamn it, Jake! If you are home, pick up the phone." After a few seconds I slammed down the receiver. This was really starting to piss me off. Jake was probably there sleeping, with the phone turned down, letting the machine do his answering. He probably had a big smile on his face, as sweet dreams fluttered through his unconscious mind.

It took only a little more than an hour to return the house to some semblance of its former self. The actual destruction was not as bad as I originally feared. I figured I could fix the broken drawer in the bedroom. The couch could be covered with a blanket, but a couple of chairs were a total loss. I dragged the broken chairs outside. These I'd put in the truck later and drive out to my burning pit. Most of the refrigerator contents would make a feast for the chickens. As I swept the kitchen, I knew I was avoiding the one task I dreaded most—out in the barn.

I slowly swept dirt, broken glass and debris into neat little piles. My mind went over and over the events of the past twenty-four hours. There had to be a reason for this mess I was cleaning up. And the only reason I could think of kept bringing me back to Jake.

Jake had been my closest friend almost since the day I had hit Santa Fe. There were more times than I cared to remember when he had been there for me. He had shared my happiness when Alice was born. And he had held me through my deep despair when Anna died. Our friendship had survived the fiasco in the desert and ensuing jail time, even when my marriage to Francine hadn't. But something was gnawing at me and Jake was part of it. He had been distant lately. Brushing me off. It wasn't how he acted when we met Karen that bothered me. His actions then had been predictable. A beautiful woman gives him a glance, and it's "See you later, Hank." The thought made me smile. No, this was different. He acted like he was bothered to have me around lately.

Jake and I were different. Yet we were very much the same, closer than most brothers. Jake liked to run around but if a woman got too close, he'd make himself scarce. He said he didn't want to be tied down. I told him he was afraid of the commitment. He argued that he'd been with Carley longer than I'd been with DeDe and while he did have a point, he definitely wasn't the settling down kind of man. Jake basically wanted one thing—to stay young. Without relationships, Jake had no markers on his life to measure the passing years.

Me? I wasn't sure what I was searching for. But there were plenty of yardsticks for measuring my life—what I'd accomplished, what I hadn't. Maybe Alice was the difference between us. Jake had watched Alice grow up but from a distance, barely noting the passing of time. For me, the father, each of Alice's birthdays marked another year, another stage, another set of interests. My life with her was filled with mile markers of teddy bears and skinned knees and bikes and boys while Jake's life was one long, endless highway going nowhere.

I stopped my work and gave Jake another call. Again, I only reached his machine. I tried his cell but got his voice mail. Again.

The kitchen was the only mess I had left to finish. I swept one pile into the dustpan and dumped the contents in a grocery bag. Following suit, the other piles half filled the bag with broken glass. It was too bad DeDe wasn't here to see the place. If she hadn't already left, this episode in my life would have necessitated the final exit. This I found funny. Less than forty-eight hours ago I had been upset that she had left. Now I was relieved. Relieved and embarrassed. Maybe an eight-month marriage was nothing to be embarrassed about. But at the moment, I was. Alice had been stunned when I told her I had married DeDe. She had looked at me in complete disbelief.

"She's only seven years older than I am. She should be my *sister*, not my stepmother," she had implored.

I finished the kitchen. It didn't look too bad. There were still enough unbroken dishes for me to have a meal on. Now it was time to face the task I was avoiding.

The chickens took my early morning appearance as an opportunity to be fed. Every time they saw me leave the house, they kept a wary eye on me just in case I was carrying *their* bucket. Chickens came running from various corners of the yard at the sound of my tapping on the bucket. I tossed the remains of my refrigerator's contents to the hungry flock. The chickens scratched and pecked at the morsels. I went out to the coop to check the eggs from the day before. One old Rhode Island Red sat guarding her nest. She had gone broody and was now determined to be a mother. Even though I took her eggs every day she remained on the nest.

"Okay, you want to be a mother, be one." Today, I took pity and left the eggs she sat on. I added three to her clutch. From the rest of the nests I filled an empty coffee can with eggs. This task done, I headed for what waited in the barn.

Everything was cool and quiet in the relative darkness of the barn. A few shafts of sunlight showed through the old boards' mismatched seams. I tossed a several bales of hay out of my way. The three lambs were resting in the corner in back. They were lying up against the foundation, taking in the rocks' coolness. The lambs scattered when I got too close.

Mildred was still where I had found her.

"Poor old girl. I'm going to take you back to your home." Gently I lifted Mildred. Her body had lost its stiffness and her head hung down. I crossed the yard to the pickup and placed her in the back. It was not the way I wanted her to make her last ride. I went back to the barn, looking for a blanket to cover her. The lambs watched my search. They expected a handful of grain. I poured out a full can and the three forgot their fear and crowded around, lips scooping up the oats, corn and soya.

When I came out of the barn, a strange truck was in the drive. It was an old, black Dodge 4x4 pickup with New Mexico plates. I stood still, looking around for the occupant. Seeing no one, I shifted the blanket I'd found to my left arm and reached for my Browning with my right hand. I stood perfectly still, listening. Hearing nothing, I took a step around the corner of the barn and began to lower my aim at the back of a lone figure. When the woman turned around, I was as surprised as she.

Quickly I placed the pistol back in my jeans. "Molly!"

"Do you always carry a gun?" Her eyes flickered from my face down to my empty hand.

"Sorry, I…"

"Don't you remember your invitation from yesterday? At the liquor store?"

"Yes," I said slowly, but my mind was racing, searching for the right words. "Yes, I was. It's…I…"

"Forgot?" she said flatly, not looking happy. "Remember? You were going to show me a *real* artist's studio. You were going to show me some of your work." Molly was carrying on a one-sided conversation.

"I did forget. It's just…something happened. I'm sorry." I could tell from her look that my tone had conveyed my despair.

"What happened?" Her voice changed, it was suddenly full of concern.

"I've got to go somewhere." I was being evasive.

"Oh, I'm sorry. I was looking forward to spending the day together."

I thought for a moment, taking in Molly's presence. "Maybe you'd like to go along?"

She looked puzzled. "Maybe."

15
Jake
Monday Afternoon

We'd taken a leisurely drive around Santa Fe for about an hour. I gave Karen my quick tour of the city with a half-hearted promise to do more the following week. Then, we headed to my apartment. Manny was scheduled to call and I had to be there. As far as I could tell, no one had been following us—or her.

As I put the key into the lock, the door opened almost by itself. Inside was what was left of my earthly belongings. Everything was scattered, torn, tipped over. We walked in. Slowly. Karen held onto my arm and baby-stepped her way behind me. I listened for sounds, any kind of sounds. Running. Breathing. Ripping. I closed the now-unlockable door and surveyed the mess. At first glance, nothing major appeared to be missing so I dismissed burglary as a motive. After a second look, I discounted vandalism. There was nothing malicious about this—no Satan-slogans, no blood on the walls, no piles of shit on the carpet.

But who did this? Slim? The Mexicans? Daryl? Vegas goons? My Shiprock partners?

A terrible suspicion crept back into my mind. Karen had just taken me on an unplanned joy ride and while we were gone, my place had been trashed. I turned and stared at her, trying to figure out if or when or why she'd been a part of this.

She'd been taking tentative steps around the apartment, being careful not to trip over the debris, when she noticed me looking at her.

131

"What?"

"Why'd you take me for that ride?"

She stared, as if trying to interpret my words.

I stepped toward her, pointing my finger in her face. "What the hell was that all about?"

She swallowed. "What?"

The phone rang, jolting my attention away from Karen. I looked for it but couldn't see it right away. I waited for the next ring and zeroed in on its new location. By the third ring, I had it in my hands and was connected with Manny.

"You sound out of breath. Are you okay?"

"Fine," I wheezed. "You?" I tried to calm myself down.

"Good. Very good." He sounded friendly. "I'm at a pay phone so I can talk more freely. Did you get the truck?"

"It's been ordered." I turned and found Karen riveted to the same spot, as if afraid to move.

"Are you still coming down this weekend?"

"My travel plans are just as they were the last time we spoke." They weren't but now was not the time to tell him.

"*Travel plans?*" he questioned. "You sound so formal. Is someone there?"

"Yes." I answered curtly. "That would be correct."

"Now I know why you are out of breath." Manny laughed. "I hope she is more beautiful than the last one I saw you with."

I looked at Karen and did a quick evaluation. Even though I had no recollection of whom I was with the last time I'd seen Manny—and despite what I'd just been considering about Karen—I still had to give a positive answer.

The laughter faded. "Now, my friend, everything is in order, is it not?"

An old, familiar chill shot up my spine. It wasn't a question. It only sounded like one. I immediately canceled any thoughts I'd had of telling Manny about big black cars or changes in plans.

"Of course." I swallowed. Hard.

"Good, my friend, because that would spoil everything."

"And we wouldn't want that," I added, more for my comfort than his.

"Very good." He'd been reassured, now it was time for him to go.

"I want you to call me every day this week and keep me aware of what's going on."

"Sure," I muttered.

He laughed, but I got his underlying message. Manny was getting nervous. That was what this phone call was about. He hung up without saying another word and I replaced the receiver in the cradle.

"You think I had something to do with this, don't you?" Karen's question startled me, and for a few moments all I could do was stare at her.

"Wouldn't you?" I finally asked.

"Maybe." She stepped closer, a little at a time, gaining confidence as she neared me. "And maybe not."

I challenged her. "Suppose you tell me why not."

Her eyes took a slow sweep of my disheveled apartment. "I'd say someone figured you have something hidden in here. Something valuable or important."

I raised my eyebrows in mock surprise. "You sure you're not a cop?" Even as I said it, the thought took on life. Was that possible? Karen was a cop?

She let my statement pass without comment and continued her assessment. "Unless you've forgotten, I've already been here. Twice. If I was looking for something—which I wasn't—I've had two opportunities to poke around in your underwear drawer."

She was right. She could have robbed me blind. Twice. But why couldn't I get rid of the notion that her little joy ride was somehow connected to my newly redecorated apartment?

I gave her a tentative half smile. "Sorry."

"So, you *are* going on a trip?"

"A trip?" Her question caught me off guard.

"You were talking about travel plans on the phone."

"Oh. That." I replayed as much of the conversation as I could remember. I'd thought I was being careful with what I'd said but evidently not as careful as I thought. "Just like you predicted." I went back to being glib.

"And is the rest of what I *saw* true, too?" She touched my arm and I felt her concern.

"The rest?" I was momentarily lost.

"The money? The danger?" Her eyes locked with mine. "Unless this..." She swept her free arm over my ransacked apartment. "Unless this is normal?"

Here we were. Again. Truth or consequences. Tell her the whole story or tell a lie. I smiled at her. Half of me wished I could tell her so that I could have an ally, someone to help me figure this out. I was feeling more and more alone. The other half of me vetoed any such plans and locked the truth away.

"Well, Karen, it's like this. I'm going into the desert in a couple of days and come out with sixteen million dollars in rare gold coins. Wanna come along?"

"Jake!" Her foot stomped the floor. "Don't lie to me. Please. I want you to tell me the truth."

I thought of Nicholson in *A Few Good Men*—how he sat there on the witness stand and spat his words at Cruise—"*You can't handle the truth!*" I wanted to say that, but didn't.

I noticed how serious my mood had suddenly become. And why not? My world was falling apart. Manny was calling every day and making unexpected visits. Cloud kept changing things. My apartment had been trashed. My life had been threatened. And, I'd just given Karen a thumbnail sketch of what was going to happen later this week. How smart was that?

"Karen," I put my arm around her. "This is all really none of your business. Drop it."

She pulled away and her eyes searched mine. Looking for what? Truth? Trust? A reason to leave?

I didn't have time to figure it out. Or to worry about who trashed my place. Not now. "Look. I need to get someplace. Can you give me a ride?"

She stared. Evaluating. Thinking. Then she nodded. Slowly, almost imperceptibly. Close enough. For now. I grabbed her arm and hustled her out the door and down to her car.

* * *

We rounded the curve just before Smiley's and I motioned for her to slow down and pull in. She down-shifted and angled into the parking lot.

"What?" she asked sarcastically. "Another poker game?"

She did have a nasty sense of humor and I liked that. It was everything else about her that worried me. In a few minutes, if Smiley had gotten my message and done what I'd asked, I'd have a few more answers.

Smiley, Rufus and a couple of ancient regulars were the only ones in the bar. The jukebox played the Eagles' "Desperado," a song Hank had always maintained was written about me. Smiley headed for the cooler to grab a Heiney but I waved him off.

"Too early?" he asked, almost incredulous at the thought of me turning down a beer.

"No," I said as I sat on the nearest bar stool. "No time."

Smiley rested his meaty hands on the mahogany bar. He gave a quick nod to Karen. "Anything for you?"

She shook her head and looked down, avoiding Smiley's inspecting glare.

I tapped the bar to get Smiley's attention. "I'd like to pick up my share of the poker winnings—and that other envelope I gave you."

He broke away from staring at Karen and nodded to Rufus who rolled off his barstool and headed toward the back room.

Smiley pivoted back toward Karen. "And just how is ol' Clarence?" Smiley's voice took on a tone that only sounded friendly.

She swallowed. "Fine. He's..."

"Let's see," he cut her off, running his right hand over his bald head. "I haven't talked to him for a while. In fact, I tried calling him today but he wasn't around," he said with a slight nod toward me." But the last time I talked with Clarence he was telling me something about one of his kids—the oldest one I think—had won some kind of award." He stopped rubbing his head and looked right at Karen. "You wouldn't know what that was, would you?"

I swiveled toward her. Smiley was testing her, something he should have done more of Saturday night. If I was going to keep her around, this was one test she'd have to pass.

"Unless we're talking about two different people," her voice was slow and cool and confident, "the Clarence I know," she lifted her wrist and let it fall limply forward, "doesn't have a wife, any kids or anything in his life except his bar."

Smiley paused, and then shrugged. "Right. I must have been having a senior moment there."

His attempt at playing detective had only proved that Karen did know Clarence but not that she wasn't some kind of fraud who'd slipped past his normal scrutiny. I raised an eyebrow, asking a silent question. He stared for a second and then got it.

"I didn't have any luck on the other calls, either."

"Nobody home?"

"More like nobody talking. I'll try again later."

Rufus brought out my share of the winnings and Manny's envelope. "You ever see those two Mexicans again, Jake?"

"No." But, I wondered if they'd been inside of that black Ford. Or the ones who'd trashed my place. "They been back here?" I stuck the envelope in my shirt.

Rufus and Smiley both shook their heads.

I got up. "Figures. Once the big dog barks, the little pups listen."

Rufus rolled his eyes. Smiley just turned and walked away. No respect.

I headed for the door, Karen following right behind me. As we stepped out into the sunlight, I heard Smiley tell me to be careful.

16
Hank
Monday Afternoon

A tear ran down Molly's cheek as she looked down at a dead goat lying in the pickup's bed. She gently caressed her neck and asked what the goat's name was.

"Her name is Mildred," I said softly and dabbed at my eyes. "Someone shot her. And I'm taking her home." I had been wondering what to tell Molly. I wanted to be honest with her and not start to weave a tangled web of lies. I looked down at my old friend and pulled a blanket over her.

I leaned on the truck and looked at Molly. She looked beautiful to me. Not a trace of makeup was on her face. Her eyes were large, deep brown pools, and the lashes long and thick. Her black hair hung loose to her shoulders with only the last couple inches caught in a silver and turquoise clasp, creating a short ponytail at the end. Large silver hoop earrings accented her hair and gently grazed her high cheekbones when she moved her head. She had removed an old faded jean jacket, which she had placed on the truck's tailgate. A white sleeveless blouse revealed her bare arms. I marveled at the muscles in them. A full print skirt almost reached her ankles, covering her legs. While many men would find her plain, I thought she was lovely.

"I'm sorry; I forgot you were coming over this morning but with Mildred and…" I fought the tears before they came.

Molly looked out across the yard for a long time before responding. "Hank, I understand why you would have forgotten I was coming over."

Molly smiled slightly. "But when I showed up at your place, I was greeted by the barrel of a gun. Is there something going on here that I need to know about?"

I pulled the truck's door open and sat in the cab's shade. Molly did the same on the passenger side.

"Molly, I'm not going to lie to you." I reached over and took her hand in mine. "I'll answer any questions you have, as best I can. There are some things I may choose not to tell you right now." My eyes met hers, gazing into their deep darkness.

She held my look. "Okay, Hank. There's something about you that I trust, but I do want to know what happened."

"I'm taking Mildred home. I have an old Navajo friend who lives on the rez. It's a pleasant ride."

Molly smiled again. Her smile made me melt. "I know the rez and it is a nice drive. But please tell me what happened to Mildred and what you're doing with a gun."

"Like I said, someone shot Mildred. When I got home yesterday someone had broken into my house and trashed it. I found Mildred in the barn. I don't know who did it or why. Nothing was taken, just stuff busted up. Someone might have a vendetta against me. I can't think of who or why, though. Or it could be a stupid prank. Either way, I plan to find out." I took the gun from my lap and placed it under the seat. "That's why I had the gun. In case it is a vendetta and they come back looking for me. You still want to go with me?" I hoped that she did.

"Killing your goat is cruel. Someone must be really mad at you."

"I can't think of anyone, except a cowpoke who lost some money to me in a card game the other night."

"Was it crooked?"

The question made me grin. "I don't need to cheat at cards."

"Oh, you're that good?"

"No. Most players just don't really know the game. If you want to come, we should get started."

Molly closed the door on her side. "Yes, I want to go with you."

I shut my door and started the truck. We began the first leg of our journey a fifteen-minute ride to Pojoaque. There was no traffic in either direction, except us. Molly asked me to tell my story again.

"Late yesterday, I came home and found that someone had basically ripped my place apart." I kept my eyes on the highway. "I don't know if they were looking for something or just making a mess. If they were looking for something, I don't know what it was. I just hope they found it and they don't come back. If the cowboy did it, I want to settle the score."

"How are you going to settle the score? With the gun?"

"No, not with the gun. But somehow he'll pay."

"You can't think of anything you have that someone would want from you?"

"No. Nothing was taken that I can tell. But a possible connection might be a friend of mine. Someone might have us confused."

"Who's the friend?"

"Just a guy named Jake." But I gave no more details. Molly shrugged and motioned me to continue. So, I gave Molly the long version of the story, starting on Monday, the day DeDe left for the last time. Molly reached over, brushed my hand very softly with hers and looked down to see where they touched. *Okay*, I thought to myself, *I haven't scared her off yet.*

So I continued and told her about the black mystery car and Jake. Molly didn't interrupt me. She sat and listened while I told her about W.E., Elmore, the hit-and-run accident, and what appeared to have been the same mysterious black car.

At this point she asked only one question. "What do the police think?"

It seemed like a simple question to her, but it really opened another closet of skeletons.

"They weren't very helpful," I said flatly.

She nodded as if she understood.

By the time I had finished explaining, we had passed through both Pojoaque and Los Alamos and were high in the mountains, almost to the Sulphur Springs. Other than the one question, Molly hadn't said a word, only nodding whenever I looked her way.

As we turned north towards Cuba, I asked, "So, do you want to get out?"

She laughed. Her laughter was infectious. "Not while the truck is moving." Then she turned serious. "You're a good man, Hank Djumpstrom. I can sense it." She took my right hand from the wheel and held it to her cheek for a second. "I would like to stop for a minute."

"Okay, I'll stop for gas."

We made our pit stop and picked up something to drink and snack on. Molly ripped open a bag of pretzels and twisted the cap off a bottle of Ginseng tea.

"DeDe just left last week?" Molly giggled. "That means I'm riding around the back roads of New Mexico with a married man. So much for my feelings about you being a good man." She broke into laughter, dropping pretzels and partially spilling the tea.

My smile was huge, but I could feel my embarrassment as my face flushed.

"Oh, poor baby." Molly leaned over and kissed my cheek.

I looked at Molly. I wanted to pull over and stop the truck. I wanted to kiss her lips and hold her.

Molly quit laughing and thought for a second. "Djumpstrom. That's the last name of the woman who owns Frank Galleries, where I first met you."

The statement altered my mood immediately. My head rolled back.

"A sister?" Molly raised her eyebrows to emphasize the question.

I let the question sit for a moment while I took the turn off 126 at Cuba and caught County Road 197 south to Torreon.

My tone turned serious. "I was married to Francine a long time ago."

Her eyes had gotten big, but she seemed fascinated by my story. "Wow, married twice."

This made me wince. "Francine was my second wife."

"Whoa, you mean that DeDe is wife number three? There aren't any more, are there?"

"No." I was suddenly sad.

"Who was wife number one?"

"Are you sure you want to hear all this?"

"Only if you want to tell me."

I drove a ways without responding. Then the floodgates opened and my past came tumbling out. I had met Anna Huettner in Taos shortly after I'd first arrived in New Mexico. She was an art student from Albuquerque spending the summer in the art colony, searching for what had inspired Georgia O'Keefe. This was a common bond between us. We became lovers and moved back to Santa Fe when we tired of Taos' trendiness. When Anna found out she was pregnant, I told her I wanted to marry her. Anna cried and said we were too young to get married. Our daughter, Alice, was born in November and was the image of Anna. We married a couple months later.

Molly sat against the door attentively listening. I could tell she understood that this was painful for me but didn't know why.

"Anna wanted to go on a trip, have sort of a honeymoon. She wanted to see the Alamo." I paused and looked at Molly. "I guess she wanted to see where John Wayne died." I gave a half-hearted laugh. Molly gazed into my eyes and nodded. "Well, Alice rode in a backpack as we took in the sites of San Antonio. To 'Remember the Alamo,'" I said in my best Texas drawl.

I glanced at Molly and she gave me a small grin.

"Anna wanted to stay in a campground. I wanted to stay in a motel with creature comforts. We stayed in a tent. When I woke up in the morning, Anna was dead." A tear ran down my cheek and came to rest on my chin. I brushed it away with the back of my hand. "She was nineteen years old. She died on January 6th, 1972. I'd known her for less than two years." I wiped away another tear, and then another.

"What happened?"

"A coral snake had crawled into the tent, probably attracted by her body heat. I suppose she rolled over on it and it bit her. Anna never knew; she just never woke up."

We rode in silence the rest of the way to Torreon. County 197 is a two-lane blacktop road that the Rand McNally atlas lists as "conditions vary—local inquiry suggested." I turned west towards Star Lake, where the Continental Divide is.

"Hank, I'm sorry." Molly's voice was soothing.

"It's okay. I didn't have to tell you. I wanted you to know. When people hear I was married three times, well…"

"How did you meet Francine?"

"Francine is Anna's sister." I paused. "I guess it was our mutual grief that brought us together as well as our love for Alice. When we divorced, Alice went to live with Francine. That's why she kept my name. We've stayed friends, but we never should have been married."

We drove to Star Lake, chatting idly about nothing, and then on to Pueblo Pintado, where I turned south towards White Horse.

"Where exactly are we going?" questioned Molly.

"North of Standing Rock. Now it's my turn to ask you about your past."

"So you want my life history. Okay. I grew up near Red Rock."

I turned to look at her.

"I'm mostly Navajo. My father's mother was white. I grew up on the reservation and lived there until I went to college at New Mexico State." Her voice was very matter-of-fact.

It was my turn to stay quiet and not interrupt.

"My father ran a store on the reservation. He was several years older than my mother. Her family was not happy when they first got married."

"Do your parents still live there? I mean at the store."

"My mother has never lived anywhere except on the reservation. My older sister and her husband run the store now. Mother helps out, but mostly she just sits on the porch and greets the customers. My father died almost twenty years ago." Molly's voice had a faraway sound to it. "He drank himself to death."

"I'm sorry."

"Don't be. I loved him and so did everyone who knew him. He liked to drink. But he liked it too much. He was almost seventy when his liver finally gave out. He lived a long time and he might have lived longer if he didn't drink so much." Molly sounded philosophical.

She kicked off her moccasins, put her bare feet up on the dash, and looked out the window, watching the sagebrush go by. I enjoyed looking at her toes as she wiggled them.

We were almost to the Crownpoint bypass where we turned northwest, only a few miles from Standing Rock and the reservation border. The sun had passed its mid-point in the day, and we had been on the road for almost four hours. We passed by the four buildings that are Standing Rock. The truck kicked up a tail of dust as we headed due north. Even though we rode in silence, a bond was developing between us.

After about five miles, I left the road and headed west out into the desert, on what some people wouldn't even consider a trail. I had to slow the truck as we bumped along the ruts and rocks.

"We're going to see Walter Ravenfeather. He's the one I got Mildred from. I want to return her to where she was born."

"How did you meet this Walter Ravenfeather?"

"When I was living in Taos, I tried to make a living as a potter. I used to go out to the pueblo and study the pottery. This one shop had an amazing collection from the different pueblos and reservations. There were some Navajo carved pots that were particularly nice. Walter's name, Ravenfeather, was etched in the bottom. The woman running the shop told me that Walter was from somewhere around Crownpoint. After Anna died, I remembered the pots and decided I had to meet him. I came out to Crownpoint and someone told me to check at the Chapter House in Standing Rock. And someone there told me how to find his hogan. But when I found the hogan, there was a fire going but he was nowhere around. So I started looking for him. After searching for an hour or so, I heard someone calling for help. I followed the voice and found Walter. He had fallen down in an arroyo and broken his leg. Well, I took him to Window Rock to the clinic. They put his leg in a cast and told him he'd have to stay for a week or so. Walter told them he couldn't, that his sheep and goats needed him. When the nurse asked him who was going to help him, he looked at me. I ended up living out here with him for the summer. His wife Corrine was visiting a daughter and new grandchild on the other side of the reservation at the time. He neglected to tell me she would be returning in a few days." I smiled at the memory of the sly old fox. "During my stay with Walter, he taught me about his art and life in the desert. I've been coming back ever since. I guess you and I have both lived on the rez—and even at the same time." The statement made Molly smile.

* * *

Walter was sitting outside his hogan in the shade when we arrived, his straw cowboy hat tipped down over his eyes. Barney, his dog, was lying at his feet. Walter didn't make a movement until I had brought the truck to a halt twenty yards from the hogan. It was the Navajo tradition to wait at a distance until your host was ready to notice your presence. Slowly, Walter raised the brim of his hat and a smile crept across his face. I knew Walter was happy to see me. I'd spent a lot of time with him and his wife since we'd first met. Walter's wife, Corrine, had died of cancer ten years earlier. When she passed away, I felt like my grandmother had died. Corrine and Walter had two children, a son and a married daughter who provided several grandchildren for him to spoil.

Molly and I sat in the truck and waited until Walter stood and waved to us. I could smell pinon smoke from the cooking fire. The sun was past its peak, but still blared down on us; the day had reached its boiling point. While we were riding the last few miles, Molly put her hair in two braids and wrapped them around the back of her head. I pushed my sunglasses up on my nose.

"*Yaa' eh t'eeh!*" I greeted Walter.

Walter returned the greeting. He beamed at me and gave Molly a broad smile. "Hank, how did you know I would be home?"

"Walter, you're always home. This is Molly Kiyanee."

"Molly, I am very happy to meet you." Walter's smile had a question in it.

"DeDe and I are not together any longer." I took a quick glance to see Molly's reaction. She looked to Walter, who nodded and looked up at the sky.

"We should get out of this sun. Come sit under my porch." Walter led the way. His porch consisted of several old blankets stretched across a frame of poles that were attached to the hogan's roof, making a lean-to. We sat in the shade and Walter offered us water.

Walter could not keep the smile off his face. His mouth was usually just one of the many lines that creased his face. Today his smile was full of teeth and laughter. Walter's gray hair was usually worn long, but today it was in a tight bun at the back of his head.

"Molly, how did you come to meet my young friend?"

Molly exchanged a smile with the old man. I could tell the two instantly liked each other.

"I met Hank at an art opening. Then I ran into him in a liquor store parking lot yesterday."

This made Walter howl with laughter, and he slapped his leg.

"Kiyanee. I think I know that name…when I was a boy I lived up near Mexican Water."

"I was born to the Two Trees Dinee," Molly responded. "They have lived near Red Rock for many years. Maybe you know the Single Stop Trading Post?"

144

Walter nodded. "Yes, I remember it. It has been there for many years. A man," Walter thought for a moment, "and his wife ran the store."

"Yes," Molly smiled. "That was my father. He has been dead for many years. But my mother and sister still have the store."

"Then I know of your family. You have an uncle who is a *hataallii*? I remember him singing the Blessing Way when I was a child."

"I did have an uncle who was a shaman. He is dead now. But my cousin has learned to sing."

"That is good. Not many young people want to learn the songs of the *hataallii*. I will have to remember your cousin if I need a singer."

"His name is David Redhawk. He lives near Many Farms."

"Do you have any other brothers or sisters?"

"I have a brother who is a policeman. He works out of Window Rock."

Walter nodded with satisfaction. "I have a son who is a police officer. He's stationed at Tuba City."

For a second something flashed across Molly's eyes. "I've heard his name. I'm sure my brother must know him."

"My son is unmarried." Walter smiled at me.

Molly giggled.

I didn't like where he was taking this conversation.

Walter turned his attention to me. He asked about Alice and Francine, but DeDe's name didn't come up again. He wanted to know if I had been working on my art, doing any pottery. How the lambs were he had given me to raise. He caught up on the last couple months of my life. Finally I told Walter about Mildred's untimely death. I avoided filling in any of the theories that I had. But I could tell by Walter's reaction that he knew there was more than I was telling.

Walter and I walked out to the truck to see the goat. There was a low humming coming from Walter. He gently rocked back and forth when I pulled back the blanket for him to see.

"This is very bad, Hank. You must be careful. You must watch out for that girl, protect her. She is a special one." He looked back at the hogan where Molly sat in the shade. "I know where we can take the goat."

I smiled and took Walter's hand. "Thank you, Hosteen Ravenfeather. You are a good friend."

* * *

Molly and I sat with Walter for an hour after Mildred's burial. He told Molly of his grandchildren and about his son, the police officer. He told her about his courtship of Corrine and how happy they had been for almost fifty years. I knew this story was for my benefit.

When we left, Walter made Molly promise to come back and see him, with or without me. He opened his jish pouch and took out what looked liked a large coin. The object glittered and sparkled in the sunlight. Walter took Molly's hand and pressed his treasure into it. Molly smiled and bent forward, kissing the old man on the cheek.

We retraced our path back to Standing Rock and headed east. Molly dug into her purse and retrieved the gift. She held her hand out for me to see.

"Where do you think he got this? It must be solid gold. Here, hold this."

Molly handed the object to me. I held it in my left hand, feeling its weight. It looked like an old coin.

"Yeah, it looks like gold to me." The coin was larger than a half-dollar. The edges were smooth and it looked old. "Walter finds all kinds of things out in the desert." I handed it back to her.

Molly was carefully examining her prize. "But, this is a gold coin."

"Yeah," I shrugged my shoulders at the statement, not knowing what more to say.

* * *

The sun had set and the beginnings of darkness were falling when we arrived at my farm. The moon was up, playing hide and seek in a bank of clouds. I parked the truck next to the house. With the engine off, all was silent. Molly was nestled in my arms. I gently tipped her head back and kissed her on the lips. We kissed for several seconds, enjoying every moment.

"Show me your house," she said.

We strolled around to the back porch. I put the key in the lock and was relieved to find the door solidly shut. We stepped into the kitchen. I glanced around, and everything looked peaceful. I hoped there weren't any unwelcome guests lurking in the shadows.

"Come on in. Things are a little messy."

Molly responded with a smile and stepped through the doorway. It was a good thing I had finished straightening up because I had forgotten I was going to be having a guest. The house looked a bit sparse without the two chairs. Molly looked around as I turned on lights. She gravitated to a drawing I had done of a horned toad.

"This one is yours! I recognize the style."

"Yes. All the animal drawings are mine."

Molly moved from one small drawing to the next. "I like them. You're very good." She moved around the room, picking up my pottery and admiring each piece before moving on to the next. I felt proud as Molly examined my art and fortunate that the invaders had actually broken very few pieces. Then Molly picked up a carved pot. Turning it over, she discovered Walter's name. "Ravenfeather," she read out loud. Molly flashed me a smile.

Molly moved to the bedroom where she tossed her jean jacket and purse on the bed. I stood in the doorway watching. She moved around the room looking at the meager furnishings.

"I'd really like to take a shower." Without waiting for my response, Molly started to unbutton her blouse and moved in the direction of the bathroom. I stepped out of her way as she passed. I was sure a sly smile graced her face. She dropped the blouse after she had passed and stopped long enough to step out of her skirt. I followed and found the discarded skirt surrounding her moccasins in the doorway to the bathroom. She was standing with her back to me, wearing just a white bra and matching panties. She gracefully undid the braids that surrounded her head. With her back still to me she unfastened her bra and let it fall to the floor. Then she stepped out of her panties. There was no hint of a tan line, just an even dark coloring over her entire body. She quickly slipped behind the shower curtain. I heard the water start and then the spray of the shower. I stood in the door wondering what I should do.

"Is there some shampoo?"

I looked around and didn't see any.

"I'll check." I looked under the sink and found none. "Are you sure it's not in a corner?"

"Oh, here it is." Molly giggled. "How about some soap?"

"That I can manage. Here." I put my hand behind the curtain.

Molly didn't take the soap, but instead grabbed my wrist and half pulled me into the shower. To keep from falling I put one foot into the tub. A spray of water hit me in the face, blinding me momentarily. Molly laughed with glee.

"I'm getting all wet," I protested.

Molly kept trying to pull me into the shower.

"I'm still dressed."

"Quit complaining and get in here!"

Molly put her arms around my neck and kissed me on the lips. I could feel her breasts against my chest. She loosened her arms and started to push my shirt up over my head. It was difficult to remove the wet shirt, so I helped. While I was pulling off my shirt, Molly started on my jeans.

"Just a second." I sat down on the tub's edge and started to take off my shoes.

We stood in the spray of the shower. Her hair was wet and washed down over her shoulders past her breasts. I took in her form. Her breasts were small and nicely shaped. Her pubic hair was as dark as that on her head and looked straight in the running water. Her thighs were well defined and I wanted to put my hands around them and run my tongue over them.

"Hurry up and get those jeans off," she laughed.

I fought my way out of the wet clothes and tossed them out onto the floor. I could already feel the effect of this naked woman on my desire.

As I stood, Molly took me in her hand. I was hard and excited. Her tongue explored my mouth and found my tongue. She pulled me against her slick body and rubbed back and forth. My hands covered her body. I wanted to touch everything all at once. My mouth found her breast and I played gently with her nipple. It rose to meet my tongue.

Falling back under the spray, Molly put one leg up on the tub's rim. She led me into her. I moaned with excitement. She licked my ear and pressed her breasts against my chest. Instinctively, I moved my hips. Before I could really get started, Molly gently pushed me back, breaking our grasp. She picked up the soap and lathered my body. I did the same to hers. Then she poured a dab of shampoo into her hand and washed my hair. I copied as if we were playing a game of follow the leader. With our bodies slick with soap she led me inside her again. After a few thrusts, she quickly broke us apart.

Molly pointed the showerhead at me and rinsed my body. She turned and rinsed hers. I reached around and took the small breasts in my hands and gently caressed them. Then she turned off the water and stepped from the tub.

She pulled a couple towels off the rack, tossed me one and began wrapping her hair in a towel. I took in the sight. Then she took a third towel and patted her body.

"Let me do that for you," I responded.

"No, you go turn off the lights."

I raced through the house flicking off lights. I kicked shut the back door and turned the lock. I unplugged the phone and headed back to the bathroom. It was empty. I stepped quickly into the bedroom. Molly was already between the sheets. I joined her. She pressed one hand against my chest to slow my advance.

"Here." In her left hand was a condom. She smiled.

I tore the packet with my teeth, slipped on the protection, and glided back under the sheets. We found each other. Molly's body was still moist from the shower. I kissed her and she kissed me back. My knee was between her legs and she was pressing to get under me. My breaths were coming too quickly; I was becoming faint with desire. We tangled and rolled back and forth on the bed. Molly's hips rose to meet me and hold me. We wore each other out. Finally I fell back onto the pillows and begged for mercy. She laughed.

* * *

I woke with a start. Molly was still next to me, sound asleep. I rubbed my eyes, and then the pounding started again.

"What the heck?" Someone was pounding on my door. I checked the clock. It was 1:07 a.m. I pulled on my jeans and searched for the Browning. I clicked off the safety and headed towards the kitchen. The pounding started again. I flicked on the outside light. Officer Wayne Wayne was at the back door. I opened the door.

"What's with the gun, Hank?" Wayne snarled at me.

I looked down at the gun in my hand and shrugged.

"Where the fuck is your friend Jake?"

149

"Gee-ze, Wayne, it's past one o'clock in the morning. I was sleeping."
I was irritated.

"And not alone. Who's the squaw, Hank?" Wayne had a menacing smile
on his face, but suddenly it changed to a look of concern.

I turned to see Molly with my robe on and a .38 caliber service revolver
in her right hand.

"The name is Sergeant Kiyanee. I'm a police officer, deputy." Molly
raised her left hand to reveal a badge.

17
Jake
Tuesday Morning

Karen slept, a dainty snore escaping every now and then. For some reason, that amused me. Maybe it made her more human, less sinister.

We'd gone from Smiley's to her hotel room and picked up the rest of her things. Since I didn't want her staying there and didn't want to go back to my place, I rented a hotel suite on the other end of town and we spent the rest of the day together. For now, I felt like we were safe.

I climbed out of bed and quietly headed for the couch. I thought about going out and sitting on the balcony but decided against it. It would put me out in the open. And even though I was pretty sure nobody knew where I was, I didn't like the idea that I'd be exposed. I didn't know what was out there. All I knew was that I didn't want it to find me. Or us.

Us. I couldn't believe I was already thinking in terms of us. Other than my on-again, off-again relationship with Carley, it'd been a long time since I had thought in those terms. Not since college. Not since marrying Jeannie...

I wondered, for the billionth time, what ever happened to her. Was she all right? Had she remarried? Did she ever think about me? And for the billionth time, I put it away. It was a long time ago. People made choices. Not always good ones. All the endless analyzing in the world wouldn't change that. Jeannie'd made her choices and both of us were still living with the consequences.

And I wondered, again for the billionth time, how long I was going to carry this around with me. How long were these hateful memories from my past going to nibble away at my future? Future! Hell, they were gnawing away at my present. They were keeping me from having a life.

I did what I'd always done. I put it all away and promised myself I'd deal with it some other time.

Karen stirred a bit, turning slightly and pulling the sheet up over her shoulder. I just watched, my eyes taking in everything about her. So much had happened in such a short time. I couldn't believe that I'd just met her Saturday night or that I was behaving like some sensitive new-age kind of guy just watching her sleep.

It was all wrong. It was all right. I knew I could debate this for hours and get nowhere. I resolved that I'd relax a bit and see how things went from here. I already knew what it took to get out of relationships. Maybe it was time I learned what it took to stay in one.

I didn't know what made Hank come into my mind but, suddenly, there he was. DeDe had left him. I was happy about that. I didn't know anyone who actually liked the woman. I could understand if Hank was embarrassed and that he needed to talk.

And what kind of friend had I been? At my first opportunity, I turned him over for a chance to get laid. Not that I was sorry it had worked out like it did. Not at all. I just figured I had some fences to mend with Hank Djumpstrom. I made a mental note to give him a call.

I started planning the rest of my day. I had to get the truck and the extra batteries for the portable GPS. I wondered about guns. I didn't like them, but could I trust the others not to have them? Or use them?

Karen stirred again. She turned slowly and the sheet slipped off her shoulder, revealing the tops of her breasts. Her eyes opened and, when they found me, she smiled.

"Still here, huh?"

"Like I said before," I whispered as I moved toward her, "I'm right where I want to be."

She lifted up the sheets and welcomed me back to bed. "Now," she said as she maneuvered her way under me, "you're right where *I* want you to be."

* * *

Later, as we lay side by side, Karen asked if she could ask me a serious question.

Shit. "Like how serious?" I had never liked conversations that started off that way. If you said "no," you were hiding something or you weren't being open. If you said "yes," you left yourself wide open.

"Like real serious." Her expression mirrored her words.

This had to be about my apartment being trashed, my behavior, and my "treasure hunting" escapade in the desert. Had she been thinking about my quick little comment?

"Sure," I answered, lining up my responses to her anticipated questions.

"Who was she?"

Wait. There was no "she" in this Shiprock deal.

"Who was *who*?"

"The woman who hurt you."

I rolled away from her. I was not going to do this.

"Jake," one hand lightly touched my shoulder. "Someone hurt you…"

I slid my shoulder away from her hand.

She sat up and angled her body toward mine. Both of her hands found my shoulder and began rubbing. "It's okay. You can tell me."

"It was a long time ago."

I expected a rebuttal but heard nothing. Instead, she gently pushed me forward until I was lying on my stomach. Her hands went to work on the various knots in my neck and shoulders. She kneaded and pressed and rubbed until I felt my tension starting to ease.

"How long ago?"

I immediately tightened. *I didn't want to get into this.* There wasn't anything anyone could do. Not now. Not after this long.

"It helps to talk about it." Her hands were already focusing on the newly formed knots.

"Like I said, it was a long time ago."

"But it still hurts?" Her hands worked on my neck.

Yes. It still hurt. I just couldn't bring myself to say it. Out loud.

"Jake," she whispered, "I told you about my marriage. It wasn't easy for me to do that."

She spoke in slow, carefully measured sentences. Not rushing. Not selling. Just talking. Letting her words find their way through my maze of defenses while her fingers found their way through layers and layers of tension.

She stopped massaging. "We've both had a lot of pain in our lives. It doesn't matter if it was last week or last year or whatever. Pain is pain. You have to let it out," she pleaded. "It never goes away."

I sighed. I hadn't let anyone get this close in a long, long time. And now she was knocking on the door. Part of me wanted to let her in, to tell her everything. But the rest of me refused.

"What was her name?"

I wriggled my shoulders. She took the hint and started working her fingers across other taut muscles. "Her name was Jeannie," I answered in a tone that signaled my reluctance to talk. "And that's all I want to say."

"Jeannie." She repeated the name as if saying it out loud made it easier to evaluate, to measure. "Jake and Jeannie. Jake and Jeannie. I don't like it. It sounds too cute."

I didn't answer.

"And what is it that this Jeannie person did to you?"

This had gone far enough. "Look!" I said as I rolled over and faced her. "I told you I don't want to talk about this!"

Karen edged back. She stuck her palms out, signaling surrender. "Okay. Okay."

We stared at each other, neither one moving, neither one blinking. As I rolled onto my stomach, I wondered why I was always getting to this point with this woman. Getting to the brink?

Without saying a word, her fingers worked my neck and shoulders and back and scalp until, little by little, I started to relax. While I didn't know if I liked her digging into my past, I did know that her skillful digging into my muscles felt damn good. This was the kind of personal therapy I could relate to. The talking mumbo-jumbo wasn't for me.

I sighed. Or was it a yawn? My tension was disappearing at a phenomenal rate. I heard Karen's soothing voice talking to me, "It's all right…let go…relax…" I tried to talk back but wasn't sure if I did or not. It was like being high. Only better. I felt layers and layers of tension and pressure and anxiety lift and drift away. I closed my eyes and let myself go.

As I slowly slipped from this world, images from my past flashed in front of me. Mom and Ken. Baseball. College. The campus. My dorm room. The team. Coach Abrams. Scouts from the show.

And Jeannie.

When her face came forward, everything else moved to the background. Fitting. That's exactly what happened over two decades ago.

These images grew into scenes and the scenes knitted themselves together and formed a little movie. In it, I was the hot-shot pitcher with the full-ride scholarship, the coaches and the scouts all talking about my making it to the big leagues.

But then I met her and everything changed. I thought she was everything I'd ever wanted. Or would ever want. Beautiful. Smart. Sexy. Even though people warned me about her, I had to have her, had to make her mine. We got married almost immediately.

At first, things were fine. It was like we were on clouds, enjoying life at its fullest. My game and my grades suffered some but not enough to worry about. Everything else was perfect.

And then it all started to unravel. Coach needed me to concentrate on my game more, my advisor warned me about my slipping GPA and eligibility, the administration reminded me about the requirements of my scholarship. It all meant more time at school and less time with Jeannie.

We'd been living with my folks until we could find a place of our own. Jeannie grew more and more resentful of my being gone. I knew she was spoiled and self-centered but I never realized how far she'd go to get even. She probably figured that if she couldn't have the son, she might as well have the old man. She started having an affair with my father.

I can never be sure, but I don't think Ken even knew what hit him. I'm sure he felt flattered by all the attention. He must have just lost his head.

Afterward, she started blackmailing him. Not much. A few bucks here and there. Ken must have been worried about Mom or me finding out, so he paid her. Eventually, she really put the screws to him.

Ken finally ran out of his own money and embezzled a couple thousand from the bank. It was supposed to be one final pay-off, enough for her to get out of town and put an end to his nightmare. But one of the examiners found out about it and turned him in. It was a big deal. The newspaper and the television reporters just couldn't get enough of it. He killed himself. He put a gun in his mouth and pulled the trigger.

Jeannie just took off. Left town. Avoided the whole mess. I never saw her again. I quit school and baseball—and any chance for a pro career. I also quit trusting. Instead of becoming Jake the starting pitcher, I became Jake the hustler. It felt good to strike back at a world that had hurt me so much.

"Jake?"

My eyes flew open. I strained for more sound.

"Jake? Were you sleeping?"

I twisted up on one elbow and turned toward the sound.

Karen smiled. "I was rubbing your back to relax you, not put you to sleep."

Is that what happened? I fell asleep? I tried to smile. "Sorry."

"Don't be."

"No. We were talking…" I searched for more clues as to what might have just happened. "I wasn't talking…I mean…just now…" I'd just revisited the most devastating point of my life—had it become public?

Her fingers were tracing tiny little patterns all over my chest. "Are you asking me if you were talking in your sleep?"

"Was I?"

She smiled. It was that same smile, that "I-know-something-you-don't-know" smile and I knew she wasn't going to tell me. Whether she knew or not—and I doubted she did—she wanted to keep me guessing.

It reminded me of something *I'd* do.

* * *

After we'd showered, Karen rummaged around for something different to wear. She came out with white shorts and a hot pink blouse. I said I'd be fine in my same clothes. She wrinkled her nose but didn't say anything. I wrote it off to one of the basic differences between men and women. Men care too little about what they wear and women care too much.

Karen drove me to the Ford dealership so I could check on my truck. Ed said it would be ready first thing Tuesday morning. Guaranteed.

I'd also bought a new cell phone. Since I couldn't go back to my place,

I needed a way for Manny and Cloud to get in touch with me. The lady behind the counter was busy and not in a very good mood. I calmly explained that I had to have my new phone programmed to my old number and I had to have it done right away.

She started getting pissy about it. "These things take time. It's not our usual procedure."

So I pulled out my money clip and said, "Then let's get right to it." I peeled off hundred dollar bills and watched the expression on her face. "Just tell me when I've paid for the phone, the programming fee, and any other service charges you can think of and, of course, a little something extra for your valuable time."

She swallowed. She watched.

"But don't wait too long," I cautioned. "I can always go next door or down the street."

She smiled insincerely and stopped me. My new phone would be hooked up this afternoon.

On the way back, Karen asked about the truck and about the phone. I told her it was for business.

"What kind of business?"

"Private business."

She held back, not responding or asking any other questions. But I knew there was a lot going on in her head.

"Yesterday, at your apartment, you weren't kidding," she finally said, more matter-of-factly than anything.

"Kidding? About what?"

"About this treasure thing."

"Come on," I joked. "Don't you think I'm a little old to be running around playing treasure hunter?"

"You don't get it, do you?"

"Get what?"

"This isn't just about you anymore." Her voice held a tinge of anger. "I'm here. I'm with you now. I want you to help me make bets in Las Vegas."

I nodded. "I can't think about that right now. Besides, this doesn't concern you."

"But are you going to get in trouble?"

"No."

She studied me some more. "Jake, I can't afford any trouble."

"Okay. I got it."

She drove through northern Santa Fe, blending in with the flow of the tourists as we headed back to our hotel.

"Jake?"

"What?" I stared at her.

"Who do you know that drives a Lincoln Town Car?"

"What?" Now, I was really lost.

She motioned for me to look behind us. I turned and searched the street behind us until I saw a bright white Townie about three cars back. Brand new, from the looks of it. I stared while my brain searched through the files marked: MONEY. BIG CARS. NEW CARS. The answer came back: NO FILES FOUND.

"Why?" I asked, wondering if I should try again using different parameters.

"Because it's been following us for three blocks."

I went to turn around, to look again but stopped myself. If we were really being followed, it was all right to look once. It was not all right to look twice. Instead I asked Karen. "A driver and how many more?"

She started to turn but I stopped her. Someone else looking was definitely not all right, either. I pointed toward her rearview mirror. "Use your mirror. Drive normally and tell me what you see." I tried using my side mirror but couldn't see much.

She drove and stole glances whenever she could. I finally gave up trying to see anything and forced myself to look straight ahead. If they were following us, I wanted them to think that they hadn't been spotted. That way, their adrenaline would stay at one level. If we forced their hand, it'd shoot up a couple of notches and we didn't need that.

"The windows are tinted and I can't really see but I think there are two of them."

"Are you sure they've been following us?"

She thought for a moment and then nodded. "You just don't miss a car like that. I saw it for the first time just as we turned onto Palace. It's been back there ever since."

A lot of cars turned onto Palace and headed right through town. It was a major throughway. How could she be so sure?

"Turn right at the next corner." I pointed where I meant. She gunned the engine but I made her slow down. "Nothing fancy, sweetheart. Just make a right turn and we'll see what happens."

She made the turn, spending so much time watching the Townie that I thought we were going to hit the driver in front of us. As she straightened out the wheel, I asked what'd happened to the Lincoln.

"He looked like he was trying to get over from the left lane but couldn't. He swerved a couple of times, trying to cut in but no one would let him in. He had to go straight on Palace."

"Turn at the next corner. Right." I guided her through parts of Santa Fe that even I hadn't been in for years. After a few minutes, I pointed up the street.

"Turn in here."

"Where?" Her eyes scanned the area, looking for the place I'd selected.

"Here. In here."

She slowed and pulled into a parking lot that was filled with other cars. I searched for one particular area and nudged her in that direction.

"Pull in right next to that blue car." The questioning looks disappeared as she figured out what I'd been up to. She parked, grabbed the keys and stepped out into the bright sunshine. I was out of the car a split-second later, scanning the area for a white Town Car. Not seeing one, I relaxed a bit.

Karen caught my eye. "I guess the best place to hide an ear of corn is in a cornfield." She smiled.

I nodded, still being watchful. Cars. People. But no Town Car. We were safe. For now, at least. I noticed Smilin' Jim Wynn, Santa Fe's largest-volume Pontiac dealer, according to his many, many, many TV ads, coming down the long row of new and used Grand Prix automobiles and heading straight for us. We moved back into the row and awaited his arrival.

"Lemme guess. You rented this fine looking Grand Prix in…" His eyes focused on the back license plate. "…in Las Vegas, fell in love with it and now you've got to have one for your own." His words were aimed at me.

"I rented it," Karen stated defiantly.

"Well," he smiled and turned toward her, "then you're the one who fell in love." He held out his hand. "Miss?"

"Meyers. Karen Meyers. This is Jake."

We all shook hands and exchanged meaningless pleasantries.

"Las Vegas." His smile never really changed. "Tell me, did you win?"

She smiled. "Let's just say there was plenty of excitement."

"I hope that means what I think it means." He laughed in anticipation of doing business with a cash-rich couple fresh from Vegas. "So, would you like to look at anything in particular?" Smilin' Jim Wynn was not a time-waster.

"I like the Grand Prix but Jake says we need something a bit more..." She fumbled for the right words and then turned to me. "Jake, honey, what was it you said we needed again?"

I selected half dozen words that would have worked, would have fit into her ploy. But I declined. I wanted to see how she'd wiggle out of this spot. I just shook my head and acted dumbfounded.

"Substantive." She leaned toward Smilin' Jim Wynn. "That means substantial." She moved in a bit closer. "Like it has some meat on its bones, you know."

Smilin' Jim Wynn did a terrific job of pretending he'd just learned a new word. He said it sounded like a damn fine word and if that's what we were lookin' for, he had just the car to show us. Could we walk over to the new car showroom?

I followed behind, keeping my eyes on the lookout for white Townies. Karen enthralled our new best friend with a few Las Vegas tidbits and that we now needed a car that was more in keeping with our new image. Smilin' Jim played his role to perfection—nodding when nodding was appropriate; smiling when it was called for; laughing, but not too loudly. And getting serious when the time for serious came around.

"This is the finest American-made full-sized car in the world." His hands slapped the fender of a dark green Bonneville. "And I'm not the only one who thinks so." He went on to list the magazines and car critics who had sung the praises of Pontiac's new and improved Bonneville.

Karen hung in there and listened attentively to every word, stopping to ask about seat coverings and equipment packages and financing options. She was building that all-important trust factor, the factor that would let him give us the car keys for a test drive—without him chaperoning.

I distanced myself from Smilin' Jim's pitch. I'd heard this crap before.

Besides, we wouldn't be buying a new Bonneville, at least not today. We would, however, as soon as Karen finished ooohing and ahhhhing, be going for an extended test drive, without Smilin' Jim Wynn.

* * *

We drove the Bonneville around Santa Fe for nearly an hour. We spotted the Town Car, even followed it for a while. It was like being invisible. We could see them but they couldn't see us. Not that we learned anything new. The dark-tinted windows made it impossible for us to see inside.

But it was obvious that they were looking for us by the way they were driving. Going slow as they went through intersections, scanning up and down the streets, making sudden turns whenever a red Grand Prix came into view, following it until they decided it wasn't us.

We did learn one thing from following them. In their search, they drove by my apartment and Karen's room at La Posada. This was getting more and more dangerous.

We returned the Bonneville when we saw the Town Car heading up 590. Probably going to Hank's to see if we somehow made it out there. I figured that gave us about thirty minutes to take care of our next move.

Smilin' Jim Wynn was real disappointed that we didn't absolutely fall in love with America's favorite full-sized automobile. Karen thanked him for his hospitality and understanding but admitted that we really owed it to ourselves to do a bit more looking around before deciding.

Just like on his TV commercials, Smilin' Jim's smile never once faltered and he started refiguring this and "throwing in" that and kept coming up with lower and lower prices. When Karen finally told him, "Perhaps some other time," his smile grew even larger. I know how car sales work, and how this guy could smile in the face of never seeing us again was beyond me. I wondered what it would be like to play poker with him.

We eased the Grand Prix back into the mid-morning traffic, and I told Karen to head for the rental company at the airport. It was obvious that it was time to get something else, something less conspicuous to get us around town. We dropped off the Grand Prix, paid cash, walked out the door and headed for Global.

The lady behind the counter at Global Rental was a real talker. More than just the routine Q & A. She chatted up a storm about a half dozen different topics, not the least of which was the striking color of Karen's blouse.

The two of them talked clothes while I signed everywhere the clerk indicated. For the first time in my life, I took the rental insurance. Was that a sign of impending doom?

We drove the Buick Regal around Santa Fe. Once again, I felt invisible. Whoever was after us now had no clue as to what we were driving.

I needed to talk with Hank so I had Karen stop at a pay phone. I dialed his number and waited ten rings. No answer. No machine. I wondered if that was good or bad.

When I got back into the car, Karen asked about going into the police station to tell them that we'd been followed. I vetoed it immediately. I didn't want or need the police involved. Instead, I directed her to the closest strip mall. I needed some time to think.

We sat in the warmth of the sun. Karen turned on the radio and found an oldies station. While the Animals belted out "House of the Rising Sun," I ran the events of the day through my head. Someone *was* following us. But was it me or Karen they were after? Did it matter? Hell, yes, it mattered! If they were after Karen, then my Shiprock deal was still on track. If they were after me, then…

The sound of two doors closing broke my spell. I turned and saw the Town Car. It had just pulled in front of a convenience store in the same strip mall where we'd parked. I clued Karen. The sight of the Town Car and the two men crossing the asphalt stopped her breathing. Her eyes shot over to mine, wide with disbelief.

"They don't know," I whispered as I pointed to the dashboard of this car. I could tell she didn't understand. More hushed words. "We changed cars. Remember?" She got it but still looked terrified.

One of the men stopped near the rear of the Town Car and rested against the rear fender. The other man walked toward our car, reaching in his pocket as he neared.

Karen panicked. "It's him!"

I drew an immediate blank. *Him who?* I turned and searched for clues.

"From Smiley's." Karen shrunk deeper into my arms.

The light finally went on. The two Mexicans playing pool, hassling the three of us. Shit. Where was Rufus now?

Karen shuddered. The big man stopped right in front of us. His right hand reaching into his front pocket.

I searched for something to prevent this guy from pulling out his gun and shooting us. But I wasn't behind the wheel and there was damn little I could do. I was trapped. I felt like I was about to die.

But he didn't pull out a gun. Instead, it looked like he pulled out a handful of change. I glanced to my right and saw a pay phone. I looked to the front and saw the man counting change as he resumed walking toward the phone.

Fuck. Even though he hadn't seen us, this was still way too close for comfort. The phone was only ten feet away and if his eyes wandered around the parking lot at all, we'd be in trouble.

I reached over and grabbed Karen, pulling her into my arms.

"I don't want him to see my face," I whispered. She nodded that she understood and pressed closer to me, covering me with her body, shielding my face from the passenger side window. I held her as tightly as I could, all the while trying to keep track of both men.

Karen started to say something but I hushed her. I wanted to hear what the man would be saying. My window was open about an inch so I figured I might catch a word here and there.

I kept my eyes forward and my ears focused on the pay phone. He dropped in a whole series of quarters and punched more than seven numbers. Long distance.

Whoever it was that he was talking to must not have been very happy. While I couldn't hear a word he was saying, it looked like he was making excuses and apologizing to whomever he was talking to.

I closed my eyes and strained to hear more details, something that would tell me for certain who he was doing all this explaining to.

Just then, I heard a loud rumble. I opened my eyes and saw that a truck had just pulled in and parked in front of the convenience store, blocking my view of the Town Car. I craned my neck to look under the trailer to see the man's legs. He wasn't there. I pivoted to the left. Nothing. Then back over to the right, peeking around Karen's head.

"Miguel!" someone shouted. "Miguel!"

I looked back to the left, where the voice was coming from. It was the other man. He was pointing to our car with one hand and reaching for his gun with the other.

"Ees dem!" He pulled his gun but kept it close to his side. He edged his way along the length of the semi, slowly closing the distance between us. I saw him grab his own shirt and hold it out and then point to our car. In a second I knew what'd happened. He hadn't recognized me, he'd recognized Karen's hot pink blouse.

To my right, I heard nothing. No talking. No excuses. No explaining. They were both closing in on us.

"Drive!" I shoved Karen back in the driver's seat. For an instant she just sat there, stunned and scared. I hit the ignition. "Drive!"

Glass shattered next to me as the butt of a black revolver crashed through my window. I recoiled away from the sound. Most of the glass was in my lap and I saw Miguel turn the gun in his hand, stick it through the window and point it toward me. I lunged for the gun with my left hand, deflecting it away from us.

Karen grabbed the shift lever and hit the gas. Miguel's arm was dragged against shards of broken glass and he screamed as it ripped his flesh. He was running to keep up with the car but was losing his balance. I pressed his arm deeper into the glass until he was forced to wrestle himself free. Karen was still flooring the Regal, heading right for the man by the semi. He had his gun up, ready to fire, but he didn't. Instead, he ducked under the semi just before Karen swerved to the left and screeched for the exit. Five seconds later, we were out of the parking lot and halfway down the block.

I had to get to Hank's and warn him.

18
Hank
Tuesday Morning

I turned to see the Santa Fe police car pull into the driveway. The tires crunching on the gravel gave away its advantage. Right behind it was a county sheriff's cruiser with Deputy Wayne Wayne at the wheel. Several hours earlier I'd sent Wayne on a wild goose chase in his search for Jake. Now he was back and had found his quarry. I could see a big smile on Wayne's face.

Jake had arrived a few minutes before with Karen. After quick introductions, he'd stepped me off for a private talk while Karen and Molly headed for the house. Now, Wayne had returned with reinforcements and interrupted our conversation. We watched as the two officers got out of a dark blue squad car. One had stayed back slightly with Wayne, obviously covering the cop who was now not more than ten feet from us.

The cop looked from Jake to me and then back to Jake. "Are you Hank Djumpstrom?"

"No," was Jake's simple answer.

The cop looked in my direction.

"I'm Hank Djumpstrom. What seems to be the problem?" I could hear the edge in my voice.

"I'm Officer Reynolds and that's Officer O'Connell." The cop nodded in the direction of the shorter, older cop near the cruiser. "I believe you know Deputy Sheriff Wayne." Reynolds didn't wait for a response. "We're going to have to ask you to come down to the police station, Mr. Djumpstrom."

"What?" I was incredulous.

"I'm sorry, Mr. Djumpstrom, please get in the car."

"I'm not going anywhere until you tell me what you want. Or am I under arrest?" I was getting mad.

Jake had backed away from me and the cop. He moved slowly and deliberately, not saying a word.

"Hey, you. Don't move," the cop, O'Connell, yelled. His hand was on his still-holstered gun. Wayne Wayne had his bulk resting against his car, the shit-eating grin still plastered across his face.

Officer Reynolds and I looked in Jake's direction. He had moved ten feet from the action. Jake raised his hands to show he was no threat. My eyes met Jake's. I knew we didn't need a bunch of questions by the cops right now. The idiot Wayne probably had a bunch of his own questions for Jake. Karen had come out of the back door for a better look, but hadn't left the relative safety of the porch. I couldn't see Molly, but I figured she was watching from the house.

"I'm going to ask you just one more time." Reynolds' voice was tense. "Or we can come back with a warrant and arrest you."

"Yeah? On what charge?" I challenged. For a second Reynolds didn't seem to know how to reply.

"Look, we were told to bring you in for some questioning," Reynolds finally stated tersely.

I nodded. "I'm coming. Don't get upset."

Jake remained frozen as I ambled towards the car. Reynolds turned to follow me. O'Connell stood waiting with one of the back doors open. Wayne lifted his frame and moved in Jake's direction. I had my problems and Jake had his.

Just as we reached the car, Molly came out onto the porch.

"Is this man under arrest?" Molly's voice was stern.

Reynolds turned to see who was now questioning his authority.

"I asked you a question, Officer." Molly, with Karen following tentatively behind her, had moved up close and was now in Reynolds' face.

He looked peeved. "Lady, who are you?"

Molly met his glare and held it. Her hands were at her side. She raised the left one and flashed her badge. "Sergeant Kiyanee."

Reynolds broke eye contact and looked at the badge. "You're a long way from the rez, Sergeant. And, I think your jurisdiction ran out back around Highway 371."

"We both know the law." Molly held her ground.

"Look-ee, Sarge, Mr. Djumpstrom is not under arrest. We're just taking him in for some questioning. Okay?" Reynolds didn't wait for an answer. "Lean against the car, Mr. Djumpstrom. I need to pat you down." Reynolds did a quick search. I was glad the Browning 9mm was in the house. He put his hand on my shoulder and gave me a slight shove. I bent my head and got in the backseat.

"I'm going, too," Molly said.

Reynolds whirled in her direction. "Fine. You want to follow, I can't stop you. But, you ain't riding with us." He slammed the back door. O'Connell stood on the passenger side and smiled, amused about something.

From the back seat I could see Wayne had already started questioning Jake.

19
Jake
Tuesday Morning

There we stood. Karen. Me. And dick-brain Wayne. All watching Hank being taken off to jail with Molly in her truck following closely behind.

I tried taking Karen's arm and heading for the car but Officer Wayne Wayne stopped us. Stopped me. He probably didn't give two shits about Karen. At least not for questioning purposes.

I knew he'd be in his glory, having one of his favorite "suspects" under his thumb. If history repeated itself, he'd ask a bunch of stupid questions, try to intimidate me and then attempt to fix my whereabouts as to a certain hour of a certain night. Most likely, a crime had been committed in his jurisdiction and he'd try to see if I could possibly, remotely, be connected. I couldn't prove it but I'd long suspected that many of these questioning sessions were for his own pleasure and not part of any official investigation.

He folded his arms across his chest, attempting to appear solid, formidable. To me, he looked more like the figure of that jar of thick pancake syrup.

He narrowed his eyes. "I want you to know, Jacob Marley, that I know you are up to something."

I narrowed my eyes right back. "And just what would that be?"

"Don't know what," he tried to look menacing. "But rest assured that I'm gonna be on you like stink on rice from right now, this moment, until I figure it out."

I stifled my laugh. Usually, I'd try to bait him, to get him flustered during these little interrogations. But I didn't want to do that. Not this time. I just wanted him to go.

"You don't seem like a slob."

I frowned. "What are you talking about?"

He gave me a smile that told me he knew something that I didn't.

"Your apartment, Jake." His all-knowing smile grew exponentially. "I been looking for you. Your landlord let me in. I got to tell you, I was mighty surprised."

Shit. He'd seen my place. This wasn't looking good. Before I could make up some bullshit excuse about wild parties, he dropped his grin and got serious.

"I suspect you been holed up with her at some hotel." He pointed toward Karen.

"That's none of your business."

"Well, since your place is a mess and I know you weren't at Hank's…"

I frowned. "How'd you know that?"

He smiled. "I was here. Last night." His finger poked my chest. "Looking for you."

"Putting in a lot of overtime hours, aren't you?" Wayne Wayne working at night? This didn't make sense! The guy was notorious for working the lightest shift he could weasel.

Another smile, this one a little bigger. "Oh, Jake, I really don't mind puttin' in the extra time, especially when it concerns one of my fav-rite criminals."

"What's this all about?"

His smile faded. "Who was it that tried to kill you?"

"Kill me?" His question rattled me. Karen moved closer to me, eyes darting from me to Wayne and back again.

"Sunday. Right out here on 590." He pointed to some unseen point south of Hank's. "Someone tried to run you over."

"What do you mean?" Even though I was panicking inside, I played it as cool as I could.

Wayne Wayne spit brown juice off to his left. Most of it cleared his uniform. Karen turned away in disgust and folded herself into my left side. This was his moment and it looked like he was intent on making it last.

"Well, seems we had a report about you."

Again, I fought the urge to jump in and say something smart, something to fuck with his head. But this wasn't the time for Jake the Smart-ass.

"Least-wise, I'm pretty sure it was about you." His words were aimed for me but his eyes traveled the length of Karen's body. I felt her press into me even more. "Seems some tourists was driving on 590 Sunday past." He brought his attention back to me. Evidently my reaction to what he was telling me was more important than Karen's legs. He took a few small steps closer, never taking his eyes off mine. "Seems they seen a big black car heading towards town mighty fast, a bit reckless-like. Funny, that matches the description of the car that hit old Elmore. And, if you know anything about it that you're not sharing, that's withholding evidence." He smiled. "And that's against the law. Now why would you do something like that?"

He stopped and spit. This time, he only turned his head enough to clear my right shoulder. Barely. Again, I held my tongue—and my temper.

"They's from Minnesota. Out here on vacation. Visiting some relatives, they said. You know. Seemed like good people come from up that way." He nodded toward me, wanting me to play along.

I did. "And they did their duty and reported what they'd seen," I said, giving him the line I thought he needed.

That brought the expected smile, right on cue. I'd originally thought this was something new but it wasn't. It was the same old shit. Only the wrapping was different.

"Well," he said slowly, "that might be all there was to this story but that'd hardly make it worth my time telling you about it, would it?"

"Guess not, Officer Wayne," I replied. No sarcasm. No humor. I was desperate to get this over with.

His eyes returned to Karen. Now, they seemed to be focusing on her breasts.

"Seems they seen a fella dressed in a bright blue jacket," he pointed to mine. "Like this one here." His fingers touched the light fabric of my windbreaker. "The description they gave of the man, well, Jake, they coulda been talking about you." His eyes shot back to mine. "Even though they's a ways away, it looked like that car not only tried to run that fella' over but stopped, backed up and…" He paused. If I had to give Wayne anything, I had to admit he knew how to play his hole card. Must've been the only thing he learned in cop school.

"And?" Now I was doing more than playing along. I was hooked.

"They called it cactus."

"What?"

"Stupid. Stupid. Stupid." He backed away and pointed out to the desert.

"What?" I asked again.

"The brush." He pointed to a patch. "When they said you—this fella—jumped to the side of the road, they said he jumped into a patch of cactus." He turned back and looked at us. "Can you imagine how much that'd hurt?" He examined my face. "Why, I'd be betting that jumping into the brush would leave a scratch or two." His eyes locked in on the right side of my face. "Something like you got right there."

"Can't imagine." I turned toward Karen, making it more difficult for him to see my scratches. Besides, I was tired of this digression. I needed to hear the last part of his story. If it was heading where I thought it was heading, it just might prove I wasn't imagining what'd been happening to me lately.

"I straightened them out. Told them the difference between roadside brush and cactus. Likely they won't make that mistake again."

"That was nice of you. Officer Wayne, is it?" It was Karen, speaking soft and demure and sexy and inviting. She smiled when he faced her. "I think you have some more information that both Jake and I would like to hear." She slowly moved away from my side. "I was wondering if you could please tell us what those good people from…" she paused, her eyebrows arching. "From what state was that again?"

It took a moment but Wayne finally muttered the answer. "Minnesota."

"Minnesota. Fine." She offered him a brilliant smile. "Anyway, these people from Minnesota must've had something else to say or, like you said, you wouldn't have wasted your time. Right?"

Again, a definite lag between question and answer. This time, Wayne Wayne only gave a dimwitted nod. His mouth was now hanging open.

She stepped closer, her right hand touching the fabric of his soiled uniform. "Could you pleeeeeeese tell us what they had to say?"

I marveled at how well she was handling Wayne Wayne and how quickly she fell into her role. I also wondered how she'd gotten so good at it. Had she been doing the same thing to me?

"Ma'am," he tipped his hat and tried to sound official. His eyes rose to meet hers. Wayne Wayne was finally trying to be a cop. "These tourists reported that while they couldn't be sure, it appeared that the man in the black car had backed up and stopped, not to help the guy but to hurt him. They said it might sound odd, like not a lot to go on, but as they was pulling up on the scene, the driver of the car spotted them and took off, 'not the actions of a Good Samaritan' was exactly how they put it to me, ma'am."

Karen pressed for more. Her eyes widened, her fingers continued fondling the soiled, khaki cloth. "Did they see a gun or anything?"

"No, ma'am, not that they reported." Wayne Wayne appeared thoughtful, as if evaluating either how much or what else to say. "They just felt that, in the first place, the car was trying to run the man over. Then, it appeared to them that it was trying to do him some bodily harm. So, they reported what they'd seen. I thought it only proper to tell Jake here what'd been reported, considering what happened to Elmore. I thought Jake might know something about this, this happening."

She gave him a smile that was probably the best one he'd seen in years. "Thank you, Officer Wayne. Is there anything else?" She patted the uniform and stepped back.

He smiled and shook his head. His eyes drifted south again.

"Then," she said with a polite smile, "if you'll excuse us, we have someplace we have to be and we are already late." She sounded so sweet, so polite that I was sure Officer Wayne never knew what'd taken place.

He tipped his hat to Karen and tried to look professional. Then, he turned to me, scowled, and went right back into his same old routine. "Jake, like I said, I know you're up to something and I ain't gonna rest until I figure it out. You hear me?"

I nodded.

He gave Karen another quick glance and then headed for his car. I just stood there and watched. Wayne Wayne was finally right about something. I knew it and he knew it. Now it was just a question of which one of us would figure it out first.

As he backed out onto 590 and headed northeast, Karen turned to me.

Her charm and sweetness from a few moments ago were gone.

"Jake," Her words were cold and hard and edged with a trace of fear, "someone trashed your place. Your friend Hank was just hauled in for questioning. And now I hear that someone tried to kill you." She leveled her eyes into mine. "What's going on?"

I swallowed. Bit by bit, piece by piece, my world was crumbling before my eyes. And I had to find a way to stop it. Fast. I put both of my hands on her shoulders. "Karen, I think it's time you and I had a little talk."

20
Hank
Tuesday Afternoon

The ride into Santa Fe took about fifteen minutes. Molly was true to her word. She jumped in her truck and followed. Reynolds and O'Connell pulled into a "police only" parking spot and watched for a second as Molly looked for a place to park. O'Connell appeared greatly entertained by her frustrations.

We went in a back door and down a hall. As I walked with the two cops, I could feel the eyes of strangers following us. I wasn't in handcuffs, so I wasn't a criminal. Two guys we passed sat with their hands cuffed behind them. They were criminals and might have figured I was an undercover agent. But the other cops at the station knew better. Reynolds and O'Connell acknowledged a couple of them while I stayed in step and followed.

The two officers stopped at a desk, manned by a nearly bald sergeant. They whispered something and glanced in my direction. What hair the sergeant had, he wore in a ring of fringe that covered his ears. He picked up a clipboard and said something unintelligible to me. Reynolds called my name and I again followed. I caught a glimpse of Molly coming down the hall, just as I was led into a small room. Immediately I knew what it was. I'd been interrogated before.

O'Connell indicated that I should sit in one of the chairs surrounding the table, the only furnishings. Reynolds left the room and shut the door as he left. O'Connell moved to the far side of the ten-by-ten room. He studied his fingernails and I looked in the large mirror that covered one wall. I wondered who was on the other side. I waved, to be nice.

"Hank Djumpstrom?"

A man in an atrocious, pale blue suit was standing at the door. The suit screamed of the old maiden sisters Polly and Esther. He was about my age and of medium build. His hair was thinning a bit and he could have been a high school principal judging from his mild looks. But, I knew he wasn't. There was a badge hanging from his suit jacket breast pocket.

I didn't answer the question.

"Mr. Djumpstrom, I'm Sergeant White and this is Detective Millard." White indicated another man standing in the doorway. He was several years older than White and a lot uglier. Millard wasn't wearing a jacket, just a short-sleeved white shirt with a tie that didn't reach over his expanding gut. His pants were the same fabric as White's suit, only they were pea green. The pockets gaped as the material stretched across his butt to the point of tearing. There should have been a yellow sign on his belt announcing "wide load."

"We'd like to ask you a few questions," stated White.

I looked at White and then Millard. O'Connell was leaving the room without being asked. He didn't look amused any longer. The door closed and the room got very small.

"Am I under arrest?"

No one answered me.

"Am I being charged with something?"

Again, no answer. White sat down across from me, and placed a large manila envelope on the table. Millard stood behind me.

After a moment White asked quietly, "Should we be arresting you?"

I smiled in response.

"Did you do something that we should charge you for?" he continued.

I let out a sigh. We were playing games. I decided to wait for my turn.

White looked at me, I looked at him. He said nothing. I said nothing. Finally, I turned around to look at Millard.

"Look, Detective Millard, I don't like people reading over my shoulder. So, why don't you come over here and sit at the table with us?"

Millard snorted his contempt and continued to stand.

White broke the chess game. "Mr. Djumpstrom, we've read your file. And, you're not exactly a model citizen, are you?"

"Come on, Sergeant. What is this all about?"

"Are you married to Deidre Louise French?"

"Yes." That was an easy question. "She uses her maiden name. She thought it important for her career at the District Attorney's office." I emphasized the last three words.

"We know she's an assistant DA, Djumpstrom," added Millard, none too friendly.

I looked at White and turned my head to see Millard. There was nothing to read.

"When was the last time you saw your wife?"

I thought for a moment. Where were these guys going with this? "Sunday morning."

"Sunday, two days ago?" asked White.

"Yes."

"Are you sure?"

"Yes, I'm sure." I said somewhat tersely.

"Where? Where'd you see her?"

"At my house, our house." I was beginning to get angry.

"And what were the circumstances?"

"She had come to pick up some clothes. Why?"

"We understand she has a condo in the city. Would you like to explain that?"

"No. Not until you tell me what is going on. Has something happened to DeDe?" My answers were sounding as evasive as White's questions.

"Why'd she have a condo, if you have a house?"

I rolled my eyes. "She worked a lot. She didn't feel like making the drive sometimes."

"What, ten minutes, maybe fifteen?" White asked scornfully. "Were you and your wife having marital problems?"

I thought for a moment. White had said "were," not "are." "You two aren't checking on how happy my marriage is?"

"I'd appreciate it if you'd just answer the question, Mr. Djumpstrom." White smiled slightly, as if he was a friend.

"We're separated," I answer begrudgingly.

"So there were problems?"

"Yes, some problems."

"Did you ever beat your wife?"

"What?" I was incensed. "I never hit DeDe. Now, what is going on?"

"When was the last time you spoke with her?"

I retraced the last couple days. "Sunday. She called Sunday afternoon."

"So you saw her Sunday morning and then spoke with her later in the day?"

I didn't answer.

"Were there any witnesses to this call?"

"No. And, unless I'm being charged with something I'm not answering any more questions without my attorney here."

White looked over my shoulder at his partner. "Mr. Djumpstrom, your wife is dead. She has been murdered."

I couldn't speak. The wind had been knocked out of me. The tears were there, but they didn't come. I could feel my eyes blinking, but nothing else. Everything was a blur, out of focus. I felt numb.

"Did you hear me?" White's voice had turned calm.

It was the dumbest question I had ever heard. But I only nodded. I stared down at the small square table, worn smooth with age, most of the veneer gone. The words I'd just heard were unreal. DeDe? Murdered?

"Would you like a glass of water or something?" It was White talking.

I shook my head.

"Was your wife's life insured?"

I looked up at Millard. I hated his question. I knew what he was insinuating.

"Your wife's family has money, right, Djumpstrom?" Millard's voice was filled with malice. White let the line of questioning continue.

"You'll make out pretty well, won't you?"

"You son-of-a-bitch." My words were barely audible, but spoken with contempt.

"What? What'd you say?" Millard was in my face. When I didn't react, he stepped back. "Take a look at these pictures." He tossed a pile of black-and-white 8-x-10s in front of me. "They ain't pretty."

The top picture showed DeDe's face. Her right eye was swollen shut and there was a large bruise on her left cheek. A big piece of tape covered her mouth. Her left eye was open and stared blankly out at me. The second picture showed her tied to a wooden, straight-backed chair. Her blouse was torn, her head hanging down. I pushed the pictures away. I kept pushing them until they fell on the floor, scattering. I couldn't look anymore. My stomach lurched and lurched again. I fought the impulse to vomit. Stomach acid and bile burned my throat; a black spot appeared in my vision and grew larger. I was hot, burning. I had to get out of the room. My legs were like rubber. White and Millard were a blur at the edge of my vision. The black spot was growing larger and larger. I couldn't breathe. I tried to push myself up but fell on the table and back into the chair. Someone grabbed my arm and I tried to fight their grasp.

"Let me out of here." It sounded like my voice, but it was coming from a long way off.

"Steady. Don't fight me."

Hands were pushing me down in the chair. I quit my struggle with the hands that were trying to control me. My breathing became more regular and slowly my vision started to come back. I could see Millard standing across the table from me and White sitting to my right. The two cops waited a couple seconds.

"Are you sure you don't want a glass of water or something?" It was White asking.

"No, I'm all right now," I said softly. Tears were running down my cheeks. I wiped them away.

White looked at me and then down into a folder. "Okay then." He started his questioning again. "We have a report of two men in the parking lot of your wife's condo."

I watched White.

"Our witness said they hadn't ever seen either of these men before. Both men were said to be middle-aged, late thirties or so. One of the men was described as short and stocky. The other was maybe six-feet tall or more, weighed about two hundred pounds." White paused for my reaction, but one didn't come. "The shorter man was described as looking Hispanic or Indian, with black hair and a moustache. The other was white, clean shaven, with dark brown hair." He paused again. "Long hair, worn in a ponytail."

I returned his look, but said nothing.

"Sound like anyone you know?" he asked.

I didn't answer.

Millard butted in, "One of 'em sounds like you, Djumpstrom. Now where were you Sunday night?"

I looked at my two tormentors. "DeDe is dead and you two think I tortured her?" My voice broke and I wiped back the tears. "Killed her for insurance money?" My voice trembled with emotion, but sounded angry. "You don't even know if I'm a beneficiary." I hung my head and wiped at my eyes with both hands. The room was silent as I tried to compose myself.

After a moment I looked up, caught Millard's eyes and answered his question. "I was at W.E.'s junkyard up on 590." I paused for a long moment and continued my stare. "The whole night."

Now it was the two cops' turn to exchange looks.

"Can this W.E. verify that?" White asked.

"I just told you he could."

"He better be able to." Millard stared at me with contempt.

White waved his partner off. "Mr. Djumpstrom, if there is anything you know that could help us...you see, your wife was tortured with an electrical wire. They ripped the cord out of a lamp and plugged it in and then..." White's words came slowly and softly. "She was beaten to death."

I just met his look without comment. Inside, I was dying.

"Why would someone torture your wife?"

"I don't know. She's an assistant DA," I answered weakly.

"We know that. And, we'll check her conviction record and see what bad guys may have recently gotten out of prison," Millard snapped. "What are you into, Djumpstrom?" He didn't wait for an answer. "I got your record here. Very interesting reading. Not the bio of an artist." Millard held a manila folder. "I see a gross misdemeanor conviction after a plea bargain. Caught on reservation land with a truckload of dinosaur bones."

"Fossils," I muttered.

Millard shot me another nasty glance. "Questioned about smuggling drugs across the border, you and Jacob Marley. Another fine Boy Scout. Interesting friend you have, Djumpstrom." Millard slapped the file. "Bar fights, some drugs, arrested for flying in pot for our friend Maniandez." Millard snorted a laugh. "Charges dropped." His voice was full of sarcasm. "There's all kinds of wonderful activities in your record."

"That's all old stuff. Ancient history," I retorted.

Millard tossed the file on the table and gave me a long look. "You're not a good citizen, Djumpstrom." He circled the table and pulled out a chair. He spun the chair and sat down with his arms and chin resting on the back. "Your alibi better check out cuz we're going to be watching you. You so much as fart in public and we're going to come down hard on you."

"What Detective Millard means is, you might want to tell us anything you know about your wife's death now, before you go." White was playing the good cop. I knew the routine. "Or you might want to talk to a lawyer," he offered.

"Are you reading me my rights? Because if you are, you're not doing it correctly."

"Don't get smart, Djumpstrom. We know you're dirty. Maybe you didn't kill your wife, but there's something going on here." Millard was biting off his words. "We talked with your wife's family."

I nodded.

"Seems you're not too popular with your in-laws, Djumpstrom. Why is that?" Millard was back in my face. "Maybe they know something about you that we should."

I wanted to rip out the man's heart and feed it to him.

"Okay, okay." White was talking to Millard, not me. "There will be an autopsy this afternoon. We may have some more questions after that."

"Can I go now?" I said curtly.

The two exchanged looks.

"Yeah, you can go."

Millard gave me a wink. "We'll be in touch." He wanted to get in the last word.

"I can hardly wait."

21
Jake
Tuesday Afternoon

Karen walked off by herself toward the barn, but she stopped before she got halfway. I wanted to go with her but she waved me off. "Give me a minute or two," was all she said.

In either the smartest move of my life—or the dumbest. I'd just told her the whole story. Everything. How Williams had found the gold, how Cloud had found Williams, how I'd been brought in and how Manny had become the fourth partner. I also told her whom I thought was behind my recent problems. It was mostly speculation, but I figured it was close enough to count. Maybe telling her was dumb. Maybe it was desperation. Back-up-against-the-fucking-wall-nowhere-to-run-nowhere-to-hide desperation.

She just listened. Didn't ask any questions. Didn't get angry when my story contradicted what I had lied about before. She just sat there, eyes focused on someplace past the mountains and listened. When I was finished, she got up and headed toward the barn.

Now I sat watching her. Staring. Studying. Looking for a sign that I'd done the right thing, that I hadn't blown whatever chance I still had of pulling this off. I watched her for a reaction. Any reaction. I waited. That "minute or two" ticked by ever slower and slower and slower.

When I couldn't stand it any longer, I rose from the steps and headed carefully toward her. She heard my approach but didn't move. I was just about to say something, anything, when she spoke in a flat but strong voice.

"You lied to me."

I nodded. Normally, in situations like this, I'd say I was sorry, that telling lies was easier than telling the truth, that I had a problem that way. Normally, I'd say whatever I thought needed to be said to get past this point and onto the next. But this wasn't *normally*.

She turned and faced me. "And how do I know if I can believe you? Ever?"

"You can't."

She studied me. "Meaning?"

"Meaning you'll never know, never really know, if I'm telling the truth."

"And just how am I—?"

I cut her off. "Look. I may have twisted the truth before. I admit that. I had my reasons and I think you know that. But you asked me for the truth and I just gave it to you, both barrels. Now, you can believe me or not; that's up to you." I stepped back and locked my eyes to hers. "But this is real and I don't have time for anything else, no games, no bullshit. Just tell me now if you're in or out."

She stared. "That's asking a lot."

"I know I'm asking a lot. And I'd rather not do it this way, backing you into a corner and all…"

"Then why? Why now? Why me?"

"Because my place got ransacked. Because Hank is in jail. Because someone is trying to kill me." I took in a deep breath and shook my head as I let it slowly escape. "Because I'm not sure I have many choices left."

We stared at each other for a long time. At first, I felt better for having told her everything. But, as the minutes ticked by, I began to have second thoughts. Had I done the right thing? Had I involved her in something too dangerous? I shook it off. Once this was all over, I could debate the moral implications and ramifications till hell froze over. Right now, I had to get to Hank.

* * *

Karen drove the Buick like she was taking her driver's test. Full stops. Blinkers. Speed limits. The works. If nothing else, telling her about Shiprock had virtually guaranteed we wouldn't be getting any traffic tickets. What else had it done? My head hurt at the thought of it.

"Jake?"

"Yeah?"

"About the money?"

"Yeah?"

"You get three million, right?"

I nodded. "Williams and Cloud get two each. I figured an extra million for putting the deal together, but neither Cloud nor Williams need to know that little detail."

Karen thought for a second. "But I thought you said they'd already gotten their money?"

"They did but they didn't."

"Huh?"

"They each got some 'good faith' money. Ten thousand. That was just a little something from Manny to close the deal, to take care of any expenses."

"But not a couple million?"

"Let me explain. Williams knew he was screwed out of getting the big jackpot. He said it was the most expensive flat tire he'd ever had. But even though he was screwed, he still knew he held the only key to getting the gold."

"He has the coordinates, right?"

"Right. And before he'd turn those over, he had to be assured his money, his two million dollars, was tucked safely away in a numbered account."

"Cloud, too?"

"More or less. Manny didn't want to pay either of these mystery guys a dime until he got his gold, but I convinced him it wouldn't work any other way."

"What do you mean?"

"It's like building a house of cards. First you get two cards to lean up against each other, then you can add another and another and so on. I get Williams to agree to turn the coordinates over. But he wants to be guaranteed he'll be safe and that he'll get his money. Cloud wants to make sure he's not cut out of the deal. Manny agrees to put up the money but he doesn't want to get taken. So, I get Manny to put the money in numbered accounts in my bank. I get a copy of the wire transfer sent to Williams and Cloud verifying that the money is there."

She squinted. "Couldn't they just empty their accounts?"

"Uh-huh. Manny put the money into the account with the stipulation that it can't be withdrawn until Monday and only then by using a pass code."

"The numbers he gave you Saturday night?"

I nodded.

Karen mulled it all over. "So they've been paid but not really."

"They'll get their numbers when the gold is loaded on the truck."

"So even if Cloud got his hands on those numbers, right now, today, this second, it wouldn't do him any good?"

"Right."

"Couldn't this Manny guy freeze the account? Or empty it himself?"

I shook my head. "There's four million dollars of Manny's money that he can no longer get to."

"You've got the numbers?"

"Yeah."

"And you, not that you'd do this, couldn't get their money because you don't have access to their accounts."

"Right again." I paused. "There's another reason, too."

"What?"

"Nobody crosses Manny and lives to tell about it."

She pondered for a moment. "You thought all this up by yourself?"

"You're on a roll."

She smiled. "A house of cards."

I thought for a moment. "And someone is huffing and puffing."

"So, Jake, which one of your guys is the big bad wolf?"

A heavy silence filled the car. Who, indeed, was the big bad wolf? I mulled the possibilities over in my mind as we passed a slow-moving truck and continued on our way to Hank's. "Something on your mind?" I asked.

"I was thinking about this Shiprock deal, about who searched your place. It must be the Mexican."

"Manny?" I asked.

"Yeah, him." She quickly turned and looked me in the eyes. "There are only four people who are in on this, right?" She returned her attention to the road.

"Right."

"It's not you. It can't be the NASA guy. You trust Cloud. That only leaves Manny."

Trust? Her words had a ring of truth to them but I was skeptical. Why did I have trouble believing that Manny was capable of such treachery? After all, he was more than just a small-time drug dealer. People like Manny didn't get where they were by being nice or by playing by the rules. They did what needed to be done and didn't stop to ask if it was politically correct. Was I so blinded by what we'd been through in the past that I couldn't see the realities of today?

"It appears to me that someone has decided he wants this treasure all for himmself." Her eyes narrowed. "It only makes sense that Manny's the one."

I turned and stared out the window, unable—unwilling?—to argue.

"Or don't you see it that way?" she asked after a lengthy, uncomfortable silence.

"I don't know," I muttered. "I just don't know."

"Jake," She touched my arm. "There's something else."

I turned and stared. "What?" My frustration showed.

"Um, those guys back at the strip mall? They might be after me, not you."

I frowned my question. "What makes you say that?"

"I got worried about David and called his mother. She said he'd been released from the hospital and was looking for me. She gave me the new number where he was staying so I called him. He said he wasn't happy that I'd left but he understood I was scared by the way he'd acted. He said he was better and that he wanted to see me."

"Did you tell him where you are?"

She bit her lip. "Yes."

"Shit!" I slammed my hand on the seat. "You told him where you are? Why?"

"I don't know. I was scared. He was scared. I guess I wanted him to know in case anything happened."

"When? When did you do this?"

"Yesterday morning." Her voice grew small.

"And you're just telling me now?"

"I thought you'd get mad."

I fumed. "You do realize, don't you, that if he left Vegas right then and there, he's in Santa Fe right now looking for you. And he might not be alone."

"What do you mean?"

"Maybe they 'got' to him, convinced him to find you, to find the software."

"David wouldn't do that."

I snorted in disbelief. "You have no idea what these guys are capable of doing. With what's at stake, they could find a way to make him cooperate."

She shrank into a smaller version of herself, one that looked frightened and worried. "I'm sorry, Jake."

I shook my head. "It's too late for 'sorry' now. You can't stay in Santa Fe any longer." I couldn't let something like this happen again. "Can I see your cell phone?"

"Um, sure. Why?"

"I just need to see it."

She fished it out of her purse and handed it to me. I looked at it, turned it over a couple of times and admired how thin and sleek it was. Then, I rolled down my window and tossed it into traffic. In my mirror I could see it splinter into a dozen pieces.

"Hey!" she screamed. "What are you doing?"

"I don't need any more surprises."

We drove in silence. I wondered what to do with her. Put her on a bus? Take her up to Taos? For certain, I couldn't keep her with me, not if some bad asses were trailing her. The last thing I needed was to be caught in someone else's crossfire. I racked my brain, sifting through layers and layers of impending doom. My world was closing—collapsing?—in on me and for once in my life I honestly, truly, one hundred per cent felt I had nowhere to turn.

I shifted toward her. "Look. I need someone to drive me to Shiprock. You need to get out of town. You get me to Shiprock, I'll set you up in motel room in Farmington and I can take care of my business."

"But I'm really scared…"

"Don't worry," I said, still thinking through the finer details. "No one will know you're there. Hell, most people don't even know where Shiprock is."

"And all I have to do is drive you there?"

"That's all."

"Where is it?"

"Up by Four Corners, northwest of here. We got a deal?"

"A deal? Jake, you sound like you're trying to hire me."

"Hire you? I'm trying to protect you!"

She thought about it for a little while and then finally agreed.

There. It was done. Right or wrong, I now had a fifth partner.

* * *

We pulled into the parking lot of the Ford dealership when my cell phone rang. I answered on the first ring and whoever it was didn't speak. I was sure it was Cloud, playing it cool.

"I'm coming up for a visit." I offered. "How does tonight look?"

"Tonight?" I heard Cloud light a cigarette.

"Yeah. That a problem?"

"Not for me. Anything I need to know?"

"No," I lied.

"Good. You remember how to find me?"

"Course. At the station. On the south side of town." I was careful not to mention real places or real names.

"See you then." The line went dead. I clicked off the power and turned to Karen. Suddenly, all the talk, all the planning, all the time spent had crystallized into one bright moment. It was here. It was real.

"Cloud?" she asked, already knowing the answer.

I nodded.

"And it's tonight?" Again, saying out loud what she already knew.

"Tonight," I confirmed.

Her eyes left mine and stared ahead. "Then you've got to decide if you still want Hank in on this."

"Why wouldn't I still want Hank?"

"Because until a few minutes ago, you didn't have anyone else you could trust." She smiled. Big. "Now, you've got me."

The hair went up on the back of my neck. It does that when someone is trying to sell me something. Karen was trying to sell me on *not* bringing Hank. Why? I stared at her. *Glared* would be a better word. If there was a quick

187

answer, I was going to get it. Now! "What are you talking about?"

She blinked and stammered. "You said you didn't want to involve Hank in this because of what had happened in the past."

I maintained my intensity. "This is different."

"Or…" she said calmly, trying to back down, "…we could all work this thing out together." Her words trailed off, leaving a vacuum.

My fervor decreased, but only by small degrees. "Why did you just say that?"

Thankfully, she didn't play innocent and ask "Say what?" Instead, she swallowed and whispered, "Because I want to keep you all to myself."

I studied her. "You just tried something there, tried to sell me on something." My eyes locked with hers. "Don't ever do that again."

She nodded and after a moment added, "But I wasn't kidding. I do want to keep you all to myself."

I nodded. "Hank's in," I stated flatly.

She just nodded and said, "Whatever you say, Jake."

I had to get a hold of Hank, tell him I was in trouble, tell him I needed his help. I needed someone I could trust watching my back.

22
Hank
Tuesday Afternoon

I was in a dizzying spin. It was unimaginable that someone had murdered DeDe. How could it be? Why? I felt panic closing around my windpipe, my heart was racing.

"Hank?"

My name being called brought me out of my fog. Molly was rising from the chair where she had been waiting.

"What happened?"

I wanted to burst into tears. I wanted to roll back time and make it last week, last month, or better yet, twenty years earlier.

"Hank, are you okay? What's going on?" Molly's concern was etched in her voice. "You've been in there for almost an hour."

"DeDe's dead."

"What?"

"DeDe's dead. Someone murdered her."

Molly grasped my hand. "Can you leave?"

"Yeah," I whispered.

Molly led the way, taking me down the hall and outside to her truck. I got in the passenger's side. Molly slid behind the wheel and started the engine.

I rolled down the window of the truck and let the wind hit me in the face. "They beat her and they took an electrical cord from a lamp and…" I turned and looked at Molly. Her face was filled with concern. She drove and listened without interruption to my story about DeDe's torture and death.

"And they think you might have done it, right?"

I just looked at her.

"Hank, I'm sorry. In a murder case, it is usually someone who knew the victim."

We were headed up Paseo De Peralta and out of town.

The truck was starting to feel too small, claustrophobic, just like the interrogation room. I was gasping for breath, hyperventilating.

"Stop. Pull in here," I demanded.

Molly pulled the truck to the curb and I jumped out before she could finish parking. I stood in the grass next to the truck and took a deep breath, trying to calm myself. We were parked by the hill that led up to the Cross of the Martyrs, a giant cross that stood high above the city. I ran across the street and started up the stone steps, two at a time. Anger and confusion fueled each step. I pushed by a family of tourists reading the plaques that summarized Santa Fe's early history and the missionaries who brought Christianity to the city. When I reached the top, I stood below the large white cross and looked out at the rooftops of Santa Fe. A slight warm breeze grazed my face. The city was going about its business as if nothing was wrong. There were tourists visiting the historic plaza, buying jewelry and pottery from the Pueblo artisans. Office workers were out for lunch on their midday break. Didn't they know that something terrible had happened? DeDe was dead. Murdered!

"Damn you! Damn you, God!" I screamed at the top of my lungs to the sky. DeDe didn't deserve to be dead.

The family of tourists looked up at me, the raving lunatic. Their little boy continued to stare as his mother grabbed his hand and hustled him down the steps, away to safety. Molly picked up her pace and headed for the top. When she passed the family, they gave her a look of concern.

"Why?! Why?!" I screamed and started to cry.

When Molly reached me I was sitting with my face in my hands. The tears had finally come. She sat next to me and took my hand and held it.

"Hank, I'm sorry." Her words were soft and her body provided the human touch I needed. There was a violent storm raging in me: anger mixed with grief, mixed with guilt and self-doubt. Memories and the day's events intertwined, painting a surreal picture. Finally my breathing and pounding heart slowed and returned to normal. I tried to clear my head and make some kind of reason out of the last couple of days.

We sat for a long moment before she spoke again. "Don't blame yourself. There's nothing you could have done." Molly paused and looked into my eyes. I knew she wanted to know if I was listening to what she was saying or just hearing meaningless words. "What are you going to do?"

"I don't know. I should be making funeral arrangements or something. Call DeDe's parents." The thought made me shudder.

Molly must have felt it pass through my body into hers. "What?"

"The thought of calling DeDe's parents."

Molly squeezed my hand again, but she didn't say anything.

"They don't like me." The words made me pause. *Don't like* was too mild. "They hate me. There was a big scene when DeDe announced we were getting married. In fact, at the time, I felt that the fit her parents threw was precisely the reaction she was hoping for. After that, everything else in our relationship was downhill." I dropped my head back and looked up at the sky, fighting the tears. "What a mess."

"The other day you told me a lot of wrong reasons why you married DeDe. It sounds like she had just as many wrong reasons for marrying you. You can't take all the blame."

"Yeah, Daddy's little girl. I knew it at the time. Her parents' distaste for me fueled my desire to go ahead and marry her. DeDe's father is Eli French, the trucking magnate. Lots of money. She was supposed to become a corporate attorney in Daddy's firm. Instead she joined the DA's office. Spite. And, me, I guess that was the icing on top. Poor DeDe."

"I'm truly sorry." Molly was studying my face. "What do you think is going on?"

I looked at the woman who was talking to me. Even though I had only known her for a few days, I felt there might be something really good between us. But now my world had turned nasty and dangerous.

"I don't know," I answered, shaking my head. "I really don't know. Someone she put in jail. Someone looking for something and, for some reason, they think I have it or know something about it. But I don't know what it is!"

"Did Jake say anything to you?" Molly's tone was starting to lose some of its concern. She was beginning to sound more like a cop. "What does he know?"

I looked at Molly and took my hand back. "Jake told me someone searched his place, too."

"When?"

"Sometime the other morning."

"What else?"

"What do you mean what else?"

Molly paused and took a breath. "I'm sorry. I'm trying to help, but I know I must sound like a cop."

"You are a cop," I replied testily, remembering my earlier interrogation. Molly looked at me. "I thought I explained that last night."

"You did, but you could have told me right away."

"Hank, we met in a liquor store parking lot." Molly shook hands with an invisible person. "Hi, I'm Molly Kiyanee. I'm a reservation police officer," Molly said in a very polite tone. "We went over this last night," she pleaded.

And so we had. I didn't want to punish her for my insecurities. So what if she was a cop? I was more or less an honest citizen these days. "Molly…" I shook my head in bewilderment. "I'm sorry." I wanted to say something to ease the tension. I looked at Molly and whispered, "I'd like to see you in your uniform."

"Oh, you would?" She smiled and took my hand.

I returned her smile. "Yeah, I would." An image of DeDe entered my mind for a second and, with it, the lightness of the moment was lost. "I'm just so pissed off. Those cops think I killed DeDe. And DeDe…" I shook my head trying to shake the images that I knew would haunt me.

Molly reached over and took my hand again. She waited a moment for me to compose myself. Her eyes turned moist. "I really am sorry that DeDe's dead. I'm even sorrier for the way in which she died. But we have to figure out what is going on. And you can't blame yourself for her death. As for the cops, I don't think they believe you killed DeDe. They are just covering all the bases. The spouse is always the first person questioned. But we," she emphasized *we*, "have to figure out what is going on. You might be in serious danger. Jake, too." She rubbed my hand again to show she was still there. "You realize that now, right?"

I nodded that I had heard her. "I have to find out from Jake what is going on. Whatever it is, he's also in danger. And as long as Karen is with him, she is probably in danger." I thought for a moment. "Not probably, she *is* in danger. You're also..." I looked up at Molly's face. She was carefully scanning the park. I glanced around. Was someone watching us right now? A couple stood further up the steps, near the top of the hill. They were hugging each other and taking in the view. The man looked in our direction for a second. Had they heard my tirade? Or were they watching us? Following us? Paranoia started to burrow into my brain.

"How well do you know Karen?" Molly asked.

"What?"

"Karen." Molly reached up and gently turned my face back to her.

"I know who you mean. Why do you ask?"

"I'm curious."

"Jake met her at Smiley's bar the other night. Why?"

"She seems to be pretty close to him. And he just met her the other night?"

Her statement made me smile, in spite of how I felt.

She laughed, catching the irony. "Okay, so we just met, too. But that's different."

"How?"

"It just is," Molly replied with a squeeze of my hand.

"What did you two talk about when we were out in the yard?" I asked.

Molly thought for a second. "Jake. You. She asked me if you and Jake had been on any trips together lately." Molly made a face, wrinkling her forehead as if she were trying to understand something. "She did a lot of oohing and ahhing about Jake. She seems like she really likes him."

I thought about what Molly had just said. It really didn't matter about Karen as far as I was concerned. There were more important things at hand than whom Jake was sleeping with.

"Jake might be into something illegal. It's happened before," I cautioned. "You could get into trouble over this, your association with me." I let it drop. "The Santa Fe cops are probably going to come looking for me again. And I wouldn't be surprised if Wayne Wayne doesn't have Jake in a little square room right now. You better think this over."

"I am. But what are you going to do?" It wasn't a plea, but a good solid question.

"I don't know. The first thing I'm going to do is make a couple phone calls. I've got to talk to Francine and tell her and Alice to stay away from my farm. And, W.E., I've got to warn him. I don't think I should go back to my place." I shrugged my shoulders. "And then, I don't really know. Get in touch with Jake somehow."

I looked at Molly to see what she was thinking. I couldn't tell. I hadn't learned to read minds yet. "I don't think you should be involved in this. You should go back to Shiprock right now. You'd be safe there, from whatever this is or from losing your job because of this."

"I'm not worried."

I looked back for the couple. They were gone, or were they? I made a quick scan; there was no one else in the park that I could see. I felt the paranoia again and wished I had my gun.

"I don't want to get you in trouble over whatever is going on with Jake," I said.

"I know you don't. But I'm not going to leave you, let you go off without knowing what you plan to do."

"I'm going to find Jake. Whatever is going on, I'll have to help him get out of it and that could get messy."

"Well, damn it. Don't dismiss that I might be able to help out here." Molly was upset; storm clouds filled her dark eyes.

"I'm not saying you couldn't. But how I help Jake might not be…legal," I said. "Look, Molly, I just think you need to consider this very carefully."

We sat exchanging looks, but neither of us said anything. Finally Molly broke the silence.

"I have an aunt who lives in town. Let's go to her place and try to reach Jake."

I shook my head. "I'll make a deal with you. You give me your aunt's number and I'll call you in a few hours. In the meantime, I have some things to do. And, it's better that you aren't a witness to them." I let the thought drop. "You go to your aunt's and think." I got up and looked around. "Give me the number, please."

Molly didn't protest. She searched in her jacket pocket for something to write on. I fished a matchbook out of my shirt pocket and handed it to her.

194

"I'll call at 3:30. I promise." I bent to kiss her on the lips and then stood and started to walk away.

"Let me give you a ride."

I looked back. "No. I need to walk a bit. You be careful."

"*You* be careful," she called after me.

* * *

It had been almost two years since I'd been in the One Hand Clapping bar. The place was as wild and strange as the characters and stories in Anthony Burgess' books. A more appropriate name might have been A Clockwork Orange. The bar was a long and narrow room, with a single row of six booths running its length. A dozen or more high stools were pushed up against the bar, which curved just before it reached the front door and ended at the wall. This was a place for serious drinking, not a tourist hangout. Not a thing had changed since my last visit. Ishray still owned the place and manned the bar and Duke was still working out of the last booth. A couple of transient-looking guys were having a shot of rotgut and sitting in the lone pool of sunlight near the door. Otherwise, the place was empty and dark.

I dropped a quarter in the pay phone and dialed.

"Porter's, may I help you?"

"Betty?"

"No, this's Mary. Betty's out in the kitchen. You want me to call her?"

The voice was familiar. It was the older Mary and she knew me. "Mary, this is Hank. Have you seen Jake?"

"Hank? Oh, Hank," the voice warmed with recognition. "How you doin'? You haven't been in for a while. You naughty boy." Her voice was full of affection.

"I'm fine. Have you seen Jake?" I tried not to sound impatient.

"Sure, he was in here yesterday mornin'. Why? Is he in trouble again?" Her tone turned to concern.

"Isn't he always?" I tried to chuckle, but my voice just cracked. "Ah, he's not there now?" I knew he wasn't and didn't wait for an answer. "Listen, can you take down this number and have him call if he comes in." I checked my watch. It was five minutes past one. It wouldn't be unusual for Jake to drop

195

in around two for a late lunch. But I doubted he would be spending much time on fine dining. I gave Mary the number, thanked her and hung up.

I had tried Smiley's first, figuring Jake might be holed up in the back room with some of the regulars. But Smiley hadn't seen Jake since he'd picked up his winnings from Saturday night. I left the number with Smiley, too.

In fact, I'd left messages all over town. No one at any of Jake's haunts had seen him in the last few days. I guessed I could give his apartment a call, but that was the last place I expected him to be. I dropped a quarter into the phone and heard the familiar bong as it hit bottom.

"Hank," a voice from the back of the bar called me before I could dial again. "Come on out here. You've been on that phone long enough."

I hung up the phone and retrieved my quarter. I'd come here specifically to meet with Duke, so I figured I ought to keep my appointment.

Duke shook my hand and said, "Hey, I haven't seen you in awhile, buddy. Not since that time we went huntin' down 'round Cibola."

I gave Duke a nod that I remembered and followed him to the last booth. Duke always sat so he could keep his eye on the door. I was facing an old flower-patterned curtain covering a doorway to the kitchen. Ishray, the owner/bartender, caught Duke's eye and gave him a wink. No one would be bothering us. If anyone tried to sit at the end of the bar or in the next booth, Ishray would tell them, politely, that they couldn't. And there weren't too many people who argued with a 280-pound, six-foot-eight black man with a shaved head and a smile that revealed a diamond in one of his front teeth. I also knew Ishray kept a baseball bat behind the bar to settle any arguments. I had seen his one-handed swing put an immediate end to several brawls. I could see a big smile on his face.

Duke wasn't really a friend, not a close one at least, but he always greeted me as one. He was more of a business associate from my past life. I trusted Duke. I had known him for almost as long as I had known Jake. The man was razor thin, but looked like he could slit your throat faster than you could yell "help." He wore his black hair long, slicked straight back in a ponytail that reached past his shoulders. His moustache curved around the corners of his mouth and there was a tuft of beard on his chin. A dangling crucifix hung in his left earlobe. To complete his look, Duke always dressed in black, giving him a sinister appearance.

196

"Hank, I'm a little surprised to see you in here today. *Amigo*, you really should get a cell phone. Everyone's got one." Duke smiled, showing smoke-stained teeth. He raised his left hand and groomed his moustache with his thumb and forefinger as he studied me. An oversized briefcase sat in the middle of the table. Duke slid it up against the wall, flipped open the top and tilted it slightly to reveal its contents to me. "I'm a little low on stock today. You know—short notice." He shrugged his shoulders. "Maybe if you'd mentioned what you wanted when you called." He punctuated with a smile.

I looked at the display of guns. There were several automatics, a couple large revolvers and some cheap Saturday Night Specials.

"How much for the Berettas, the Smith and Wesson and the .32?"

"Oh, Hank. What's going on here? Four guns? You in a war? Or just some friendly target practice?" Duke laughed and Ishray looked to see what was funny.

"Target practice. How much?"

"For you, Hank," he stressed, being the consummate salesman, "let's see, the Berettas are like new. I'd have to get four apiece and at least five for the Smith and Wesson. I'll let you have the .32 for nothing and the others for eleven hundred."

I smiled. "Duke, you just quoted me thirteen hundred."

"Hank, you're my buddy." Duke smiled and tossed his head back. "I'm feeling good. Consider it a volume discount." He took a pull of his whiskey, draining the shot glass. Then he set it down with a bang. Ishray looked up from his paper and reached for a bottle of whiskey. Duke pulled out a pack of Lucky Strikes. "When was that huntin' trip…two, three years ago?" While he waited for my answer, he tapped the end of the filterless cigarette on the table twice.

"Almost two, Duke," I replied. I wanted to get back to the reason I'd come. "I'll have to owe you for the guns." The cops hadn't left me enough time to get my winnings from Smiley's before dragging me downtown. "You know I'm good for it, Duke."

Ishray came and refilled Duke's glass without a word to either of us. Duke struck a wooden match with his thumbnail. It popped and ignited, filling the air with the smell of sulfur. He lit the Lucky and inhaled deeply.

"Hank, I know. But I'm running a business here." He exhaled and a large cloud of smoke hung between us. "I don't know about no credit line." Gracefully he picked a few flecks of tobacco from his tongue.

"I need a box of shells for each of the guns. And, if you have 'em, I want 125-grain hollow points for the Berettas, and extra clips. And a box of Glaser Safety slugs for the Smith."

Duke whistled through the gap in his front teeth. "You must be after some real bad guys, Hank. Those Glasers are nasty, pre-fragmented amm-u-ni-tion. Those fuckers will blast around in someone's cranial cavity and make pulp-e-fried brain matter. Wow. What an ugly mess." Duke shut the case and slipped behind the curtain. I knew the transaction was finished and that my credit had been approved. My package would be ready in a few minutes.

I walked past Ishray and gave him a wave. He smiled and his diamond twinkled in the dim light. I returned the quarter to the slot and waited for the tone. On the third ring the phone was answered by a woman's voice.

I was surprised to get an answer.

"Is Jake there?" I asked with some timidness.

"Who is this?" came the reply.

"Tell him it's Hank."

"Oh, hi, Hank. This is Karen." The voice became friendly and almost bubbly. "Are you in jail?"

"No."

"Where are you?"

"Can I talk to Jake?"

"Oh, sure." It sounded as if she was a little hurt by my non-answer.

"Hank, where are you?" It was Jake's voice.

"You on a cell phone?"

* * *

Jake showed up with Karen about twenty minutes later. She looked a little put off by the surroundings. Ishray smiled when he saw Jake. I waited in Duke's back booth where I could watch the front door. Duke had left for an appointment. As he said goodbye, he didn't ask about when he would be paid, but just smiled, shook my hand and placed a brown paper bag, neatly taped shut, on the table. The bag was now on the seat next to me, out of view.

I sipped my rye. As Jake and Karen approached, I didn't rise to greet them.

"Hank." There was a slight twinge in Jake's voice.

I nodded to each. Before they sat I spoke again. "Karen, would you mind waiting at the bar?" It was more a demand than a question.

Karen looked around at the now empty bar, except for Ishray. He smiled at her and went back to his paper.

"Don't worry, Ishray doesn't bite. He's quite well read. You'll have a nice chat and he'll keep the riff-raff away that comes in here sometimes." I sounded cold, but it was supposed to be friendly.

"It'll only be a few minutes." Jake kissed her cheek. Karen didn't appear happy at being excluded or with the surroundings. She looked like she might pull out a tissue and wipe off the stool before sitting. Ishray gave Karen a twinkling smile, which she nervously returned and took a seat at the bar. Ishray immediately engaged her in a conversation.

"What's up?" asked Jake.

"You're asking me what's up?" I gave a laugh, but it had no humor in it. Karen looked around from her barstool. Ishray was handing her something in a cocktail glass.

Jake and I sat in silence for a moment while Ishray brought Jake a beer and refreshed my rye.

I looked Jake in the eye and held his stare until he squirmed with uneasiness. "What is it?"

"DeDe is dead."

The words hit Jake with almost the same impact they had leveled at me, but for a different reason. He knew when I said "dead," that I didn't mean she had had a heart attack or been hit by a bus. I could see the wheels spinning in his head. He was doing the same mental exercises I had been doing the last couple of hours. Trying to add up the figures and finding out they didn't compute.

"She was murdered."

Jake was losing his color. He and I had been through a lot. But mostly it was exciting and adventurous. We weren't used to real life-and-death danger.

"Hank, I'm sorry."

I looked at Jake. This was the second time today someone had said they were sorry. Sorry for me? Sorry DeDe was dead? Sorry? Sorry didn't cut it. It was weak and too late for DeDe.

"Jake, you don't understand. DeDe was tortured! Then, the bastards beat her to death." I waited for the words to penetrate. "This wasn't some mugging gone wrong. This was planned, premeditated, thought-out, torture for answers. These are very bad guys we are dealing with. When the police interrogated me, they showed me pictures. They weren't pretty. I was sick. Sick to my stomach." I raised my voice enough to draw Karen and Ishray's attention. "They tied her to a chair, they tortured her with an electrical cord, they beat her face to the point where it wasn't DeDe." I took a swig of the rye. It burned my throat like the stomach acid had.

Jake was silent. I hoped my words were drawing the images I had seen. "Are you getting the picture here?" He nodded an affirmative response. He didn't look well. "Good, Jake, very good."

I ripped open the bag, revealing my new armaments, and pulled a Beretta from the bag. I placed the automatic on the table between us. Jake's eyes grew big. "This is an automatic. It has sixteen shots. Flip off the safety and keep pulling the trigger," I instructed. "It's loaded with 125-grain hollow points. They'll put a hole in a person the size of your fist. Anyone hit is not going to be getting up." I reached into the bag. "Here's an extra clip." I pushed the gun and extra clip across the table to him. "It's loaded and the safety is on."

Jake looked down at the gun. I knew he never carried a gun. He had shot my Browning only a few times out in the desert, many years before. We'd come across a Mojave rattler, a particularly nasty snake, on one of our excursions into Mexico. I'd shot the snake twice and then handed the gun to Jake. He had missed four straight times. He came close only once.

"Take it. You might need it."

Jake didn't make a move to pick up the weapon.

"Take it," I demanded. "Someone murdered DeDe, and they weren't nice about it."

Jake picked up the Beretta without comment. He turned it over in his hands and then placed it and the clip in his lap.

I reached in the bag and brought out the Smith and Wesson .45. I spun the cylinder, checking the empty chambers. Then I loaded it. I held the gun out for Jake to see.

Jake watched my hands and then looked at me. "Hank, what are we going to need these guns for?"

"Are your ears painted on? Haven't you heard what I've been saying? You didn't see the photographs of DeDe. And you don't want to." I put the revolver back in the bag. "These are not nice people that are looking for you." I noticed Jake cringe slightly.

I pulled out the second Beretta and put in the clip, and then returned it to the bag. Finally, I brought out the little Walther .32 and loaded it.

"This is my hidey gun. I'll carry it in my boot."

"You serious?"

"I'm not only serious, I'm prepared." I put the safety on and reached under the table to slip the Walther into my boot. I closed up the bag with the two other guns. "Now, I think you have something to tell me, Jacob." I could tell by the look on Jake's face that he knew I wasn't going to listen to anything but the truth.

Jake spent the better part of the next twenty minutes telling me a tale of the Wild West, lost treasure in the desert and satellites in the sky. There were several parts of the puzzle that he wasn't privy to but he told me everything he knew, his part in the whole scheme, how each of the individuals was protected from the others by what each knew or, more importantly, didn't know. There were two letters he had hidden that told his part. Then he told me about the two Mexicans in the parking lot, the phone call, and how close he and Karen had come to being dead. He said Karen felt they might be after her, something to do with her husband, Vegas and a computer program. But this reasoning didn't tell me why DeDe was dead.

It was an interesting tale. If I wasn't in the middle of it, I might not have believed it. I remembered White's description of the two men seen at DeDe's apartment. One of the men had been Hispanic, or maybe an Indian. Maybe there was a connection.

Another piece of the puzzle that didn't fit was this man, Williams. Jake said Williams worked for NASA. Was there a connection between the two NASA men found dead on the reservation, the ones W.E. said had been in the paper, and Williams? W.E. had also mentioned a coin dealer found dead on the reservation recently. Gold coins and dead coin dealer? Was that part of this mystery, too? I asked Jake about these but he had no idea how or why they'd be connected. I think he wanted to believe they were just very strange coincidences. I wasn't so sure but we both agreed it really didn't matter right now. We could trust no one.

I looked at the bar where Karen sat nursing her second drink. She had quit pretending to ignore us and was now turned toward us, watching intently. I smiled to show there was no hostility on my part. She politely returned the gesture.

"Do you really trust her?" I was still smiling, even though I wasn't feeling friendly.

Jake took a long time to answer, long enough that I knew the answer before he spoke. "Let's just say I'm not going to be letting her out of my sight any time soon." He drained the warm beer and held the glass for Ishray to see.

While we waited for our drinks to get replenished, Jake continued.

"I'm not sure if I believe her story about the husband. And sometimes she's too smart."

"So how much of this does she know?"

Jake sat quietly, his jaw working back and forth. "Everything."

"That's not like you. What in the hell were you thinking?"

"I had my reasons." Jake sounded defensive.

I shook my head. "I hope they are good reasons."

"Me, too," he said somewhat tentatively. "She has helped me think this thing through. She's thinks Manny's the most likely to stab me in the back."

"Maybe. Manny seems to be the logical connection. But I wouldn't dismiss Cloud, either." I had met Cloud only a couple times while working for Manny. There was nothing to like about the man as far as I could see. Jake might trust him, but I didn't. I had no reason to. Manny, on the other hand, well, he had the resources to take the whole enchilada without asking, if that was what he wanted. We'd trusted Manny—at least we did a long time ago. I took a small sip of the rye. Jake looked over his shoulder to see what Karen was doing. She smiled, probably in response to Jake. He turned around to face me.

It was time to get my anger out in the open. "I'm going to say this once.

I've known you for over half my life, Jake, and in that time you've pissed me off many times. You've gotten me into fights. You got my head busted." I fingered my scar. "And, for some fucking reason you're still my closest friend." I let the words sink in. "Several years back you promised to never tempt me with any *deal* again. And you've pretty much kept that promise. I understand that this is something different. You didn't bring me in. Circumstances did. I accept that. This is my decision." I pointed my finger at him. "Don't say 'Are you sure?' or anything like that. I'm in. I have a personal stake in this now. DeDe's dead and I'm a suspect." I looked Jake squarely in the eye. I wanted to make sure he knew I was going along. "It could have been those Mexicans from Smiley's. One of the men seen near DeDe's was described as Hispanic. The other was a white guy. The other Mexican could have been waiting in the car."

Jake merely nodded an acknowledgment and listened.

"They've been following you and probably followed me home from the bar. When they saw DeDe leave with all her stuff, they must have followed her. Then after they searched my place and yours and didn't find any clues to where the gold was..."

Jake took a deep breath. "Yeah, it's all fits. They figured DeDe took something or knew something..."

"And they killed her!" I cut Jake off. "I want to be there when you cross their path again!" I said loud enough to draw both Karen and Ishray's attention. We sat in silence for a second until Karen and Ishray returned to their conversation.

"Hank..."

"Don't say anything. My decision has been made." I checked my watch. It was nearly 3:30. "I've got to make a call."

I slid out of the booth and made my way along the bar. "Hi, Karen. It will only be a few more minutes. Ishray, give the lady another drink."

I dropped quarter in the phone and dialed the number on the matchbook. "Molly?"

"Hank." She sounded pleased. "You're prompt."

"I'm with Jake."

"Where are you?"

"In a bar. Have you been thinking?"

"Yes, but I need to ask you some questions. And I want straight answers."

"Do you know the One Hand Clapping bar?"

"I know where it is."

"Meet us there. Then we'll talk. Be there around seven. There are some things Jake and I have to do."

"I'll be there." Molly hung up before I could respond. I returned the receiver to its cradle. Karen watched me as I passed to the booth. I slid back into my protective corner.

"So what is your plan, Jake?"

23
Jake
Tuesday Night

There was no direct route to Shiprock from Santa Fe. The two biggest things up there were Shiprock Mountain, which is a sacred place to the Navajo and not open to tourists, and the Four Corners National Monument, and that was nothing more than a geographical dot where four states touched each other, the only place in the country where that happens. However, if someone hadn't built a monument saying that's what it was, you'd never know. I'd heard that adventurous couples would sneak into the park after dark and screw on the monument. I'd also heard that something had been done to put a stop to that. Government!

After way too much haggling, the four of us had finally agreed on a route. Molly devised a system where we could verify if we were being followed. Each couple would drive separately to Cuba. Then, after we rendezvoused in Cuba, we would leapfrog each other the rest of the way to Shiprock. They'd lead for a few miles and then pull over. When we passed them, they'd wait and see which cars were still following. If anyone was following us, we should be able to spot them.

"And if someone is?" Karen had asked.

"Then we don't go to Shiprock. We go to Waterville."

"And?" I'd asked.

"And we wait until they make their move."

She hadn't said what we'd do next. And no one wanted to ask.

"I think it's about time for another switch." Karen's words brought me back. "I think Molly said we should switch after the Blanco Trading Post and I just saw the sign for it."

I shrugged. "Whatever."

"Let me guess," Karen offered, "you don't think much of Hank's new friend..."

"She's a cop." I was mystified by it all. "Why he has to slip beneath the sheets with a cop, especially now, is beyond me."

"But she is a reservation cop and that could come in handy, couldn't it?"

"A cop is a cop."

"What are you talking about?"

"Look at it this way. She's a cop. Good or bad, I don't know. But if she's out there helping us, she's breaking the law. Now, just how much of this is she going to go along with? Just how much can she turn her back on? If she's a good cop, then the answer is very little—maybe not at all. Her own conscience will force her to 'do the right thing.' If she's a bad cop, then we may be in deeper shit than I thought. She could waste us all, hide most of the gold, claim she was making a bust and become a hero, a very rich hero."

She sat through my tirade and then asked one pointed question that wrapped it all up. "Do you trust Hank?"

My silence was her answer. Of course I trusted Hank. I trusted him implicitly. That also meant I trusted his decisions. If he said it was all right for Molly to be along, that it was all right for her to help with the planning, all right for her to see sixteen million in gold and all right for her to help us get it to Manny, then that would have to be good enough for me.

I turned toward Karen. "What do you think of her?"

"What do you mean? Do I like her? What?" Karen looked puzzled.

"You just met her, but you must've formed some kind of opinion. First impression. Woman to woman. Anything?"

She exchanged hands on the wheel and shifted in her seat, turning more toward me. "I don't think we'll be best friends, but she seems okay. Quiet. Friendly. Smart."

"Is she all right?"

"All right?"

"Yeah. On the level. Trustworthy. You know."

She thought for a moment and then answered that from what she'd seen of her, Molly appeared to be okay. "I'd trust her."

"Anything else?"

"Yeah. She really likes Hank."

"Did she say so?"

"Yes. No. She did but she didn't."

"Now you're the one who's got me confused."

"She didn't say so with words but her actions say so. The way she looks at him when he isn't looking. The way she ran to help him when the cops came. The way she says his name. You can tell."

"But he just met her…" I slowed my argument when I realized it didn't have enough steam to make even a few more words.

Karen's smile lit up the cab of the truck. "Right! There couldn't be anything serious between them. They just met."

I smiled and laughed right along with her. Okay. She had me there. If I could be feeling something for Karen after only a few days, then Hank could do the same thing. In fact, Hank was more likely to do something like this than I was. I went through women like fat people go through candy. Hank was different. *He falls in love.* His relationships, when he has them, are passionate affairs. So Hank falling in love is nothing out of the ordinary. Falling in love with a cop. Now that was another matter. When this whole thing was over, I'd have to ask him some serious questions about that.

"Jake?" Karen's tired voice barely made it to me.

"Yeah?" I reached for her, touching her shoulder.

"I'm really getting tired…"

I looked up ahead and saw the lights of the gas station and grocery store that comprised the Blanco Trading Post. "Pull over." I directed her to the gas station. "Let's switch places."

"But…" She looked confused as she pulled in and stopped.

"But nothing. No one's following us."

"Are you sure about this?"

"I'm sure. Now switch with me."

She climbed out of her side and instead of getting in the passenger's side, she headed for the station. I tapped the horn lightly, getting her attention. She turned quickly and, squeezing her legs together, imitated someone in desperate need of relief. I smiled and motioned for her to hurry up. She responded by scurrying into the station.

As long as we'd stopped, I decided to top off the tanks. I checked my watch. We had plenty of time. If Hank and Molly passed by, they'd pull over as planned.

I checked my watch. Again. It was a bad habit I'd developed whenever I had to wait for anyone or anything. It was as if I could somehow speed the time by watching it more closely. Anal-retentive. Good. Add that to my paranoia. I didn't want to think about what that made me.

I kept guard on two fronts. One for Karen and one for Hank. Since one was in front of me and the other behind, it wasn't too long before I had the makings of a stiff neck. Shit. What the hell was taking her so long? Especially on this night. I put the pump handle back and headed inside.

"Twenty bucks," the old man behind the counter stated without looking up from the book he was reading.

I slapped a twenty on the counter. "Restroom?"

"Occupied," was his monotone response.

I looked around. "Only one?"

He looked up, his dark skin deeply wrinkled. "One's all we usually need up here. There's a pretty lady in there right now but I'm sure she'll give you the key when she's finished."

I smiled and headed toward the back. The door opened just as I got there and Karen was coming out. She had a funny look on her face. Or was it a surprised look? Or maybe a worried one?

I took the key from her and stepped inside—and stopped dead in my tracks. On the wall, the wall opposite the facilities, hung a pay phone. A phone whose long cord was still swaying slightly from its last use.

* * *

Somehow, I managed to get back to the truck. I was fuming. My heart pounded. Raced. With every moment that passed, my anger increased.

"Jake?" Karen asked tentatively. "What's going on?"

I didn't answer. I couldn't. Had I trusted her too much? Whom had she called? And now she was sitting here, using that fucking little girl voice, asking me "What's wrong?" as if she didn't know. As if she hadn't made a phone call while she was in the bathroom.

"Jake," she began again, "I know you're under a lot of stress but…"

I stopped her with a hateful glare. My hands coiled into tight fists and I wanted to hit something. And she just sat there. Looking innocent. Looking concerned. I hated her. She'd lied. Now she sat there so calm and cool. She'd said she had to pee but she really had to make a phone call. She'd lied. Was she working for someone? Who?

I figured it had to be Manny. He was the only one who had the kind of connections to procure a woman with Karen's talents. Smart. Beautiful. Yet, so utterly deceitful. It had to be Manny. It had to be.

She leaned away from me. Looking confused, she asked if she'd done something wrong.

It was now or never. "Who'd you call?" I tried sounding as normal as possible.

Looking shocked, the traitor asked what I was talking about.

I exploded. "You know fucking well what I'm talking about!" My words backed her up against the door. Looking fearful, she swore she didn't have a clue what I was talking about.

"The phone. In the bathroom. You made a call." I laid out her crime out in front of her.

"What?"

"You made a phone call."

She shook her head. "No…"

"Don't lie to me, you…" I raised my hand but stopped. I'd never been able to hit a woman. As much as I wanted this to be the first time, to make her pay for her sins, I couldn't.

"Jake, I never…"

"Don't lie to me! I saw the cord swinging. Back and forth. Back and forth." My hands mimicked the motion. "I went in there right after you. Remember?"

She thought for a second and then reached for her purse. In two heartbeats, she fished out a quarter and held it up.

"Look!" She commanded. "I found this quarter in the pay phone." She waved it in front of my face, back and forth. "It's something I do. An old habit. A superstition. A silly superstition." Her words were measured and careful. "Ever since I was a little girl, I've believed that when you find a quarter in a

209

pay phone, it means good luck. My mama used to tell me that. I did it for us. So we'd have good luck."

I hit a wall. An invisible wall of guilt, doubt, hate, love, trust and suspicion. It stopped me cold.

Review. Quick review. A few minutes ago I was ready to marry the woman. Then, in an instant, I was ready to kill her. Now, I wasn't sure about anything. What the fuck was going on? I was up, down, and had no idea, which was which. Had she just used the telephone to call someone? Manny? Or had she really gone fishing for a quarter—for luck—for us—and found one?

"Jake?" She lowered the quarter and stared at me. "Talk to me, Jake. Why are you so angry?"

"I'm not." Automatic pilot. Denial.

"Don't give me that." She was in my face. "Look, you're about to do this thing and, from what I've seen so far, it's very dangerous. You could get killed. The only security you've got is that we all trust one another. You. Me. Hank. We've got enough to worry about as it is." Another pause. Another check. Another salvo. "If we don't work together on this, it isn't gonna happen."

I nodded. She was right. But I still couldn't get over my suspicions.

"It all comes down to this, Jake. It's the same thing you've been telling me. You either trust me or you don't." She folded her arms across her chest and waited for my response.

The sudden silence stunned me. I could *feel* it. Like an enveloping mist, it was there but not really. It concealed and hid and distorted what I needed to be thinking about, what I was feeling in my gut. I faced her but she looked like she was fading away from my view.

Think. Quick. Think. Do you want to lose her? Do you trust her?

The answer to both was no. I didn't want to lose her but I couldn't say I trusted her, either. Not like I trusted Hank.

"Yes. I trust you," I lied.

Slowly, ever-so-slowly, her rigid stance melted into something more fluid, more open, more accepting. "How do I know if I can believe you?"

I wished I could be warm and sincere but I couldn't. "You don't have a choice."

24
Hank
Late Tuesday Night

Molly and I could be like hundreds, even thousands of other couples, riding along in the night going somewhere. We could be going to visit an elderly relative or to a church function or just out for a leisurely evening drive. But we weren't. We were headed deep into the desert to find sixteen million dollars in gold coins—and the men who'd murdered DeDe. I didn't know how it was all connected; I just knew that it was.

Jake and Karen had been in the lead and we were supposed to leapfrog with them a few miles past the Blanco Trading Post. Then it would be their turn to watch for suspicious cars. There hadn't been much traffic since we left Cuba. It appeared we weren't being followed, at least not yet.

After leaving One Hand Clapping earlier in the day, Karen, Jake and I had first swung by the Ford dealer and picked up the new truck. The salesman was all smiles to see Jake. I didn't bother asking Jake what the truck had cost. As he explained it, money wasn't going to be a problem soon. Even though the truck was black and nothing flashy, I had felt conspicuous sitting up high in the fully loaded F350 four-by-four. I had driven because Jake didn't want to be stopped without a license. Karen followed in the Buick to the rental lot. Then the three of us headed back to One Hand Clapping. Molly arrived a few minutes after seven. That was the last stop before heading north.

I spent fifteen minutes outlining what was going on for Molly. Jake was sitting on a pot of gold, *literally*. At first Molly had tried to talk me out of any involvement. "Are you sure you need to be in this?" she had quizzed.

I explained Jake's concern about a possible double-cross being played. He believed one of the three other partners had decided to take everything for themselves without sharing. He also told me about Karen's husband and an adventure in Vegas. But who? Who was so greedy that they'd kill? I outlined the situation, keeping it simple and not providing names or too many specific details. I told Molly I was in. Jake needed me and I was the only person Jake could trust now and that was that. And there was DeDe. I was positive that whoever the greedy bastards were that they had killed her; and sooner or later I would be coming face-to-face with them.

Molly sat in silence and held my hands, looking deep into my eyes. It felt like she was reading my soul. I knew she suspected my interest in the gold was only camouflage for the revenge I sought. Finally, she announced that she would help us reach the reservation undetected or followed. After that she would see how it played out and what her commitment would be. Now it was my turn to plead for *her* noninvolvement. But she'd been insistent. She didn't care about Jake's gold, only my well-being. On the rez, she said, the Tribal Police were the law and The People had a different view of how the world should be, different than the *bilagaana,* and that difference could come in handy. I reminded Molly that I was white and so was a part of her. Molly's eyes had narrowed and turned dark. "I am Navajo," she simply replied. From that point on, Molly acted like a general directing battle plans.

Jake was intent on getting to Shiprock the quickest, easiest way. Molly reasoned that taking back roads made more sense because it would be easier to see if we were being followed. As Molly laid out her plan, I could see Jake getting madder and madder. I knew Jake's problem. He wasn't in control. Jake had a problem with women taking the lead. And when Karen piped up, joining Molly's camp, it infuriated him.

Jake had wanted to head south to Albuquerque and then west on Interstate 40 to Gallup and, finally, north on NM 666 to Shiprock. It was the quickest route. Molly had explained that the Inter-Tribal Indian Ceremonial was going on all week at the Red Rock State Park east of Gallup. There would be more than fifty tribes from the U. S. and Mexico participating. Thousands of Indians at the pow-wow. She had planned to attend with her brother and aunt, who had left for the ceremonial a couple days earlier. Many of the reservation's residents would be headed down NM 666 to Gallup and there would be a lot of activity in the vicinity of Interstate 40 and NM 666. With all this traffic, it would be difficult to watch all the cars and detect if we were being followed. And there would also be lots of cops. This was the main reason Molly hadn't wanted to follow Jake's plan.

I could see that Jake understood Molly's point, but he wasn't going to tell her that. A compromise had been struck; Jake and Karen headed south on 25 to catch 44 north. Molly and I would take the same route we had taken to the reservation only days earlier. We would head north to Pojoaque and then cut across east to Cuba, where we would rendezvous and start the leapfrogging north along NM 44.

After the travel plans were set, Jake had announced that Molly would have a share of his gold. Molly had been dumbstruck, but said nothing. I knew what Jake meant by this gesture. If Molly was cut in, she became part of it, putting her squarely on our side of the fence.

* * *

The tension in Molly's truck was smothering me. I rolled down the window and let in the dry night air. It was cool and getting cooler by the minute. All the fresh air did was make me shiver. Finally we saw a sign for the Blanco Trading Post, five miles away. When we passed the trading post, Jake's truck was the only vehicle in view, sitting in a pool of light next to the gas pumps.

"What are they doing? They're not supposed to be stopping. We're to pass them after the trading post." There was a tinge of panic in my voice.

"We'll keep going for a few miles, slow down and see if they catch up. If they don't, we'll double back and see what's going on." Molly maintained her speed and blew by the trading post. "Maybe they needed gas or one of 'em had to use the bathroom. Don't get upset, not yet," Molly commanded.

"We agreed to get gas in Farmington," I grumbled to myself.

We drove out of sight of the trading post's lights before Molly slowed down. She watched the rearview mirror for the truck. Finally after ten miles, when they hadn't caught up, she pulled off onto the shoulder and turned off the truck.

"We'll wait for a few minutes," Molly said. She opened her door and got out. She left the ignition on so we could hear KNDN, the rez radio station. I got out and joined her; we leaned against her truck, arm in arm and waited.

"You need to relax, Hank," Molly said. "It's going to be a long night." She leaned her shoulder against me. "Are you thinking about DeDe and the police?"

"No. Yes. It's so hard to believe that she is dead."

We stood in silence for a few minutes, waiting, watching the night. She leaned into the car to switch off the radio and turned up the sound on the scanner. We listened to a dispatcher and a patrol car exchange pleasantries. Molly told me who the two voices were.

The night air was starting to relax me. I tried to focus on the task at hand and clear my mind of the past day's events. DeDe was gone. Whatever guilt and remorse I felt, it wasn't going to bring her back. Nothing I could do now would give her life again.

We got back in the truck and Molly fiddled with the scanner.

"Well, it won't be long now. Just thirty-some miles to Bloomfield. Then we'll head north to Aztec and see if anyone is following before we go to Shiprock. We should be there shortly before 1:00."

Molly looked over at me in the dim light of the instrument panel. "Are you okay?"

I fidgeted with the Walther in my boot. *Yeah,* I thought to myself, *I was okay.* I was headed out into the night desert to recover sixteen million dollars in gold coins, my wife had been murdered and there were strong indications that someone was trying to kill us. "Yeah, I'm okay," I repeated softly.

Every so often the scanner cracked and we would hear a report. It sounded like the reservation was fairly quiet. Everyone was down at Red Rock State Park, including most of the Reservation Tribal Police.

"Why did Jake make a point of saying I would get a split of the gold?"

I hesitated for a moment. I knew Jake's reason. "If you are in on this and get a split of the gold, then you won't back out and arrest us, that's his thinking. He's not sure if he can trust you." I knew the words stung, but figured Molly probably didn't care if Jake trusted her or not.

"I don't want any of the gold," she spat. "I never even mentioned the gold. I have no interest whatsoever in *his* gold!" Molly shook her head. "I can't believe this guy. Your buddy, Jake, he is some kind of a male chauvinist pig, isn't he? I get the feeling he doesn't like women giving him directions."

"You're right on all scores," I answered timidly.

"Did he tell you how he stumbled onto this gold?" she quizzed.

I turned in my seat to see Molly's profile in silhouette. Was she interrogating me now? "Why?"

"Don't get paranoid on me. I'm just trying to put this together. Jake doesn't trust me? Well, I don't trust his thinking. And it appears that one of Jake's partners shouldn't be trusted. DeDe is dead. And I don't know who these partners of Jake's are. I want to be prepared for whatever *we* might be walking into."

"I want to ask you a question first. We're breaking the law. Aren't you worried about helping us?"

Molly thought for a moment and then, picking her words carefully, explained. "I'm worried about your safety, first of all. You are carrying three guns, obviously expecting the worse, and looking to settle a score with some unknown assailants. Your friend, Jake, is caught up in gold fever and not thinking straight. The only one who seems to thinking straight is Karen." Molly thought for a moment. "But there is something about her that doesn't fit. I don't trust her." Molly looked at me. "So, you see, you are the only one I do trust."

"Thanks. But, hey, Karen supported your plan back in Santa Fe." It was a weak reply, but the only one I had. I knew Molly was right on all counts.

"Yes, she did support me. That's why I said she was the only one thinking straight. But something doesn't feel right where she's concerned." Molly gave me a stern look to emphasize the point. "As far as breaking the law, for starters, you'll be trespassing on reservation land. You guys are just treasure hunters and there are treasure hunters all over the Southwest looking for the big score. You won't be the first treasure hunters to trespass on the rez, and you won't be the last. If there are a bunch of gold coins hidden in the desert, then someone placed them there. If the Tribal Council were to get the gold and if they were to make their find public, then there could be lawsuits galore. Everyone and their mother would lay a claim to it. As you would say, I may be playing judge and jury here, which very much is the *bilagaana* way of thinking, but that gold, is only going to lead to serious trouble. And it's trouble The People don't need. I see my thinking, my actions, as the Navajo way.

I'm a Navajo first and a cop second, Hank." Molly paused for a moment and listened to the night sounds. "Getting the gold off the reservation is going to be good. Right now its presence is causing trouble. People are trying to kill you and Jake, obviously for the gold. Getting the gold off the rez is going to restore harmony, *hozho*, to the reservation. Your *bilagaana* justice is based on punishment. Navajo justice is based on fairness, making good for damage that has been done. Discovering the gold has caused damage. My actions may restore harmony and make things good again."

Molly's answer left me without a reply.

I pulled out the Beretta and flipped off the safety.

"And besides," she said suddenly, "if Jake insists that I get a split of his share of the gold, I can make some nice donations around the reservation, anonymously of course, to the clinic, the school, the Chapter House," Molly stated. "So, you see, the reservation will get its share of the gold without having to bargain with the *bilagaana* justice system."

Molly had thought through her involvement in our *excursion*, had carefully weighed her plans, options, reasons why and how she would do this. She'd even found a noble use for her portion of the gold. I liked her even more.

Molly reached over and patted my hand. "I answered your question. Now answer a couple of mine. "Do you know how to use those guns? Or are you going to shoot yourself in the foot?"

I had to smile. "I know what you think. An artist—what's he know about guns? You're stereotyping."

Molly chuckled. "Okay. So how do you know about guns?"

"My dad, he taught me how to shoot. When I was a kid, we hunted back in Wisconsin with my uncle. My father insisted that if I was going to kill an animal that I had to be a good shot. 'Make the animal's death quick,' he said. So we spent a lot of time at target practice, my uncle and me. Any more questions?"

"Where are your parents now?"

"They died in a car accident several years ago."

"I'm sorry. It's not easy losing one parent, much less two." Molly paused. "I do have another question. How is it that Jake got mixed up in this?"

"Years ago, before I met him, he used to run with a Navajo named Cloud. I only met him a couple times and..."

Molly pivoted and cut me off. "Whitney Cloud?"

Her sudden move startled me. I put the safety back on. "You know him?"

"Yes, I know him. And I don't like the fact that he has anything to do with this." Her voice was firm.

"Why? Jake seems to trust him." I dug to find Molly's concern, without revealing my own misgivings.

"No, he doesn't." Her response hit with force. "Jake said that he wanted us as backup when the gold was loaded. That's not trust. He just neglected to mention who he was meeting out in the desert." Molly's mind was at work again.

"So what's the deal with Whitney?"

"He's not what he seems. When he got out of prison he came back to the rez, pretending to be a Traditional, a real Navajo. He even says he wants to be a tribal leader. But behind the scenes, Whitney Cloud is busy doing things that are contrary to being a true Traditional. He isn't concerned about the People's heritage or what the *bilagaana* have done to us. Yes, I've heard him spout off about the atrocities inflicted by Kit Carson and about The People's proud past and about *his* plan to return the reservation to that past. But Whitney Cloud cares about one person—himself." Molly's voice was hostile with rage. "I don't know if Jake knows this about his one-time friend or not, but he's smart to want a back-up if Whitney Cloud is involved. Those guys following Jake and Karen around may not be working for this money man after all. They're probably working for Whitney Cloud."

Then, suddenly, lights appeared and the big black truck with Jake and Karen passed us.

"I wonder what they're doing."

"They're just confused," Molly replied. "We'll let them get ahead a few miles and watch for cars."

At first Jake's truck slowed as it passed and then regained its speed. He and Karen had probably figured everything was okay and continued toward Bloomfield.

"See, everything is okay," I said, the tone of my voice not supporting that statement. I was thinking about Cloud and what Molly had said. She had confirmed my suspicions about Jake's old friend.

We waited until I wasn't sure if I could still see the taillights of Jake's truck or if it was just an illusion. Molly started the truck and turned down the police scanner. We were on our way again. Just before Bloomfield, Jake's truck suddenly appeared on the side of the road. We passed, leading the way through Bloomfield and the few short miles up 544 towards Aztec.

At Farmington, we found a gas station and filled the truck. We watched as Jake and Karen went past and headed towards Shiprock. There was very little traffic between Farmington and Shiprock.

Outside Shiprock's city limits we slowed and let the distance between the two trucks increase. Jake and Karen led the way. We drove along the edge of the town that was dark as it slumbered. Just after we crossed the San Juan River, Jake turned into a 2/11/7 convenience store, pulled up alongside a public phone in the parking lot, and stopped. The store was closed and dark. A single light barely lit the parking lot, giving it an eerie feeling. Molly continued up the road, turned off the lights and doubled back. She pulled behind a line of junked cars next to a dark Exxon station and stopped. Now it was time to wait. I looked out the back window, watching for lights, for other cars, for the bad guys. I checked my watch. It was 1:10. Each passing minute felt like an eternity. I could feel the adrenaline rising in my bloodstream.

I took a deep breath and slowly blew it out. Molly turned to look at me. "You wait here; I want to see what's going on."

"Hey, where are you going? You can't go wandering around," I protested.

"Don't worry, Hank. No one is going to see me. I'll be back in a minute." Molly reached up to the dome light and switched it off. She left the door slightly ajar and disappeared into the dark without a sound.

I looked at my watch. It was 1:11.

25
Jake
Wednesday AM

I drove to Shiprock and parked the truck near the phone Cloud had designated. I'd told Karen I'd changed our plans. Originally, I was going to drop her off at a motel once we'd gotten this far. Now, because of the phone call incident, that didn't seem like such a great idea. Whatever it was that she was up to, it might be better—safer?—to keep her close to me. She'd argued about it, about not wanting to get involved with this. I'd told her I was sorry but things had changed, that she was staying with me.

"How long?" she'd asked.

"Until I get the gold," I replied. "And if you don't like it, you can always get out right now and take your chances on the open road."

She'd fussed and fumed but not as much as I'd expected. Finally, after she'd gotten me to promise that nothing bad was going to happen to her, she'd relented. "But after you get done with this thing, then what?"

"Then you can go, you can stay. I just don't know right now and I sure as hell don't have time to figure it out."

After a few minutes, I got tired of sitting and went out by the phone. I made Karen wait in the truck with the doors locked. I paced. Four steps north. Four steps south. The pay phone stood as a silent sentinel, marking my slow-paced vigil with each passing. It'd been nearly five minutes already and no word from Cloud. I tried to be rational. At this stage of the game, five minutes was nothing. He'd call. I knew he'd call.

A car rounded the corner and headed right for us. It slowed as it neared but not by much. I counted about six kids, teenagers, crammed inside. Two of them yelled something as they passed by but their muffler was so loud I couldn't understand what they said. Just as well. I didn't need any distractions. A light tap of the truck horn brought my attention back to Karen. She looked frightened and was signaling me to come over. I turned and checked the phone thinking that my attentiveness might cause it to ring. It didn't.

"Who were those boys?" she asked as I approached the driver's side.

"Kids…"

"I thought Cloud said everyone was busy with that pow-wow thing."

"Like I said, they were kids, too old to want to go with mom and dad to the Intra-Tribal Ceremony and too good of an opportunity to just stay home. They won't interfere."

"I wish I could be so sure. Aren't you cold?"

I shook my head. Cold. Tired. Hungry. None of those things had even entered my mind. I had only one goal and that was to answer that phone as soon as it rang.

"Where's Hank? Do you know?"

I turned and looked behind us. Seeing nothing but wide open spaces, a few rough buildings and a short stretch of highway, I smiled. "No, Karen, I sure don't."

She panicked at my words. "But he's supposed to…"

I brought my full attention back to her. "He's supposed to do exactly what he's doing. He's watching us."

"But you can't see him."

"Right. Because if I could see him, so could Mr. Whitney Cloud."

"Oh, right," she said as she slumped back. She grabbed a pillow and hugged it in her arms.

I leaned into the cab and tried to ease her tension. "Now aren't you glad I insisted that we bring those pillows?"

"I'd rather have you in here with me than some stuffy pillow."

I smiled. Not a real smile but a passable one. Her possible phone call at Blanco still lingered. Hell, everything about her lingered. Good and bad. Maybe that's what I liked about her. She was like a truly great perfume, always subtly there but never overpowering.

A half-ounce of sincerity had started creeping into my smile when the telephone jarred me from one world and shoved me into another. I reached the phone in two steps and had the receiver in my hand before the second ring was over.

I froze. Just for a second, I froze. The enormity of what was about to happen hit me like an avalanche, paralyzed my body, my soul and my mind. Only a healthy measure of greed pulled me back and made everything function again.

"Yeah."

"Jake." It wasn't a question. He knew who it was. Was he watching? From where?

"Whitney."

"Who's the bitch?" His words were cold and hard. I looked around. He was close by, but I couldn't see him. Shit. He *was* watching us. I wondered how long he'd been watching. I had to keep my cool.

I answered firm and direct. "She's with me. It's okay."

"No, Jake, it's not okay. It's you and me and Williams. That was the deal." He was pissed.

I shot back. "The deal's changed."

"Not for me, *amigo*." He sounded like he was getting ready to hang up. "We laid this out. Hell, Jake, you laid this out so shit like this wouldn't happen."

"Right, *amigo*," I cut him off. "I laid this out and I can change it." I switched the phone to my other ear and checked on Karen at the same time.

Cloud was quiet for a long while and then finally asked, "Who is she?"

"A friend," I answered coldly.

"You never mentioned her."

"You never asked."

"I'm asking now." Cloud was sounding edgy.

Enough of this. "Look. She's with me. That's all you need to know."

"She's hot, too hot for you." I could feel his lust over the phone. *He was close*. Cloud always did have a thing for beautiful women and had gotten into trouble more than once because he couldn't control himself.

An uncomfortable silence fell over both of us. I wanted to get on with it. Hell or high water. It didn't matter. But I knew I couldn't push my old friend and partner. He didn't operate that way. Never had. He made his own decisions in his own way and time. I'd said my piece. Now, I had to wait for his.

Finally. "You got a big enough truck?"

I said I did. "Extra batteries, too. Just like Williams asked for."

"Good." Cloud laughed. "I don't think he trusts me."

I was tempted to tell him that if I was Williams I wouldn't trust him either. But I didn't. "C'mon, Whitney, he's just following the plan. Remember? No one gets too much information. Too much information creates too much temptation. Too much temptation…"

"Fine." He cut me off. "I saw that movie, too. It's just that the sooner we get this over with, the happier I'll be."

I lightened up a little. "You and me both."

"You got my money?" Cloud's hard edge hadn't softened.

"Money? Cloud, you know how this works."

"I know how this works but I don't like it. I can't spend numbers."

"But, come Monday, those numbers will be worth two million dollars and I'm sure you won't have any trouble spending that."

Silence. "Monday?"

"Right. Monday."

"Why not tomorrow?"

"Cause it's not set up that way."

"Jake, you better not be fucking with me."

"Look. No one's fucking with you."

"Then why Monday? Haven't you told the other guy about the change in time?"

Shit. I didn't want to get into this with him. Manny didn't know about the change and I sure as hell wasn't going to tell him. I didn't need Cloud screwing things up. "The money man hasn't got anything to do with this part of the deal. He put the money in your bank a week ago with explicit instructions that it couldn't be touched until Monday. And now that it's in there, an act of Congress couldn't budge it until Monday. *Comprende?*"

Silence. Then the sound of a lighter flicking followed by hard drawing on a cigarette. "If you say so."

"I say so."

More silence. A deep inhale. "What's her name again?"

"You mean 'the bitch'?" I mocked his earlier title while I stole another glance at her.

"Yeah, her."

"Her name is Karen."

"I'd like to meet her. Find out what she sees in you."

I smiled. We were on. "You just name the time and place, Cloud, and we'll be there."

"Here's what I want you to do. Go down 666 until the four lanes turn into two."

"And?" I asked, expecting a lengthy and detailed list of instructions.

"And wait. I'll be along as soon as I'm sure no one has followed you."

Shit. I panicked. We'd take off, Hank and Molly would be right behind us and Cloud would spot them right away. "Okay, Cloud." I tried not to let my fear show. "This part of the operation is up to you. Just don't take too long."

"Why? Worried about the time?"

"No," I improvised. "It's just that Karen brought these pillows and..." I let my words trail off, hoping I'd fueled his imagination.

He laughed, sort of. "Just go there and wait." The line went dead.

I hung up and cursed out loud. Slowly, ever-so-slowly, I headed back to the truck. I needed time to think and time was one thing I didn't have much of. Cloud was watching, had been watching for God knows how long. I'd forgotten how sharp he was. I made a quick promise to myself that if I ever got past this crisis, I'd never underestimate Mr. Whitney Cloud again.

Karen leaned out the truck window. She could tell by my expression that something had gone wrong but she was smart enough not to say anything. One way or another, I had to signal Hank without signaling Cloud. Whatever I did, it had to be clear, but normal. And I had to do it *now*!

Think! Time was running out. I was nearly at the truck. Cloud was watching. Hank was waiting. Karen was wondering. I was panicking. Then it hit me. I knew exactly what to do.

I walked to the back of the truck, unzipped my fly and took a piss on the back tire. Wordlessly, I got in the truck, turned the key, put it in gear and headed south on 666.

26
Hank
Wednesday Morning

What the hell! was that? I watched through the binoculars as Jake appeared to pee on the rear tire. We had two set signals and Jake hadn't given me either one. What the hell?

The call had come at 1:21 and lasted for what seemed like forever. And now they were leaving. The big black truck's lights came on and illuminated the parking lot. Slowly it lumbered towards the highway.

"Damn, Molly. Where are you?" I said out loud. I pounded the dashboard in frustration. I looked from side to side hoping to catch sight of her.

The truck was now sitting, waiting as if there was some traffic to pass by before they could turn onto the highway.

Nervously I drummed my fingers, sitting in the dark, watching and wishing I had a cigarette. It had been over ten years since I had my last one. Now I wanted a cigarette!

The sound of a shot made me almost jump out of my skin. An old beige car careened around the corner and whizzed past me, as if I wasn't there. "It's just a car, backfiring," I said to myself.

The car headed towards the closed convenience store and the waiting truck in a taunting fashion. *It was the same kids out joyriding who'd passed by a few minutes earlier,* I thought to myself. Just in case the second pass-by was more than it seemed, I had my hand on the Beretta. The car was a beat-up Chevy Caprice, more gray primer than paint. It veered down the center of the empty street, and seemed to be aimed right at Jake's new truck.

For a second the car's headlights flashed across the windshield and I saw Jake and Karen. Then they were lost in the blackness.

Jake hesitated a second longer and then pulled from the parking lot and headed west, the opposite direction of the Caprice. It looked like they were following the main drag out of town. I watched as their red taillights became barely visible.

"Well, I guess you're going to miss this adventure, Ms. Kiyanee. I can't wait any longer." I slid over to the driver's seat and was just about to start the Dodge, when a rock landed in the bed of the truck and rattled around. Moments later, Molly stepped from the shadows and sprinted to the driver's door.

"Move over," she demanded. She was out of breath.

"I can drive," I protested.

Molly waved me over. "Just move over and don't turn on the lights." She was huffing and puffing for breath. I slid over so Molly could get in.

"Well?"

"Just a second," she gulped air. "He's in a black Bronco," she panted. "He was just across the highway at the shopping center sitting in the shadows, watching, using a cell phone."

"Who? Cloud?" I questioned.

"Yes, and he's not alone. There's someone with him." Tension filled the truck.

"It must be the guy who originally found the gold."

"Did Jake give you a signal?"

"Yes and no."

"What?" Molly questioned.

"He stopped to take a pee on the truck tire," I answered somewhat exasperated. "There was no signal."

Molly chuckled. "He took a pee?"

"That's what it looked like. And, it's not so funny."

"I know."

Jake wasn't stupid, I thought to myself. The peeing had to be a signal; it had to mean something. Then it hit me. "Piss on it. That's what he meant. Piss on it. He couldn't use one of the agreed upon signals. I think he was trying to tell us Cloud was watching." I was proud of my deductive thinking.

Just then, a set of headlights came on in the shopping center parking lot. They were from an old, beat-up, black Bronco.

"Get down," Molly commanded.

A second later the lights slowly swept across the line of junk cars and the truck. After the lights passed, I looked over the dashboard. The taillights of the Bronco were disappearing in the direction Jake had gone and then appeared to turn south.

"That was Cloud," Molly announced.

"Do you think he saw us?"

"Did he stop?"

"No."

"Then I don't think he saw us."

"What are we going to do?" There was a bit of confusion in my voice.

"Follow him. He'll lead us to Jake, and to the gold."

* * *

We took the same route as Cloud; headed west out of town and then turned south on NM 666, driving with our lights off. For a few miles 666 is four lanes then it narrows down to two. It was at this point that Cloud pulled off the road. Molly quickly turned off the engine and rolled the truck to a stop a hundred yards behind him. Sitting in the darkness a couple car lengths in front of the Bronco was Jake's truck. Cloud sat in the Bronco for several minutes.

"What's he waiting for?" I whispered.

"He wants to see if anyone is following."

I knew that. Now I felt stupid for asking.

"Do you think he can see us?"

"No," Molly said sternly. "Hank, don't worry so much."

After a couple more minutes we saw the Bronco's headlights break the inky blackness. Cloud pulled up alongside Jake's truck, hesitated a moment and then led the way south on 666. We followed. After about three miles, Cloud headed off the highway and into the desert.

We watched the two vehicles' lights show their location as they drove into the night, one vehicle following the other. The red dots grew smaller and smaller, until they disappeared over a rise. Molly started the truck, turned it around and headed out into the desert. I hoped she hadn't lost sight of the taillights, but I said nothing. She'd been doing just fine so far. The night sky was littered with gray-blue clouds that the full moon played hide and seek in.

I looked back at the road and saw a Jeep drive by slowly and then disappear down the highway. For a second I wished I was in the Jeep, headed home to a warm bed and a good night's sleep.

We rode in darkness and silence. It seemed Molly was guided by some unknown sense. I was completely lost as we moved tediously forward. My eyes had adjusted to the dim moonlight so that I could see the outlines of rocks and sagebrush. Suddenly the truck lurched as we hit a deep pothole.

"Shit, I didn't see that one," exclaimed Molly.

"I can barely see anything. Are we on a road or anything?"

Molly found this funny. "Not really, just a well-worn path. We're headed out into the desert. Things are going to get rougher."

As we came over a small hill we could see two sets of headlights off in the distance. They had swung to our left and seemed to be circling back.

"What are they doing?" I asked.

"It looks like Whitney's coming back to retrace his tracks."

"Shit, what do we do?" I reached for the Beretta, preparing for the worst.

Molly started to turn in the opposite direction, away from the oncoming Bronco. "We're going to head toward that stand of rocks and hope he doesn't see us." Her voice was anxious.

"What rocks?" I couldn't see where Molly was going.

"Over to the right." Molly pointed into the darkness and accelerated. The truck jumped to the challenge. We had been tracking the bouncing lights a half mile ahead of us, following in their lead. Now we were headed off into uncharted territory. I hoped Molly could see where she wanted to go. The four-wheel drive truck climbed over the sagebrush without any trouble. It scraped along the bottom of the truck. I looked back to see the headlights of the two other vehicles making their wide arc. Molly coasted to a stop, not using the brakes and turned off the engine. We waited for them to pass. I realized I was holding my breath. The whole escapade was turning out to be much more difficult than either Jake or I had predicted. If Molly hadn't been along, I would be alone now, lost in the desert, waiting for the sun to come up. Or dead.

227

"I don't suppose you have any idea where we are?" I said in a hushed tone.

"We're headed southeast. Hogback Mountain is just to the north. There's not much out here except rocks, sagebrush and snakes," Molly answered. "If we go far enough, we'll run into the San Juan River."

We continued to watch the circling headlights as they bounced up and down, but they didn't come anywhere close to us. After they were a safe distance away, Molly started the little truck and we were, once again, in slow pursuit.

We bumped along over some very rough terrain, almost crawling at some points, the truck's engine groaning its complaint. Molly concentrated on her driving, while I searched for Hogback Mountain. I couldn't see a thing.

"It looks like they're coming around again," I said anxiously.

Without answering me, Molly turned the truck hard to the left this time. I tightly gripped the armrest. It looked like we were heading right into the headlights of Cloud's Bronco. Again, Molly allowed the truck to coast to a stop, safely out of range of the probing lights. Cloud repeated his searching maneuver two more times, driving a couple miles and then circling back. Each time Molly skillfully dodged his search. Eventually he must have felt secure, because he gave up the pattern and headed directly out into the desert with Jake not far behind, and Molly and I still on their tail. We rode in silence, traveling at about ten miles an hour. The grade was getting steeper, the bumps bigger and more severe.

"Are we climbing?"

"Yes, I think we are, gradually," Molly answered.

The truck bounced along, tossing us from our seats. The little four-by-four pitched violently as it stepped over the rocks in our way. I had completely lost sight of the taillights when Molly pulled the truck up against a rock formation.

"Why are we stopping?"

"Because they did."

I looked off into the night and could only make out dark shapes that appeared to be large rock formations.

"I figure they are a few hundred yards from where we are. It's time to hoof it." Molly reached around for a small pack behind the seat. It contained a

228

Thermos, compass, matches, and binoculars. I handed her the flashlight and checked my three guns.

The night air was still and chilly but it felt fresh as we set out. After a few minutes, the brisk walk began to warm me and I finally stopped shivering. While my eyes had adjusted to the dark, I wasn't sure I could see the dim light Molly said was straight ahead. It was hard enough making out rocks and plants right in front of me. She led and I followed. The only sounds were those of our feet against the hard windswept ground and the occasional coyote puncturing the evening air with its sad song. The sound in the dark gave me a strange sensation. A moment later, from another direction, the song was answered with a long, low howl. Instinctively I turned in the direction of the cry.

"Can you see the light yet?" she whispered.

"Light?" I whispered back. "I can barely see you." The moon was peeking through some clouds, providing a bit more help. I reached out to feel Molly's sleeve. My other hand felt for the Beretta's grip. The Walther in my boot was starting to rub the bone on my ankle. I stopped and stooped to readjust it.

"What are you doing?" Molly's voice came from somewhere in front of me.

"I'm pulling up my socks. They're bunched up." I didn't mention the gun because I had already gotten a long lecture about carrying three guns. It was true, now that we were on foot I did feel weighted down, but I also felt secure with my firepower.

"Come on, hurry up. And be careful. There are snakes out here. They don't like to be wakened from their sleep." Molly laughed softly.

"I know there are snakes out here." I didn't want to think about their possible presence. I knew enough about snakes to know that they would have snuggled up to a warm rock as the sun went down and weren't out here on the sand. Not this late, hopefully.

I thought I could see Molly waving for me to follow. We moved along in silence for another fifty yards until we saw a dim light. I couldn't make out whether it was a fire, the headlights of a car, or both. Whatever, it was definitely a light.

Molly stopped, dug out the binoculars from her pack and scanned the horizon. After a moment she motioned for me to follow. She was scouting our approach. Molly moved off to the right, skirting a stand of mesquite as cover. My heart was pounding. We were getting close. I wondered how Jake and Cloud were doing, how Cloud had reacted to Karen tagging along. I knew very little about Whitney Cloud, just that I didn't like him. And Molly didn't trust him one bit. I checked the Beretta again.

Molly led the way toward the light. It was just a glow on the desert, barely visible to my eye. Molly had homed in on it, like a ship following the beacon from a lighthouse. But, now, the light was moving. Then I realized that there were several lights. They were on foot. Finding their way with flashlights. Then the light disappeared.

"Where'd they go?"

"I don't know, Hank."

We walked another thirty yards and could see the truck and Bronco parked at the entrance to an arroyo. We headed away from the vehicles and climbed over rocks to the rim above the arroyo floor. As we approached the top, we hunched down behind a small stand of pinon trees and peeked over the edge. We could see four figures picking their way along the dried valley bottom, heading toward a dead end. A slab of rock at the end of the arroyo rose out of the desert, nearly a hundred feet high, blocking their path. The one I assumed to be Williams was taking baby steps while concentrating on his portable GPS. He stopped and put his hands on the massive slab while the others just stared.

"Holy shit!" I whispered, the enormity of the slab and what we were about to do hitting me with full force.

Molly reached for my hand. "This is it."

27
Jake
The Middle of the Night

We crept along slowly, our flashlights guiding our way through the arroyo's rocks, brush and loose sand. It took us about fifteen minutes to get to the other end, stopping to check the GPS coordinates whenever Williams needed more verification.

Fifteen minutes! Shit. It seemed like fifteen hours. We were so close, so anxious and yet time slowed exponentially. It already seemed like days ago that we'd started jostling our way across the desert. *Why was this part taking so long?*

I felt Karen nestle in tight. She'd been hanging very close to me ever since getting out of Cloud's truck. About an hour before, we'd stopped for a break. Williams had said he was sick of Cloud and his bullshit and didn't want to ride with him anymore. I'd said Williams could come in with us but Cloud had complained long and hard about that.

"Another case of the *bilagaana* teaming up against the red man." That was how he'd put it. But I knew that he was really worried about the three of us suddenly having all the information and dealing him out.

Against my better judgment, I'd told Karen to get in Cloud's truck. I didn't like letting her out of my sight but couldn't see any other way to keep us moving. She protested but did it anyway. As soon as the trucks had stopped, she'd raced over to me.

"Are you all right?" I'd asked as I opened my door.

She'd cemented herself to my side and told me that he hadn't touched her; just that she got a real creepy feeling from the way he looked at her.

"Did he say anything?"

"No. Not a word."

That didn't sound like Whitney, especially where women were concerned. Especially a woman like Karen. I'd reassured her that nothing bad was going to happen. We only had a few more hours and this deal would be all but over.

Now, we were all gathered in a small semi-circle, staring at the face of a seemingly impenetrable cliff. Williams stepped slowly forward until he was at the base of the rocks. He moved to the left, to the biggest rock, his hands caressing it like it was an old friend. He turned to the rest of us and announced, "We're here."

I couldn't see anything that would indicate a cave or a treasure. All I saw was one big fucking rock.

"Here?" Cloud sounded stunned. "This is it?"

Williams just kept touching the rock, slowly inching his way to the left.

"Shit!" Cloud spat. "I've been by this place a hundred times…" He never finished his thought, but I knew what he would have said. I knew what I'd have said, being this close to this much gold and not even knowing it.

I turned to Williams. "What do we need to do?"

He never looked up but answered, "Just follow me."

Silently, Williams checked the GPS and moved to his left. A few steps. Stop. Check. A few more steps. Stop. Check. He dropped to his knees and touched the ground. One by one, he moved a dozen smaller rocks. I went to help but he waved me off. Evidently, he wanted to do this part himself, the treasure hunter staking his claim. This was his moment.

After he moved another batch of small rocks, my flashlight detected the bars of a carefully hidden metal grate. It looked like the door of an old jail cell.

Williams picked up his flashlight and scanned the area to his left. He found a fallen branch about six feet long and went to get it. The three of us watched as he used the branch as a fulcrum and almost effortlessly lifted the heavy grate completely off. He gave it a healthy shove to get it out of our way.

We all turned our attention to the cave opening. It was wide enough for a man to squeeze through but there was no way a wheelbarrow would fit. That meant we'd have to carry the gold by hand and load the wheelbarrow outside the cave. And that meant extra work and extra time.

We all looked at each other one last time before entering the cave. *This was it.* We were finally here. While I wanted to savor this moment, Cloud ducked into the cave and disappeared into the darkness of the earth, his flashlight sending only flashes of light back to us. Williams followed and, to my surprise, Karen quickly filed right behind him. I grabbed my flashlight and edged my way into the cavern. So much for savoring the moment.

As our four beams of light independently searched the cave's boundaries, I was amazed by how big it was. And dry. We all stood there. Upright. Somehow, I'd imagined a small, swampy cave with bats and snakes and God knows what else. But this reminded me of a small garage, only much deeper and with more irregular features. Beams of light illuminated four different angles, forming eerie portraits of people on the brink of something extraordinary.

Williams headed to the rear of the cave. "It's over here." I immediately started to follow but Karen slowed me. She nodded covertly toward Cloud, who was holding back.

She whispered to me, "Better not let him get behind us."

I nodded and agreed. "C'mon, Whitney, let's share this moment together."

I sensed a mountain of reluctance on his part but eventually he joined us and we all followed Williams. We took slow and careful steps across the rough cavern floor. We were so close to the gold, none of us wanted to risk a broken leg or twisted ankle. Our beams went on ahead of us, crisscrossing in a staccato-like pattern until they finally converged on one spot. One golden spot.

It was hard to get an accurate image of the entire picture. Our flashlights were ricocheting from right to left and back again, holding for an instant and then moving, searching for more. Ten bags. Twenty. I'd see a half-opened bag of gold coins and then go look for more. Thirty bags. Cloud's light was doing the same thing. So were Williams' and Karen's. We were like kids in a candy store.

We stood there, the four of us, transfixed by the magic of our beams highlighting millions and millions and millions of dollars of gold. Karen's one word comment rang true.

"Cool."

* * *

I didn't feel like a multi-millionaire. I didn't feel independently wealthy or like I was going to be the next subject on *Lifestyles of the Rich and Famous*. I just felt tired. My muscles ached and my back hurt. *Seeing* the treasure had been mind-boggling, euphoric, even overwhelming.

Carrying that same treasure was none of those things. Instead, it was one of the worst experiences in my life. First, gold is *heavy*. A bag of gold is even heavier. Forty bags of gold were almost unimaginably heavy. Getting it out of the cave and into the wheelbarrows proved to be harder and more time-consuming than I was prepared for. As Williams had told us, the bags were rotted and weakened to the point where we wouldn't be able to use them. That meant we had to scoop up the coins and fill some of them into new sacks and hand-carry them through the narrow entrance and stack them in the wheelbarrows.

Second, pushing those wheelbarrows back and forth through a hundred yards of loose sand was damned near impossible. The weight we were carrying made it difficult to steer and we were struggling against a small incline all the way back to the truck.

Third, Williams started complaining almost immediately, saying he couldn't carry very much and that he was tired and didn't feel very good. Karen did her best but she just didn't have the physical strength to haul much. At least she didn't whine about it. So Cloud and I were left to do most of the work.

Fourth, I didn't trust Cloud. I'd taken his keys and had his truck blocked with mine. That didn't mean he wasn't planning something. But that's where Hank came in. I hoped.

On several of my trips, when I was sure no one else was around, I scanned the area for Hank. I stood out in the open, making myself very visible, looking for some sign that Hank was there. That he'd made it out here. That he hadn't fallen victim to some Cloud-fueled double-cross.

I scared myself with that last thought. Suppose Hank hadn't figured out my "pissing on the tire" signal? Suppose he'd started to follow but had been cut off by Cloud's cohorts? Suppose he was dead?

I stopped myself from going any further down that path. I had to trust that

Hank and Molly were out there. I also had to keep a close eye on Cloud, just in case.

The final trip was about to take place. Williams had stopped his whining and was scouring the cave floor for the last remaining coins. I sat down and waited for Cloud and Karen to return.

"You going to do this again? Look for more treasures?" I asked, making small talk.

"Maybe," Williams answered without looking up.

"If you do, what would you do different?"

He smiled in the dim light. "Make sure it's not on a reservation."

I smiled back. I was about to tell him to give me a call if he ever needed any help but I didn't. I'd had enough adventure to last me for a long, long time.

Williams grabbed his flashlight and headed out, saying something about being "damn glad to be getting out of here."

I wanted to respond but I was too tired. Besides, I needed to sit and think through the next steps of the plan. If Cloud was going to pull something, I wanted to be ready. I checked my gun and faced the entrance.

Karen came through the narrow entrance and slumped down beside me. "Hot tub. Then a massage. Yeah. In that order."

I turned and faced her. "And about twelve hours of uninterrupted sleep," I added, picking up on her wavelength.

"And room service. And chocolate." Her eyes were closed, apparently visualizing what lay ahead.

I watched her face. So beautiful, so inviting. "And a bit of the bubbly…"

That brought a smile to her face. Her eyes remained closed. "And something very 'spensive…" Karen was so tired that she was having trouble pronouncing her words. "…I want some of that Dom Per-ig-nam…Peer-ik-nerm…" She gave a tired little giggle.

"Dom Perignon." It was Cloud, directly behind us. We both turned at the same time. He stood there, looking twelve feet tall, blocking the opening of the cavern. I made a move to get up but Karen pulled me back.

"He's got a gun!"

I looked. It was at his side. My eyes shot to his, searching for a sign that this wasn't what I thought it was, that we weren't about to die.

"Whitney?" I mocked. "This isn't part of the plan."

He didn't answer. Not with words. He just moved steadily closer, raising his weapon as he neared. Karen edged in closer and I could feel her heart racing as she hugged me. I had to keep my head. I made a slow move to stand up, but a deliberate wave of his gun convinced me I'd be better off right where I was.

Okay. I could deal with this sitting down. "So," I began, not sure where I was heading. "Now you're greedy and think you can have it all?" I waited for a response but didn't get one. He seemed more preoccupied with Karen than with my challenge.

I tried again. "Let me guess. Mr. Williams is out reprogramming my security system and the two of you are going to ride off into the sunset." I remembered the time and tried to see if that would get his attention. "Or into the sunrise. It's getting light out there. Aren't you worried?"

Cloud pulled out a cigarette and lit it. The sulfur and tobacco smell filled the cavern and I desperately wanted a cigarette. *Does the condemned man have any last requests?* "These coins aren't going to be very easy to get…"

He glared at me. "I'm not worried. Now, shut the fuck up and give me the pass codes!"

"Who'd you cut a deal with?"

A lazy puff of smoke was his only response. And then it hit me. Manny wasn't the enemy. Manny hadn't double-crossed me. It was Cloud, making me think it was Manny, getting me to look everywhere but where I should have been looking. I kicked myself for not seeing it sooner. Or at all.

"So," I eased into a more comfortable tone, "…let ol' Jake do all the work and then take it away from him. That ain't very nice." Having figured out that Cloud was more greedy than smart gave me something to work with. "What are you gonna do with all this, Cloud? Go door-to-door selling gold coins?" I faked a smile. "Or melt 'em down and sell it to some assay office?" I kept going, trying to get a reaction. "Or bring in a handful to the local pawn shop. That ought to turn about a thousand a day—until the Feds come looking for you." I paused. No reaction. "Or hadn't you thought about that? Hadn't you figured that sooner or later, someone would realize that some poor Indian bastard trading Double Eagles like they were cheap fucking trinkets maybe ought to be brought in for questioning?" I couldn't be sure, but I thought I was starting to get to him. I took a left turn with my logic. "It's not too late, Whitney. We could still work something out."

He took a step closer. "Jake, you're not in a position to do much bargaining. I want those pass codes." His words were cold and hard. "And I don't want you to call me Whitney ever again."

I didn't like the way this was going. For the first time, I figured he was actually going to kill us. True, unbridled panic washed over me. I repeated my last statement, slower this time. "You don't have to do this. We can work something out. I could help you fence them." My brain raced with other, desperate thoughts. "What about the three million in cash I'm getting when I deliver the coins.? You want to just throw that away?"

Cloud looked at me through slit eyes and dragged deep on his cigarette. "Three million?" He half smiled. "Now ain't that just like you, Jake? Gettin' yourself a bigger slice of pie." He shook his head. "Sorry, Jake, but getting your cash ain't part of my plan."

"Or," I countered, "you can take the gold. All of it. Just let us go."

The flashlight I'd set on the ground cast its light upward, revealing a frightful sneer. "I already got the gold."

"Okay. You got the gold. You got nothing to gain by…"

"By what? Killing you?"

I swallowed and nodded. The threat of death had coated us like an oily film but the word hadn't been spoken. Now that it had, my fear multiplied and I reached for my trump card. "You sure you wanna fuck with Manny?" I asked.

Cloud froze. "What?"

"Manny's the money man."

"Shit…" Cloud rubbed his forehead.

"Yeah, Manny. Who else do you think has the money to pull off this deal? He won't be happy to lose out on the gold. He'll hunt you down and kill you, Cloud."

Cloud became frantic. "He doesn't know who your partners are. You said so yourself, Jake." He began to pace. "You fuckin' weasel. You'd say anything right now to save your skin." He smoked and paced and fretted. "Manny doesn't know how to find me." Cloud stopped and took two steps toward me.

"If you want to believe that, you go right ahead." My confidence was building. "But deep down, you know as well as I do that as soon as these coins hit the market, Manny will hear about it. And when he does…"

Cloud stared at me, evaluating my every word. I stared back; this was not the time to show any weakness. Finally, Cloud gave me an almost imperceptible nod.

"You, Jake Marley, are a liar. Manny would never get involved in something like this and even if he was, he won't find me—ever!" Cloud raised the gun and pointed it first at my head then slowly over to Karen's. I felt sick. It was bad enough that some long-forgotten cave in the middle of nowhere was going to be my final resting place, but I hadn't counted on this for her.

"You." He pointed the barrel in Karen's face. "Tie up lover-boy." He tossed her a length of rope. She nervously reached for it, her eyes going from Cloud's to mine. "Then you and I can have some fun while Jake watches."

She gasped and shook. I glared at Cloud. "Hey, man, she ain't nothin' to you. Just let her go. Do whatever you're gonna do to me but let her go."

He turned his attention to me. Fully. "Jake…" His eyes narrowed again to tiny, menacing slits. "Seems like every so often I just have to kick the shit out of you…"

In an instant, he swung the gun from in front of Karen's face and slammed it into the side of my head. The pain of metal against flesh and bone buckled my universe. I toppled over, sprawling on the ground.

More pain. More confusion. What? Where? My head throbbed with pain. Thud! A kick to my ribs…

"Jake!" Karen screamed.

I fought to stay with it, to hold on. All around darkness encircled me, covering me with its comforting, pain-easing oblivion. The more I gave in to it, the less my head pounded.

"Jake! Help!"

The voice drifted away as the blackness enveloped me and made the pain fade away.

A piercing scream was the last thing I heard.

28
Hank
Dawn Wednesday

"Hank, give me the binoculars." Molly raised her voice. "Quick!" she demanded.

I turned around and handed them over. "What?"

Molly had the binoculars to her eyes, her hushed voice was alarmed. "Cloud has a gun."

"Shit!" Now she had my attention.

"I just saw Cloud go into the cave with a gun."

"Are you sure?"

"Yes. We'd better get down there. Now!" Molly was already on her feet, digging through her pack. She pulled out the .38 she'd waved at Wayne Wayne a few nights earlier. I scrambled to my feet and Molly led the way over the edge of our hiding place. Small rocks were sent tumbling down the side of the arroyo. Molly picked her way like a mountain goat, gracefully using the smallest hold of a root or rock to balance on, just long enough to make the next step. Within seconds she had a lead of several yards. I slid and stumbled and lost my balance, skidding down the loose sand and rock like a surfer. Molly had reached the gentle slope near the bottom and was now almost at a full run.

A scream echoed from underground. I grabbed at a sagebrush branch and regained my balance. Molly was only twenty yards from the cave. She danced from rock to rock for cover, closing in, the gun held in her right hand, pointed at the sky. Another scream rose, intensifying our urgency. I reached

239

the arroyo floor and quickly hid behind a large pile of rocks. I immediately pulled out the Beretta and flipped off the safety. The Walther had dug into my ankle on the descent and I quickly rearranged it. Molly was working her way forward, toward the den.

Karen came screaming from the cave's mouth. Yelling and cursing. Her blouse was torn and hung loose. She stumbled and fell to the ground. Not a step behind came Cloud, a big ugly Magnum in his right hand.

"Stop, you bitch, or I'll kill you right now." Cloud's hair was a tangled mess. His shirt was open and revealed muscles developed from hours of pumping weights or hard labor. Karen scrambled to her feet.

"Help!" Karen quickly looked around to see if we had heard her call. "Stay away from me!" Cloud towered over Karen as she stepped back from him. "Don't touch me, you filthy pig!" she screamed. "I'll kill you!"

Cloud laughed and shook his head. "And how you going to do that, bitch?" For his size, Cloud was surprisingly quick. He reached out and caught a handful of Karen's hair as she tried to maneuver away from his outstretched hand. One fast yank and he had her in a one-armed bear hug. He tore at what remained of her blouse, while holding her tight against his body. Karen kicked and clawed. Scratching at his eyes, she broke from his grip but Cloud was too swift for her retreat. He clutched her wrist and swung her around, as if he was playing a game of crack the whip. Karen spun in a circle and landed hard on the dirt near the entrance to the cave.

Cloud turned to face her. "You don't even have the decency to talk to me while you ride in my truck," he spat toward her. "I'm going to make you regret that." He started to undo his belt buckle and stepped toward Karen. Karen threw a handful of sand at his face. Cloud merely covered his eyes and continued moving forward. Karen crab-walked backwards toward the cave.

"Quit moving or I'll put a bullet in you right now."

Karen stopped. She tried to cover herself but there wasn't enough of her blouse left.

"We're gonna have some fun now. I only wish lover boy was out here to see it."

Molly had worked her way within fifteen feet of Cloud. I was still a good thirty feet away. I raised the Beretta and brought Cloud's back into my sight.

My finger tensed on the trigger and I started to squeeze. The big man began to drop his pants. Molly moved from her hiding place and quickly took three steps closer.

"Now, take off the rest of your clothes." Cloud raised the Magnum and pointed it at Karen.

Karen looked up and saw Molly. Cloud realized Karen had seen something and started to turn. Just as he did, Molly took the last couple steps. She raised the .38 and slammed it into the side of his head. I could hear the force of the blow. Blood splattered on his face. Cloud staggered back one step, trying to maintain his balance, his trousers now around his ankles. Karen scurried to get out of his way, as he teetered back and forth. Cloud blinked and wiped at the blood in his eyes. He took one step toward Molly and started to raise his gun. Molly caught him square in the groin with her right foot. I could *feel* the impact and flinched. Cloud gave out a harrowing cry of agony and fell to his knees. His face showed the sheer pain he felt. He dropped his gun and covered his crotch with his hands, as if this would help his suffering. Molly stepped forward and kicked him right on the end of his chin. The sound of teeth breaking made me cringe. Blood flew from his mouth. Cloud's eyes rolled back, he swayed a couple times and he fell forward, landing with a thud, face down in the sand.

Karen crouched on the ground, hugging herself. Tears were rolling down her cheeks. She started to shake and then the sobs came. Molly stepped over Cloud and picked up his gun. Then she bent down to comfort Karen. She took off her jean jacket and put it around Karen's shoulders.

I flipped the safety back on the Beretta and walked toward Cloud's body. Blood had started to pool on the ground around his head. His breathing was shallow and labored. I rolled him over before he smothered in the sand. Blood was coming from the corners of his mouth and nose. I looked down at the flattened nose that was pushed too far to the left side of his face to ever be normal again. Either the fall or Molly's kick had broken it. Ants were already starting to gather at the edges of the blood pool. A white tooth in the pool gleamed in the morning sun.

"*Holy shit,*" I said to myself. I bent over Cloud and then patted him down for other weapons. I lifted a large Bowie knife from his belt. There was fresh blood along the blade. I immediately turned and looked around for Jake.

Molly was helping Karen to her feet. Karen put her arms into the jean jacket, revealing her bare breasts. I looked away for a moment. When Karen had herself covered I quickly moved towards the two women.

"Where's Jake?" I asked with urgency.

"He's in the cave," Karen sobbed, her eyes fixed on Cloud's body.

I stepped past her and touched Molly's arm. "Holy shit, lady. I'll never cross you," I whispered. She was breathing heavily, trying to get the violence under wraps.

Karen slowly moved to Cloud's body. I could see her saying something but couldn't hear it at first. Then she kicked him in the side and started to scream. "You fucker! You fucker!" Karen kicked him a second time. Molly let her kick him a third time, before she interceded. She pointed Karen in the direction of the cave and then grabbed a length of rope and started tying Cloud's hands behind his back.

I stepped into the cave. My eyes hadn't adjusted to the dark, but Jake's moans told me he was alive.

29
Jake
Wednesday Morning

I could feel sand stuck to my lips and tongue. I spit—or tried to—but my mouth was too dry. Instead, I rolled over and started to get up. Pain! Torture-chamber pain. I dropped back to the ground, the back of my head hitting a small stone, igniting another barrage of pain-induced fireworks.

The massive throbbing slowly relented and I opened my eyes. I saw the figure of a large man with a flashlight edging toward me. For some reason, I *knew* he wasn't going to hurt me. I tried to focus, to get a clear view of who it was but it took too much work. After a few confusing seconds, I just closed my eyes and gave up.

While I lay there, a vision of a partially assembled jigsaw puzzle came to mind. The corner pieces and the ones along the edges were already in place, framing a dark-hued tableau. I picked up other pieces, looking for clues. One showed stacks of gold coins. Another held a woman's face with a Mona Lisa-inspired smile. One had a police badge. Another had Hank's face on it. That made me feel better. If Hank was here, I was going to be all right.

A few other pieces started to fall into place, connecting names and objects and meanings and places. The woman with the smile was Karen. Gold. There was lots of gold. The badge belonged to someone named Molly. She was a cop—with Hank? I mentally put that one back down, deciding it was too weird.

From someplace so far away that it surely couldn't have been in this universe, I heard someone calling my name. Faint, at first, almost unrecognizable, it grew in strength and intensity.

"Jake?"

Other words. Other questions.

"Are you all right?"

Someone touching me. Someone lifting me up.

"Jake?"

More voices. More questions. More noise. More people.

"Jake, sweetheart, talk to me."

Sweetheart? I could have sworn the first voice was Hank's.

"Jake, lover, are you all right?"

However confused I was about my immediate surroundings, there were a few things I knew with dead-on certainty. Hank had never called me sweetheart or lover. I opened my eyes, slowly.

"Jake?"

It was the woman named Karen. Her face was about a foot away from mine, making it hard for me to focus. I could feel her warm breath on my face. I tried to smile. Her hair was ruffled and she had dirt smeared on one side of her face. Dried blood caked one corner of her mouth. I shifted my eyes to the left and found Hank. A dark-haired woman stood behind him. Molly. Her name is Molly. Molly the cop.

"Talk to me." Karen's hands went to some place on the top of my head, lightly touching the epicenter of my pain. That one touch did two things. It set off yet another wave of throbbing torment throughout my body. It also triggered a flood of memories, instantly bringing them up from wherever they'd been hiding.

Gold. The cave. Williams. Manny. "Cloud!" I tried to get up, my anger pushing forward and driving my uncoordinated limbs to get up. Cloud had done this to me. I had to get him.

Two pair of hands held me down. I looked to see who was keeping me from settling the score.

"Slow down, buddy," Hank cautioned.

"Take it easy, lover," Karen spoke soothingly, her hands leaving little traces across my forehead.

"Don't worry about Cloud," Molly said as she glanced toward the opening of the cave. "He isn't going anywhere." Her words had an air of certainty that made me believe her.

I relaxed—collapsed?—back to the earthen floor. "What just happened here?" Even though I was sure I knew what'd happened to me, I wanted to hear from someone, anyone, what I'd missed while I was *away*.

Hank supplied me with necessary details, making sure I knew that Cloud had his dick in the dirt and that Molly had been the one who put it there.

"Williams?"

"Don't know." Hank looked to Molly as if to ask for any new information and then quickly back to me. "Cloud had a knife with fresh blood on it but that's all we know."

Molly's shadow crossed over me. "I think Williams is dead. And both of you would be dead if he hadn't..." She looked at Karen, thought for a moment and then continued. "...hadn't been distracted." She turned toward Hank. "I told you Cloud was bad news."

Molly's statement struck me hard. The two of us were alive only because of Cloud's animal lust for Karen. If he'd been thinking straight, if he hadn't wanted to fuck Karen, the two of us would be dead right now. Our little get-rich-quick trip to the desert had turned more than ugly. Cloud had killed Williams. He probably had something to do with DeDe's murder. And I was the one who brought him to the table. I glanced from Molly's eyes to Karen's and finally to Hank's. "I'm sorry, Hank. This is my fault. All of it."

Hank nodded. "Let's sort this out some other time." He put a comforting hand on shoulder. "Right now, I say it's time we put this hell-hole a couple of hundred miles behind us."

I stood up and tested the stability of my legs. Not bad. Not for someone who had just glimpsed the other side. My head hurt more than I could measure but I still pushed myself to get to the cave entrance and out into the world.

Molly was bent over Cloud making sure the knot was still tight. He rested face down, his arms tied behind him, his pants down around his ankles.

"What about Cloud?" Molly asked. It wasn't as much a question as it was a challenge.

Hank answered for me. "Cloud isn't invited." He looked at me to verify that we were on the same track.

Outside, Karen pointed at her attacker. "What are we going to do with him?"

"I don't know. Leave him here, I suppose." I ran a couple of other scenarios through my brain but none seemed as good or as easy as leaving him here to fend for himself. Before he could mount any kind of threat, we'd all be long gone, turning gold into greenbacks and on our way to the good life.

A mixture of laughter and coughing interrupted my thoughts. Low, maniacal, not-of-this-earth laughter. A millisecond later I realized it was coming from Cloud. I looked at my partners, partly to confirm that they were hearing the same thing I was.

Cloud's laughter subsided to a point where he could speak. "Jake…" he coughed out, "you aren't going to leave your ol' buddy out here to die, are you?"

I tensed. I wanted to kick him in the head, but I controlled myself. I figured the bastard probably was just pushing my buttons. I forced myself to cool down.

I nudged him with my boot. "Quiet down, ol' buddy." I put an extra helping of sarcasm on my salutation, "Or I'll let super-cop here use you for kung fu practice…"

Molly stepped silently closer and stood over Whitney. "Where's Williams?"

He flinched but immediately tried to regain his cool. "You mean *computer head*?" Cloud attempted to move but found the ropes too restrictive and gave up. As bad as he looked, he was surprisingly coherent.

"I mean Williams." She nudged his side with her boot.

Cloud tried to smile. His mouth revealing large, empty spaces. "I *deleted* him."

"He's dead?" she affirmed. "You killed him?"

"Aren't you supposed to read me my rights before you ask me questions like that?" Whitney Cloud was suddenly more alert.

"Only if you're going to be arrested."

"You're not going to arrest me?"

"You have to be alive to be arrested." Her words were so flat and cold that even I felt a chill.

For the first time, Cloud showed signs of panic. "Cut the shit! You're a cop, you can't just kill me."

She kneeled, bent forward and said something to him in Navajo. While I didn't know the exact interpretation, I knew it was an insult of the highest order. Then, in English, "Don't be so sure of what we may or may not do." She reached over and touched him on the shoulder. "People die from *natural causes* out here in the desert all the time. They fall down and break a leg. They get lost. Confused. They run out of water…" She patted his shoulder, mocking some kind of caring response.

I stood up and motioned everyone to follow me. We had to figure out exactly what we were going to do with Whitney and I didn't want him in on the process.

Karen spoke up first. "What are we going to do with him?"

"We leave him," I answered as firmly as I could. "We leave him to his own resources. I'll drain his gas tank so he can't follow us." To me, it was our only option. It wasn't murder and it wasn't something stupid like bringing him in. Whitney *could* survive out here. I also knew he could die, especially in the shape he was in. And like it or not, we would all be responsible for his death. But it was the only way out. It was a solution I could live with.

"Any objections?" I looked at each of my partners for their response. Hank immediately agreed, adding that we should leave him tied him up to make it that much harder for him to survive.

Molly reluctantly shook her head. "I can't support this. Cloud might die out here and he might not. Either way, he killed a man and I can't just let him walk away from that."

Karen mumbled something about cutting off body parts.

I was about to respond when I saw the glint of metal catch the sun. A tenth of a second later, I *felt* a bullet whiz over my head and immediately heard the shot and the ricochet. A second shot. It ricocheted off some rocks. I grabbed Karen and dove for the ground.

30
Hank
Early Wednesday Morning

The crack of gunfire was deafening as it echoed among the rocks. I ducked behind a large boulder and Molly dove for cover behind a pile of rocks. Bullets were making the sand dance everywhere.

The action brought sudden life to Cloud. He raised his head to see where the bullets were coming from and then wriggled and squirmed his way toward the opening of the cave. More shots splat into the sand. I searched for Molly but only saw Jake and Karen scurrying for cover, back toward the sagebrush.

More shots caused Cloud to hurry his furtive struggle. I pressed my back tightly against the boulder that was now my survival raft and slid down to a sitting position. I took a deep breath and realized that it was now eerily quiet. I looked around for Molly. She was still nowhere in sight.

Someone had been waiting for us to cross the open ground. Their aim had been off and, for the moment, we had escaped. Who were they? Manny's cohorts? Cloud's posse? Why hadn't we seen them while we were watching? Had they followed us?

I pulled out the Beretta and checked the clip. I slapped it back into place and then reached for the Smith and Wesson and spun the cylinder. It still held six rounds. I placed it on the ground and checked the Walther in my boot. Having the three guns did little to make me feel better. I wondered what Jake had done with the Beretta I had given him.

Cloud hadn't been able to move much from where he'd fallen. Two quick shots shattered the momentary silence. The first tore a hole through an overturned wheelbarrow. The second raised the sand near Cloud's head. He dug the toes of his boots into the earth, inching himself toward cover. A third shot snapped and a fourth found its mark. Cloud screamed in pain as a large dark stain grew around a tattered hole in his jeans. Two more shots in rapid succession made the sand dance near his head. Then it was quiet again.

I couldn't tell exactly where the sniper was. The angle of the shots suggested he was above us. I searched the rim's ridge, but saw no one. The sun was still low in the sky. A man could be standing in the open and still be hidden in a deep shadow. But I seriously doubted anyone would be standing out where they might be seen. I looked around for a sign of Molly. Jake and Karen were together, but separated from both Molly and me. Whoever was doing the shooting either knew where we all were, was secure in his position, or both. We had been effectively cut off from each other. Two more shots interrupted my thinking. Again, Cloud was the target. His cry of anguish told me that at least one of the bullets had found its mark. Cloud was almost to the edge of the cave. His progress had been painstakingly slow. It appeared to me that Cloud's assassin was only toying with him, allowing him to reach the edge of safety before putting a bullet in him. There was only twenty yards of open ground between Cloud and me, but there was nothing I could do. A mad dash to help him would only bring my own death. I watched Cloud lying in the rays of the rising sun, powerless.

Then, a solitary shot rang out, splitting the back of Cloud's head. It *exploded* like an overripe melon rolling off the kitchen counter and hitting the floor. A fountain of blood erupted from where the back of his head had been, turning the sand black as it pooled. I recoiled from the hideous sight, pressing tight against my rock. Now that the assassin had found the exact distance, he pumped two more shots into what was left of Cloud's head. A succession of three more shots shredded his lifeless body, making it recoil in response.

I could tell by the sound that the shots were coming from a high-powered rifle. But the sound just bounced around the rocks and didn't help me pinpoint the distance. The marksman could be using a scope and be a mile away. But, knowing the layout of our predicament, I figured our assassin was near the arroyo's entrance, making the distance no more than a hundred yards. He probably had taken to high ground and had been watching us, waiting for us to get close enough for an easy kill. Jake had made the right decision to find cover in the sagebrush. Frantically I searched for Molly. There was still no sign of her. She could have gone back the way Jake had. Or headed to the right, where a stand of chaparral provided good cover.

I carefully searched the steep sides of the arroyo again, looking for the hiding place of the person trying to kill us. Then it dawned on me there could be two, three, a whole army of armed killers out there, each taking turns using Cloud for target practice. I pressed tighter against the rock, feeling more vulnerable than ever. Everything was quiet, everyone was waiting.

I squeezed the grip on the Beretta. Slowly I peeked around the bottom of the boulder. My heart began to pound. My teeth were clenched tight, working the muscles in my jaw. I saw nothing and nothing happened. I pulled back. My mind raced with the same questions. *How long had we been watched? Did they follow us here? Did they know who we were? Or that we were armed?* It was beginning to appear that my hand had been called and I would have to show my cards. But not just yet.

I figured I had three options. I could wait and see if Molly had taken care of the bad guys. I could wait for the bad guys to come looking for me, which made me a sitting duck. Or I could go looking for them.

I picked up the Chief Special .45, put it in my waistband and took a deep breath. I wasn't going to wait for Molly or for the bad guys to come looking for me. There were several yards of open ground between my boulder and the chaparral the way Molly might have gone. The other way was mostly large rocks, which would provide good cover, but the rocks led to a wall that was almost straight up to the rim. I glanced back to the right. The several yards of open ground looked farther across than before. My other choice was to pick my way along the wall of rocks, skirting the open patch of sand that was now Cloud's grave and heading back to search for Jake and Karen.

I wiped the sweat from my brow. How many were out there waiting? They could be moving in tandem, communicating with walkie-talkies. They could be anywhere by now.

A trickle of sweat worked its way down my back. I had to move. If I retreated towards Jake, I'd just be circling the wagons. If I broke into the open and drew some fire, it might help Molly or Jake pinpoint where our nemesis was. If I kept thinking, I'd just twist my mind into a pretzel. I crouched and readied for my sprint across the open ground.

I ran. My legs felt heavy in the soft sand as I ran for a solid hiding place. I was almost across to safety when the first shot whizzed past and ricocheted off the large rock I was heading for. I dove head first, as if stealing second base, landing on my belly behind the rock. Two more shots rang out, but they were too late to find their mark. I was winded and my adrenaline was rushing. My ears pounded. But now was no time to rest. I jumped from the rock into the chaparral. It tore at my shirt and hair. My face was scratched and blood trickled from my left ear. I waited a second, listening, hoping for a sound, anything. I got down on my hands and knees and crawled under the thick evergreen growth.

Two shots shattered the silence. They came from the opposite end of the arroyo. Who was shooting? It sounded like a Beretta or maybe Molly's .38. Had Jake or Molly joined in? Were they shooting at anyone or just drawing the attention their way? The rifle answered with a single shot. I used the diversion to work my way in the direction of the trucks. I figured they were not more than fifty or sixty yards away.

I was huffing and puffing now. All I could see was underbrush. I fell back on my haunches when a jackrabbit burst from its hiding place, almost in my face. I sat down. I had to catch my breath. As my breathing returned to normal, I thought I could hear a voice. I strained to catch the sound. It was a man whispering loudly. He was trying to get someone's attention. I couldn't hear what was being said. The valley distorted sound, making something distant appear closer than it really was. I hoped the whispering was near.

My shirt clung to my back, soaked in sweat. I crawled through the undergrowth on my hands and knees, the Beretta in my right hand. Every couple of yards I stopped and strained to hear the whispering. My progress was tedious, as I tried to move without making a sound. I reached the edge of the chaparral and rested against a formation of rocks that blocked my way. I tried to control my breathing so that I could hear. I shut my eyes and concentrated on listening. There was nothing, and then, metal against metal, the sound of a clip being inserted in a rifle. Then the sound of a bolt-action lever. I waited. No other sounds came. I pressed against the rocks, slowly rose and peeked up through the vegetation. Fifteen feet in front of me was a man. He was dressed in a black t-shirt and camouflage pants. His hair was pulled back in a ponytail and dark sunglasses hid his eyes. He had a high-powered rifle with a scope. Today, he didn't look like a rodeo cowboy or a hard-luck poker player. Slim looked every bit the part of a cold-blooded killer.

I slid back down the rocks to my hiding place. Was Slim alone? Was he the whisperer? How close was the person he was talking to? Should I spring from my cover, shoot him and draw the others out? Should I wait for Molly? What was I supposed to do, demand that he throw down the rifle and surrender? *Hands behind your head?* I thought of Cloud and realized these guys weren't here to reason with.

Enough! I checked the safety on the Beretta. Surprise was on my side. I stood up. The rocks shielded me to chest height. I rested my two-handed grip on the rock ledge to steady my aim. Just as my finger tightened on the trigger, my quarry turned to see what had caused the commotion from the underbrush. Our eyes locked and I squeezed off three quick rounds. Slim's chest exploded from the impact. The hollow points took out most of his lungs and heart as they exited his back. He was dead before he hit the deck. Blood gushed from his body, covering where he lay.

I stared wide-eyed at what I had done. Several shots rang out and ricocheted along the rocks near where I stood. I fell back into the chaparral. The branches tore my flesh and poked at me. I scurried into its protection, diving against the ground. I covered my head with my hands, as if they would shield me from the bullets that were flying. The chaparral hid me but did not stop the bullets that tore through the vegetation. I quickly reversed my direction and crawled back towards the rock ledge. Once I reached the solid mass, I pressed tightly against it. I doubted if my assassins would come into the briar patch looking for me.

After I caught my breath, I started to crawl along the rocks away from where the shooting had taken place. I headed for the far side of the arroyo. I tucked the Beretta in my belt and started to climb hand over hand up the side towards the rim. If I was quick, maybe I'd reach the top before I was spotted. I hoped this maneuver wouldn't be expected and the others would still be hunting for me in the chaparral. I wanted to circle around to where the trucks were parked.

I looked up the steep rock. This side of the arroyo went almost straight up. As I climbed, my hands ached, gripping for a hold among the loose rock. I hugged my body as close to the steep side as I could, using every muscle to keep from falling to my death. When I finally reached the top I stopped for a quick second to catch my breath and look around. I could see the path we had taken from the cave, but I couldn't spy Jake and Karen or Molly in the deep underbrush. This was good. If I couldn't see them maybe our pursuers couldn't either. There hadn't been any shots since my flight through the chaparral.

I started the descent. Small rocks tumbled ahead of me. It was either a choice of going slow and quiet or reaching the bottom as quickly as possible. I chose to run. The guns in my belt stabbed at me. I was moving faster than I could keep my balance. Several times I fell and rolled, only righting myself through sheer determination and fear. I reached the bottom without doing much damage to myself. I headed for a large rock and rested. I looked back to see if my escape had brought any observers. I pulled out the Beretta and took a deep breath. When I decided the coast was clear, I headed for the mouth of the arroyo.

Carefully I picked my way, dancing from rock to rock as quietly as I could. Nervously my thumb rubbed the texture of the safety. I figured that the opening to the arroyo was just ahead. There might be guards waiting with the vehicles. I took a quick look around the rock and pulled back. A man was sitting on the ground just on the other side. He appeared to also be hiding. Moving quickly, I stepped out and leveled the gun at the man. He was a spindly little man with his throat slit; his head had almost been severed. Blood covered his shirt. He was tucked back into the rocks. If it hadn't been for all the blood, he might have been mistaken for a napper. But he was dead, sleeping the eternal rest. Was this Williams? Even though I had never actually seen his face, I figured it must be the guy who started this mess.

Twenty yards away, a black Jeep was parked near Jake's truck and the Bronco. It could have been the Jeep I'd seen on the highway the previous night. We'd followed Jake and Cloud, and Slim had followed us. I shook my head in disbelief, crept to the driver's side near the rear and leaned against the door. In the back was a pair of night vision binoculars. It had been easy for them. They had probably sat by the side of the road and watched as Cloud circled in the night.

I squeezed the Beretta and headed for the path to the entrance. I hoped that I was now at their backs and that I could surprise whoever had been stalking us. I made my way along to the narrow entrance, listening for a clue to their whereabouts. Fifteen feet ahead the path took a jog and I didn't have a clear view of what was around the corner. I gripped the gun with both hands and jumped to the opposite side of the path. The first shot nipped my arm, making me drop the Beretta. A second shot was wide of my head. I dove for the ground, searching for my lost pistol.

"Stop! Don't move," a voice screamed. "Or you're dead!"

I quit moving and stayed bent over. I could feel the big .45 cutting into my stomach. With my right hand I gripped the handle of the revolver and waited for what would happen next.

"Now ge-et up, slow and easy," the voice growled. "Where de others?"

I raised my head just enough to see that not more than twenty feet away stood a dark-haired man with a large moustache and a rifle pointed in my direction. I froze. It was the one of the two Mexicans from Smiley's.

"Slowly." He gestured with the rifle barrel for me to stand.

As I rose, so did the rifle. As soon as I got to my feet, a shot rang out from the other side of the arroyo. When the Mexican snapped to look, I had just enough time to draw my Smith and Wesson and hide it behind my back.

When he turned back to me, a smile slowly creased the rifleman's face. "You should have let us dance with de pretty lady. Now I'm going to keel you, *Señor*, just like the cute little lady we had to keel. Was she your wife?" The man gave a vile laugh.

My hand squeezed tight on the .45's grip.

"Don't shoot him," came another voice. The second Mexican from Smiley's stepped into view. He held a large revolver in his right hand and a cigarette in his left. He took a drag and slowly let the smoke out through his nose and mouth as he spoke. "He's our bait to bring the others in," he muttered as his head nodded toward the deep end of the arroyo.

I knew I'd be dead in a matter of minutes but I desperately wanted to take one or both of them with me. I kept my eyes locked with the first man, Miguel. Suddenly a shot rang out and the back of Miguel's head exploded. Before he hit the dirt, I drew my Smith and Wesson and fired at the other man. The big gun kicked like a mule. My first shot caught him square in the side of his face and he fell with a thud. Both men lay perfectly still, their blood joining in a dark pool in the sand.

"Don't shoot, Hank, it's me!" Molly stepped from the shadows with Cloud's .44 Magnum locked in both her hands.

* * *

"Holy, shit. Is that all of them?" Jake asked.

"Yeah," Molly answered. "There're these two and another that Hank shot over there." Molly pointed toward the rocks that rose to our right.

"There's nothing left of that one guy's face," grimaced Jake.

I looked at the Smith and Wesson still in my hand. Then toward Molly, our eyes met.

Karen hid her face in Jake's shoulder as he stroked her hair. She hadn't looked directly at the two dead men.

"I can't believe those are the guys from Smiley's." Jake shook his head. "And Slim. I guess this was one time when Smiley's picking fish wasn't so good. What the hell?"

"I don't know, Jake," I replied.

"What do we do now?" Jake asked.

Molly bent down and picked up my Beretta. "Come on, we've got some work to do," she directed. "We should get moving, just in case someone heard those gunshots."

We walked back to Cloud's body. Karen took one look and started to throw up. Jake helped her to the side of the path and gently patted her back.

"Hank, help me get Cloud into the wheelbarrow," Molly requested.

After we had Cloud in the wheelbarrow, Molly kicked the blood-soaked sand and ran a branch of sage over it, covering his death bed. We returned Cloud to the scene where the two dead men were. Molly took my Beretta, wiped it clean and put it in Cloud's hand, leaving his fingerprints. Then, carefully using a stick, she tossed it a foot from where he lay.

"Cloud killed these men and in turn they killed him," she stated.

"It doesn't look right. Cloud's been shot half a dozen times," protested Jake.

"Don't worry, Jake. Hopefully no one is going to come by right away.

255

After he's been out in the sun for a day or two and the coyotes come…" Molly looked at Karen. "No one's going to be spending a lot of time trying to figure out who shot whom. They'll be more interested in why these men were out here in the first place and who they are." Molly rested for a moment. We were all watching her, taking our lead from her experience.

"Okay, Hank, go check the guy back on the rocks and see if you can find any ID. I'll check the two over there and the Jeep."

I didn't really want to return to see the first person I had ever killed. I rose to my feet and made my way through the chaparral. When I arrived at the rock platform, Slim was still lying face down. A large pool of dark red blood glistened in the morning's rising sun. I half expected Slim to roll over and get up. His rifle lay a few feet from where he had fallen. I kicked the weapon away from his outstretched hand. First I checked his pant leg and found the knife I knew was stuck in his boot. It was one of those hunting knives in a leather sheath. I left it in the boot. It took a minute for me to work up my courage to roll him over. His dead weight provided some resistance. When I finally got him over his eyes were open. They weren't focused on anything, just looking off into infinite space and time. Slim's shirt was covered with blood. His life-giving fluid had been released through the large holes in his chest. A quick search came up with no identification. He had a red Swiss Army knife in one front pocket. It was the kind with scissors, toothpick and tweezers. There was also a set of three keys on a generic ring in the other pocket. One looked like it might fit the Jeep. He also had two sticks of Doublemint gum and a clip for the semi-automatic rifle. In a back pocket was a black leather wallet. The corners were frayed with age. It held one hundred and twenty-seven dollars in bills, a picture of a redheaded woman with Slim from one of those instant photo booths, and an empty matchbook from the Old Saloon. A phone number was scribbled on the inside in pencil. The numbers were smeared but I recognized DeDe's number and address. I put everything back in his pockets, being careful to wipe off my fingerprints. I kept the matchbook. This was the sum of Slim's existence as I knew it: a pocketknife, a hunting knife, three keys, two pieces of gum, enough money for one last poker game, bullets of death, and DeDe's phone number. Looking down at Slim, I could see he had a slight resemblance to me. He was about my height and build. His hair color was lighter than mine, almost blonde, and he was

256

probably a few years younger. Now he would never be any older. Who would miss him? Who would wonder what happened to him? I studied Slim's face for another second or two. I wondered if this was the man who had killed DeDe. Or was it one of the other two? Whether he killed her or not, he had certainly been involved. I turned and walked back to the others.

Molly was returning from the trucks as I arrived. She didn't appear to have anything with her.

"Did you find anything?" she asked.

"Yes."

"What?"

I handed the matchbook to Molly. She looked at the cover and then opened it.

"That's DeDe's phone number and address," I said.

Jake looked up at me. "What was he doing with it?"

"I obviously don't know," I said angrily. "Maybe they were calling her condo to see if she was home. Maybe she came home and found them searching her condo, looking for whatever they didn't find at my place or yours." My voice had risen almost to shouting.

Everyone was silent, looking at me.

Molly waited a second before she spoke. "Hank," she said softly, "we need to decide what we are going to do."

I looked from Molly to Jake. He looked like he wanted to say something but didn't. I glanced off into the distance, watching a large white cloud hanging motionless in an otherwise clear blue sky.

After several moments, I asked Molly what she had found.

She studied me for a second before she spoke. "I didn't find anything on either of the other two, and nothing in the Jeep to identify anyone. The Jeep had Texas license plates."

"Texas?" I questioned, trying to show no emotion.

"Yes," Molly replied.

"Anything else?" My voice sounded almost normal.

"They had enough supplies and ammunition for an army, but nothing that would tell us who they are." Molly seemed perplexed.

"Sounds like paid assassins," offered Jake.

"Who do you think they were?" asked Karen weakly, still recovering from seeing Cloud's bullet-riddled body.

"I don't know. They could be friends of Cloud's who decided to cut him out." Molly looked at Jake. "Any other ideas?"

Jake sat down and ran his hand through his hair. "Molly, these are the men who murdered DeDe. We're not helping Hank's cause by covering this up."

At the mention of my name, I looked at Jake. "I'm not worried."

Molly looked in my direction. "I'm Hank's alibi. I was with him when DeDe was killed. Wasn't I?"

"I don't know. The police didn't pinpoint when she was killed. It might have been when I was with Buggs," I answered.

"Yeah, finding these guys might be Hank's only chance." Jake rubbed his head.

"Listen, if the police had any hard evidence, they wouldn't have let Hank go," said Molly. "Husbands don't suddenly start torturing their wives with bare electrical wires. There would be some history of abuse. If it was a domestic fight, he wouldn't have tortured her. The way DeDe was killed doesn't fit with Hank doing it. The police know that. They were just trying to rattle him. See if there was maybe a long shot that he was somehow involved." Molly's voice had a bit of desperation in it. "What do you want to do, bring the reservation police out here?" Molly looked around for a response. "I can bring them. I'll explain that it was self-defense. I'm a witness, I was here. Just remember that when there are deaths like these on the rez, the FBI is probably going to claim jurisdiction."

Jake and I exchanged silent looks.

"And how are you going to explain the gold?" asked Molly.

I looked at Jake again. He shrugged his shoulders in reply. Our thinking was stumped by our greed.

Molly continued. "It's up to you two. You can try and hide the gold and I'll get the cops. But where are you going to hide it? And you better do it right now. There was a lot of shooting and someone may have heard it." She paused, but no one interrupted her. "Here's the story. You're out here treasure hunting and these guys jumped you. They shoot at you, you shoot at them. Self-defense. You might get charged with trespassing and having unregistered firearms but that might be about it." Molly raised her eyebrows in question. "But once a story about gold being found breaks, do I need to tell you how hard it will be to get the gold out of here after you bring in the police? If you tell the police you found the gold, you will probably lose it because it once belonged to some bank or mint. Or at best, you might get a finder's fee. But what about your other partner?"

Jake and I exchanged quick glances. What about Manny? He wouldn't like it if we lost the gold to the reservation police or anyone else.

Molly continued, "I don't see any way to play it but for all of us to leave right now, with the gold. If these bodies are ever found, then let the police speculate why they were out here, why they killed each other." Molly turned toward Hank. "These guys killed DeDe. If you want, we can find some other way to do this, some way that officially clears your name." She touched his shoulder. "But that's your call."

I wanted to do what was right for DeDe, for her family. And I sure as shit wanted to clear my name. I looked over at the lifeless bodies. Part of me, the right is right part, wanted to file police reports, drag the press out here and let the whole wide world know what had happened to DeDe and who had done it. But another part of me, the realist part, knew these guys weren't going to get any deader, weren't going to suffer one iota more and that none of it would bring DeDe back. Still…

Karen, who had been standing on the sidelines, silent up to this point, spoke up. "When are you supposed to meet Manny?"

"We're supposed to meet him on Sunday," Jake answered. "This was all supposed to go down on Friday. Now we have a couple days to lay low and think about this."

"No," came, Molly's reply. "No, you don't. If you're going to bring in the police it has to be now."

Jake looked at me. "What's it going to be, buddy?"

My voice didn't come as I mouthed the words.

"What's it going to be?" Jake asked again.

"Let's go," I said. "Now." My lips were dry. What had happened during the last half-hour was starting to sink in. My hands were shaking again and I felt sick to my stomach. It had been surrealistic, happening in slow motion in my mind as I played it back, over and over, not unlike a painting by Salvador Dali. But it was real. I had killed two men. One part of me was glad, but it was fighting the uncertainty that was drowning me.

"Hank, are you all right?" Molly asked as she took my hand.

I snapped back to the present. She had sensed my despair.

"Yes, I was just thinking about…" I mumbled.

"It was self-defense. It was them or us," Molly spoke softly.

Jake and Karen watched for my reaction.

"I know," I said angrily. "It's just…Jesus Christ, they deserved it…I never shot anyone…never killed a human being…"

Molly squeezed my hand. "They weren't human beings. You saw what they did to Cloud. And what they did to…"

"Molly's right. They deserved it," Jake piped in quickly. "You saved our lives today."

Jake stepped up to me and put his arms around me. We held each other for a moment, our hearts pounding blood through our veins. It felt good to be alive.

31
Jake
After Sunrise, Wednesday

There it was. The gold. *My* gold. *Our* gold. I stood and stared at the hard-won treasure, my mind now suddenly reeling with the size and scope of it all. What I saw was a four-lane superhighway that led straight to the good life, no traffic, no stop lights, no speed limits, no cops—just me and Karen in a silver Boxster going wherever we wanted. Life had just become one hundred percent endless possibilities.

Molly made the first move. "We should get out of here. If anyone heard the gunshots, they could be getting here any time." She headed for the truck. Hank followed, turning once more to survey the devastation. I wondered how this was going to affect him. While I was ready to move on and never give this another thought, it didn't mean Hank was. He'd ended two people's lives. I made a note to keep an eye on him.

Karen reached for my left hand. "Molly's right. We should get out of here."

I nodded and held her hand, adding, "And never come back."

We squared off when we reached the truck, standing like people do when making travel plans. Who went in what truck? Who would lead? Where would we rendezvous? Molly took control and did most of the planning.

"Remember," she stated, her eyes going from one person to the next, "if we get stopped, let me do the talking. Nobody knows what happened out here except for us. We start acting guilty and the cops will pick up on that immediately."

Her eyes had stopped at Karen's, like she was delivering that message directly to her. Molly probably figured she could cover for Hank and that I was so used to *schmoozing* my way out of tight situations I didn't need any warnings. I guessed she'd pegged Karen as the weak link and wanted to impress on her exactly what to do if there was any trouble.

"Are we clear on what to do?" Her eyes were still locked with Karen's.

"We're clear." Karen glared back.

"One more thing." Molly faced Hank and me. "Did anyone touch that?" She pointed to the black Jeep.

Both Karen and I shook our heads. Hank closed his eyes for a moment, apparently concentrating.

"I went up to it," he opened his eyes, "but I don't think I touched it."

Molly stepped toward him. "Don't think or don't know?"

More concentration. He shrugged. "Everything happened so fast I..."

"Hank, you need to be sure. Sooner or later someone is going to find the bodies—and this Jeep. If your prints are on it..." Her sentence hung in the air.

"No." Hank stated. "I didn't touch the Jeep."

Molly stared, her eyes asking the question, *Are you absolutely sure?*

Hank nodded. "I looked inside, saw the night vision glasses but didn't touch anything."

Made aware of the implications, Karen and I joined Molly in her questioning stare.

"I didn't," Hank stated emphatically.

I pictured Hank sneaking up behind the Jeep and realized the only prints he'd be leaving behind would be footprints. The desert would take care of those. "Maybe we should wipe it down, just to be sure." I nudged Karen and she headed for the Jeep.

"Then let's grab the wheelbarrows and get moving." Molly pointed to Hank and then the cave, signaling his task. I headed for the wheelbarrows. I was about to ask why when the answer came to me. They were metal. Our hands had been all over them, touching places we wouldn't think of wiping. I knew I didn't want to spend even a second wondering if we'd done a good enough job of erasing our ties to this desolate scene. A quick scan of the area told me there wasn't anything else we'd left or touched that could incriminate us.

As I hoisted the second wheelbarrow into the back of my truck I realized that they'd come in handy for unloading when we got where we were going.

Where were we going? I knew we were *leaving* here but I hadn't given any thought to where we were *going*. I turned to face Molly and immediately resented myself for doing that. I'd given over too much of the decision-making to her and, while she'd done a great job, I wanted it back. Before I could make a stand, she turned toward me.

"Where to?" Her hands were tucked into her jean pockets.

Damn. Standing up and taking control of a situation was one thing. Having someone neatly hand it to you was another. She frustrated me and I wondered what Hank saw in her. I also wondered what the answer to her question was. *Where to?*

"Nowhere until Hank gets back." I turned and headed to the front of the truck, making it look like I had to get something. What I really needed was some time to think.

Originally, we were going to head south. Manny would meet us, inspect the gold, give me a pile of money and I'd be on my way. But that suddenly didn't seem wise.

Someone had crossed us. Manny *had* been number one on my suspect list but recent events had changed that. Because of what Whitney Cloud had done, I'd moved him to the head of the pack.

Now, however, since I'd had time to think it over, I wasn't so sure. If Cloud had been the betrayer, he'd done a piss-poor job of it. No real plan that I could see. No escape provisions. Maybe he'd just gone crazy when he saw the gold. Like Bogie did in *Treasure of the Sierra Madre*. Or maybe he hadn't chosen his friends very carefully.

And I didn't see how it could have been Williams. He didn't seem like the type to have those three dead *hombres* as buddies. Cloud had kept Williams wrapped up tighter than a newborn since day one. He'd had no chance to contact anyone. And even if he had, there was no way he could have told them who was involved or when it was going to take place. Only Whitney and I had known that. Besides, Williams was dead. I'd like to believe that anyone ballsy enough to go for the whole thing would also be smart enough to stay alive.

Present company excepted, that left Juan Maniandez. He had to be the one. *How* he knew we were going early was something I'd want to find out someday. Right now, I had to assume that he *knew* we were going early, that he'd used his considerable resources to get a step or two ahead of us and take the gold for himself, without having to pay me the three million I had coming. I wondered if Manny and Cloud had secretly mended fences and formed a partnership against me. Given their history, that was highly unlikely but I didn't see how I could rule anything out.

It had to be Manny. I couldn't deny the facts. And knowing that didn't make me feel any better. If anything, a darker depiction of what lay ahead loomed before me.

If we did what we'd planned, we'd be walking right into whatever trap he had waiting. We'd already done our best to make sure the trail stopped in the desert. I was positive Manny could be just as thorough, if not more so, in ensuring there were no telltale signs that four people named Jake and Karen and Molly and Hank once had sixteen million in gold in the back of a beefed-up truck.

But how could we *not* continue as planned? Certainly, Manny was watching, or at least aware of what was happening. And if he had people in this area, it'd only be a matter of time before they were looking for us full-time.

Where to go?

Before I could answer my own question, I sensed Karen's presence.

"You okay?" Her hands were in the pockets of the jean jacket.

I turned. "No. Not really."

"What's wrong?" She stepped closer.

I started to answer but realized I didn't know how to say what I wanted to say. If it was bullshit or bar talk or flirting, I always knew what to say. But this was none of those, this was real life. I shook my head and turned back to the truck.

"Jake?" She inched closer to me. "I'm scared. I want to get out of here…"

"Me, too," I answered without turning. Exactly where we were going or what we were going to do next I couldn't be sure.

"Hank's back." She sounded apprehensive. "We're all ready…"

"I'll be there in a minute." I nodded my head toward the rear of the trucks, motioning Karen to join the others. I still needed some time. I needed to put my brain into high gear and find some answers. Fast.

I heard Molly yell something to Hank but couldn't tell what his response was. He was still probably too far away. Or I wasn't listening. Or concentrating. Or letting *things work.*

I closed my eyes and filtered out any unnecessary noise and thoughts. The Zen masters say the mind is like a drunken monkey. Those who can tame this wild animal will find truth. I mentally made a pot of black coffee and invited my inebriated friend in for some conversation.

Over the course of the next few minutes, too short a time for me, too long for the others, I tamed the monkey just enough to glean one simple fact: Staying with our original plan would be the end for all of us.

The monkey tried to tell me another truth. He tried to tell me that double-crossing Manny was very dangerous. I sent him away. Even if it was true, I didn't want to hear it.

Someone came up behind me and I turned, expecting to see Karen. Instead, I found Hank.

"We're ready," he said matter-of-factly. He was so calm that I wondered if he was in shock. I looked into his eyes and found they were cloudy and unfocused.

"You okay?" I asked, placing my hand on his shoulder.

"No." He shook his head. "I'm not sure…" His voice stopped but his hands kept trying to explain. His fingers flexed and clasped one another and finally knotted themselves together.

"You saved our lives, Hank. All our lives."

Hank's eyes frowned. "I just need to get away from…"

His words dropped off but I knew what the rest of the sentence was. *Away from the death and destruction.* I was about to tell him that I couldn't agree more, but I still hadn't figured out where we could go. I never got the chance.

"Molly said we could go to her place," he said. "It's not far."

Molly's place. That's right. She lives in Shiprock. It's close. We could rest. Eat. Most of all, we could think.

"C'mon, partner." I put my arm around him and headed for the trucks. "Let's go see where your friend Molly lives."

32
Hank
Midday Wednesday

Molly's house was on Cottonwood, a couple blocks from the community college and hospital. The house was a rambler with an adobe exterior that looked well worn. All the other houses on the block were similarly styled. None of the yards showed any signs of a gardener living there. Molly owned one of the few houses on the block with a garage. She parked her truck on the street. She went to open the garage door for Jake's truck and the gold. I gunned the engine of the big truck and barely squeezed it into the single-car garage.

The house had that stale smell to it from being shut up for too long. Molly moved about, opening windows and turning on fans. The effort created a pleasant breeze.

"There's the shower, or I can rustle up some food. What's your pleasure?" Molly asked us.

Jake and Karen were sagging on the couch. Karen had her eyes closed and was leaning on Jake's shoulder. Her makeup was almost gone and her hair was wind-blown from being in the desert for twenty-four hours. She still had on Molly's jean jacket with nothing underneath it. Even in her disheveled state I could see her natural beauty. A beauty I had only seen a couple times before in person. She could be a model in a *Victoria's Secret* catalog. For a moment, I wondered what she saw in Jake.

Jake growled, "I'm beat and my head hurts. In fact, I hurt all over. I need to sleep."

My adrenaline rush was over and the hours without food and sleep were taking their toll on me. My body ached from the over-exertion and tense situation I'd just been through. I had been trying to put the two men I killed out of my mind. But every so often I would see their faces. The terror and fear of the moment made my heart pound again. The memory of the black-and-white photos of DeDe's battered face helped resolve my quandary about killing another human being.

Karen stroked Jake's temple. "Jake, I think you should have something to eat." She looked at me. "And don't you think he should have his head looked at?"

"I've said that for years."

Ignoring me, Jake whined, "I don't need my head looked at. I need to lie down and sleep." He absentmindedly played with a stack of the gold coins. They made a pleasant clinking noise in his hands.

"I'll see what's in the kitchen." Molly took the few steps to the other room and disappeared.

I didn't respond to Karen's question, not wanting to get involved in this domestic disagreement.

"No, Molly, let me. I can be of some use," Karen protested. "Jake, we'll talk about you seeing a doctor after I have fed you."

Jake made a face towards Karen's back, as she headed to the kitchen.

A knock at the door made us all jump.

Karen turned, took a couple steps back to grab Jake's hand and pull him from the couch. "Come on in the kitchen with me," Karen said in a hushed tone. "And keep quiet."

Jake returned quickly to the couch and gathered his stash of coins.

There was a second knock and Molly reappeared. I stayed put in a sling-back chair. She waited until Karen and Jake were safely hidden in the kitchen. The third knock was louder.

"Hi, Molly. I saw your truck out front." The bright backlight in the door provided only a silhouette of the man standing there. He was almost a foot taller than Molly, making him a couple inches taller than me. I could see that he had his hand on Molly's shoulder. "Mind if I come in?" Before she could respond, a large Indian stepped into the room. His hair was loose and reached past his shoulders. His facial features were sharp, chiseled. His good looks rivaled a male model's. He was wearing black cowboy boots, jeans and a denim shirt. There was a gun on his right hip and the silver star of a reservation police officer on his chest. My body became rigid with tension.

"Jim, this is Hank Djumpstrom," Molly said. Turning to me, she introduced the big cop. "And Hank, this is Jim Laughinghorse. We work together."

I stood to shake his hand. Jim hesitated a second and then gave my hand a firm grip, but no pump. His eyes met mine.

"Hank, how you doing?" His voice was even, but not friendly. "You have a few scratches on your face."

I nodded, "I'm okay, had a fight with a bush." My hand rubbed my ear, feeling the dried blood.

"So when did you get back?" asked Laughinghorse, returning his attention to Molly.

"Just now, a few minutes ago," Molly answered with a smile. "Hank came up from Santa Fe with me."

I strained to see if I could hear any sounds from the kitchen.

"So you were in Santa Fe? I thought you were going to the pow-wow with your aunt." Laughinghorse watched me as he spoke.

"I was, but I changed my mind. Hank and I got together down in Santa Fe. Hank's an artist. He wanted to do some painting of the bluffs and I said I'd show him around." Molly held her hands apart and shrugged her shoulders. "Ah, listen, we're kind of busy."

Jim's dark brown eyes scanned the room and came back to find me. They bore into me. I tried to meet the scrutiny, but I didn't know what was going on and glanced away.

"Thanks for coming by," Molly smiled and took Jim's arm, leading him back to the door.

"I just wanted to say hello." Jim stopped at the door. "When are you coming back to work?"

"I have the rest of the week off and I may take next week off, too. I have a lot of vacation built up. Need to use it. I'll see you when I get back."

He was still looking at me as he turned to go. Molly shut the door and turned the deadbolt.

"Who was that?" I asked.

"Jim's a patrolman. Works out of Shiprock."

I ran my hand through my hair. It was filled with sand. I needed a shower. "So who is he?" I stressed. "He's a patrolman, right? So, since you're a sergeant, are you his boss?"

"I just told you. He's a cop I work with." Molly gave me a sly smile. "You jealous?"

I didn't know what I was. I was exhausted. "He just seemed to be a little, I don't know…" I looked for Molly to complete the sentence.

Our eyes met and locked.

"Okay, maybe I am jealous."

"What are you going to start, twenty questions? You have nothing to be jealous about. Okay? Don't start that macho bullshit."

She was right.

"Who was the cop?" Jake stepped into the room. "What'd he want?"

Molly laughed. "Ask Hank."

* * *

Karen had helped Jake take a long, warm bath. She said his muscles needed to relax. When he had dried, he came into the living room with a towel wrapped around his waist to show off his bruises. A large purple one had appeared at the base of his skull and covered much of his neck. He also had a couple good-sized bruises on his ribs.

"Wow, you look like you hurt." I grimaced. "Jake, Karen might be right. Maybe someone should look at your head."

"Okay, Doctor Djumpstrom, you come take a look."

I made a face of anguish. "Your head could be cracked. If you had any brains, they might be leaking out."

"My head is okay. I think I took most of the blow on my neck. I'm not seeing any stars or blacking out. I just need some rest." Jake yawned and stretched. "That bath sure felt good. Molly, you certain that truck is safe out in your garage? I wouldn't want it to get stolen." He laughed and Molly laughed with him. Maybe now that the pressure was off, these two would learn to like each other.

"Come on, Jake." Karen stroked his temple. "You need some sleep," she mothered.

"What about something to eat?"

"There are some eggs. You go get in bed and I'll scramble some and bring them to you." Karen wrapped a towel around his bare shoulders.

"You can use that bedroom on the right." Molly pointed in the direction. "The bed should have clean sheets on it. My mother always changes them after she stays with me."

Jake padded down the hall and disappeared. Karen went back in the kitchen and I could hear her getting dishes and starting the eggs.

"How about you? You ready for a shower?" There was a glint in Molly's eye. "I'll start it."

I sat back down in the chair and listened for the water to start running.

* * *

Molly was wearing a short cotton robe when I entered the bathroom. The shower curtain was pulled back slightly and I could see the spray hitting the wall.

"Get undressed and get in," Molly directed.

I smiled and pulled my shirt out of my jeans. Sand flew everywhere, making the floor feel gritty under my bare feet. I carefully dumped my clothes into a pile on the floor and stood naked before her.

"Very impressive," she smiled. "Now get in." She pulled the curtain back and I stepped into the water. It felt cold at first and raised goose bumps on my skin. I let the spray splash on my face and soak my hair. Molly stepped in behind me, soaped me up and started washing my back. It felt great. Then she started to wash herself. I enjoyed the view.

"Don't get any ideas, big boy. You need some food and rest. Maybe later. Just look, no touching," she teased.

I washed the sand from my hair. I couldn't believe how good it felt to be clean.

* * *

When I woke I could tell the sun was going down. The shadows were long on the wall. One shadow looked like a giant spiderweb that was swaying

270

back and forth. I turned my head and saw a dream catcher blowing gently in the breeze from the open window. I had fallen into a deep sleep, with the dream catcher trapping my bad thoughts before they became nightmares. Molly was sleeping beside me. Her breathing was deep and slow. I studied her face in the fading light—her high cheekbones, the fullness of her lips. I wanted to kiss her but resisted. Her hair was thick and black, void of color. I wanted to reach out and touch it, to feel its texture. I pushed back the sheet and took in her perfect body. "I have every reason to be jealous," I whispered to myself. Who *was* this woman who had come into my life?

I sat on the edge of the bed and rubbed the sleep from my eyes. There was a sound coming from the other room. I stopped and listened. It sounded like someone talking. I got up and carefully slipped on my jeans, trying not to wake Molly and stepped to the door. When I opened the door, there was light coming down the hall and I caught a glimpse of Karen moving around in the kitchen. I listened, but didn't hear any more talking.

Karen had her back to me as I entered the kitchen. She was standing at the sink in a borrowed bathrobe. It appeared she was deep in thought. When she turned and saw me, she jumped.

"Jesus, Hank, you scared me," she put her hand to her throat. "I didn't hear you. How long have you been standing there?"

"Just a second. Are you all right?"

"Yes, I just got up to get a drink of water."

"How's Jake?"

"Oh, he's still sleeping. He seems fine. I think he needed to sleep." She nodded her head knowingly.

"You sure you're okay?"

"Yes, it's just everything. Nothing was like I expected it to be…" Karen let the sentence drop and looked at me. She had showered and combed her hair. But she still didn't have any makeup on. She looked soft and vulnerable.

"I thought I heard somebody talking."

Karen looked at me for a long second and then shook her head. "No."

"Well, I'm going back to bed. Sorry I startled you." I turned and went back to Molly's bedroom and gently shut the door.

* * *

It was completely dark the next time I awoke. I couldn't hear Molly's breathing, but I knew she was still next to me. Her hand found me and gently stroked my chest.

"Hi, sleepyhead. Our sleep patterns are going to be all screwed up."

There was the sound of a match striking. It popped and for a second the spark blinded me. Molly lit a candle that gave off a nice intimate glow. She sat in the flickering glow and looked at me for a long time. Then she gave me a knowing smile.

I yawned and stretched.

"Get enough sleep?"

"Yeah, thanks."

"I want to talk. I want to know why you and Jake are so close."

"That's kind of a big question."

"Come on. Do you have something to hide?"

"No. Is that why you're sitting there looking so beautiful, to loosen my tongue so your interrogation will be easier?"

"No, I have rubber hoses for that."

We both laughed.

"That's very kinky. I didn't know you were that kind of girl." I leaned over and kissed Molly on the mouth. "Where are your handcuffs?"

"We can play later." She laughed and pulled away. "Now answer my question."

I looked into the darkness. The candle cast just enough light so I could see the dream catcher turning gently in the night air. "Jake…" I thought for a moment. "He came out to my farm to write a story about me. Someone had told him there was an interesting new artist in town. Why did Jake come to write about me," I asked, chuckling to myself, remembering, "when just about every other person in Santa Fe is an artist? My farm is near Smiley's Old Saloon, his home away from home. He figured he could swing by, ask a couple quick questions, and then spend the rest of the day at Smiley's working on the story and have it done before the serious drinking started." I answered my own question. "Sometimes, many times, Jake is motivated by laziness." I turned back to see if Molly was engrossed in my tale. "By the time we—and I emphasize 'we'—got to Smiley's that first day, a lot of serious drinking and other chemicals had already been consumed."

"So, Jake's a writer? I never would have believed that. I thought he was a…" Molly laughed. "I don't know, I guess I thought he was a crook or something."

We both laughed.

"A bum maybe?" I asked.

"I don't know. Not a bum. I didn't think about it until now. I guess I thought he was some kind of leech, someone looking for the easy life."

"Oh, he is looking for the easy life. But he's not a leech." I smiled. "Jake is actually quite talented. He just puts a lot of effort into finding the easy way. If he put as much effort into his writing…"I stopped and looked at Molly.

She was sitting back into the pillows and making herself comfortable and fetching. She caught my leer. "Oh, no." She smiled. "You finish your story and then maybe, just maybe, you'll get lucky."

"For some reason Jake and I hit it off immediately. Something clicked. In a lot of ways we have the same outlook on life."

"And, what would that be?"

I thought for a moment. "While it appears from the outside that Jake is basically looking for the easy score, he is more complex than that. This is going to sound hokey, but he wants to leave a notch with his passing, to create something worthwhile. Not that anyone'd notice by what he has done so far. But that's why he writes. That's one of the reasons I do art." I looked again at Molly. She was so beautiful in the candlelight. "I don't really know why I have to create. I just do. Telling someone it's for fame and fortune makes it tangible, but that's not really the reason. It is very hard to explain in words. Sometimes I just have to put something down on paper or take some twisted pieces of metal and put them together or feel the clay between my fingers. It's the process. When I'm working, fame, fortune and the audience aren't even a thought. Most people think that an artist creates for recognition, but that's only a by-product. It really is the process, the journey that's important, not the arriving. An adoring audience is just gratification. Critical success is money in your pocket and possibly the opportunity to do art full-time. That's what got me into trouble."

"What?"

"Doing art for the sake of the almighty dollar. Sometimes I lose touch with reality."

Molly stifled a laugh.

"No, really. I mean Jake and I were talking about art and people not really appreciating art, but getting caught up in all the bullshit. He came up with this idea to make me famous and to make us some money all at the same time. First, Jake does his 'interesting new artist' profile on me. Then Jake got this guy we know, Ishray, the guy who runs One Hand Clapping, to play a New York art critic. So then Jake gets the art critic from the *New Mexican* to meet with Ishray. Ishray is very convincing. He tells this critic that I'm the next Picasso; that I've had some small shows in New York, San Francisco and Paris, and that, while my work is highly respected, if only by the small circles that have seen it, I'm somewhat of a recluse." I smiled, remembering the lie. "He says that is why the critic probably hadn't heard of me. So Jake brings the critic out to the farm to see some of my work. He's very impressed. Now, looking back, I'm not sure if he was impressed with me or with Ishray's performance. Anyway, the critic writes an article and starts telling some gallery owners about *his* great discovery. The critic does another article telling of my successes in Paris and New York and San Francisco, entirely based on what Ishray had said. During the interview with this guy, I'm making up stories about my travels. I've never even been to Europe and he's eating it up. Jake is beside himself. He is having a great time watching this stuffy critic go for the hoax. Later I found out Jake really hates this guy for his condescending attitude. So one day I get a call from a gallery owner who wants to see some of my work. Next thing I know I have to fill this guy's gallery for an opening. At the opening all these so-called patrons of the arts are gushing all over me and my work."

"I'd have thought you'd love that."

"At the time I did. I had just started experimenting with large clay sculptures and I made several for the opening. My stuff was selling at prices I had only dreamed of. The gallery owner sold about half my work on the opening night. Well, not all the patrons were as excited as Jake and I had hoped they would be. There are always some naysayers. Someone did a little checking and found out that no one in New York or San Francisco had ever heard of me, nor had anyone in Paris. When the critic was clued in, he went directly to his editor. The editor was furious, calls Jake's editor at the *Reporter* and well…what could he do? The editors agreed everyone should just keep quiet and neither paper would write another word about me. But somehow the word got out and not much more of my work sold. Some of the opening night sales fell through. The gallery owner closed my show early and I was done. No one likes being duped. But there was one of the patrons who didn't care about critical acclaim. He still liked my work. He had bought quite a few pieces of the clay sculptures and a few paintings. That's how I first met Manny."

"Manny?"

"Yeah, Manny is the guy putting up the money for the gold."

"The guy you and Jake are supposed to meet? The guy buying the gold?"

"The same."

"Wow. So, Manny liked your work?"

"Very much so. He actually has a very good collection. He has works by a wide variety of artists. But the rest of the so-called patrons were only buying my work because they thought I was a new important name and that my work would be worth something someday. They were investing, buying at a low price. It didn't matter if they liked it or not. There was no love of art. But it was my own fault. I got caught up in the game of making money. I ran smack into the ugly side of art, the game, while paintings of Elvis on velvet are called art because they sell."

"Hank, that's not all art is." Molly was frowning. "Look at Navajo art. It is part of our religion, its part of our daily life, it tells our history."

"Exactly, it wasn't created to be sold. It was created for a purpose. That's why I don't care about selling anything I do anymore. It's nice but…I enjoy the process and if it sells, great. If not, so what?"

Molly ran her fingers through my hair and touched my face. "So, Manny became your patron?"

"Well, not really. He bought some of my work and I believe he really liked it. He had been employing Jake. I became one of his employees for a while."

"Manny was your employer?"

"We used to bring pot in from Mexico for him. When he started in the cocaine business, we got out. Among other things, Manny was a drug dealer. Now, who knows? He may still be. He's a criminal who has gotten very rich and very powerful. And…"

275

"And what?" Molly waited for my reaction. Her face was impassive. I couldn't read how she was feeling about me.

I thought for a moment. It had started to fit together. "What if those guys out in the desert weren't friends of Cloud's? What if they really did work for Manny? What if he's the partner pulling the double-cross?" The thought made me shudder with fear.

"I thought Manny was your *friend*," stated Molly. "He bought your art."

"Friend? Molly, pot was business. When you're in the drug business, you don't have any friends. This may not be drugs, but it is still business."

"Exactly. I think we better re-think this. I don't like what I'm hearing. Manny sounds like he's serious trouble. If those men in the desert weren't Cloud's associates, you and Jake could be driving the gold to your death sentence."

Molly had a stone serious look on her face. I knew she was turning this over in her mind, examining the angles. She was concerned. She was concerned about my safety. She might even be concerned about Jake. What she didn't know was there was good reason for this worry. I knew Manny believed in one simple edict: Don't fuck with him and you would be okay. Had someone fucked with him? Maybe Manny's men were double-crossing him? Maybe they were freelancing now? Did he think Jake had double-crossed him? If he believed it, even suspected it, then we had better be ready. But why would he suspect it? I knew what would happen if Manny had lost his *trust* in us. I had witnessed it once. So had Jake. It hadn't been pretty.

33
Jake
Late Wednesday Night

I'd been awake for hours. Molly's house was quiet and, with the bedroom door closed, I'd finally gotten some sleep.

Which was fine; I'd needed it. I'd slept for a short time. One of those deep, coma-like sleeps that renders you unconscious for a couple of hours, repairing whatever damage you've done to yourself and your psyche. And then lets you wake up, not healed, but somewhat healthier.

When I opened my eyes, I took a quick inventory. My head and most of my body hurt like hell. I cursed Cloud. He'd caused this pain. In fact, he'd caused all of our current problems. If only he hadn't gotten greedy…

There were a few things I was certain of. Karen was next to me, sleeping peacefully. We were at Molly's house. Hank was here. We had a truckload of gold in the garage. And, thanks to Hank and Molly, we were lucky to be alive.

I wasn't as sure about anything else. A thousand questions marched across my mind, some coming in logical, predictable columns, while others raced in out of nowhere.

I figured I had two choices. I could nuzzle up to Karen. A touch here, a caress there, a light kiss on the back of the neck…

Or, I could be as still as the moon at midnight and try to work out those unanswered questions.

Sorry, Karen, I bet it would have been terrific.

* * *

I lost track of how long I'd been there. Thinking. Random thoughts. Scattered ideas. Wild theories. This had to stop. It was going nowhere. I took in a deep breath and cleared my brain. I'd use *the exercise*.

I exhaled and took control. Like I'd done a hundred times before, I imagined myself at Smiley's. The dark paneling, the long bar, the poker room in the back. At first, it's just me and Smiley. Then, slowly, carefully, the door opened and the *visitors* came in.

Another deep breath. Another slow exhale. One by one, my thoughts, now in the personage of Smiley's customers, sauntered in and bellied up to the bar. Some looked like regulars, others more like occasional drop-ins, while others seemed totally new. Whatever their status, they stayed for a while, had a beer or two, said their piece and then headed out. Some were hardly noticed while others left their mark. What usually happened was that in all the coming and going, all the noise, all the drivel, some truth would come forth; some cream would rise to the top. Some *thing* of importance would be gleaned from the minutiae.

And then the memory of Ralphie came strolling in.

I could feel my blood pressure rise and my breathing increase. I forced myself to calm down, to relax, to let this exercise do its work, to watch and not participate. Slowly, ever-so-slowly, I returned to my trance-like state.

Ralphie's image walked up to the bar and, crowded as it was, a space opened up. The room grew quiet. Smiley slowly walked over and asked him what he wanted.

Ralphie looked across the bar, his eyes sad. He wore the clothing of a homeless man, of someone down on his luck. His filthy hands scraped the stubble on his face, his cracked lips quivered as he tried to speak. "Another chance…" he whispered softly.

Smiley bowed his head for a moment and then looked up. "You know the rules."

Even more sadness filled Ralphie's eyes. His mouth made a move like he was going to say something more, but nothing came out. He dropped his head down, turned and walked out.

In this vision, Smiley walked over to where I'd been watching all this. He looked right at me, all serious-like. "When it comes to dying, a guy only gets so many chances to beat it. Sooner or later, you flat run out of chances.

Sooner or later, you die." He leaned in even closer. "You can't cheat the odds forever, boy."

Okay. Enough of that. If Smiley was trying to tell me not to fuck with Manny, he was wasting his time. I already knew what happened when you crossed Manny. I was there when Ralphie tried to skim more than his share. And that was fifteen years ago. It might as well have been yesterday. The way Manny called Ralphie out. The way he laid out all the evidence. The way he gave him one more chance to tell the truth. The way he put the gun to Ralphie's head. The way he told him to come clean, to say he was sorry, to say he'd never, ever, ever do anything stupid like that again. The way he asked him not to force him to do what he must do to those who *transgress*. The way Ralphie refused to admit his sins.

And, finally, the way Manny had pulled the trigger, splattering Ralphie's brains all over the room and then calmly, and I mean calmly, turned to Hank and me, wiping the blood from his hands and asking us what we wanted for lunch. I already knew Manny was dangerous.

Or did I? Did I realize exactly how dangerous he was? Had I considered how much trouble we'd all be in if we tried to double-cross him? Even if we did manage to get out of here with the gold, he'd hunt us down and kill us all.

Sooner or later, you run out of chances.

Okay. Trying to run off with the gold was not smart. But what else could we do? If we went ahead with our slightly altered plan, we'd still be walking right into Manny's hands. Had he tried to kill us in the desert? Had we escaped only by the narrowest of margins? Why should we march right into his camp and meet the same fate?

Or were the desert assassins friends of Cloud's who had then decided to get rid of everyone, Cloud included, and take all the money for themselves?

Like lightning flashes, one reality crashed into the next, until I sorted it into a believable order. I forced my aching body to crawl out of bed, lightly tapped Karen's rear end and told her to get up and get dressed. "We've got work to do."

* * *

For the second time, I started telling my theory. Only more slowly. The first time had been met with stunned silence and about an ounce of comprehension. Karen was still half-asleep and Hank's mind was somewhere else. Only Molly had been paying any attention.

I slapped the table. "Listen to me!"

Molly jumped, looking pissed. "Jake, it's the middle of the night..."

"I know!" I raised my voice. "And I've been hit on the head and I need some rest. If it was that simple, I'd be back in bed snuggling up to Miss Perky here." I pointed to Karen, who was still not fully awake.

Molly stared back. She must've seen something in my eyes that told her I was serious. "Okay. I'll make some coffee."

I turned to Hank. "Listen. I don't think it is Manny we've got to worry about."

Karen sat up, faster than I thought possible. "What are you talking about?"

Hank's eyes flashed open.

I pulled up the fourth chair and sat at the table. "Manny isn't our problem. It was Cloud."

Molly rejoined us. "How?" She was being a cop now.

I propped my arms on the table. "Like I've been trying to tell you. It's Cloud. He knew everything. Manny knew squat."

More silence.

"Look. If someone's going to do something—rob a bank, steal a car, have an affair and get away with it—they've got to know everything that's involved."

Two people nodded their heads. Karen just stared.

I continued. "If Manny was going to make a play for the gold, he'd have to know everything about it."

More nods, more interest.

"But Manny didn't know any of the details. He provided the front-end money and he knew when and where to meet me once I had the gold. That was it. I made sure he had no idea where we were going. Hell, I had only a general idea myself."

No more nods, just complete and total interest.

"Cloud is the only one who knew all the details of this part of the plan."

Hank finally spoke. "But Cloud is dead."

I waved him off. "I know he's dead. I'll get to that in a minute." Karen went to tend to the coffee while Hank and Molly remained intent on my story.

"Let's go back to the beginning." I looked at Hank. "Remember the black Thunderbird? The one that tried to run me over?"

He nodded. "And nearly killed Elmore."

"I'm thinking it must've been one of Cloud's boys."

"Why?" Hank asked. "Why would he do that?"

"Keeping an eye on you?" Molly speculated.

I shook my head. "More than that. I think they wanted to scare me, to rattle me, to make me *think* someone was trying to kill me."

Molly leaned in. "But why?"

"So Cloud could start planting seeds of doubt. At that time he didn't know who the money man was. But it didn't matter. He was trying to make that person, whoever it was, look bad in my eyes."

Hank stared and then shook his head. "I need more."

"Okay. How about this? Cloud wanted me off-balance, looking over my shoulder. That way, he'd be free to sneak in, snoop around, see if he could find out who the money man was so he could make a better deal on his own."

Molly leaned back, shaking her head. "So he has one of his goons try to run you over?"

"Yes! And that starts me thinking that someone's out to get me and right away I'm payin' less attention to the Shiprock details and more to which jealous husband or angry boyfriend or pissed off cowboy is tryin' to fry my bacon."

"So you get distracted." Molly sat back, looking at Hank for his reaction.

"And it worked. But that ain't all," I continued. "My place got trashed. And so did Hank's." I turned to face him, knowing this next part would cut deeper than a reminder of a messy house with broken furniture. "And DeDe." I paused. "That raises the stakes to a point where nobody's thinking about anything except stayin' alive."

Nothing was said for a while. By bringing up DeDe's death, I'd given them plenty to think about. Karen returned with four cups of coffee and we all let our thoughts mingle with the steaming vapors.

Karen was the first to speak. "There were those two guys who followed us downtown. Remember, Jake?"

"I remember."

"I thought they might have been after me. You said they worked for Manny. Now you think they worked for Cloud? Why?"

"It makes more sense."

"How?"

"Trust. I know it seems hard to believe. Especially after all that's happened, but I still trust Manny. As far as he knows, our original deal is still good. He doesn't know about any of the changes." I looked around the table for confirmation. Nods of agreement came slowly but they still came. "And this isn't Manny's style. This was sloppy work. Manny may be a lot of things, but he isn't a street thug who tortures women."

We were all quiet for a long time until Molly spoke up. "Listen. Jake." Her words were careful and measured. "I'm not saying that your theory isn't without merit, but I still don't see how you can rule out Manny. From what Hank tells me, this Manny is a very powerful man. And powerful people have a way of getting what they want. And that includes finding out when and where you're going into the desert."

Okay. She might be right. Partially right. I lowered my enthusiasm and tried to fortify my argument with more logic. "I know Manny can do just about anything he wants, including having someone tail me. But in this case, he has no motive."

"You don't call sixteen million in gold a motive?"

I smiled. "You bet I do. But in this case, it's in Manny's best interest to keep me alive, to keep me on track and on schedule."

"And why is that?"

"Because without me, getting the gold becomes a bigger risk. There's no connection to Cloud, no deal with Williams and there sure as shit ain't no gold. Manny gets *nada*."

Again, the room grew silent. As fired up as I was, I needed to take a breather. It all seemed so simple, so obvious. Had I missed anything? Had I transposed any facts? If I had, I hoped one of the others would point it out.

This time Hank spoke first. "So why is Cloud dead?"

"Good question." I shrugged. "Probably greed. Wanting a bigger piece of the pie. Not choosing his friends carefully. A double-cross. It's a hell of a lot of money."

Hank stared and looked like he was going to say something, but didn't. He went back to sipping his coffee.

I turned to Karen. "And you?"

She bowed her head, reminding me of some kid in class who hadn't been paying attention and didn't know the answer. "Sounds all right, I guess."

Next was Molly. If anyone could substantiate my theory or shoot it down, I figured it'd be her. "What do you think?"

"Even though it's too dangerous to totally discount Manny, I think it sounds pretty damn good," she answered without hesitation, and that surprised me. I thought she'd need more proof before she got on board.

"Why?" Now it was my turn to ask some questions.

"It's simple," she said. "Manny needs you alive."

"And?"

"And Cloud only needed you alive so that Williams would lead everyone to the gold. Then, like Williams, you became expendable. He probably figured any deal he could make on his own would be better than turning the gold over and splitting with you and Williams."

I stared at her, at everyone. That was it. It was that simple. Cloud had tried to take it all and his plan had backfired. I should have felt terrific for having figured this all out. But, for some reason, part of me was still unsettled, still questioning.

Molly interrupted my apprehension. "And?"

I drew a blank. "And what?"

"And what does this all mean?"

"It means we don't have as much to worry about. Cloud and his friends are all dead."

"Are they?"

"Of course they are. I saw them myself."

Her silence told me I had missed something. But what?

Hank leaned forward, carrying the look of the newly inspired. "I think she means there might be *more* friends."

Molly nodded. "Cloud had a reputation for getting drunk and shooting his mouth off. Who knows how many people he told about this?"

Karen perked up. "Shit."

I sat back. Molly was right. We had no way of knowing how many people

Cloud had involved in his double-cross, or how many people they'd told. And that meant we were only fooling ourselves if we thought this was a done deal.

We sat and thought. Karen wrapped her arms around herself, Molly and Hank toyed with their coffee cups, and I just stared. For all I knew, the house could be surrounded right now by a dozen or a hundred of Cloud's personal army.

Maybe she read my mind or maybe she just couldn't sit still any longer, but Karen got up and headed for a window. Her hand was on the drawstring when Molly stopped her.

"You open that curtain and you're going to be one pretty target."

Karen's hands dropped to her side and she stood there. "So what are we going to do? Wait here for them to come and get us?" The strain of panic edged her voice. "We can't just stay here."

Even though we all knew she was right, no one answered. Like me, neither Hank nor Molly knew what we were going to do next. We couldn't stay put and we had no place to go.

"Jake?" Karen asked. "Now that you know it was Cloud who's been causing all the trouble, why can't you just go meet this Manny guy like you planned?"

Sure. I could do that. I wanted to do that. After all, I was the one preaching that Manny could be trusted.

"Jake?" Karen was almost pleading now. "People are dead. Why can't you just do it like you planned? Otherwise," her voice cracked, "I'm afraid for us."

I stood up and went to her. My arms folded around her and I pulled her close to me. She'd held up pretty well so far and I couldn't blame her for being afraid.

Molly suddenly gasped. "I've got it!" She closed her eyes and her hands went to her head. "Yes!" she said as she opened her eyes. "It's perfect. I know exactly what we need to do!"

"What?" Hank's chair skidded backwards as he moved toward her. "What is it?"

"We need to leave here, right?" She had our complete attention.

"But you really don't trust Manny enough to just drive right up to him and say 'Here we are.' Right?" She looked at each of us. "We need to find out if anyone else is out there and we need a safe place to think this through. Someplace that no one knows about. Someplace where we can plan our next move."

I nodded, waiting for more details. Karen was still snuggled in close and quiet. Hank was the only one who looked like he was tracking what Molly was saying.

His hand found hers. "Are you thinking what I'm thinking?"

She smiled. "I think it's time we paid our respects to Mildred."

Hank returned her smile with an even bigger one. It took me a second but then I remembered. Mildred. The goat, the one that'd been murdered.

"Who's Mildred?" Karen asked, rejoining the conversation.

"A friend," Molly squeezed Hank's hand. "If we can get to Mildred's resting place without being followed, I know we'll all be safe there."

"It's still dark," Hank noted. "I don't know about any of you, but I'd rather try now than later."

Molly studied his words. I was dead tired. I disagreed at first but quickly changed my mind. I liked the dark, too. We turn off our lights and blend in with the night. Karen remained silent.

Molly finally spoke her approval. "It'll work."

I checked the wall clock. 3:30. "It gets light about what? Five?"

Molly nodded, looking at the same clock.

I turned to Hank. "How far is it?"

He made a few mental calculations. "Daytime? On the highway? Two hours. Maybe more. But at night, on back roads? Much longer."

"How much?" I prodded.

He thought but couldn't give me an answer. "I've never gone to Walter's from here."

"Walter?" Karen piped in. "I thought we were going to Mildred's?"

I realized her confusion but didn't want to deal with it. "I'll explain it all later." My half-smile wasn't warmly received.

"If anyone's following us," Hank added, "I don't want to lead them to Walter."

I returned to Hank. "Look, if anyone's following us, we should know long before we get there. Anyplace where we can see the curve of the earth should also let us see if we're being followed."

"And then what?" Molly asked, her eyes locking with mine.

I stood up. "Try to lose 'em."

"And if we can't?" Her gaze growing in intensity.

I finally snapped. "How the fuck am I supposed to know!"

Hank stood up. "Take it easy, Jake. She has a point. If we're going to do this, then we better have all the angles figured out."

I put my hands in the air, surrender-style. "Okay. I know. I'm sorry. It's just that…"

Molly waved me off and Hank sat down.

I dropped my arms to my side. "It's just that we don't have many options."

Hank's face brightened and he turned to Molly. "How well do you know the road to Walter's?"

"Which one?"

He shrugged. "There's more than one?"

"Route 666 is the main road. 371 goes there, too. Sort of. But it's not much of a road."

Hank and I looked at each other and answered her simultaneously. "Three-seventy-one."

She cocked her head, picturing the road that led to Standing Rock. "I know it well. It's probably the best choice."

Hank got her attention. "Listen to me. This is very important. Is there any place on 371 that we could stop?" He pointed to me. "Or, like Jake says, double-back or do something to guarantee we aren't leading trouble to Walter's doorstep?"

Again, her head tilted as she mentally made her way south. "About halfway, there's a good-sized hill. You can see for miles in every direction. If we left right now, we'd probably get there just about sun-up."

Silence. The die had been cast. We were going.

I had to admit, it felt right. Not reckless. Not some desperate attempt. But planned. Calculated. Safe.

Karen ruined my mood. "But what if someone is following us?"

Molly stood up. "Like Jake says, we'll try to lose 'em."

Karen thought for a moment and then softly asked the obvious question, "And if we can't?"

Molly was half out of the room when she answered. "Let's just hope we can. There's been enough killing."

34
Hank
Thursday Before Dawn

I was glad the discussion was over. Jake seemed placated that Molly agreed his theory was probably correct. Also, we all agreed it was better to be paranoid and alive than smug and dead. There would be no good reason, old *friends* or not, to extend any trust to Manny.

Molly located some thermoses and started some fresh coffee brewing, while Karen found the fixings to make sandwiches for our trip. I took out the guns and set about cleaning them.

"Jake, where's the Beretta I gave you?" I asked.

"It's in the bedroom somewhere," Jake said, his voice sounding not so sure.

"Get it and bring the extra clip I gave you."

Jake grumbled something under his breath, pushed back his chair and went to retrieve the gun.

Karen turned from where she was busy preparing our "picnic." I had my bag on the kitchen table. There were various boxes of shells and the two guns sitting center stage. I spun the cylinder on the .45. There were three spent cartridges. One had blown away Miguel's face and the other two had missed the third man, who was now dead, thanks to Molly. I put in three live rounds. I checked the Walther, even though it hadn't been fired. I popped the clip from the Beretta.

"Molly, do you still have Cloud's Magnum?"

"No, I left it in the desert." She was checking the batteries in a couple flashlights. "I have my .38."

"Everyone has a gun but me." There was a bit of anger in Karen's voice as she made the pronouncement.

I looked up from the guns and my eyes met Molly's. She had a look of concern on her face.

I turned so I could see Karen. "I don't think you'll be needing a gun. Hopefully none of us will."

The room was silent. Karen didn't respond.

Jake returned and noticed the silence. "What's up?"

I looked at Jake but was cut off by Karen.

"Nothing. Just getting ready." She gave him a smile.

Molly moved past Karen and started pouring the fresh coffee into one of the thermoses. Jake handed me the automatic and clip. He had fired two shots. I wondered if one of them had been the shot that had distracted Miguel long enough for me to pull my Smith and Wesson. I'd have to ask him about that one of these days but not now. I reloaded the gun. The extra clip still held sixteen shots. "Here, Jake, you take the Smith and Wesson. Up close, this will do fine for you. I'll keep the Beretta," I stated.

* * *

Jake had ordered a fully loaded Ford F350 crew cab. The pickup was the size of a small semi and could haul an army. Jake and Karen fit comfortably in the back seat with our traveling supplies. I drove and Molly provided directions. We headed west on 64 to Kirkland and then south on an unpaved road to Burnham. No one followed us and we passed no other travelers. As the sun came up, we could see Hogback Mountain. Out there, Cloud's spirit had met his ancestors. I wondered how his reception had been.

In Burnham we got out and stretched. Karen set up coffee and sandwiches on the Ford's hood. The sun was bright and warming. We could see for miles across the desert. Molly was scanning the horizon with a pair of binoculars. No one was following us. Of that, we were certain.

"Jake," I whispered. I motioned for him to follow me. As we headed away from the truck, we caught Karen's attention.

"Just going to take a pee," I responded before she could ask. "Good coffee." I held up the cup I was drinking from.

Jake and I walked thirty yards from the truck. Karen and now Molly were watching us. Maybe they thought we might run off into the desert, abandoning them.

"Jake, we can't go to Walter's and sit out there and just think forever. Eventually we have to call Manny."

"I know." Jake stared off into the pre-dawn sky. "Kind of ironic, isn't it? I've got a truckload of gold coins to deliver to him on Saturday, just as we planned. However, I now have three brand new partners—one is his old friend Hank and one is a cop."

"We know that no one is following us now. We either take the gold and run, or we call Manny."

"I know."

"Well, what's it going to be?"

"I dreamed about Ralphie last night."

The name made me shudder with a sudden chill. "Ralphie," I spoke the name in a hushed tone. "I can still hear the gun going off and the sound of his body hitting the ground. And I can still feel his blood on my face."

Jake let my words sink in. I knew the same images were haunting him. Having a man's brains splattered on you made a lasting impression.

"If we run, Hank, there is never any going back. We'll be hiding for the rest of our lives. If it was Manny's men we killed out in the desert, then that means he doesn't trust us. And, we can't trust him, no matter what. I don't know what's going on. This was supposed to be simple. Go out in the desert, pick up some gold, turn it over to Manny for cash and I'm rich."

All of Jake's schemes were supposed to be simple. Easy moneymakers. You'd think he'd learn.

"Well, things have changed," I stated. "We've got the gold and if Manny wants it, he'll have to pay for it. And he'll have to do it on our terms. It is the only way we can come out of this alive. We're not trying to cheat him. We just don't want to be dead. Let's call him and set up a time and place."

"There already is a time and place," Jake answered quickly.

"I know, but it's a time and place that Manny controls. We have to change the game to our advantage."

"But where?"

"Walter will know a place down by Standing Rock, somewhere out in the desert where we can watch Manny's approach. A situation we can control," I stressed.

"Manny isn't going to like us changing things."

"I know. But let's call and tell him we had to make some *adjustments*. It's all different now."

* * *

We headed west and then south on 666 for only a few miles before heading back east on another unpaved road. Our ride to Standing Rock was virtually in silence. Neither Molly nor Karen asked us about our conversation. I figured as soon as Molly and I were alone, she would quiz me and Karen would do the same with Jake. Finally our zig-zagging route came out on an old two-lane blacktop, only a few miles from our destination. If anyone was following us, we hadn't seen them.

I pulled off the highway and crossed the cattle guard that was the entry to Standing Rock. The truck kicked up a trail of dust as we pulled into the first and only gas station, the Mini Mart. It was closed. As soon as I stopped the truck, Jake grabbed his phone and we both hopped out.

I shut the door before either Karen or Molly started to get out. "Gotta make a call, ladies," I said. "Be back in a minute."

Jake walked several feet from the truck and started digging in his pocket. He pulled out a small piece of paper and looked at it. With one hand he held the paper and in the other the phone. He punched in a series of numbers with his thumb.

"This is Jake. Let me talk to Manny."

35
Jake
Thursday Morning

I heard the phone clank on the marble tabletop. At least it sounded like the marble table. While I waited for Manny to come to the phone, I visualized the foyer at his place. The big double doors, the ceramic tile, and the curved staircase. The marble table. The one with the telephone on it.

Of course that had been over fifteen years ago. Rationally, I knew things changed. Fifteen years. There had to have been some changes. But right now, I didn't care about interior decorating. Right now I was looking for things to be very much the same.

Part of me figured that if Manny hadn't replaced that marble table, then maybe other things hadn't changed either. Maybe he'd still be as friendly, as understanding, as he'd always been when I'd come to him with something other than what'd been planned, some little wrinkle, some angle.

Sure, Jake, whatever you say. I trust you. You know that.

And he had. As long as what I was telling him made sense, he'd been willing to listen. Manny could always get behind a smart move.

I wondered about that. He ran a tight ship. Nobody crossed him. Nobody else changed things. Nobody else really ever asked. Except me. For some reason, he tolerated my schemes. I secretly thought that he even admired me for my audacity.

Not that I didn't fear him. I did. All I had to do was think of what happened to Ralphie and I'd remember how ruthless Juan Maniandez could be.

Hank poked me, wondering what was going on.

I shook my head and shrugged my shoulders.

"What are you going to tell Manny?" he whispered.

"I don't know. I'm going to see which way the wind is blowing first."

I could tell Hank was nervous. I knew he wished we had a definite plan, one we could explain to Manny, one he might not like but would see the wisdom of and agree to, one that would get us all out of this alive. Fact was we only had a concept, nothing exact. That, and a few guns, some food, a truckload of gold, the remnants of our unworkable original plan and a burden the size of Texas.

I looked past Hank to see that Karen and Molly had stepped out of the truck. The wind had come up with the sun and I could see it tugging at their clothes. Both of them had their arms folded across themselves, the way women do whenever they stand by a car. Both of them were staring at us.

"*Hola.*"

Manny's voice sent a chill through me.

"Jake? Are you there?"

Time to put on the razzle-dazzle. "Manny. I'm here."

"Well, Jake, how are you?" His voice seemed pleasant enough.

I relaxed. A little. "I'm fine. You?"

"I, too, am fine. It's awfully early to be calling about my health. Is that what you wanted to know?"

A nervous laugh escaped. "No."

"Then what, my friend? Has this something to do with your little *vacation*?"

Manny was choosing his words carefully. I supposed years of wiretapping did that to a person. *Never directly say what you mean.* I'd do the same.

"Yeah, as a matter of fact, I am calling about my vacation plans."

He paused. I could feel the tension growing.

He cleared his throat and continued. "Are you leaving as scheduled?"

Okay. Here we were. Manny sounding like he didn't know we'd already left and me wondering if I should continue this thin charade, wondering if I should just come right out and tell him everything, wondering if I should just hint at a few problems, see what his reaction would be and go from there.

Okay. Make a decision. Quick. If too much time passes before answering, Manny will get his answer anyway. Don't let that happen. Take control. Don't let Manny get an advantage.

I took in a deep breath. "We've already been to our first," I exhaled, "…destination."

"But I thought you weren't leaving for another two days?" Manny suddenly sounded as cold as an iceberg.

"We had to leave early." I tried to sound confident but Manny's lengthy pause made me wonder how I was doing.

After half an eternity, Manny finally moved forward. "Did you get what you went for?"

"Yeah."

"Jake, I sense that there is some kind of problem—"

"Look," I interrupted, "there were a few problems. It's a long, long story. Some things happened a few days ago."

"Things? What things?" A brittle edge framed his voice.

"More things than I can go into *on the phone…*" I let my words hang in the air.

"I understand completely," the edge was gone but a steeled coolness remained. "You will have to give me all the details when you get here."

Okay. Here we were. Again. I wanted to think this through, to have more time to work up the right words. I didn't have the time or the patience. Besides, I felt like I was on a roll.

"That's just it, Manny." I tried as hard as I could not to sound even one tenth as frightened as I was. "Our plans have changed. We won't be going to the same place we talked about." Pause. No. More than a pause. Silence. Deadly silence.

"Not staying with the itinerary? What a pity." I could practically hear the wheels turning in his head. Wondering. Planning. Scheming. Or was that me?

"Jake?" he whispered, his voice now having a totally different quality to it. "If you can't come here, then what?"

"Here's the deal, Manny." Again, I tried not sounding as terrified as I was. "We've got to get together. Soon. But because of some unforeseen circumstances," I let those words linger before continuing, "we can't keep to our planned schedule."

"Can't?" he interrupted. "Or won't?"

"Can't."

"You sure about this, Jake?"

"I'm sure."

"Because you know how much I was looking forward to seeing you again. As we had planned."

"Things have changed. Trust me."

"I trust you, Jake. If I didn't, I never would have sent you money for the trip. I never would have agreed to any of this in the first place."

We were both quiet for a while. I knew it was my move. I just wished I knew what to do next.

"You aren't alone, are you?"

"No," I answered. I guess I'd used "we" one too many times.

"But you're still traveling with the same group, no?"

"No." Even though it had been a long time since I'd been in a conversation like this with Manny, I knew that when he got to this point, it was the time for the truth. No extras. No tangents. No lies. Just answers. Truthful answers.

"Then who?"

"I'd rather not go into that right now."

"Jake, I don't like surprises."

I thought about the look on Manny's face when he would meet our group. His old friend Hank, the artist. That wouldn't be too much of a surprise. Karen, the good-looking woman on my arm. I knew Manny might not approve of the circumstances but he'd probably understand. But Molly. Molly the cop. Manny would have a hard time with that one.

"Listen. Even though our plans have changed, everything will still come out the same." I paused, searching for just the right words. "I'm doing the only thing I know how to do. I'm staying healthy until we can get together."

After a short pause he offered, "Healthy? Jake, should I be worried about you?"

My silence was his answer.

He backed off his aggressive tone and adapted the manner of someone resigned to the fact that he really had no control of the situation. "First of all, my friend, do whatever it is you need to do to make sure you stay healthy."

"I plan to."

"Second, I want to see you as soon as possible."

Through his gentle demeanor, I got his meaning: *Stay alive and bring me my gold.* This reminded me that I'd better tell him something about the gold. I wanted to keep him in a good mood. "I do have some very nice gifts for you."

He sighed. I knew it was on his mind but he had waited for me to bring it up. "When, Jake," he shifted from backing off to being anxious, "am I going to see you? It's been so long that I don't think I can wait another day."

"I'm going to have to get back to you on that."

"What?"

"I'll have to call you later."

"Why can you not tell me now?"

"Because," I stopped just short of saying...*because a half dozen people are already dead and I don't want to join them,* "...because I'm not sure where we're going."

"Is there a number I can reach you at?"

"No. No number."

"What about your cell?"

"No. You can't call me. I keep it turned off until I need it."

Another silence. Then, in cold, calculated tones, "Jake, I need to hear from you within twenty-four hours. Do you hear me? Twenty-four hours." He took a lengthy pause. "This had better go well. Remember, making last minute changes can be costly, very costly. I hope you can remain well."

"I'll call. I promise."

36
Hank
Thursday Morning

Three crows were sitting on the edge of the gas station roof. They were taking turns swooping down on a discarded bag of garbage. One of the opportunists had something in its beak. The other two were eyeing various morsels, as if trying to decide if it would be easier to fight for a portion or look for their own reward.

Many people think of crows as scavengers, standing along the highway centerline picking on road kill. I have always found the large black birds to be regal. Crows play an important part in many Native American legends and are held in high esteem for their cunning and intelligence. Some legends say that crows carry the souls of the dead to their final resting place. I wondered whose souls these three waited for.

"Look at those crows," said Jake, breaking my meditation. "They're on top of the world, not a care. They have everything they need right now."

"Yeah, until the snow comes or a fox catches 'em."

"Yeah, life's a bitch. We've got a ton of gold but can't spend it. Sometimes I wish I were a crow or a fox. Life would be much simpler." Jake slapped at his jeans and a little cloud of dust rose.

"Manny was that understanding, huh?"

Jake looked at me and gave a snort. "Oh, yeah. He isn't going to make it easy. He told me that changing things can be costly—costly to one's health."

"*That* understanding." I gazed at the great expanse of the Navajo reservation. We had all the room in the world, but Manny was making that world feel awfully small. "Did he sound surprised that things have changed?"

"Surprised? Let's just say he was not happy."

I knew how that made Jake feel. No one liked to make Manny unhappy.

Karen and Molly had stayed with the truck during the entire phone call. They stood watching us, just as they were now. Molly was leaning ever so slightly in Karen's direction and talking to her. I could tell by the look on Karen's face that she was concentrating on what Molly was saying.

As we ambled up to the truck, their conversation ended abruptly and I could see that Karen was ready to pounce.

"Molly says there is no bathroom at Walter's place. And there isn't any running water." Karen looked hard at Jake. "Can't we go to a motel somewhere, Jake? Why do we have to go out into the middle of the desert again?"

Molly took my arm and watched the exchange. Jake looked our way for support. I wasn't about to get in the middle of this squabble if I could help it, and I figured Molly had already done her part to create this stir.

"Don't worry. It will be all right. It'll be like camping or something." Again Jake looked in my direction. I kept my lips zipped.

"I don't want to go camping. I don't see why we can't go to a motel and work this out. No one will find us. We can register under false names." Karen's voice was becoming loud and shrill. "Jake, I'm not going back out in the desert. I'm not. If you want to go, then go! I'll go to a motel by myself."

I could sense that a major panic attack was about to take place.

"Karen," Jake said in a soft, even tone, "we can't go to a motel."

"Why not?" Karen screamed, "Why not?" she repeated with a stamp of her foot. "You told me once you got your stupid gold that I could leave."

Jake stepped in close to her to put his arms around her. "Don't worry. The worst is over. It'll be okay."

"No, it won't!" Karen brought her arms up close to her body. Her hands were now clenched. She twisted back and forth, thwarting Jake's attempt to hug her. "Don't you remember what happened out there? Please, Jake, please," she pleaded, "I want to go to a motel. Let Hank and Molly go out to Walter's. They can set things up. Please, Jake!"

I could see that Jake was weakening. He glanced in my direction for an answer.

"Jake…"I started to respond.

"No, Hank!" Karen snapped at me. "You stay out of this!" She turned back to Jake and placed her hand gently on his chest and smoothed his shirt. "I just can't go back into the desert. I can't. I won't!"

Jake took her hand and stopped the motion. "Karen, we're all in this together now. Hank and I have to set this up. We have to be in touch. It'll only take a couple days and then we'll be on our way."

Karen pulled her hand from Jake's grasp. She held her hands down at her sides in fists. "Let Hank take that goddamn cell phone. He can stay in touch. Jake, I won't go. I won't. You'll just have to drive me in to Gallup or someplace and leave me at a motel. When you're done with Manny you can come and pick me up. If I'm still there. If you're still alive."

Karen looked like she was on the brink of breaking.

"Karen," Jake said in a whisper.

The scene was mesmerizing. I didn't know which way Jake was going to go. He looked at me, but not for an answer. I could see the anguish in his eyes. I felt Molly gently tug at my arm.

"Come on," she said softly.

I resisted the pull. It was like watching an accident scene. I wanted to see the outcome.

"Hank," Molly said sternly. She pulled at my arm again. "Would you come on?"

She led me to the side of the gas station where the crows were enjoying their picnic. We could still see Jake and Karen but they were now out of earshot. I expected Molly to exclaim what a nut case and prima donna Karen had become.

"I think we were about to see a meltdown there," I exclaimed. I was under the impression that the only thing Molly and Karen had in common was their gender.

"That woman went through hell out in the desert less than forty-eight hours ago. What did you expect?" Molly glared at me. "She was just about raped. She wasn't twenty feet from where Cloud was shot to death. And she saw men with their faces blown off, lying in their own blood and excrement." Molly took a deep breath, blew it out and slowed her staccato delivery. "Why do *you* think she doesn't want to go off on Jake's camping expedition?

Because she might break a nail?" She caught my eyes. "You know, I'm not sure I like the possibilities that might be on the horizon, either."

I pulled Molly into my arms and hugged her, just holding her, feeling the warmth of her body against me. I wondered again, *Who is this woman?* Suddenly there was a chorus of cawing, followed by a flurry of black wings. I watched the three marauders take off, circle and then head into the sun. Within seconds, they were merely dots in the sky. Was this some kind of omen?

When I looked back at Jake and Karen, he was holding her at arm's length, talking to the top of her head. Karen was looking at her feet. I could see Jake was doing all the talking. Finally she looked up at him. He took her in his arms, she nuzzled in close and he kissed the top of her head while they slowly rocked back and forth.

* * *

When we got to Walter's, the sun was high in the sky. A hawk was riding the rising heat waves over his hogan. Walter was out on a ridge watching the bird gently swaying, slowly circling, and not moving a feather to speed its journey.

"*Taa' eh t'eeh*! *Taa' eh t'eeh*!" Walter called when he saw it was me. The sight of Molly brought a beaming smile to his face.

Walter took my hand in both of his and looked into my eyes. "It is good to see you again so soon, Hank. And it is even better to see you again, Molly." He took her hand and patted it. He looked beyond us to our two companions.

I turned to make the introductions. "Walter, this is Jake. You met him several years ago."

Walter nodded to Jake. "Yes, I remember you, Jake. You are Hank's friend. Welcome."

"And, this is Karen."

"Karen, it is nice to meet you." Walter took Karen's hand and held it for a second. He smiled as he looked into her eyes. "Come, everyone. Let's go into the shade. I have some coffee."

* * *

We spent an hour discussing our plan. Jake would draw a scenario and I would disagree. Molly would tell us to keep it simple and then matter-of-factly explain how it would be. Karen sat in silence her eyes occasionally moving to whoever was speaking. Walter just listened, nodding occasionally and then announced he knew the place we were looking for.

"Great," Jake exclaimed at Walter's description of the place. "You three go and check it out. Karen and I are going to Window Rock and spend the night in a motel, if we can borrow Walter's truck."

"The keys are in the truck, Jake," answered Walter.

I was surprised that Jake was dismissing us to carry out a mission this important without his supervision. My attention was drawn to Karen. Her stare was like a laser boring into Jake's mind. I was happy to embark on our expedition, leaving the two lovebirds at each other's throats.

The afternoon sun was resting on a large bank of clouds, painting the sky an even hue of deep indigo, when Walter, Molly and I set off in the truck. We were going to see the place where we would meet Manny and exchange the gold. While Walter gave directions, Molly kept an eye on the odometer and carefully wrote down distances, directions and landmarks. All the details would be given to Manny so he could find us in the middle of the desert.

We followed a shallow wash, dodging the small junipers that were struggling to survive in the arid land. The truck, heavy with gold, crept along, bouncing us from our seats and making Walter laugh. After a few more miles, he told me to cross the wash. He pointed toward a large outcropping of rock that looked like a cracked coffee cup. As we got closer, the formation grew in size. It stood fifty or sixty feet high. A crack ran from top to bottom, barely big enough for a man to squeeze through.

"This entrance leads to the center of the rocks," Walter stated, "but we want to drive to the other side."

As we drove around the rocks, a series of arroyos spread out from the base. They were shallow enough for the truck to cross, but quickly got deeper as they stretched out into the desert. Once I crossed to the back of the rock formation, I saw where Walter was taking us. There was another entrance big enough to hide the truck. We came up over a small rise and I pulled the truck into the shade of some high rocks and got out.

I walked back up the rise and looked out at the desert. It was beautiful.

And it was empty. There was no sign of another human being, just sagebrush and junipers dotting the horizon. I looked back and discovered that I couldn't see the truck. Perfect.

Walter led us along a narrow path through the rocks to the center, which opened to a flat area about thirty feet in diameter. He walked ahead to another opening in the rocks.

"This leads to the entrance we saw from the other side," he stated.

It looked barely wide enough for a man to fit through. Walter looked up at the fortress and picked a handhold. He started to climb up the rocks. Molly and I followed. At about fifteen feet up there was an opening in the rocks where we could look out and see the approach to our new rendezvous spot. I looked along the road that we had traveled. Tomorrow, we would be able to see Manny's approach for at least a mile. I scouted the place where he would have to park his car. I imagined him squeezing through the rock's opening with our money. We would have the drop on him the entire way.

Molly smiled, "This is perfect, Walter."

He returned her smile.

"Hank, see that pile of fallen rock and the stand of cottonwoods?" Molly asked. "That will be a good hiding place."

I looked over the edge to where Molly pointed. The cottonwoods' shade left the rocks deep in shadow.

Molly nudged me. "Karen could hide down there."

"What about you?"

"I thought of something else for me. I'll tell you about it later."

It unnerved me when she did that but I had learned to trust her instincts. "What were you saying about Karen hiding in the rocks?"

"Someone needs to make sure no one's hiding in the back seat of Manny's car. The rocks by the trees are a good place for someone to hide and check the car once it's parked. Like Karen," Molly stated. "Walter, this is perfect."

Walter smiled. "I told you I found a good spot."

Molly's approval settled my apprehension. I could believe that it was all going to come off okay. Then she came up with yet another wrinkle.

"Let's unload the gold. There's an overhang back where the truck is parked. It'll be protected." Molly led me back to the narrow path. "You and

Jake can show Manny the gold and leave. He'll have to reload the gold into the truck and that will provide you with plenty of time to escape and not be followed."

"It won't take long to unload the bags." Molly pulled some dried sagebrush aside. "The gold can be hidden right here." She noticed my hesitation in answering her. "We could stay up here tonight and sleep in the truck if you're worried about the gold," she suggested.

I knew leaving the gold wasn't going to make Jake happy.

"We'll go back and see what Jake thinks."

Her eyes brimmed with enthusiasm. "Let's do it now. I'm sure Jake has already left for the motel with Karen. Walter, we can run you back to your place." She reached over and placed her hand on my forearm. "It'll be okay, Hank."

Watching Molly take control made Walter smile broadly. "This place reminds me of Shiprock, the *Tsebida'hi*, the rock-with-wings. It is the great bird that brought the Navajo to our homeland."

Molly and I listened to Walter's soft tone. We both knew the story, but didn't interrupt.

"The great stoneship brought The People from the underworld." Walter looked out over the desert. "This is the land that the stoneship brought us to many, many centuries ago. This land." He raised his arms and spread them towards the desert. "This is our homeland." Walter turned and faced us. "The Spanish came looking for the seven cities of gold. When they didn't find them, they tried to take the land of the Pueblo Indians. The Spanish stayed in this land for three hundred years." Walter shook his head, as if to say, these were troubled times. "Why does the white man want to be so rich? Look at what the search for gold has done for the *bilagaana*, and what the *bilagaana* has done to the Indian. We don't need the *bilagaana's* gold or greed." Walter turned and his eyes met mine. "Hank, you remove the gold from the reservation tomorrow. That will be good. But you must be careful."

The flap of wings caused us to all look to the sky. A crow circled our hiding place and then disappeared.

"You be careful," repeated Walter.

* * *

The last hints of purple just barely grazed the edge of the earth. Molly and I headed back to the outcropping of rock after leaving Walter at his hogan. I thought I knew the way but found that I needed the directions and distances Molly had carefully written down. It was pretty dark by the time we found the rock formation. I left the headlights on, pointed to where we had hidden the gold. The brush we had piled on it looked undisturbed, but I had to see it for myself. I pulled back a couple of pieces of sagebrush and surveyed the bags that I knew were filled with gold coins. Molly sat in the truck and watched me. When I turned and smiled, she cut the headlights and sat in the glow of the dome light.

I reached through the open door for Molly's hand. Molly slid across the seat and pressed up against me. When the door shut, darkness enveloped us. Finally my eyes adjusted to the blackness. The moon was rising and casting its glow on our secret spot in the middle of millions-of-years-old rocks. I could barely make out the features of Molly's face, even though it was only inches from mine. But I could tell she was smiling. She pulled me close and hugged me.

"Look at those stars." I pointed up. The sky was littered with pinpoints of light. Thousands of stars surrounded the Big and Little Dippers. "The two Dippers are the only constellations I actually know," I said.

Molly laughed. "Those are technically not constellations, they're called asterisms. Let's take off the topper and sleep in the truck bed. We can lie and watch the stars. I'll tell you some of the star patterns' names," she said.

It sounded like a great idea. We got out of the truck and worked quickly, undoing the topper's clamps and fasteners.

"You like it out here, don't you?" Molly asked as we worked.

"Yeah, I do. When I met Walter it was the first time I had spent any time out in the desert. I've always enjoyed solitude. That's why I have my little place out of town. It used to be nowhere before all the developers got greedy. The desert provides seclusion. When I started staying with Walter, we could go weeks without seeing anyone. But then I don't need to tell you about life on the rez."

Molly smiled in the moonlight. "I'm glad you like it out here." She squeezed my hand. "Tomorrow, I want you to be careful."

"I will. I feel comfortable with the plan. And I want you to be careful when you go into Standing Rock."

"Don't worry. I'll look just like any other Indian on the rez. Walter's old truck will provide the perfect disguise. Just a squaw visiting the Chapter House. Manny won't even give me a nod."

"Oh, I don't know. He always had an eye for a pretty girl."

Molly smiled again. "Thanks. But I won't be pretty tomorrow. And don't forget I'll be looking for him. He'll be the one out of place. I'll be carrying my .38, so I will have the advantage."

"Yeah, he is going to stick out," I agreed.

Molly sat in silence for a couple minutes. I knew she was deep in thought.

"Do you think Manny will come alone?"

"No, he never goes anywhere alone. There will be someone with him or at least covering his back. That's why your plan is so good. Jake will call Manny and tell him to go to Gallup and wait. Manny will go to the El Rancho, have a meal and wait. Then tomorrow we'll call him and tell him to drive to the gas station in Standing Rock and to be there by noon. Then we'll call and give him the final directions. He won't have time to pull any surprises."

"How do you think he'll react when he sees you?"

"He'll be surprised, but it'll be okay. He knows me and that all we want is to exchange the gold for the money and come out of this alive. Manny is going to get what he came for. We're not changing the deal. And no one is raising the stakes."

37
Jake
Thursday Evening

Karen and I had borrowed Walter's beat-up truck and headed for Window Rock. I didn't like doing this but knew I had to keep my part of the bargain. Earlier, against my better judgment, I'd agreed to take her to town, rent a motel room, take showers and pick up some supplies. That would provide her a way to meet whatever daily cleanliness requirements she had and give me a chance to call Manny. I had to tell him his travel plans and, with secrecy being so important, I wanted to use a land line. I also had to tell Manny to come alone.

She immediately slipped into the bathroom and our tiny room was soon filled with the sound of running water. I went directly to the bed and stared at the phone.

Just pick it up, dial the numbers, tell Manny exactly what needs to happen and then hang up.

It was that simple. Just do it. The longer I waited, the more nervous I'd get. The more nervous, the more likely it was that I'd crack, that I'd screw up, that I'd give away whatever advantage we held.

Even though three other people were with me on this deal, right now I felt very much alone. Just me. My fears. And Manny. I felt the weight of the world on my shoulders. I'd been the one who'd brought them all into this. I'd be the one responsible for any and all fuck-ups.

I grabbed the phone, went through the half-page list of instructions for making a long distance call and got so involved in the details that I nearly lost my nervousness.

"*Hola.*"

"Tell Manny that Jake is on the phone." I heard footsteps, some rustling and then Manny.

"Jake?" He sounded friendly, even cheerful.

"Yes. It's me."

"I can't wait to see you, my friend. When will we be able to get together?" No beating around the bush this time. I responded in kind.

"Tomorrow. Noon."

"Excellent. Are you coming here?"

"No." So far, so good. I felt good, confident. But I was afraid that it wasn't going to get any easier.

"No?" A long pause. "Where then?" I sensed the tension returning.

"I have some instructions. They are a bit complicated so you may want to write them down."

"Are you sure you cannot stick to our original plans?"

He was giving me an out, a chance to return to what had been planned, to what worked best for him. Just liked he'd done with Ralphie.

"No. It has to be this way or I'm afraid we won't get to see you."

"Jake," he lowered his voice and I could practically feel him squeezing the telephone, "are you sure you know what you are doing? Changing one's travel plans at the last minute can be very expensive."

No. No, Manny, I'm not sure. I'm scared shitless and I wish this whole fucking mess was over with. That's what I wanted to say. That's what I was feeling. But I lied. I mustered up every dishonest bone I had. "As sure as I've ever been about anything."

I heard muffled voices on his end of the line and then, "Go ahead. Tell me where."

If I could have just given him freeways and highways and county roads, this would have been very simple. But if anyone was listening in, I had to make it something only he'd understand.

"You remember the city where we first met?"

He paused, thinking, and then said he remembered. "I do."

I asked another question, just to make sure. "What happened that night?"

I heard a small chuckle. "We met two ladies. A mother and her daughter."

I wanted to share in his chuckle but I was too nervous. "I want you to go there, tomorrow morning, to that same hotel. And bring my money."

"Anything else?" The moment had passed. He was pissed.

I cleared my throat. *As a matter of fact...Oh, by the way...Now that you mention it...*

Here we were, at the crux of this whole deal and I was trying to think of nice, cordial ways to start telling him.

I finally just blurted it out. "You have to come alone."

He laughed. "You can't be serious."

"Manny, I'm deadly serious."

"But you will have a friend with you, won't you? I'm afraid I'll feel like a third wheel if I don't bring someone."

"Manny, this is one of those times when you're just going to have to trust me. You have to come by yourself. You *have* to trust me."

"That is getting to be a familiar theme, is it not?"

He was right. I'd asked him that quite a few times already. "Manny, I wish it didn't have to be this way, but it does."

"You sure, my friend?" His edginess increased.

"Yes," I said, more convincingly than I felt. "I'm sure."

"And everything is going to be all right? No more surprises?"

"Everything is going to be just fine. You be there tomorrow and I'll call you with the rest of the instructions."

"Tomorrow morning, then. Goodbye, Jake."

Manny hung up the phone without waiting for my reply. I imagined him standing for a moment by the telephone, wondering if Jake Marley was being straight with him, wondering if the change in plans was necessary, wondering if he'd have to kill me.

I cradled my own phone, wondering who the hell I thought I was, wondering what I'd gotten into, wondering if there wasn't another way out.

* * *

I had no idea a motel room could be so small. A bed. A table with two chairs. A couple of cheap lamps. Me.

And Karen.

"Jake," she said without looking up. "I'm worried. I don't like these changes."

I thought about answering but I didn't. I'd grown tired of her droning on and on about this latest change. She must've brought it up a half dozen times. For someone who had hardly said "boo" for the last couple of days, she'd suddenly come to life. Questioning. Arguing. Pleading with me not to pull any more tricks on Manny.

"Tricks?" I asked, immediately regretting that I was actually taking part in this.

She bristled. "You know what I mean. Changes. More and more changes." She was leaning, arms folded across her chest, against the wall. I was semi-sprawled on the bed. She was as tight as I was loose.

"You keep telling me that this Manny guy is dangerous, that he's capable of just about anything."

"He is," I answered absentmindedly.

"And that he doesn't like changes."

"He doesn't." I sat up. It was time to put a stop to this. "Look. Manny doesn't know about any of this. We could have changed things two dozen times between ourselves." I waved my arms, trying to emphasize my point. "But he doesn't know that. There's no way he could know any of that. And, as long as we stick to what we've just told him, we won't have any problems."

She grew strangely silent, like I'd touched a nerve.

Since day one, she'd cast big shadows about herself. Folding with four aces. The phones. Showing up at Porter's. On and on. But I'd kept her around. At first, because she'd thrown away eleven grand in the poker game, I thought there might be more money. If what she'd told me about the football betting software was true, then there might be even more money than I'd originally thought. And she was sharp, fun, great in bed—and she had a car. Mostly, it was easier to keep an eye on her when she was right next to me. And, even though I hated to admit it, she'd grown on me. I *wanted* her to be with me.

But now this.

"Changing the plan isn't a problem," I said, stopping just short of telling her that *she* was.

She shrugged, as if indicating I was foolish for being so trusting. I watched her as she continued meandering about the room. She moved. She stopped.

Her casual manner belied the tension that was continuing to grow between us. Was she doing this on purpose? Manipulating me? Trying to make me tense? Throw me off?

My curiosity magnified. "Why are you suddenly so interested in how this thing is going down?"

She stopped walking but didn't look at me. "Don't you know?"

"If I knew, I wouldn't ask."

She turned slowly, hands folded prayer-like in front of her. "Don't you know that I'm worried about losing you?"

She was fabulous. One moment inviting me to play a dangerous game of "Who Do You Trust?" and the next acting like "The Woman He Left Behind." When this was all over, I'd see to it that she got a nomination for best actress in a supporting role. But right now, I had to see where this was going. "You're worried about me?"

She inched closer. "It's more than just that." Her words came out slowly, carefully, saying little but conveying more. "I think we've got something. You and me."

"You think we've got something?"

"I do." She kept closing the distance between us, her eyes locked with mine. "And I don't want to lose it."

"And I'd like to believe you." I reached out and grabbed her shoulders. "But your bullshit…"

She wrestled herself free. "It's not bullshit!"

"Then what is it?"

"I'm worried."

I cut her off. "All you're worried about is not getting a cut of the money."

"That's cold." She stiffened. "Even for you."

"It might be cold but it's still the truth. Isn't it?"

She turned her back to me. "What I was going to say was that I'm worried about you. But I'm also worried about the rest of us. If something goes wrong, it won't just be you that pays the price. There's Hank and Molly and Walter. And me. It's not just you that's laying it on the line."

Okay. That hit home. A little. But I still wasn't buying what she was selling. Even though the wrapping gave the appearance of concern, underneath, where it counted, she was only worried about herself. "Look. With the possible exception of you, everyone that's here has chosen to be here. We know what we're doing. It's gonna work!"

"So no matter what I say, you're still going to go through with this."

"It's like this, Karen." I wished she'd turn around. "Out there in those rocks is more money than I can imagine. You and I both know that chances to grab the brass ring don't come around very often. This is my chance. I've worked for it. I've earned it. I've waited a long time for my chance and I'm not going to let it get away."

"So that's what this is all about? Jake Marley grabbing the brass ring?" She pivoted and faced me. "It's a good thing we're all going to be here so we can be a witness to your greatness. I just hope your triumph doesn't turn into our tragedy."

I shrugged and deflected yet another attack from her. I had to give her credit. She was using all her weapons. "There's more."

"More?"

"Yeah. One more thing." This time, I leveled my eyes into hers. "Don't think I haven't thought about taking this for myself. I have. But I know Manny. And I know that not going through with this would be the same thing as signing all of our death warrants."

She paused. I'd gotten her attention with that last statement. "But…"

"But nothing. I'm doing it. I have to."

"No matter what?"

I noticed a hint of challenge in her words. *Where was she going with this?* While a thousand thoughts ricocheted across my brain, only one made sense. "We stick to this plan; we'll all be out of here right after noon."

She arched a skeptical eyebrow. "And Manny is going to just let us all walk away."

I nodded. "I know him. He'll keep his word."

"Then why not tell him where the gold is and leave a little note so he can just send you the money?"

"Very funny."

"No. Really."

"Karen. This is business. It's done face to face. Man to man."

She quickly picked another tack. "You're scared shitless and deep down you know you can't pull this off by yourself. You need me. You need us."

"You're crazy, woman."

"Am I?" She stopped right in front of me. "Then why aren't you here by yourself? Why are you up to your elbows in this with three other people, two of whom you just met? Why did you drag your ol' buddy Hank into this cesspool? Why?"

"Enough!"

"Enough what? Enough of your bullshit?"

"No! Enough of your bullshit."

She glared at me. I glared right back. "Nobody is forcing anybody to be here. True. I'm not letting you go. Not right now. But you came here of your own free will."

"I offered to give you a ride. A fucking ride! Then people started getting killed."

"And that's why you're not going anywhere. People have been killed. I don't want any more deaths. If we all stick together, we'll be all right."

"That's what you said in the desert."

"And that's what I'm still saying."

"Then how come I don't feel any safer?"

"Maybe the question you want to ask yourself is this: How come we're all still alive and those other assholes are getting chewed up by the coyotes right now?" I let my words hang in the air, become part of what we breathed, what we felt, what we were. "You should be fucking glad Hank had his guns, that Molly was there." Karen stiffened, still ready for battle. But ever so gradually she relaxed. We were still alive. If we stuck together, we'd still be alive tomorrow. And, we'd have the money. This would be over.

We stared at each other. Nothing was said but I could *feel* the wheels turning in her head. She was searching for her next avenue.

I didn't give her the chance. "Why are you suddenly so interested?"

She perked up. "Because there's still time."

"For what? To run off with the gold?"

"Yes!" She stepped forward, recharged. "There's enough for both—for all of us. Hank and Molly. Walter, even. And there's still time."

"So you're doing all this, saying all this, to get me to take the gold?"

"Yes! Jake! Can't you see that it would be so easy to do?" She was half-pleading, half-selling.

"No, Karen. I can't." I turned away from her and neither of us spoke for an eternity. The silence lingered, multiplied, until it filled the room. I stared at her. Who was she?

It seemed more likely all the time that she was a pro. She was a not-so-small-time con artist who had drifted into town looking for big money. Maybe she'd been in the women's john at Smiley's last Saturday and overheard me and Manny talking. Maybe our voices carried through the walls. Maybe she'd done some quick digging, asked a few questions of the regulars. Maybe she'd simply been smart enough to keep her eyes and ears open and her mouth shut. Hell, I'd even made it easy for her. I'd told her the whole story a few days after meeting her. All she had to do was pick up a few more details and she had enough information to run a scam on me.

Was I right? Was she making her big play? Was she taking all of my own suspicions, mixing them together with a generous portion of my own greed and trying to get me to see her way of ending this little duel in the desert?

If so, I'd had enough. I turned and faced her. "So, you want to pack up the gold and leave tonight?"

She slowly nodded, still playing the part.

I just smiled. A half-smile but a smile nonetheless. No point in showing all my cards. "Sorry, doll. This is one hand I'm playing to the end."

"Fine." She stared at me, into me. "Have it your way, Jake. I'm going for a walk."

I stood up. "You're not going anywhere."

Her hand found the doorknob and opened it. "Think about it, Jake. You've got the keys to the truck and we're fifteen miles from the next town. Just where the fuck do you think I'm going to go?"

I didn't answer her. I just sat in the dark, fingering the truck keys and wondering how this was all going to turn out.

38
Hank
Dawn Friday

I could feel the warmth from the rising sun on my closed eyelids. It had just broken the horizon enough to reach the truck and fall on my face. I opened one eye and was blinded. The blazing tip of the sun was slanting through the outcropping's opening. Molly was still in the shadows, protected from the crack of dawn.

My neck was stiff and my arm had gone to sleep. It was wrapped around Molly, who had somehow made herself comfortable. While the Ford was about as big a pickup as you could buy, it didn't make for a very good place to sleep. The sleeping bags had provided little cushion against the metal-ribbed truck bed.

It had been fun camping out with Molly, even with the building anticipation. The day we'd been waiting for had finally come. Before, it had been something remotely in the distance, like your high school graduation, your wedding day, the birth of your first child. Now, the day was upon us.

I stirred slightly and Molly smiled without opening her eyes. I ran my tongue around my teeth and tried to suck the morning breath from my mouth.

"Good morning." Molly rose up on one elbow and shielded her eyes from the sun with her other hand.

"Sorry I woke you. My arm was asleep."

"Poor, baby. I was awake." Molly stood and stretched. Her shirt rode up and revealed her brown stomach and belly button. I leaned into it and kissed her warm flesh. She held my head to her stomach and gently swayed from side to side.

"I want you to be careful today."

"You've told me that a dozen times," I replied gently.

"Yeah, well, I just want to say it enough so that I'm sure you've heard me." She walked to the tailgate and jumped down. "We should probably get back. I'm sure Jake is going to be pretty antsy this morning. And Karen has been…"

"Amen to that." I cut Molly off. She gave me an all-knowing smile and turned to jump down from the tailgate.

We were surrounded by rock. Less than ten feet away was sixteen million dollars in gold. I needed to see it one more time before we drove back. I pulled a couple pieces of brush off the pile. There it was. Just like it had been the other times I had looked at it. Bags filled with gold, still as the dead. I replaced the brush and the gold was gone. We were once again in a stand of rock, nothing special, just home to a few lonely desert varmints.

"Seen enough?" Molly asked.

I laughed. "Yeah. It just doesn't seem real."

Molly walked to me and took my face in her hands. She looked at me for a long moment. "You…"

"I know. Be careful," I finished for her. "I will."

"Okay, let's go."

* * *

Jake was standing outside Walter's hogan. No one else was in sight. I brought the truck to a halt and jumped out.

"You're back already?" I asked.

Jake shrugged his shoulders, not stating the obvious.

"Where is everybody?" asked Molly.

Jake nodded towards the hogan. "Karen went inside to get some more sleep," replied Jake.

Molly and I exchanged a quick glance.

"Walter left a note saying he was going out to check his sheep or something."

"I think I'll go see if I can find him," Molly said as she reached over and gave my hand a reassuring squeeze. "I won't be long."

After Molly had disappeared, Jake gave me a long look and then gazed out into the desert.

"Hank, you are my best friend. I want to say that first. I didn't want you to be involved in this. I wanted to keep my promise to you."

"Yeah, I know, Jake." I could tell that Jake was feeling the weight of the day.

"Everything was so simple at the beginning. Go out in the desert, collect the gold, give it to Manny and he gives me the cash." Jake looked at me and I nodded. "Easy money. Simple. Except that DeDe is dead, Cloud is dead, Williams is dead, and so are three other guys out there, and you're involved up to your ass. I'm sorry."

"Well," I said to be saying something, "today is the day, huh?"

Jake looked at me, but didn't respond. Then he turned and looked off in the distance and blew out a long breath.

"I was thinking we might as well just spend the morning up at the rocks until its time to call," I said.

"We'll call now," answered Jake.

"What? You're not supposed to call until noon."

"Well I'm changing things, again." Jake shot a look in the direction of the hogan. "It will give him less..." Jake let it drop. His voice was testy and he looked as if he hadn't slept. "He's probably in Gallup right now. What's the difference when he gets to Standing Rock? It'll take him over an hour once I call and tell him where to go." Jake waited for a reply.

"I suppose it doesn't make any difference." I shrugged. Something was going on. A lover's quarrel? A bad night's sleep? Too much anticipation?

"You okay?"

"Yeah. I'm just tried of waiting."

Molly's return interrupted our conversation. "Hey, I found Walter," called Molly. "He'll be back shortly."

Jake and I turned to watch Molly approach.

"Molly, we're going to drive up to the hide-out and call Manny."

"I thought you were calling at noon?"

"Well, I'm tired of waiting," replied Jake. "No reason to not get going."

Molly looked around for Karen, but didn't question where she was. "Okay, then I'd better get going."

"Do you have your gun?" I asked.

"Right, here." Molly turned around and pulled up her white t-shirt. The .38 was stuck in the back of her jeans. The t-shirt was gray with age and too big. She was also wearing an old jean jacket that was almost as white as the t-shirt had once been. There was a tear in the knee of her jeans. She hadn't combed her hair. To add a final touch to her look, she had tied a red kerchief around her neck.

"How do I look?" she asked me.

"Beautiful."

She shot me a broad smile of white teeth and her eyes showed the beauty I was falling in love with.

"You be careful," we both said at the same time. I kissed her quickly on the lips and looked at her.

"I should get going." Molly's statement broke our moment.

I looked around at Walter's old green pickup. "The keys are in it. Are you sure Manny won't…"

Molly cut me off, "I will be all right. He won't even see me."

* * *

There was no talking on the ride to our rendezvous spot. I had tried carrying on a one-sided conversation for a while and then gave up. Karen sat between Jake and me. I could feel the tension radiating from her body. She looked straight ahead during the entire trip.

When we arrived, Jake's mood brightened. I could tell when we pulled into the rocks that he liked the new location. He jumped from the truck and immediately asked where the gold was. I walked around to his side.

"Well?"

I raised my eyebrows and bent down and pulled up a couple a branches of sagebrush. Jake had almost landed on the gold when he had jumped from the truck. We all surveyed the stash.

"Jake?" Karen said, standing by the passenger door. "There's still time." Her voice was small. The look on her face told me that there had been a lot of conversation about the gold the night before.

"No, there isn't," Jake said defiantly.

I held my breath, waiting for her response. None came. Maybe she'd figured out it wasn't worth arguing anymore.

"I'm going to make the call and then you can show us around." Jake turned back to the truck and went for the phone.

Karen walked back to the opening in the rock and looked out at the desert.

Jake punched a long distance number and waited.

"Can I have Juan Maniandez's room?…Manny?…Yes, it's Jake….Yeah, I know. It's early. What's the matter? You have other plans this morning?"

Jake was trying to make his voice sound light and friendly. I wished I had joined Karen out of earshot and not heard this conversation.

"It's time to get moving. We're wasting daylight. No, nothing's wrong. There is just no reason to wait. Yes. Yes. Look, Manny, it is now or never. I've got your gifts. You either come and get them or I'm gone. Yeah. It's very simple. I'm not playing games. You bring the money and I give you your gifts. Just like we originally planned. That part hasn't changed one bit. Not one bit."

I wished I had a cigarette. I quickly glanced in Karen's direction. She hadn't moved. I turned back to Jake. He was listening. His face didn't give me any kind of read. Then, he gave Manny the directions.

"You drive to Standing Rock. You know where it is? Stop at the gas station. Yeah, the Mini Mart. You got a cell phone?" Jake snapped his fingers and made a writing motion. I dug in my pocket and found a pencil to hand him, along with a map to write on. Jake jotted down some numbers.

"Good. I'll call you in an hour and fifteen minutes with the final instructions. No. Don't worry. There's no one out here listening to our calls. This is the reservation. I'm just being careful. No, Manny. All I want is my money. I'm not changing anything. You should have no problem getting to Standing Rock in time." Jake hung up the phone and smiled. "It's happening."

* * *

The three of us killed the next hour by taking a slow walk around the perimeter of the outcropping and going over our plan. Except for the crack in the front and the large opening in the back, the formation was almost a perfect circle of solid rock. The inside consisted of two large, open areas with a narrow path between them. From the back, there was a series of arroyos that spread out and gave the illusion of several escape paths. But if you took the wrong one, it might be a dead end. Molly and I had scouted them and knew which one to take if things got hairy. But I didn't figure we would need to.

I showed Jake the perch where we could watch Manny's approach. Then we squeezed through the crack and I showed Karen the cottonwoods and rocks where we expected her to wait. Manny would be told to leave his car with the key in it near the trees. Once he had gone into the outcropping, Karen was supposed to make sure no one else was in the car and then get in it, turn it around and be ready to leave. If there was someone else in the car, we'd wait to see how it played out.

As I spoke she watched me, but every so often her eyes found Jake. She listened to the instructions without comment.

"Do you understand everything you're supposed to do?"

Karen simply nodded.

"Okay," I answered, wondering what was going on between these two. "Once Manny sees there isn't anything to be concerned about, everything will go smoothly." I looked to Jake for confirmation for my next move. "But here's a gun just in case." I handed her the .32 I'd carried with me.

"Yeah," he responded. "You won't need it but…"

I checked my watch. "He should be there in fifteen minutes or so. Let's go back to the truck and get out of the sun."

We went back through the rocks. Once we were surrounded, the height of the encirclement of rocks provided almost complete shade and cooled the air.

"Jake, everything—"

Suddenly there was a ringing. We all jumped at the same time. It was the phone. I looked at Jake and he looked at me.

"Well, answer it," I said.

"Hello?" Jake nodded and then held the phone out to me. "It's Molly."

"What? Already?"

I took the phone. "Molly, is anything wrong?"

Her voice was soft. "He's here."

"He's there? Already?"

"Yeah. He just pulled in."

"Is he alone?"

"It looks like it. He's driving a gray Le Sabre. I can't see anyone else in the car. He's standing in front of the Mini Mart looking around."

"Where are you?"

"I'm up the hill at the Chapter House looking out a window."

"Is there anyone else around?"

"No. Just a couple kids at the school playing on the swings. The Mini Mart is still closed. There're some sheep in the road."

"Very funny."

"There are." Molly stifled a laugh. "Now they're moving away from him. He's just standing there, looking around."

"You're sure he's alone?"

"It appears that way. You call him and I'll wait until he leaves town. I'll hang back and see if he's being followed. I'll call again about fifteen minutes after he leaves. Okay?"

"Yeah, you be—"

"Careful," she finished for me.

I hung up the phone and handed it to Jake. "Game on."

39
Jake
Friday Mid-morning

I looked for Karen but she wasn't where I'd last seen her. A quick three-sixty found her walking toward the road. I turned back to Hank, gave him the "Now what's going on?" shrug and took off after her. She hadn't been walking very fast and I was next to her in a few seconds. "Goin' somewhere?"

"No," she answered without looking at me.

Okay. She was still being cool. Ever since last night. Ever since she tried to get me to take the gold and run.

"I want to get out of here." More talking, still no eye contact.

"No can do."

She stopped walking. "Can't? Or won't?"

"Can't!" I snapped. "And you know all the reasons."

She turned and faced me, her eyes burning into mine. "You know I'm right. You know we could do this."

"Not and live to tell about it."

Her hands went up in frustration. "Jake. There's still time."

I stepped back and stared at her. It was time to expose her. "You're a pro. Just like me. You hit town. You kept your eyes open. People like you and me can spot a fish a mile away." I stepped closer. "You spotted me. Shit," I shrugged, "I must've stuck out like a chimp in church."

"Don't flatter yourself." She turned her head.

I smiled. "You *smelled* the money, didn't you?"

321

No reply. Just contempt.

I pressed on. "You smelled big money, bigger than the eleven grand in that poker game, so you decided to stick around for the long haul. Hell, I've done the same thing myself. Dozens of times. Let the fish win a few small ones 'cause you know—you can *feel*—that there's a much bigger payoff just down the road." I paused. "That about it?"

No reply. Just her head crooked to one side, staring off at the horizon. Seconds ticked by, turning into minutes. The wind did its best to push us around, bothering us with dust and dirt and the occasional tumbleweed.

"You've got some ego, Jake Marley." She turned and faced me.

"If you say so," I said flatly.

She shook her head and started to walk away. I grabbed her arm and pulled her back.

"I see it like this. However you got involved, you were thinking that sixteen million is worth whatever the risks might be. You were thinking that you could bat your eyelashes and somehow con ol' Jake into double-crossing Manny." I stepped closer. "And when that didn't work, you figured you'd use my own suspicions to build a case against Manny, that you'd turn me against him."

She tried to wriggle free from my grasp but I held on.

"But what you didn't know, what you hadn't counted on, was that Manny would never and I mean *never,* let this go. It's impossible to double-cross Manny and live to tell about it."

"Stop!" She broke free and put her hands up. "No more!" She pivoted and took a few steps away from me. "Don't you see? It's not the money. I don't want the money."

"C'mon," I protested. "People like you and me are *only* interested in the money. It's what makes us tick."

"Not anymore."

"Don't bullshit me."

She stood, quietly, her back toward me. The wind tugged at her clothes, pushed her hair all in one direction. "I told you the night we met." Her voice was barely audible above the wind. "I could tell people's fortunes."

"I remember."

"And what did I tell you?"

I thought. That night. The poker game. Afterward, in the bar. "Something about travel and money."

She quickly added, "And danger."

"So you said."

"It's real. The danger. I can feel it."

I scoffed. "Now you're telling me that you really are a psychic?"

"I'm telling you that I got the creeps when I was reading your palm."

"Nice try." I grabbed her shoulders. "First you tell me you've got the only copy of some miracle software but there might be some Las Vegas bad guys after you. Now you tell me you're Madame Zola the stargazer. What's next? A space creature on holiday?"

She stomped her foot. "Jake, I'm telling you the truth!"

"And which truth is it? Which story?"

"All of it."

"And the part about Las Vegas?"

"I made that up."

"You made that up?"

"I had to tell you something to get your attention, to get you to keep me around."

"So there's no software? No half million dollars?"

"And no math-genius husband named David." She cocked her head to one side. "Come on, Jake, you didn't really buy that story, did you?"

I sidestepped her question and plowed forward. "And the rest?"

"It's all true. I swear it!"

I didn't believe her. There was too much that didn't add up. I checked my watch. Pretty soon it wouldn't matter. Manny would be here. The deal would go down. Just like I planned.

"There's no more time, Karen. He'll be here in a few minutes."

She looked off into the distance. "And you think it's all gonna go like clockwork?"

"I do."

She turned and studied my face, searching for clues that I was quoting from the Gospel and not the *Fantasyland Gazette*. She stared, apparently multiplying whatever facts she had against whatever she was thinking, and dividing it by whatever she was feeling. "What happens to me—to us—after this is over?"

I shook my head. "I don't know. I suppose it depends on what happens in the next half hour."

She nodded. It was as if our entire week had crystallized down to this one moment. She was in or she was out. Finally, she stood up straight. "The way things stand; I guess I don't have much of a choice."

"I guess you don't."

She closed her eyes. I couldn't tell if she was shielding herself from the glare of the sun or from the glare of truth. She sighed as she opened her eyes and faced me. "What do you want me to do?"

I explained it all once again.

"And I won't be in any danger?"

"None." When this was all over, I was going to have a ton of questions for her.

I led her to her spot and helped her get into position. She got out her gun and I showed how to release the safety, how to hold it, how to aim. She acted like she was cooperating but I'd given up trying to figure where her head was at. All I knew, all I cared about, was that she'd be tucked into this little stand of cottonwoods and finally out of my way.

40
Hank
Friday Noon

After Molly made her second call and said that Manny was on his way, a knot started to tie itself in my stomach. When the little tail of dust began to grow, heading our way, the knot became unbearably tight.

"It must be him," I said. Jake nodded that he had heard me. Karen had been in her hiding place, out of sight, for about ten minutes. I glanced quickly toward the cottonwoods. I couldn't see her.

I looked back across the desert. It had to be Manny. This was the first time I had seen anyone even near here in the last two days. I checked my watch. It had been just over thirty minutes since Molly had called. He was making good time. I was happy to see he had finally arrived to get *his* gold.

I spun the binoculars' focus ring, bringing the dust storm in and out of view. The image became clear. It was a gray Le Sabre going faster than it should across the desert. The car bounced over sagebrush and kicked up sand. It looked like an uncomfortable ride.

"It's him," stated Jake, flatly.

If we had any second thoughts, it was now too late to change our minds. We continued to watch the approaching car in silence. Finally it was close enough to see that only a driver was visible. It came to the left of the small rise where Karen was hiding in the rocks and stopped. No one got out of the car.

"We'd better go down and meet him," Jake whispered.

We scampered down the rocks and took our places just inside the small entrance crack. It was cool and dark in the shade of the surrounding rocks, but there were beads of sweat on Jake's brow. I wiped my own forehead, dried my hand on my jeans and pulled out my automatic. We stood and listened. There wasn't a sound. Finally, a car door opened.

Jake poked his head around the entrance and took a quick look out the crack. "It's Manny. He's just standing there with the door open, looking around."

"What's he doing now?"

Jake looked again. "He's leaning over in the car. Now he's taking a briefcase out." There was excitement in his voice. "He's putting the briefcase on the roof. He's opening it. Now he's shutting it." Jake pulled his head back. "He's coming," he whispered excitedly.

I was sure my heart could be seen pounding through my shirt. My hand tightened on the gun's grip. I could hear Manny's steps coming closer on the pieces of loose rock. And then he was through the crack looking at Jake.

"*Buenos Dias*, Jake." He held out his right hand. Jake took it and gave a quick shake. "I hope there are no snakes in here." Manny smiled. He'd put on a few pounds since the last time I had seen him, but he still looked to be in very good shape. His short, black hair was colored by only a few gray ones. I wondered if he dyed it.

He must have caught me looking at him out of the corner of his eye. Slowly, he turned in my direction. First he looked at the gun and then me.

"Hank, *amigo*. I didn't know you'd be here. It has been a long time." His eyes held mine. Then he glanced at the gun, again. "You don't need the gun."

He held out his right hand. I looked at it and shifted the gun to my left and shook hands.

"It's just a precaution, Manny. Nothing personal, just business." I nodded to Jake, who stepped forward and quickly frisked Manny. He lifted a Glock 9mm from a shoulder holster.

"You're a little overdressed for the desert. It's a bit too hot for a jacket out here today," I said in response to the automatic.

"Hank, you know I always carry a gun." Manny's voice was matter-of-fact. He might have been ordering a Belgian waffle. "Especially, when I'm alone and carrying all this money."

"Well, we'll keep the gun for you until it's time to go," I answered.

Jake stuck the pistol in his jeans. And I put mine back in my belt to show there was no maliciousness on our part.

"Manny," said Jake, "let me show you your gold." There wasn't time for pleasantries between old friends.

Manny looked from me to Jake. "Yes, that would be nice. You lead the way." Manny turned to me. "Would you actually shoot me, Hank? I thought you were my *amigo*." Manny smiled.

I returned the smile and shook my head in a noncommittal way. "Let's go, Manny."

"*Si*, all business. No time to talk about art or life?" Manny smiled. He was always smiling. I knew that his smile did not always mean he was happy or pleased. "If you have any new work, I would like to see it some day." Manny was a lot more calm than Jake or I.

"Sure, anytime."

Jake led the way to the narrow passage and through to the other side. I followed Manny.

The big black truck sat in its spot, the topper still resting against the rock wall where Molly and I had left it.

"Come around here," Jake indicated.

We all stood looking at a pile of brush. Jake stooped and pulled back a couple of branches revealing our efforts.

"There are forty bags," Jake said. He ripped open a bag and brought out a handful of coins and showed them to Manny.

"They are very nice, but how do I know each bag is full of gold?"

Jake shot me a look and stood. "What do you want me to do, empty each one?"

Manny laughed. "No, Jake, just open a couple. That one there." He pointed with his right hand. "And that one. Open a few more and show me. I've waited a long time to see these gold coins. Now I want to enjoy the moment."

Jake hopped to a bag near the back, tossing branches from his way. He pulled open eight bags and revealed the gold that was within.

"Satisfied?" He slapped his hands together, causing a small cloud of dust.

"For now. Is it sixteen million?"

"Every coin is a Double Eagle twenty-dollar gold piece, weighing an ounce. Forty bags, each about fifty pounds. Depending on the price of gold, the melt value alone is at least sixteen million. But to coin collectors, it's worth way more than that," Jake answered. "Now let's see the money."

Manny stepped round to the open tailgate of the truck and faced us. He set down the briefcase and started to work the combination locks. Something in his manner made me jump. I drew the Beretta. When Jake saw me, he moved back and gave me a clear shot. Manny looked up and stopped his action.

"Jake, step over there and help our friend with the locks," I directed.

Jake moved over next to Manny. I had the gun leveled at Manny's chest. I wasn't ten feet away. Manny knew I wouldn't miss.

"Open the briefcase very slowly," said Jake in an even tone.

Manny finished the locks and popped the lid. For a second, neither moved. I couldn't see the contents. Jake reached in and brought out a second Glock and quickly stepped away from Manny.

"Where's the money?" Jake's voice was tight and angry.

Manny answered with a growing grin. It grew until his teeth showed bright.

"Where's the money?" Jake demanded. "We're standing here with sixteen million in gold. You could just as soon be dead and we'd be long gone by the time the coyotes finished gnawing on your bones."

"Jake, such a nasty picture you paint. And I thought Hank was the artist." The smile stayed on Manny's face, but his voice showed he was annoyed.

"Anything else in the case?" I asked.

Manny turned to look at me and the gun that was still pointed at him.

"Well, this." Jake held up a phone.

"What?"

Jake held the Glock at his side. "A phone," he repeated.

Manny shrugged. "Jake told me to bring a phone. This is the one I used when he called to give me directions."

"We also told you to bring the money. Now where's the money?" I asked. Then it hit me. Maybe Karen had found it in the car. But if she had, why hadn't she brought it in?

"Jake, go check the car," I directed. "I'll stay with our friend." I leveled the gun at his chest.

Manny smiled at me. Then his phone rang.

Jake and I froze.

"Should I get it?" Manny laughed and didn't wait for an answer. He flipped the receiver open and listened. "*Si,*" was all he said. The smile on Manny's face grew. "The money will be here shortly," he said to us as he hung up the phone.

Jake looked at Manny, his face full of questions. "What do you mean?"

"You didn't really think I'd bring three million dollars out into the desert by myself, did you?" The smile was now gone. "I'm not stupid."

Jake turned and started to run for the passage. He obviously had the same misgivings I did. We had more visitors coming.

"Follow him," I said. "Hurry." Manny closed the briefcase and slowly turned to follow. I gave him a shove to get him started. Manny shot me a look of contempt.

Jake was already through the passage and out of sight when Manny started to press through. When we came out the other side, Jake was standing outside the entrance looking through the binoculars.

"There's a black Jeep coming," Jake said. "There are four people in it." He described to us the sight the binoculars revealed. "Walter and Molly are in it."

"What?" My voice was filled with fear. "How'd they get Molly?"

Manny smiled at me. I was getting sick of his teeth. "Insurance."

I raised the gun so I could sight it at the center of his forehead. "I ought to blow your fucking brains all over these rocks." As my thumb pulled back on the hammer I could see a bead of sweat drop from Manny's brow.

"If you kill me, my men will kill your friends, Hank," he answered evenly.

"If anything happens to Molly or Walter, I'll end your life right here and right now."

He snorted in contempt. "They have their orders and I think you already know, Hank, that they do what I tell them to do."

"They're almost here." Jake's voice was constricted. He rubbed the day's growth on his chin nervously.

"But they're not going to kill anyone when they see I have a gun to your head." I pushed the gun's barrel harder between Manny's eyes, until his head moved away.

"Do you really want to take the gamble?" Manny's voice didn't indicate an ounce of fear. "You have a gun to my head." His eyes pierced my stare. "Just as there is a gun to your woman's head. And maybe my man's finger is not as steady as yours." Manny's eyes didn't even blink as I let my thumb slowly return the hammer to its resting place.

We heard the squeak of the Jeep's brakes as it came to a halt. Then there was silence.

"Okay, Manny, you go through first." I pushed the gun hard against his head for emphasis. He shot me a look of hatred. I knew he couldn't stand the position he was in. This was humiliating for Manny. Every time I shoved my gun in his face, he showed no fear, only hostility. I stepped back and gave him room to move past me. Jake stepped behind me and followed.

When we came out from the rock's shade, the mid-morning sun was blinding. The Jeep was less than thirty yards away, parked next to the Le Sabre. I looked for Karen, but she was nowhere in sight. I noticed Jake also quickly searching the area. Next to the open-topped Jeep were two men standing with guns trained on Molly and Walter. Molly looked like she had been hit in the face several times. I imagined she hadn't made it easy for them.

"Ah, I see we have a stand-off," Manny spit at me. "They seem to have more guns than you do."

I kept my eyes on Manny. It didn't matter how many guns they had. His head was less than two inches from the barrel of my gun. "Jake has several guns."

Manny turned his head just enough to see Jake. In response Jake pulled out one of the Glocks and pointed in the direction of the Jeep.

Manny snorted. "Jake can't hit anything."

Jake walked over and planted the barrel of his gun to Manny's temple. "But even I can hit something from this distance."

I turned and aimed my Beretta at the Jeep. "Hand me that other Glock," I said.

Jake pulled Manny's second Glock from his jeans and handed it to me. I took it with my left hand and placed it against Manny's right temple. He now had the barrel of a gun in each ear. I could almost see his blood pressure rise with the indignity he was suffering. "Where's the money, Manny?" I jabbed the gun into his ear.

Manny signaled to his men and one of them, the one behind Walter, moved to the back of the Jeep. His muscles stretched the black t-shirt he wore. He felt around the seat and pulled out a briefcase similar to the one Manny had brought. He walked back towards the front of the Jeep and shoved Walter from his seat. Walter stumbled from the vehicle but caught himself before he fell. I pushed my gun into Manny's ear in response. The other man grabbed Molly and pulled her in front of him, providing a shield. He took a handful of hair and yanked her head back, shoving his gun under her chin. Blood was pounding in my temples. I was hot. Anger, fueled with adrenaline, pumped through my veins. The photos of DeDe flashed through my memory. Then the man placed the case on the hood and opened it. He turned it to face us. It appeared to be filled with money. He stepped back to the side of the Jeep and pushed Walter ahead of him. Jake looked at me. I didn't have the answer he sought. I raised the automatic slightly and sighted in on the man's head.

I looked from Walter to Molly. Her face was filled with rage. Her eyes told me to kill the son-of-a-bitch.

Both Manny's men were frozen with their human shields.

Manny turned and faced me. The gun was less than six inches from his face. Our eyes where locked.

"I told you change was expensive," Manny said over his shoulder. "Didn't, I Jake?"

My finger tightened on the trigger, pulling the hammer back.

41
Jake
Friday Noon

Here we were once again, on the edge of the abyss, staring at death. One flawed move and we could all be dead.

Walter stiffened as one of Manny's thugs buried his gun a little deeper into the old man's throat. Molly tried to protest but the other man yanked on her hair, snapping her head back to an unnatural position.

I turned just in time to see Hank respond in kind. He matched the ante by pressing his gun a little deeper into Manny's left temple. If this hurt Manny, he didn't let it show. His face burned with anger.

I had to do something.

I checked Hank one more time. I had to know if he was with me or if he was consumed with getting revenge on Manny. I'd seen what the two thugs had done to Molly and I was sure Hank was ready to explode. But he looked steady. Whether he was or not didn't really matter. For now, all that mattered was that he *looked* like he could blow Manny away without so much as a second thought.

Don't just stand there. Do something.

Time slowed, then stopped. Each of us became a chess piece, holding our individual powers in check, waiting for someone, anyone to make a move, any move. I looked from player to player, each one tied to the other, ready for action, frozen until someone made that first move.

I took a step forward and slowly, ever-so-slowly, lowered my gun. Nobody moved. Nothing changed.

And Karen? Where the hell was Karen? Without moving too quickly, I scanned the rock pile where I'd left her. Nothing.

Think, Jake ol' boy. What is it you do best? What have you been doing all your life? What can you do—right now?

And then I knew. I smiled, like I was back on home turf, like I was right where I wanted to be.

Call me a liar. Call me a criminal. Call me a dope-head. Call me anything you like. But never underestimate the power of Jake Marley when his back is up against the fucking wall.

I slowly turned toward Hank and Manny. I had something to say to Manny, something that could end this madness, but I had to get close enough without alarming his boys.

With the confidence of the true believers—or the truly desperate—I tucked my gun into my waistband, raised my arms out to my sides and turned from side to side, showing anyone and everyone that I wasn't going to fire the first shot. Sweat beaded on my forehead and trickled down my face and neck. *This was it*!

Letting my arms ease back to my side, I inched my way over to Manny. His eyes followed my every step, every move, every blink. Hank soldiered his role, his gun keeping Manny in check. Everyone and everything was frozen in time. Only the wind moved.

The last few steps were the hardest. They brought me that much closer to ending this, one way or another.

I took that final, last step and stopped a few feet in front of him. One deep breath. One half-smile. One chance.

"I came here looking for an old friend and this is what I find?" I tried to broaden my smile, to let him know it didn't have to be this way.

His eyes bored into mine. No smile. "I, too, came looking for a friend." He shifted his eyes to the right, toward Hank. "And this is what I find!"

No smiles. No relief. Only anger and contempt. The clock was ticking. Get to the point. Lay down your hand.

"Remember Ralphie?" I asked, returning his stare. If there was a way to get his attention, the memory of Ralphie should do it.

He blinked. He remembered. I felt the level of tension decrease ever so slightly.

"Ralphie isn't with us today because—"

Manny cut me off. "Ralphie *died* because he broke the rules, because he tried to steal from me."

It was my turn to interrupt. "And that's exactly my point." I stepped a half-foot closer.

"Your point?"

"I haven't broken any rules!" I said louder than I'd intended. "There have been a few changes, but the deal is still as good as it was when I first told you about it."

He thought. He scowled. Finally, he blinked.

I leaned in closer. "So why are we doing all this?" I raised my right arm and swept it over our tableau. "Why are the three of us standing here ready to blow each other's brains out? I thought we were friends, *amigos, compadres.* I thought we had history—"

Manny interrupted. "I'll get right to the point." Still no smiles. "We're doing this," he nodded his head toward the Jeep, "because I wasn't sure I could trust you anymore. It's been a long, long time."

Good. Now we were getting somewhere. "Well, isn't that a fine coincidence?" I backed off. A little. "I wasn't sure I could trust you, either."

His expression changed slightly. "Tell me, *Señor*, how is it then that good friends such as us are in such a dangerous predicament?"

I dropped any pretense of warmth. It was time to close this deal. "I can only think of two reasons, *Señor*." I stopped and made sure he was listening. "Women. Or money."

His eyebrows arched. "And sometimes," he smiled maliciously, "the two are tied together, no?"

I relaxed even more. "And when that happens, watch out."

"I want my gold," Manny stated quietly.

I nodded. "And I want my money." I faked a smile. "Well, then, I believe we have a deal." I checked his face for any reaction. None. Stone-cold. I kept up my line, figuring bullshit was better than bullets. "Now, some of the particulars may have changed but we'll save those details for another time and another place." Keep talking. Keep working. Keep everyone alive. "It comes down to this: You have something for me and I have something for you. Nothing else really matters at this point. Does it?"

Manny's eyes narrowed and I took that to mean I was reaching him. Keep going. More of the same. I pointed to Hank and then over to the Jeep. "All of this is a little unnecessary, don't you think?"

"No, Jake." Anger framed his words. "I think all of this is extremely rude. I think you are pissing me off. I think I will not soon forget how you are treating me."

If there had been a lowering of the tension, it was now back to where it'd been before. Or worse.

"Manny," Hank whispered in Manny's ear. "Tell your guys to drop their guns." Hank's voice was strong and clear.

"And if I don't?" Manny challenged.

"And if you don't," Hank uttered each word methodically. "I'm gonna pull this trigger and blow your fucking brains all over this desert."

Manny swallowed. "But you'll—"

"But nothing!" Hank interrupted. "This hasn't got shit to do with anything else. Maybe I'll die. Maybe not. Maybe Jake will. Maybe not."

"And your lady friend?" Manny tried to gain an advantage but Hank wouldn't let it take hold.

"And maybe she'll get killed. And maybe not." He moved around in front of Manny and locked eyes with him. "A lot of things could happen but only one thing will happen for sure." He pressed the barrel even harder into Manny's flesh. "You are gonna be the first motherfucker to die!"

I reached slowly for my gun. We were at the brink again. Hank glared, his eyes forcing the issue.

Manny finally blinked. "I don't think you've got the guts, Hank." He blinked again. "And I did not come out here to be killed by a fucking artist."

I relaxed. I let my hand fall away from my gun.

"Tell them to drop their guns." Hank kept up his edge.

"Get your piece out of my ear and I will."

Hank thought for a second and then slowly backed off. The world was suddenly extremely quiet. Both men continued their death stare until Manny cleared his throat and shouted orders in Spanish. The guns hit the sand and I learned to breathe again.

Molly immediately ran to check on Walter and then headed for Hank.

I nodded to Hank that he should drop his gun. I relaxed a little more. The

335

worst was over. First, evidently, we had to have this not-so-little pissing contest. Now, we could get down to why we were all here.

As Molly brushed by me on her way to Hank, she hastily nodded toward the rock pile behind me and mouthed the word "Karen." I wanted to turn, to look, to see for myself. But I didn't. That might have raised more than eyebrows. And, it might have upset this fragile truce. Besides, the rock pile behind me wasn't the same one I'd put Karen in. Molly must have been mistaken.

Hank wrapped his arms around Molly as she threw herself into his embrace. Then, he pulled back and checked her bruised face. An instant later, he glared at the man responsible for Molly's pain.

Molly leaned forward, breaking the spell between the two men. "I'm fine. Really." She patted Hank on the shoulder and looked him squarely in the eyes. "Really." Hank handed her one of his guns.

I stepped back. Watching. Waiting. I told myself that I had to stay focused, keep my eyes open, see which way the various winds were blowing. If trouble was coming, either from Manny or Hank, I wanted to be the first to know about it.

Manny turned to me. "I want my gold."

"And I want my money."

It was our turn to stare each other down. Okay. I could play this game. I could, but I wasn't going to. I wanted my money as much as Manny wanted the gold. I could feel it. All I had to do was make the first move.

"You know where the gold is. There's a truck big enough to haul it out of here, there's enough gas to get you to Gallup or wherever, and the keys are in the ignition. All you gotta do is pick the stuff up off the ground and put it in the back." I stepped in front of him. "Now, hand over my money."

"Jake," he said evenly, "I hope there are no more problems." He paused, as if to let his words sink in. "Because all of this is making me very angry. I will not forget what has happened here today. Not ever."

I knew what he meant but fired right back. "And neither will I!"

He glared. Another moment of truth. Who would blink first? Who would cave in? Who would hold the upper hand?

"Tell your men that if they hustle, they should be able to load the gold in fifteen, maybe twenty minutes." I was tired of fucking around. I wanted this over and done with. And I wanted my money. "And it won't take you nearly as long to give me my three million dollars."

Without hesitation, Manny signaled his men. One grabbed the briefcase from the Jeep's hood while the other fetched their guns. Hank and Molly reacted by leveling their own pieces at the two men. The men stopped but Manny motioned for them to continue. Evidently, this was more about money than guns.

He took the briefcase and told them to go through the crease and load the gold. They tucked their guns back in their holsters and silently took off. As I watched them disappear, I wondered if we should have sent Hank or Molly to guard them. After all, I had no idea what Manny might have told them before they'd arrived. He could have just ordered them to circle back and kill us. I turned back to ask Hank if we were doing the right thing. He must've anticipated my question because he smiled and raised his gun back to Manny's temple.

"I don't think they'll try anything." The barrel tapped lightly next to Manny's ear. "Do you?"

I wanted to return the smile but couldn't. Deep down, I knew we were doing what we needed to do to stay alive. But not so deep down, not so buried that I couldn't feel it, I knew we were also fucking with one of the most dangerous men I knew. *There would be consequences.*

"Your Indian friend isn't looking very good." Manny pointed his head toward Walter. "I think someone ought to see to him."

We all turned. Except Hank. He kept his eyes focused on Manny's every move. Molly headed back to Walter, who looked to be in bad shape. I hoped it was nothing serious. Cold-hearted as it sounded, we just flat-out didn't have time for anything more.

"Hear that?" Manny asked.

I strained to hear what he was talking about. First, nothing. Then, from through the crease, I heard the sound of the truck being loaded. Bags of gold were landing in the metal bed of the truck. I smiled. Another step closer to being done with this. To being out of here.

"It appears my men are very busy doing exactly what I ordered them to do." Manny edged out each word. "Obviously, they are not coming around the corner to shoot you."

I nodded. It made sense.

"So, do us all a favor, Hank. Drop the hardware."

Hank pulled his gun back and dropped it to his side. I started to relax but remembered that I still hadn't seen Karen. Molly said she'd seen her in the rock pile but was she still there? Was she hiding? Afraid? What?

Wherever she was, whatever she was doing would have to wait. Manny was getting his gold coins. I wanted my money.

"And now, Manny, you have something for me."

"Of course." He smiled as he handed me the briefcase. "A deal's a deal."

I took it from him and juggled it up and down a few times. Heavy. Sort of. Like a briefcase filled with paper. Only more. *So this is what three million dollars in cash feels like.*

"Count it, if you like." Manny's offer sounded like a challenge.

"Do I need to?" I asked, returning his challenge.

"Only if you don't trust me."

"It's not that I don't trust you," I said as I released the locks. "It's just that Hank here has never seen this much money and I thought he might like a peek." I opened the lid and stared at enough money to take care of me for life. Bright green, a mixture of old and new bills. I was so impressed that I almost forgot to show it to Hank.

"Satisfied?" Manny asked.

I locked the briefcase and nodded. I turned to Hank. "Let's get out of here."

"Jake?" Manny sounded hurt. "You leaving already?"

I turned. I couldn't think of anything I wanted to do more than get the hell out of here.

He stepped toward me. "But we may never see each other again."

He was right. Too much had happened this time for either of us to ever consider there being a next time.

"And I think you owe me an explanation."

He was right again. This was Manny's way of closing the deal. If I didn't give him what he wanted now, there could be consequences later. I motioned for the others to go to the car that I'd be along in a few minutes.

Hank declined. "I'm staying." He told Molly to make sure Walter was comfortable. Even though I wasn't expecting any more trouble, I felt better knowing Hank was with me.

"First of all," I began. "I decided not to tell you that Cloud was involved in this because of your history with him. Whether you trusted him, liked him, hated him; it didn't matter. He was our only conduit to the gold."

Manny simply shrugged and that surprised me. This was the first he'd heard about Cloud being a part of the deal and I expected a bigger reaction from him.

Time was tight so I plunged forward. "Second, we were forced to make changes because people were following us, trashing our houses, trying to kill me." I looked him squarely in the eyes. "And they tortured Hank's wife to death."

He turned toward Hank. "You know that wasn't me."

"I wasn't so sure," he answered, "until now."

Manny checked his watch and looked toward the crease. Our time was running out. He turned back to me. "Tell me, old friend, how did we come to be in this shithole?"

I checked the car before answering. Molly had started it and was waiting with Walter. Where was Karen?

Even though this next part wasn't going to be easy—telling him we hadn't trusted him—I'd try to get it over and done with quickly so we could all be on our way. I took in a deep breath and slowly let it out. "Manny, six people died for this gold. I didn't want there to be any more."

He thought for a moment and then gave me a half-smile. "What you're really saying is that you didn't trust me."

No more bullshit. "What I'm really saying is that I got to the point where I didn't trust *anybody*."

His eyes remained riveted to mine. Searching. Evaluating. Analyzing. Finally, he nodded toward Hank. "But you trusted him?" I noted another challenge in his voice.

"Manny," I said as forcefully as I could. "I trust Hank with my life."

"And the others?" He nodded toward the car.

"Them, too."

"Does this complete trust of yours include Karen?"

"Karen?" How did he know about her?

"Yes. Karen. You know she works for me, don't you?" He spoke matter-of-factly, like he was talking about the weather. His words twisted my insides.

I stared. "I don't believe you."

He chuckled. "Look at you, Jake. Your words say one thing but your body says another. Look. You are sweating. Your hands are shaking." But Manny wasn't finished with telling his story and destroying what little hope I'd had for Karen. "She called me the other night. Reporting in." No smiles. No grins. Just life-altering words. "She told me about the change in plans, about how to find Walter Ravenfeather. And about Molly. She also told me that I had nothing to worry about. That even though things had changed, the deal was still solid, that I'd get my gold."

I was pissed. *She had worked for him all along.* I felt enraged and embarrassed and stupid.

He looked me squarely in the eyes. "You didn't know?"

I shrugged, still trying to maintain some sense of control. "She kept me guessing."

He grinned and put his hand on my shoulder. "She's very good. The best I've ever hired. That's why I brought her in for this."

"Yeah," I muttered, still not recovered from the shock. That explained why Manny wasn't outraged at the mention of Cloud's name. He'd known all along.

"Jake. Jake. Jake. I thought you had more sense than to let a woman get under your skin. I thought if your gut told you it was time to run, you ran. That if something smelled fishy, you put it in the garbage, not in your bed."

Before I could answer, two shots rang out. I hit the dirt and drew my gun. Hank and Manny landed right beside me an instant later.

Manny's eyes burned into mine. "Jake, if you are trying something here, it'll be the last thing you ever do."

"Molly?" I heard Hank yell. "Are you okay?"

"Yeah!" she answered. "You?"

"Okay!" he hollered back. Then, he looked at me, raised his gun toward Manny and whispered through clenched teeth, "If you're trying something here—"

"The shots came from back in the rocks," Molly yelled. "Where the truck is."

"That's what I heard," Hank answered, his eyes and gun still occupying Manny's full attention.

I scanned the area. "Where's Karen?"

"Karen?" Manny shouted. "She's here?"

Hank and I looked at each other and then at Manny. "Yeah," I answered. "Of course, she's here."

Manny rolled back against a big rock. "That lyin' little bitch!" His eyes held the fires of hell. "That lyin' double-crossing little bitch!"

Hank moved with him and got in his face. "What the fuck is going on?"

Manny could barely control himself. "She told me she wasn't going to be here."

"What?" Hank and I asked at the same time.

"The last time she called, she said she had no reason to be here. She said she was done and that I could send her the rest of her money to some place in Tucson."

I jumped in. "But you didn't know she was here? That she was still with us?"

"No."

Hank waved his gun in front of Manny's eyes. "No bullshit!"

His eyes bore into Hank's, giving him the kind of look that was bedrock solid. "She works for me. I hired her to keep an eye on Jake, on the gold, to report to me."

"Then what's this about?" I asked for both of us.

"I think that's pretty clear," Manny's eyes shifted from mine to Hank's. "She's gone into business for herself."

Again, I was about to protest when Hank agreed. "She's probably killed your men and taken their guns. Plus, she's got position on us. We can't move. She can."

"More than that," Manny added. "She's got a truck already loaded with sixteen million in gold and pointed toward Mexico."

We all sat in stunned silence. Mentally, the wheels turned, tumblers clicked into place, words and actions that had been cloudy suddenly cleared.

"Manny," I offered the obvious. "I don't think she's working for you anymore."

He mumbled something in Spanish and then turned to both of us. "We've got to stop her." He moved to get up when Hank grabbed his arm.

"You sure you're being straight with us?"

Again, the look on Manny's face told all. "You have my word."

Hank slowly nodded. "'Cause if this turns out to be a trick, I swear I'll take your head off the instant I get the chance."

Manny turned and stood up. I couldn't vouch for Hank but I was holding back to see if any more shots were going to be fired. None came and we ventured carefully toward the crease.

Hank angled toward Molly and Walter. I wasn't sure but I reasoned that he was telling her to stay there, take care of Walter and guard the cars. A few seconds later, Hank was next to me as he entered the crease.

I had never been in a war. I never had the terrifying experience of trying to get from A to B knowing that someone might have me in their sights, just waiting for the right moment to pull the trigger. But here I was, ready to file into what could certainly be a death trap.

Hank stopped us before we entered. "One of us should circle around."

It sounded good to me but before I could answer, Manny cursed. "That will take too long. She's got the gold. My gold! I'm not going to let her get away." He grabbed the gun from my hand and plunged into the crease. I ran after him, briefcase still in hand, partly to get my gun back and partly to stay with him. If this was some sort of trick, I had a much better chance of staying alive if I was with Manny than being hunted by him. Hank followed.

In blinding seconds, we made it to the other side. Manny immediately headed for a small rock pile and I scooted in directly behind him. Hank held back, finding shelter in the shadows of the crease.

"The truck is still here," Manny noted in whispers. "So is the gold." He nodded at the fully loaded bed of the truck. I scanned the area and saw the lifeless forms of two men. I pointed them out to Manny. He shook his head and then turned to me. "Now do you believe me?"

I nodded. Manny would do a lot of things to gain an advantage but I doubted he would kill his own men.

"Can you see her?" Hank whispered.

Manny and I both surveyed the area, looking for anything that gave away Karen's presence. Before we could answer, the world exploded with sound. Guns shots. Glass breaking. More shots. Bullets hitting metal. Loud, deafening shots.

I hugged the rocks. Manny did the same. We both tried to pinpoint the source. I turned to see if Hank was all right. He was standing in the crease, pointing back to the other side, to where Molly and Walter and the cars were.

"The shots are coming from there. I'm going back. You two stay here." And then he was gone.

As a reflex, I grabbed my gun back from Manny. If we were going to guard the truck, I wanted to be the one with the gun. Even though I now believed Manny one hundred percent, I still wanted the control that came with holding the gun.

I figured the best thing we could do was sit tight and wait. Hank would let us know what happened or if he needed help. Until then, we hugged the rocks and stayed alive.

We looked at each other. In one of those flashes of understanding that people talk about, we realized what'd happened.

We'd both been taken by a pro. A real pro. Manny had hired her but it was clear she was working for herself now. She'd discovered the one flaw in both our plans. Manny and I said we trusted each other. Only in reality, we didn't. She'd seen that and manipulated us into using it against each other.

I had to give her credit. She'd run a near-perfect double-cross and was just a few moments from getting it all.

I smiled at Manny. I found some solace knowing that she had duped Manny, too. At least I wasn't the only fool out here in the desert.

Manny returned my smile and put his hand on my shoulder. "I should have trusted you, my friend." He smiled.

I nodded. That was as close to an apology as I was going to get. And all that I needed.

"It's awfully quiet," Manny stated, looking toward the crease. "I think one of us should check on Hank."

Before I could tell him I didn't think that was such a good idea, he slowly stood up. An instant later, a shot blistered the air and a split second after that, Manny collapsed on the sand next to my feet. Half his head was gone. His body twitched once, twice, and then stopped.

Out of pure stupidity and shock, I started to stand up. My eyes were locked on Manny's bloodied corpse the entire time. When I straightened up, I turned toward the truck. All I could see was the barrel of a gun pointed at the spot between my eyes.

"Hand me that briefcase." Karen's hard-edged voice left little doubt that she wasn't playing games. Automatically, I handed it to her. Why had I ever let her get this close, this involved?

"Now tell your buddy Hank that I'm coming around the other side!"

I looked at the truck, then back to her. "Why not just leave? You've got everything you came for."

"Do it! Now!" The barrel touched my forehead and the look in her eyes told me she wasn't kidding. I also saw a hint of fear. She knew Hank and Molly were armed and that the truck couldn't outrun bullets.

"No!" I said through clenched teeth, mustering every ounce of courage I could find. I wasn't going to help her set up Hank.

She pressed the gun against my sweating forehead. "I've worked and planned for this gold from the moment Manny called me." An icy edge coated her words. "I've already killed three people. One more isn't going to make much difference."

She *would* kill me. I could feel it. But I still wasn't going to help her get to Hank. I slowly straightened myself and locked my eyes with hers. "Then go ahead. Pull the trigger. If you can." At least I was going to die with some measure of dignity.

She returned my glare. "Is that what you want? To die out here?" She softened her tone a little. "We could have had this all, Jake. You and me. And all that money. But you wouldn't listen."

I didn't respond. She wasn't making me an offer. She was simply rubbing my nose in it and I hated her for it.

Seconds turned into millennia as we stared at each other, neither of us making a move. Even the ever-present wind died. The desert and everything in it was completely still.

But I was in a rage. My insides were boiling. She'd used me. She'd taken me. Big time. I knew I had to put an end to it. Right now. And, I knew, one way or another, I was going to find a way to get even with her.

A small smile crept across my lips. "Karen," I whispered, "I want you to know that I—"

Suddenly, her eyes shifted to the opening of the crease. She recoiled and gasped. Hank. It must be Hank. I turned, looking for Hank, looking for help.

But no one was there. And then I knew. She'd set me up, tricked me one more time. An instant later, the butt of her gun crashed into my skull and the back of my head exploded with pain. My knees buckled and I collapsed on top of a lifeless, bloodied Manny. I fought to remain conscious.

I heard the truck start and roar off into the desert. Sand and rocks and dust filled the air, making it hard to breathe and harder to see. I tried to get up but couldn't. My head hurt and my muscles wouldn't obey my brain's commands. I felt like I was going to pass out. A stilled darkness slowly began covering me.

I heard noises. Loud noises. Wham! Wham-wham! Wham!

Gunshots. From behind me.

Wham! Wham! Wham!

Then quiet.

Then someone calling my name.

"Jake?"

It was Hank. Molly, too. They knelt next to me, one on each side.

"Did you get her?" I tried to smile.

"Once. Maybe." Hank didn't sound very confident. "Or maybe not."

42
Hank
Seven Weeks Later

"Okay, Djumpstrom, don't go away. We'll be with you right away."
Millard let out a cackle and shut the door. I was back in the same ten-by-
ten room where I had first met White and his crazed partner, Millard. Only
this time, I knew why I had been brought in.

"Just routine questioning," was how the patrol officer put it when he came
to pick me up.

"Yeah, sure," I had replied. I didn't fight the invitation for a ride
downtown, but I said I'd drive my own car.

"Suit yourself," the officer had said.

I leaned back in the chair and pulled my hair into a ponytail, using a rubber
band to hold it in place. I checked the mirror to see how I looked, ran my
hand over the table and was out of things to do. The police brought me in for
questioning because Manny's body had been found two weeks earlier. The
coyotes had made a positive identification difficult, but once it was
established that one of northern Mexico's biggest drug lords had been killed
in the desert, it was front-page headlines. The various news stories were
mostly speculation. Officers from several branches of law enforcement were
interviewed, and all they really had was a sketchy look at Manny's past. They
surmised that Manny's death in the desert came during a drug deal that had
gone bad. The newspaper said police and federal authorities were following
several leads. I figured I was one of those "leads."

There wasn't a clock on the wall and I hadn't worn a watch. I didn't know how much time had passed since the portly cop had left. *What game were Millard and White playing?* I thought to myself. *They either had Jake in another room and were questioning him, or were just trying to wear me down.* But I hadn't seen Jake in over a week, so I doubted they had him. I did know they'd be comparing our stories at some point. The thought made me smile.

The door popped open and Millard strolled in. He had a donut with chocolate glaze in his left hand and a cup of coffee in his right. "Something funny, Djumpstrom?"

"Where's Sergeant White? I like his attitude better."

"Hah." Millard spit bits of donut. "Hah, that's funny." The dumpy detective kicked back a chair and spilled a puddle of liquid on the table as he sat down. "You're a funny guy," Millard said without any humor. He shoved the last morsel of donut into his mouth and licked his fingers.

"Why is it cops are always eating donuts?" I quizzed.

Millard gave me a glance and shook his head. He made a slurping sound as he tested the coffee's temperature.

I rolled up the sleeves of my denim shirt. The room was getting warm. Millard and I sat in silence, enjoying each other's company. I inspected the paint on my hands.

"I didn't have time to clean up before I came in," I said, holding my hands out for Millard to see.

The door slowly swung open with a creak. Sergeant White entered, reading from a manila folder. He was wearing a pair of reading glasses, the half-lens kind, making him appear older than he was. I let out a breath and both police officers looked at me.

"Mr. Djumpstrom," White addressed me before he sat down. "Is it okay if we tape this conversation?"

"No, it's not."

White paused a second and sat on the edge of the table, then asked his next question. "Do you know why we asked you to come in?"

I considered the question for a moment and shook my head.

"Juan Maniandez is dead. He and two of his men. Do you know anything about it?" White asked.

"Am I under arrest?" I replied.

Millard slammed his hand down on the table, making his coffee cup jump and spill. "Shit! Are you going to start playing games like last time?"

"Tim," said White sternly. "Take it easy. Okay?" White studied his partner.

Millard pushed back his chair and crossed his arms defiantly. He kept his eyes on me.

"Listen, Hank, maybe you can help us." White's voice was calm.

I smiled at White's use of my first name.

"We just want to ask you some questions. You are not under arrest. If you want, you can have an attorney present. Okay?"

I nodded.

"Now, we know you and Maniandez used to know each other a few years ago."

"A long time ago," I corrected. "Over ten years. He bought some artwork from me a couple times."

"Hah. Art." It was Millard, showing disrespect for my craft.

I glanced at him, and looked back at White, the good cop.

"When was the last time you saw him?" continued White.

"Over ten years ago," I repeated.

Millard shook his head.

"Hank, I'm going to tell you what we know. Maniandez and two other men," White checked his folder, "…flew into Gallup Municipal Airport and rented a car and a Jeep. They stayed at the El Rancho Hotel on Route 66 for one morning. Motel records showed that Manny's room received two phone calls. Two days later the two rental vehicles were reported stolen by the rental agency. Couple of weeks ago, the bodies was found by a kid herding sheep. The car and Jeep had several gunshots in the radiators and in a couple tires." White closed the folder and looked to me for a response. "Any of this sound familiar?"

"No."

"Would you know why they rented two cars?"

I shook my head.

"Okay. DEA is investigating." White gave a sigh. "And the FBI has asked a couple questions. Since the bodies were found on reservation land, it's their jurisdiction. We're helping out the FBI here. They could be the ones asking you these questions. But to be honest, no one really cares who killed Maniandez. Someone did the Feds a favor. They figure some other big-time drug dealer had it in for Maniandez."

"Sergeant, I don't know anything about Manny's death. I haven't seen him in over ten years," I stressed.

"That's what you said." Without missing a beat White continued. "Where were you August 11th through the 14th?"

"That's almost two months ago. I can't be sure."

"Let me tell you where you weren't," interjected Millard, in a gruff tone. "You weren't at your wife's funeral."

The statement hurt. I lost a bit of my cockiness.

"Where were you, Djumpstrom?" growled Millard.

"I knew I wasn't welcome at the funeral, so I made myself scarce."

"Where were you?" repeated Millard.

"I was in Las Vegas. Trying to forget," I said softly.

"Hah. Vegas. Forget. Shit," growled Millard.

"Where did you stay?" asked White.

"In a tent," I responded. "I camped out in the desert."

"Anyone see you in Vegas?"

"Lots of people."

"Anyone we can ask?" wondered White.

"Jake Marley."

"Hah. I'll bet." Millard glared. He looked at White, who returned his partner's stare.

White considered the answer for a moment. "How'd you do in Vegas?"

"I won a few bucks. Jake lost a few."

"Blackjack?" asked White.

"No. Roulette."

Sergeant White rose from the table and pulled back the third chair. He sat and opened the folder; shuffling through the pages he found a couple small pieces of paper. He placed them side-by-side on the table so I could see them.

"These are telephone records from two digital phones. One belongs to Manny and the other, your friend Jake Marley. The bill shows the number called. A call was made early on Thursday the 11th to Manny's home in

Mexico from Jake's phone. Then late that evening, Manny received a couple calls in his room at the El Rancho, in Gallup. We don't know where these calls came from. Friday morning Manny receives another call from Jake's cell phone to his motel room. Then this call is very interesting." White pointed at one line and then ran his finger across to the second bill. "A call is made from Jake's phone on Saturday and at the same time Manny's cell phone receives an incoming call. About the same time, Jake receives two incoming calls on his phone."

I looked down and read the damaging evidence. Jake and I had talked about this possibility. I looked across the table into White's eyes. He returned my stare. "Jake lost that phone just before we left for Vegas," I said flatly.

"Hah," popped Millard. His arms were still crossed, his face flushed with disgust.

"I didn't ask you about his phone." White broke the stare and pushed back his chair. "We'll be right back."

Millard got up without taking his eyes off me. Then he crossed to the door, looked back once and shut the door after him.

I waited. Glancing at the mirror, I wondered if the two officers were watching me, or checking my answers with Jake in another room.

I was sure that the authorities had been very frustrated by what they found in the desert: three dead men, two disabled vehicles, an empty briefcase and a bunch of guns. Everything else was purely conjecture on White and Millard's part. The official files had more questions than answers. I knew this because we had helped to create the questions.

Manny's men had done a good job of loading the truck. They hadn't dropped a single coin and had even put the topper back on before Karen sent them to meet their maker. Molly made sure we wiped down everything that might have had our fingerprints on it. There were no signs of us or the gold when we left. We just walked away. It wasn't even discussed what we would say until we got back to Walter's, and then the discussion was just about how deeply we were into this. We couldn't tell anyone about why we had met Manny in the desert because that would lead to Cloud's final resting place and that would lead to… We had woven a very tangled web.

The door's creak announced the return of my two interrogators. It was

Millard who spoke, "We don't have enough evidence to arrest you."

"You can go," White interrupted. "But watch yourself."

* * *

I drove north, towards my place. W.E. was expecting me to help him part-out a couple cars in the afternoon. As I passed Smiley's I slowed slightly to see if there was any sign of Jake. The parking lot was almost empty. I stepped on the gas and continued on my way home.

When we first got back, Jake had only one focus in his life.

"I'll find her some day, somewhere. She'll be there and then I'll get even." Jake had made the statement to me more than once. There were often times when he would disappear for days. When he came back, it would be from Denver or Houston. His wrath fueled three or four such excursions, but after a couple weeks he knew his search for Karen was useless. She and the gold were long gone. Karen had three million in cash and probably was well on her way to fencing the gold. As far as Jake could tell, she hadn't been able to get the four million from the numbered accounts. But even Jake had to admit that if it was possible, she'd be the one to find a way. I hoped Jake's most recent disappearance was not another one of these sojourns.

I turned left and pulled into my drive, stopped the truck and checked the mailbox. There was only junk mail and bills. I parked the truck next to the house and listened to the wind in the trees. A storm seemed to be kicking up. I rolled up the truck's windows, walked to the porch and left the mail on a table. I had been working on a series of paintings since the episode in the desert and wanted to make use of the afternoon sun.

The sun had warmed the closed-up studio but there was too much wind to leave the door open to cool things off. I took off my shirt and tossed it on the couch. An easel stood in the middle of the room; the painting it held was covered with an old sheet. I pulled back the protective sheath and studied the painting that was underneath. The background was unfinished. I squeezed some cadmium yellow into a pie tin, loaded up a wide brush with the vibrant color and added a couple bold strokes to the sky. The canvas was almost eight feet high. The image of a rose-tinted nude dominated the painting. She was almost life-sized. I took down a photo tacked along the side and studied the woman's face in the picture.

As I painted, I thought about Molly. It had been almost a month since I had seen her. We were taking time out. Molly said we had to do some serious thinking. She had even said, "We should see other people; too much has happened, we should slow down some and look at it." *It*, being our relationship. I knew Molly had been out with Laughinghorse because she told me. When I asked her if they had slept together, she only gave me a long look. We both knew that our relationship was at a critical turning point. I wasn't sure if there was any going back. Maybe she was right, maybe too much had happened.

Hours later, the sun was setting and I was just turning on the studio's overhead lights when a knock at the door startled me.

Jake opened the door. "Hey, can I come in?" He entered without waiting for my reply. His hair hadn't been combed and stuck out on the sides. There were patchy beginnings of a beard on his chin. He looked tired, but happy. "Whoa! What is this?" Jake stared at the large painting. Then his eyes scanned the several other paintings around the studio. He put down a large bundle of papers and moved to the nude. A big smile grew across his face. "Irene," he said excitedly. He reached up and took down the photo. "This should be in *Playboy*. There anymore?" Jake spied a series of photos pinned to a corkboard. "Hank, these are beautiful."

I smiled at the compliment. "I didn't think you liked art," I teased.

"Man, these are good," exclaimed Jake. He moved to one of the paintings and then the next. He studied each of the half dozen paintings, all of Irene. "You've been busy. These are really good. I'm getting excited. Irene looks," Jake paused, searching for the right words, "…nice out of her clothes. How'd you get her to pose?"

"I just asked her. You know I am an artist, Jake. This isn't some sex-thing."

"Yeah." Jake looked at me, his eyes dancing. "Do you think you could teach me how to paint?"

"Very funny," I answered. "Where have you been?"

"I haven't been looking for Karen again, if that's what you're wondering." Jake crossed the room to the bundle of paper. "I've been at the Ghost Ranch, hanging out with the Presbyterians, writing." Jake slapped the stack of paper. "It's only a rough draft. But it's done. I want you to read it."

I crossed the room and looked down at the stack of papers. I picked up the top sheet with my paint-stained hands. "*Two Guys* by Jake Marley," I read out loud. I put down the cover sheet and realized I'd left a yellow thumbprint next to the bold letters. I absentmindedly wiped my brush with a rag as I read the first page.

"That's just a working title," Jake said excitedly.

For the next three hours, I read. Jake paced back and forth, looking at the paintings and photos, but mostly kept an eye on me, waiting for a response. When I took the book to an old recliner and sat down, Jake went off to the house and brought back sandwiches and a twelve-pack of beer. After he ate, he curled up on a couch in the studio's corner and slept. The book was typed and had been corrected with a red pen. The story gave me a chill. It was about double-crosses and lost artifacts in the desert. I had a feeling I knew how it would end.

Jake woke with a yawn and stretched. "What do you think?"

"It hits a little close to home, don't you think?"

"Nah, not a bit. It's set in Mexico. It's very different."

I raised my eyebrows and shook my head. "You did a good job. Nice writing."

"You think so? You know, you should write about what you know," Jake said, trying to sound dead serious.

I shook my head at Jake's statement. "It's very good, Jake." I paused. I didn't want to dampen Jake's spirits with what I had to say next. "I had a question-and-answer session with the cops today."

Jake didn't say anything.

"They wanted to know where I was August 11th through the 14th."

"Shit! What'd you tell 'em?"

"Just what we planned."

"Vegas?"

I nodded. "They also had a couple phone bills to show me."

"Oh, man."

"I told them you lost your phone. There is no way for them to prove you actually made the calls. They don't even seem all that interested in who killed Manny."

Jake stood up and walked over to the painting of Irene. He appeared to be admiring her image. But I knew he was thinking about what I said.

"One of the cops asked me how I did in Vegas."

"What?"

"I told them I won and you lost."

"Oh, thanks. There goes my reputation."

"I told them we played roulette."

* * *

The next morning I pulled the old truck to the curb in front of Jake's apartment and turned off the engine. This was the same spot at which I had let Jake out back in August, before I knew what a dangerous path my life was going to be taking. There was a better than fifty-fifty chance that he was still asleep and had forgotten our plan to have breakfast at Porter's. I had promised not to show up before nine.

The night before we had decided to get on with *our* lives. In reality, it was Jake who was taking our misadventure the hardest. His book was a good start at returning to his life. While he bitched about the money, I knew that it was really Karen that was at the center of his unhappiness. Maybe with time, he would resolve the damage she had done.

I entered the courtyard and its overgrown garden. Dead brown leaves were beginning to accumulate in the corners. Everything was quiet as I headed up the wooden steps to Jake's apartment. I knocked twice and then tried the knob. It turned easily and I let myself in.

"Jake?"

The apartment seemed to be lit only by the morning sun.

"Jake," I called again a bit louder, "are you up? It's time for breakfast."

He was dressed and sitting at his computer, with the blue screen blank.

"Writer's block?"

He turned to look at me. His face was etched in despair.

"What's up?"

Jake handed me a letter. "Read it. It was in my pile of mail from when I was up at the Ghost Ranch."

I skimmed the first couple sentences and moved to the couch and sat down heavily. My skin crawled and I shuddered as if a ghost had passed through my body as I read the rest of the letter.

> *Dear Jake,*
>
> *I know you've been trying to find me. Don't bother. You're out of your league, honey. I know you hate me and probably would like to kill me. I can't say I blame you. If the roles were reversed, I would feel the same way.*
>
> *You had your opportunity. Now, you'll just have to realize that we were both going for the same brass ring. I won, that's all.*
>
> *In case you were wondering, I had no trouble finding a buyer for the coins. I didn't get as much as I wanted but, all in all, I'm happy. I have plenty of money, and I'm having fun spending it.*
>
> *I'm sure you've checked the postmark. I won't be staying in this part of the world for long.*
>
> *Got to go, lover.*
>
> *Karen*

I held the letter for a few seconds and reread the last paragraph. Silently, I handed the letter back to Jake. I looked at my friend and studied his face. I wasn't getting any clues.

Jake handed me the envelope. The address was in proper cursive script. I checked the cancellation, the Cayman Islands.

"I doubt she's anywhere near there now." Jake's tone was sharp. "She was a pro. She had the connections to sell the gold."

"Jake," my voice was full of no, no, no.

"Don't worry; I'm not going out on any more wild goose chases. If anything, this letter just proves how fruitless all my excursions have been."

We sat in silence for a few seconds.

"What'd she mean, you had your opportunity?"

"Yeah, well, at one point, she suggested that we could take the gold and run. And then, that morning, out in the rocks she said there was still time."

I had to think about this for a moment. Jake waited while I ran the thought through my gray matter a couple times. "Why didn't you?"

"I didn't think I could find a buyer." Jake looked me straight in the eye when he said it. He was using his gift.

"Yeah, sure." I knew he didn't mean it. I knew this because I know who Jacob Marley really is. "Yeah, sure, Jake."

Then Jake was still for a moment and stared at the blue screen. He laughed, "I just wish I could answer that letter." Jake made a gun with his finger and pointed it at me, "Pow!" He shook his head and smiled. "I need a big breakfast and then its time to go to Smiley's for a drink. Let's go, buddy."

* * *

"Well, look at this, a coupla new faces." Smiley looked thoroughly surprised to see Jake and me. He pushed up his sleeve and looked at his watch. Winny gave a low woof in reply from behind the bar. I could hear her toenails clicking along the wooden floor. "And it is barely noon. Irene, look who's here," he called.

Irene looked up from a booth she was waiting on and gave us a smile.

"Well, well, what brings you boys to this neck of the woods?" asked Smiley.

"Knock it off, Smiley," Jake said. "We'd just like a couple of beers."

"Guinness," I chimed in.

"Coming right up." Smiley stepped down the bar to retrieve our drinks. "I understand Irene's been doing some posing for you, Hank. This wouldn't be like Wyeth's Helga series would it?" He chuckled to himself. Obviously he had been let in on the secret. "When is there going to be an opening?"

I looked around to see if Irene had heard Smiley. She had and was just shaking her head slightly in amusement.

"I didn't know you were so well versed in art, Smiley."

"Well, you know, Hank, I get ah, *Art America* and ah," Smiley grinned, "oh, some other art magazines."

"Yeah, sure. Art magazines…like *Playboy* and *Penthouse*?" I had to laugh at Smiley's little act.

He was glad to see Jake and me, even if he hadn't actually said, "It's nice to see you guys."

"Been a while since there has been a card game..." Smiley stopped and looked past us.

When I turned, Wayne Wayne was lumbering through the door, headed directly toward our stools.

"Yessir-ree! If it isn't Santa Fe's favorite two criminals. Sure is hot out there in the sun for October." The growing stains under his arms attested to his statement. When he got closer so did his aroma. He took off his hat and wiped his hand through his sweat-soaked hair. There was a big grin plastered across his face. He lifted one leg and rested it against the stool next to mine. I figured it was too much effort for him to hoist his bulk and actually sit. "I understand, Hank, you had a conversation with the boys down at Camino Street."

I took a swig of the dark liquor and returned the grin. Jake stared straight ahead into the mirror that reflected our three images.

"So old Manny's dead and no one knows nothing about his d-e-e-mise. And he was such a close friend," Wayne mocked. Then he tossed down a newspaper on the bar. The headlines caught my attention. "Five bodies found on Navajo Reservation."

Jake must have felt my body tense because he looked down at the bold print.

"A bunch more dead guys found up near Shiprock." Wayne had emphasized *more*. "Some NASA computer programmer name of Williams, a couple Mexican maintenance guys, also from NASA, a bad ass ex-con from Houston, and Whitney Cloud." Wayne Wayne spit the words, his tone full of accusations. Neither Jake nor I said a word. Smiley settled back against the counter and watched.

"Story in the paper says the bodies had been out in the desert for couple of months. Animals had been eating them." He waited for a response. "Bunch of guns found. Looks like there was a shoot-out. Whitney'd been shot a whole buncha times. Everyone shot. Bam, dead." His last two words exploded. "Except that Williams guy. There weren't no bullets in him." Wayne leaned forward and tried to catch my eye. I lifted the bottle and took a slow swallow. He leaned further forward and looked around me at Jake. "Strange, a NASA computer guy being out in the desert with Whitney Cloud. Wasn't Cloud a friend of yours, Jake?"

Jake took a gulp of his beer.

Wayne gave a snort. "Yeah, you don't know nothing about Manny dying and I'll bet you don't know nothing about this, neither." Wayne slapped the newspaper. "Shit!" He pushed himself up and turned to go. "I'll be checking into this myself, boys. Be seeing you around."

I reached and pulled the paper over to where Jake and I could both see it. I scanned the first couple paragraphs. Wayne had given us the essence of the story. It was another unsolved mystery.

Jake drained his beer and held up the bottle. "Smiley, we'll have another round."

"Guinness," I added.

Jake turned to me and held out his empty bottle. I clinked mine against his in a silent toast.

* * *

That night, after I got home, I lay in my bed thinking about Jake and the police. They certainly weren't done with us. I thought about Molly and Irene and Walter. Suddenly the big cat jumped up on the bed and nuzzled into the curve of my leg, disturbing my thought patterns. His motor started running at the prospect of a comfortable night indoors on the bed. I gave him a slight shove so he would stop his grooming.

"Fred, what are you doing in here?" I asked in the dark. He answered with a "yeow" and went back to his licking. "Why aren't you out eating rodents in the barn, doing your job?" The big yellow tom yeowed again and squeezed in tighter. I reached down and gave him a couple pats and pulled the blanket up over us. In a few seconds he would come crawling up from under the covers and reclaim his spot, next to me. The curtains flapped in the gentle breeze. It was cooler at night now, the heat of summer had faded away and been replaced with the shorter days of October. Early mornings were crisp and I frequently awoke searching for an extra blanket.

In the dark, I waited, but no one came. There were no gunshots to break the quiet. It had been almost two months since that fateful day in the desert. Sometimes in the black, demons rose from the haunts of my subconscious. Their visits had lessened, but some nights they still came lurking. At first the visitor was the anguished face of Slim. His eyes were filled with terror and his mouth was open, but no sound would come out. Other nights I would see Manny, laughing at me, mocking my efforts to stop his men from raping Molly and killing Walter. I'd pull and pull the gun's trigger, but no bullets would come out. Manny was dead. I had seen him, lying in his blood; his life stilled along with his two henchmen. Only once did the tortured spirit of DeDe come to call. She looked beautiful, as she had in life, not like her tortured body in the grisly black and white photographs that I had seen. Her cheeks were stained with tears, but she smiled when she saw me. Not a word was spoken in the dream, but something had been communicated, because DeDe had not returned.

I pulled the blanket up around my chin and waited for Fred. A few seconds later he gave out a cry of displeasure and crawled towards the surface. He stopped by my face and announced his annoyance at being covered up after he had gotten comfortable. The cat walked back along my body towards the foot of the bed and lay down, rested on my leg and started licking himself again. I turned on my side and shut my eyes, but the faces and memories wouldn't go away.

* * *

"Hank," Rufus said my name softly. "The guys would like to get started." I turned and surveyed tonight's filets, five *cowboys*—each one thinking tonight was *their* night. It was strange not seeing my friend, Jake. But time heals all wounds, even if it doesn't cure the memory. And with enough time, Jake would be playing again.

Who would Lady Luck smile on this evening? Probably none of them, I thought to myself.

I took a place at the table and opened a new deck, shuffled several times and fanned the cards face down across the green felt. "High card deals. Ante fifty and three raises. Here, we play five and seven card games. Nothing wild. You can high-low split a pot, but no games named after animals or states."

I smiled and put a cigar in the corner of my mouth. Everyone took a turn drawing their card for the deal. I pulled a spade from the fan, the ace. Perhaps the Lady had chosen the artist after all.

Printed in the United States
49505LVS00007B/84

9 781413 795813